SOME THINGS HIT A MAN
WHERE IT HURTS. . . .

An unfamiliar voice drew Jack's gaze upward. At the head of the stairs, there appeared a vision.

It was a woman, tall and slender, as gracefully formed as a willow branch. She was clad from chin to toe in a white muslin dressing gown. Its pearl buttons were carelessly unfastened, revealing an embroidered nightgown underneath. She wore a delicate lace nightcap, and a few rebellious wisps of gold hair had slipped free from it to curl against her brow.

She wasn't a beauty in the traditional sense. Still her face glowed with color, and if her features were somewhat irregular, they also bespoke quiet strength and patience. As his eyes lingered over her full, soft lips, Jack found himself all at once conjuring up images of them curved with laughter, then parting to welcome a kiss. *His* kiss. God, he'd been too long without a woman's company. No doubt about it.

NOW HE JUST HAD TO TAKE CARE
OF THE SITUATION. . . .

* * *

Praise for This Author's
Previous Work

"Exceptional, a tremendously satisfying experience!"
—Diane Potwin, *The Literary Times*

"A charming love story . . . !"
—*The Paperback Forum*

"Intriguing plot and well-crafted characters. . . . Gives readers a new perspective on history. . . ."
—*Romantic Times*

DREAM WEAVER

LAUREL COLLINS

ZEBRA BOOKS
KENSINGTON PUBLISHING CORP.

ZEBRA BOOKS are published by

Kensington Publishing Corp.
850 Third Avenue
New York, NY 10022

First Printing: June, 1995

Printed in the United States of America

For my brother, Jim,
with love.

One

Could it be that, after three long years of searching, she'd come across the black-hearted bastard at last? And wholly by accident? Charlotte Devereaux stepped closer to the broad tent that served as both saloon and meeting hall for the mining camp at Six Mile Canyon and cautiously peered around the rolled canvas flap.

At once, her eyes were drawn to the man at the far end of the tent. He'd settled his compact, muscular frame onto an upturned crate now and was deftly dealing a hand of cards to himself and his companions upon a table, which had been constructed of a signboard placed atop a barrel head.

Charlotte stood there in the night shadows and studied him for a long while, still doubtful. True, this man had the same cocksure look about him, the same close-set amber eyes, peering out from under the wide brim of his black felt hat, but a ruddy beard now shaded the distinctive line of his jaw, and she just couldn't be certain . . . until he lifted his hand to fan his cards, and she saw it, glittering in the lamplight. With that, she shuddered and caught her breath.

The ring, fashioned out of a ten-dollar gold piece, had been Marcus Gideon's trademark in New Orleans. Everyone on the levee had heard the tale of how he'd had it made from the winnings of the first hand of cards he'd ever played at Price McGrath's. He'd always claimed it was his good luck charm, but tonight it would prove to be his undoing, Charlotte vowed as she stepped around to the side of the tent, checked to see that the chambers of her revolver were full, and then slipped it back into her belt.

From her hiding place, she could hear the upraised voices of the miners, chagrined that Gideon had so easily won the hand, and demanding that they play another. Charlotte shook her head as she scuffed the toe of her boot in the mud, then restlessly began to pace a stretch of uneven ground. She was prepared to wait all night, if she had to, to get the gambler alone.

Overhead, the night wind scattered a clutch of black clouds that had been obscuring the full moon, and as its bright blue light shone down over all, Charlotte's eye was captured by a glimpse of her own reflection in the water of the nearby rain barrel. She stood still before it and dragged the battered brown felt hat from her head, scarcely able to credit that she was the grim-faced young man in buckskins that she saw before her.

A trembling, calloused hand edged upward to touch the short thatch of sweat-dampened curls. She hadn't seen herself in so long. So this is what she'd become. She certainly wasn't the same naive, young girl she'd been when she'd started out on this quest. And that was all the more reason to make Marcus Gideon pay.

Through the thin canvas walls, Charlotte heard him direct the bartender to serve up his best whiskey for his friends, and with a weary sigh, she made a seat for herself on the woodpile and prepared for a long wait. Patience wasn't a virtue with which she'd been born, but after eighteen months standing ankle-deep in icy mountain streams, sifting through tons of sandy riverbed in search of a bit of "color," she was learning. She'd spent longer nights waiting, with less reason.

It was well after midnight when Marcus Gideon appeared at last. His miner friends had shuffled off a short while before, grumbling at their losses as they headed for their tents. Charlotte was ready and waiting just out of sight, with her weapon drawn, when the gambler emerged and headed down the camp's muddy main thoroughfare for the clearing where he had picketed his horse.

Following him at a distance, she felt the full weight of the revolver, heavy in her hand, and considered taking her shot now, while his back was turned. He deserved to die, one way or another. But no, she wanted to see his face, wanted him to know precisely why he was about to lose his life.

He'd reached his horse now, and Charlotte quickened her pace. She caught up with the gambler just as he mounted. She raised the barrel of the gun and pointed it at the man before he could ride away.

"Gideon!"

Slowly he turned to her, those amber eyes of his flickering for a brief moment over the weapon in her hand. His calm only served to irritate her more.

"Do I know you, boy?"

"You don't need to know me," she spat, the chill night air dropping her voice to an even huskier pitch than usual. "But how about Justin Devereaux? Is that name at all familiar to you?"

Gideon's hard face showed neither fear nor recognition. Reaching into the breast pocket of his frock coat, he withdrew a long cheroot and clamped it between his teeth. Next, he produced a match, struck it alight with his thumbnail, and held it to the cigar's tip, inhaling until the tobacco began to glow.

"Can't say it is," he replied, as he shook the flame from the match.

Charlotte's hand tightened on the revolver's grip as suppressed rage swept through her. "Well, let me refresh your memory then, shall I? You murdered him, in cold blood, back in New Orleans. I've been following you ever since, just so I could send your damned, black soul to hell where it belongs!"

This was it, the moment for which Charlotte had waited three long years. She pulled back the hammer, but as she looked up the barrel of the revolver and took aim at Gideon's top vest button, she hesitated. Her mouth had gone dry, her heart was drumming in her ears, her hand clutching the gun's grip was slick with sweat.

"What's the matter, boy?" Gideon taunted. "Lose your nerve?" The harsh bite of his laughter carried far on the still air. "It'll take more than a scrawny coward like you to kill me."

Charlotte squeezed the trigger as he turned the horse to walk away. Her first shot fell short of its mark, splashing up mud at the gambler's heels. She noticed a flash as he whirled back toward her, and then something sharp bit through her buckskins and along the flesh of her thigh. Instinctively, she raised her weapon and fired again and again, until finally the hammer clicked as it struck an empty chamber.

Gideon's horse stamped and reared, its frenzied hoof-beats shaking the ground like thunder. Gideon fell from the saddle, his foot caught in the stirrup. The horse panicked, and galloped into the night, dragging the wounded gambler behind him. The air was thick with the acrid smell of gunpowder and the screams of the horse and its rider. Charlotte narrowed her eyes, but could discern next to nothing in the smoky darkness.

He must be dead, she told herself. She'd pumped five bullets into him. But she had to be sure. She moved to take a step forward, but her leg crumpled, useless, beneath her. Her shoulder struck the muddy ground hard, and she rolled heavily onto her back in the rutted path. The fall forced the air from her lungs and left her gasping for breath. Gathering her remaining strength, she endeavored to rise, but the thick mountain mud had the consistency of glue, and so she could only lie there, stuck fast.

The gunshots and the noise had awakened the denizens of the mining camp, and Charlotte heard them as, one-by-one, they straggled out of their rude dwellings, muttering and swearing, grabbing for their weapons and pulling on their trousers all at the same time.

"What in the sweet hell's goin' on out here?"

" 'Tain't Injuns, you don't suppose?"

"Damned if I know—"

"Look! Over there! It's Charlie. Somebody's gone and shot young Charlie."

The pain in the side of Charlotte's thigh had worsened. She didn't have much strength left now; she could feel the blood seeping from the wound. When she opened her eyes again, she noticed that the air had cleared. How bright the stars were tonight, like a field of black velvet, shot with silver. And then as she grew more and more lightheaded, the silvery points of light began to spin. The sound of scuffling footsteps drew nearer.

"He's bleedin' real bad," Charlotte heard Vernon Taylor call out as he knelt down beside her. Vernon had been a friend to her—well, to Charlie, at least—ever since she'd come here. "We gotta get him to a doctor."

"There's a doctor down in Cedar Creek," Vernon's partner, Ira Jenkins, piped in. "Reckon we could have him there by morning."

"Think the boy'll hold out till then?"

"Yeah, Charlie's a tough one. He'll be all right if'n we bandage him up tight."

It took a monumental effort for Charlotte to reach up and tug on Vernon's shirt sleeve. "No," she whispered hoarsely. "No doctor."

Only a few years ago, Charlotte Devereaux would never have dreamed that she'd breathe her last breath wearing buckskins, lying helplessly in a muddy mule path in a rough mining camp located in the middle of the Colorado Territory. But, it was no less than she deserved, she supposed. After all, hadn't she just killed a man?

Funny thing was, having done the deed, she didn't feel any different. She'd dreamt of having her revenge for so long, but now that it was all over, she didn't feel the satisfaction that she'd expected.

What she did feel was regret: regret for the innocent young woman who'd disappeared so completely three years ago, regret that her short life had been filled with more hatred than love, regret that she'd never have another chance to do things differently. . . .

Jackson Cordell pounded the last nail into the newly-painted signboard, then climbed down the ladder, tossed aside his hammer, and stepped out into the middle of the street to admire his handiwork. *General Merchandise, J. Cordell, Proprietor,* the sign above the long, covered porch announced in bold, black letters. It had taken two months and a hefty chunk of his savings to have the two-story building constructed, but as he surveyed the completed project, he decided that it had been worth it after all.

Cedar Creek was beginning to look more like a real town already, he told himself, and less like the rough-and-tumble mining camp it had once been. There were more than a dozen businesses clustered on either side of the street now, including two saloons, a meat market, an assayer's office, a livery stable, a hardware supply store, and the Widow Murphy's boarding house.

True, most of them were little more than log structures with false fronts made of clapboards, but Jack had no doubt that Cedar Creek could be made into a first-class town, at least as fine as Denver, if only folk would wipe the gold dust out of their eyes, and get down to work.

Of course, his optimistic survey didn't include the

boarded-up stamp mill on the south end of town, nor the weathered headframes dotting the landscape in the distance, grim reminders of several abandoned lode mines. And he was also careful to refrain from lifting his eyes to the scarred hillside nearby, which had been so zealously stripped of timber in order to provide shoring for mineshafts and housing for the miners.

If he'd looked there, he'd have had to acknowledge the patches of uneven ground, evidence of the prospect holes that had been dug up, then quickly filled in when the high-grade ore failed to materialize.

It was the hope for instant riches that had first attracted most folk to this valley in '59. After the placers had played out, though, and the hard rock mines had proven too expensive to operate, the serious prospectors had gone west to Six Mile Canyon, and the rest had gone home. Only the hardiest toughed it out here; some because they hoped for better days, others because they had no hope left at all.

But it hadn't been the promise of gold that lured Jack Cordell here some six years ago. He'd only gotten tired of wandering. And on the day he'd first seen this place, nestled in the foothills of the majestic mountains of the Front Range, near the creek from which it took its name, he'd vowed that it was here that he aimed to spend the rest of his days.

A familiar voice cut through his thoughts. "Jack? Come on over here. There's someone I want you to meet."

Jack quit his musing and turned to see Henry Sutton, standing outside of his hardware shop across the street. Beside him was a middle-aged, bearded fellow in a rumpled suit, whose proportions closely resembled that of the pot-bellied stove that Jack had just set up in the store.

" 'Morning, Henry," Jack called out as he strode over to join them.

He nodded politely to the stranger, willing himself not

to stare. But he couldn't deny that he was curious about any newcomer to Cedar Creek, especially one who didn't appear to be a dirty, trailworn prospector.

Sutton ran a hand through his lank, blond hair, then made the introductions. "This here is Nathaniel Phillips. He's come down from Denver in response to our advertisement. Mr. Phillips, this is Jackson Cordell, the chairman of our town council."

Jack grinned—he couldn't help himself—and pumped the man's hand with unbridled enthusiasm. "Well now, sir, it is certainly a pleasure to meet you," he said. "Cedar Creek is sorely in need of a newspaper. I'm glad to see that someone has risen to the challenge. How soon do you propose to get started?"

"Just as soon as the press and my supplies arrive. They're being shipped down from Denver."

"Mr. Phillips got in only last night," Sutton put in. "He's staying at the Widow Murphy's."

The newcomer regarded Jack with a businesslike air. "I believe that your advertisement promised that you'd provide a place for me to set up shop."

"That would be the *Rio D'Oro*," Jack replied, extending an arm to point the way. "It's the last building there on your left. You'll see the sign. The doors are padlocked, but Henry can give you the key."

Phillips's brow lifted in interest. *"Rio D'Oro,* eh?"

"It was a saloon in its former life," Sutton revealed.

"The owner was kind enough to deed it to the town," Jack countered quickly. "It'll serve well enough for your purposes, I'm sure."

But Henry Sutton wasn't finished. As usual, the garrulous young man didn't know when to keep his mouth shut. He felt compelled to tell the whole tale.

"Poor old Nestor Cruz, shot by a disgruntled customer. He didn't have any family, and so, when it looked like he wasn't goin' to make it, Jack persuaded him to give the *Rio D'Oro* to the town."

"And of course, the town felt there was more need of a newspaper than a saloon," Phillips surmised.

"Oh, we still got a pair of saloons for those fellows who feel the need to kick up their heels a bit now and then. And it does get a mite raucous at times, I can tell you."

Jack shot Sutton an irritated glance. This was not at all the image he was hoping to cultivate for Cedar Creek, and so he promptly changed the subject.

"Where do you come from originally, Mr. Phillips?"

"Boston," the man replied. "I emigrated in forty-nine, though, and have been out West ever since. Wanted to run my own paper for as long as I can remember. Somehow, though, I always ended up working for somebody else— Sacramento, San Francisco, and just lately, Denver. But as soon as I saw your advertisement, I knew I had to seize the opportunity."

Jack once more offered the gentleman his hand. "Well, we're glad that you have. And if there's anything that I can do for you, please don't hesitate to call on me."

Phillips thanked him and was about to follow Henry Sutton into his shop, but hesitated, and after a moment of silent consideration, voiced an afterthought: "Have you ever been to California, Mr. Cordell? It strikes me that you look familiar somehow."

At this, Jack's heart thrummed a rapid tattoo against his breastbone. "California?" he echoed, managing a thoughtful frown. "I'm afraid not. Mine are rather commonplace features, though. You've most likely mistaken me for someone else."

"Most likely," Phillips agreed and then finally turned away.

Jack exhaled long and low as he made his way back across the muddy street. He was still shaking off the dis-

quiet when he caught sight of a pair of filthy, rough-looking
miners in the distance. One was short and sported a red
flannel shirt. His companion had a lanky build and wore
a coat stitched out of an Indian blanket.

They'd come from the south, on the path that led out
of the mountains, and were heading down the street in
Jack's direction. They were leading a bay mare upon
which a third man, wearing buckskins, was riding. To be
truthful, he was not so much riding as slumped in the
saddle, either dead or too drunk to stir.

Jack cast his eyes heavenward and shook his head. So
long as riff-raff of this sort kept drifting in from the mining camps in the mountains, Cedar Creek would never be
able to call itself a peaceful town.

Turning his attention to his own chores, he put away
the ladder and his tools, then opened out his doors to
signal the start of another business day. He was still standing there, in the doorway, when the miners he'd noticed
a few minutes before drew up, and a commotion erupted
in the street.

The young man slumped in the saddle sprang suddenly
to life. Sliding down from his perch, he stumbled about
awkwardly, and then began to lead his companions on a
merry chase through the center of town.

Jack could see now that the boy was wounded; there
was a dirty, bloodstained rag wrapped tightly around one
of his legs, and he was limping badly. Nevertheless, bent
on escape, he ducked behind the wagon that stood outside
of the livery stable, then scrambled over the lumber pile
set beside the assayer's office.

"Come along now, Charlie," his red-shirted partner ca-
joled. "You gotta see the doctor. You been shot. Why, jes'
look at all the blood you lost already."

"No doctor!" the boy wailed.

Along the street, townsmen peered out of windows and
doors, wondering what all the commotion was about. The

boy darted off again, and as he prepared to cut past Jack's porch posts, the taller miner called: "Stop him, mister! He's comin' your way."

At first, this little scene had been amusing, but now Jack found himself irritated that the peace of Cedar Creek should be disturbed by yet another pack of dirty miners. As the boy they'd called Charlie ran past, Jack pounced on him, and consequently found himself rolling in the muddy street in an attempt to subdue the writhing tangle of arms and legs. It wasn't long before his neat, white apron and the clothes beneath it were caked with mud.

"Lie still, you God-damned fool!" he shouted.

Young Charlie had lost his hat in the scuffle, and Jack noticed at once how his greasy, blond curls were plastered against his head with sweat. It was likely the boy was delirious with fever.

The exertion was telling on the boy, for soon thereafter, he gave up the fight, and his breathing went rapid and shallow. Jack glanced at the bandage on the kid's thigh. It was bright red with fresh blood.

"If you don't let the doctor have a look at that leg, you're going to die," he told the child.

For the first time, he looked into the boy's eyes. They were pale blue, eerily reflective, and as he'd expected, glassy with delirium. His brother Matthew's eyes had been that color blue. The thought came to him unbidden. And Matthew had been just about this boy's age when they'd both first come West looking for gold. Jack swallowed hard and shoved the memories back into the dark recesses of his mind.

"You aren't ready to die yet, are you?" he asked the young miner, surprised at the note of concern he heard in his own voice.

Jack's attention was drawn next to the necklace that the boy wore around his neck, a length of rawhide strung with animal claws. He'd seen Indians wear trophies of this sort.

"I deserve to die," came a breathless reply. "I've killed a man."

Jack considered this for a long while and then shook his head. "If every man out West who'd killed another were to up and die tomorrow, we'd have a tragedy of Biblical proportions.

"Now, I'm going to take you to see Doc Kelsey," he continued, as he hoisted the boy up and slung him over his shoulder. "He's a friend of mine. He doesn't bite, and I can personally vouch for the fact that he won't hack off any body parts you might be needing later on, so just lie still."

Charlie was in no condition to argue, and Jack was struck by how easy it was to lift him. Despite the boy's wiry strength, he was painfully thin. Jack had almost forgotten how grueling the life of a prospector could be, especially for one who was little used to hardships.

"Thanks for your help, mister," the man wearing the Indian blanket said as he drew up beside them.

"Cussed, stubborn boy, don't even know what's good for him," his companion piped in, following at their heels. He had gotten hold of the reins of Charlie's horse, and it trailed close behind him now.

"He's not cut out for the prospecting life," Jack remarked harshly. "Just look at him, shot up and near to starving. It would be best if he went back to the States as soon as he's able."

"Charlie?" The man beside him sounded incredulous. "Naw, he's a regular mountain man. A little quiet maybe, but an all right fella. You'd think different 'bout him, if'n you coulda seen him up at Six Mile that time he tangled with a wildcat."

Tangled with a wildcat? Jack didn't find that so hard to believe. While they'd been wrestling, the boy had squirmed and scratched and spit, rather like a wildcat himself, as Jack came to think on it.

"It was last fall. We was workin' our claim late one afternoon and had the misfortune to meet up with a mountain lion," the miner went on to explain. "Damned cat took a swipe at Charlie, but the boy rolled away, drew his pistol and shot it square betwixt the eyes."

The red-shirted miner let go a wheezy chuckle, and sweeping off his battered felt hat, ran a hand through his thinning black hair. "You talk about one lucky shot. Eh, Vernon?"

"Luck or skill, don't make much difference the way I see it, Ira. He saved our skin. You see them claws strung around Charlie's neck, mister? That's all that's left of that cat. He was modest as could be about what he'd done, so we made up that necklace as a gift—to show that the boy had proved his manhood."

One corner of Jack's mouth twisted upward, forming a wry smile in spite of all his irritation. It was a colorful tale, and he *had* been wondering about that claw necklace. As he pondered the matter further, he supposed he might have been wrong about the boy. . . .

This must be heaven, Charlotte thought to herself as she drifted back to consciousness. All around her, the air was scented with lavender and rosewater. She was nestled in warm comfort, resting on a perch so soft that she was sure it must have been a cloud.

She blinked hard, eager for her first glimpse of Paradise. The light was blindingly brilliant, and it took a moment for shapes to take form, but when at last her eyes had made the adjustment, she saw that it wasn't heaven after all.

She lay in a bed, in a sunny room with a sloped ceiling, its walls papered in a cheery floral print. Concentrating hard, she tried to think what had happened to her and found that her head was as thick as if it had been chock-full of cotton.

She could remember only a man's face, drawn in bold, angular lines and set with a pair of steel-gray eyes sharp enough to cut through to her soul, and a deep voice asking her if she was ready to die. He might have been an angel or the devil himself, just which she could not say. Yet here she lay, clearly not in paradise, purgatory or perdition.

Maybe somehow I've been given another chance, she told herself, as she rose upright in the bed. The action made her head swim, and then the wound in her thigh begin to throb. She pulled back the sheet, pulled up the hem of her night gear, and examined the bandage. A quick peek underneath reassured her. She wasn't going to die today. She may have deserved to, but it looked like she'd been dealt another chance.

And then she noticed the trimming of lace at her wrists. She'd been bathed and perfumed, and she was wearing a nightgown—a frilly lady's nightgown. Lifting a hand to her head, her fingers skimmed over a lacy nightcap, which now disguised her indecently-short hair. As her thoughts became sharper, Charlotte remembered that Vernon and Ira had insisted on taking her down to the doctor. She'd been afraid of that, afraid that if a doctor examined her, he would learn her secret. Apparently he had.

There was only one thing to do, she decided: get up and get out before she had to make any long-winded explanations. She couldn't go back to the camp at Six Mile. Even miners didn't take kindly to murderers, and that's what she was now. She'd have to go elsewhere.

Her claw necklace and the rawhide pouch in which she kept her gold were on the nighttable beside the bed, but her revolver was missing, and where were her clothes? Where were the buckskins that had come to be as familiar to her as a second skin?

She couldn't very well ride out of town wearing this

scanty muslin nightgown. Not that it wasn't pretty, with its rows of tucks and pleating on the placket and tiny embroidered rosebuds and lace. Not that Charlotte hadn't spent her long, lonely nights dreaming of possessing such dainties, of feeling such softness next to her skin again. But they simply couldn't be a part of her life anymore. It wasn't practical. It wasn't safe.

Another chance. The words echoed in her head like one of the religious chants she'd learned from the sisters at the convent school in New Orleans and then recited each morning at mass. *Another chance.*

Charlotte wasn't listening, though. Sliding her legs over the edge of the mattress, she got to her feet, and as quietly as she could, took a careful step, then coiled an arm around the tall bedpost for support.

The wound in her thigh was a tight, burning knot of pain. Her head swam, but she fought against her giddiness and attempted to put weight on the leg again. The pain seemed a bit less intense this time. It wasn't going to be easy, but she had to find her clothes and get out of here before the doctor realized that she was up and about.

"You'll not get half a mile, given the shape you're in right now."

The voice came from behind her. Charlotte clung tighter to the bedpost, and whirled around to see a man, in a vest and shirtsleeves, seated in the opposite corner of the room. His dark eyes seemed cold, and even his thick, reddish moustache couldn't soften the hard line of his mouth. He was standing between her and the door, and as he slowly rose to his feet, he folded his arms over his chest, as if daring her to try and get past him.

"I don't I know what you're running from . . . or after," he said next, "but you're going to have to stay put for a while. You've been feverish for the past two days, and you've lost a lot of blood."

"Two days?" Charlotte echoed in dismay. "I can't have been here that long."

"You were delirious for most of that time. But you needn't worry about the bullet, at least. It went clean through."

"Are you the doctor then?"

He nodded brusquely. "Noah Kelsey."

Charlotte was feeling lightheaded again. Having given up all hope of a quiet escape, she loosed her hold on the bedpost. Settling herself beneath the quilt, she propped the pillow against the headboard to support her back. She couldn't understand why the man continued to glower at her, even now that she'd slipped obligingly back into her sickbed.

For her part, she thought Doctor Kelsey's bedside manner was appalling. Did he treat all of his patients so callously, or was there something about her that he disliked in particular? Maybe Vernon or Ira had told him that she had killed a man. That might explain his attitude. While she pondered the question, he spoke again.

"I understand your name is Charlie. Your friends didn't seem to know much more than that."

One russet brow was arched high in disbelief. Ah, so that was it. She ought to have guessed at once. It was likely she would have, if her head hadn't still been so stuffed full of cotton.

"Charlotte," she corrected, "Charlotte Devereaux."

Disquiet welled in her as she realized that she had little memory of the past two days, almost none since the moment she'd ended Marcus Gideon's life.

"My companions," she posed, "the two gentlemen who brought me here. You . . . They didn't . . ."

"Discover your little secret? No. Once I'd decided that they truly were ignorant of the fact that you were a woman, I sent them back up to their camp. I told them that you needed time to recuperate."

Charlotte didn't like the feeling of being at the mercy of a stranger, and especially not one whose distaste for her was so apparent. "Where are my clothes?" she demanded. "And my pistol?"

"You won't be needing either for a while."

"But I can't stay here," she protested, reaching up to brush her fingertips over the lace nightcap, "not like this."

Her panic was increasing by the minute. Without her gun and her disguise to hide behind, she'd be helpless on her own out here, easy prey for any filthy bastard whose eye she happened to catch.

Doctor Kelsey let go an impatient breath. "You'll stay here until you're healed, and I'll give you back the pistol when you leave. You've no need for it here."

Charlotte wondered if he knew that she had already used it to kill a man. *No, Vernon and Ira must have decided to keep quiet about Marcus Gideon's murder.* On the whole, her miner friends bore little fondness for professional gamblers, and Gideon hadn't made any friends that night at Six Mile.

Probably whoever had stumbled first across his bloodstained body had stripped him of his winnings and then dumped him in the nearest mine shaft. It wouldn't be the first time such a thing had happened and no less than the bastard deserved. And if it were so, then maybe Charlotte could finally put the past behind her.

Kelsey still hadn't tempered his disapproving glare, but she wasn't about to let herself be cowed by him.

"What about my clothes?" she asked.

"I don't suppose you're aware, Miss Devereaux, that what you've done—passing yourself off as a man—goes not only against the laws of God, but also those of man?"

She considered whether Doctor Kelsey would have been half so self-righteous had he been made to live even one day of his life as a helpless woman. But much as she might have wanted to make him understand, just now she hadn't the strength. Likely he wouldn't have believed her anyway. Men of his sort only thought of women as decorative creatures, made for a man's pleasure.

Regarding him, she narrowed her eyes. "Do you plan to turn me in to the sheriff then, doctor?"

Kelsey frowned, and after a long moment's consideration, he let go an exasperated breath. "Cedar Creek doesn't have a sheriff yet, only a town council that does double-duty as a vigilance committee. God knows, if they were to find out about you, they'd run you out of town in a minute."

He strode to the window, shaking his head as he continued to speak, as if to himself. "No respectable woman dresses herself up in men's clothing. Why, not even the lowest saloon girl would think to do such a thing!"

Charlotte couldn't miss the disgust threading through his words. Strong as she thought herself to be, it still hurt her to hear it. She'd known all along that people would react this way if her secret were ever to be revealed, but somehow she hadn't wanted to believe it.

"Oh, yes," she replied, words dripping heavily with sarcasm. "Better that a woman should sell her body to any filthy, diseased wretch with the right number of coins in his pocket than to dare to flaunt God's laws and pass herself off as her better.

"I don't aspire to be a man, Doctor Kelsey, heaven knows that, but it's the best way I've found for a woman alone in the world to get by."

When he turned back toward her at last, it was apparent that he had already steeled himself against her. His expression was as unrevealing as a painted carnival mask.

"I'd be a liar if I said that I wasn't curious about your situation," he admitted. "But it's no business of mine how you choose to conduct your life. You're welcome to stay here until you've mended, and you may rest assured, my wife and I will keep your secret between us."

"Wife?" Charlotte repeated, her interest piqued. There were precious few women out here in the Colorado territory. She hadn't seen one, outside of Indian squaws and camp whores, since she'd come here.

"Of course. You don't think I keep a lady's wardrobe on hand for every 'peculiar' patient who happens my way, do you?"

She lifted the lace collar at her throat with a calloused finger. So the pretty nightgown belonged to Kelsey's wife.

"I might as well tell you now that Rachel is the one who bathed you and dressed you up like a china doll," he said next. "She's gotten it into her head that you're a poor, young lady who's been laid low by unfortunate circumstances. She has quite a penchant for manufacturing romantic tales, and to be honest, I indulge her because it's lonely for her out here, especially now that she's with child."

If Doctor Kelsey's glare had been cold before, it was doubly so now. "You and I, however, know that she is only being fanciful. I warn you, Miss Devereaux. Do not even think of taking advantage of my wife's generous spirit while you are under our roof or you'll have me to answer to. Is that understood?"

With the way that Kelsey had looked at her and the manner with which he addressed her, Charlotte felt no better than a criminal. But then, in his eyes, she supposed that that's precisely what she was.

Charlotte met him, glare for glare. "Don't worry, doctor. I don't intend to stay here a moment longer than necessary, and I won't allow my 'peculiarity' to sully your precious wife."

Kelsey seemed satisfied with that statement. "I'd advise you to get some rest," he went on to say, "and put away any ideas you might have of going back to that mining camp any time soon. Believe me, there'll still be enough gold up there for you to make your fortune after you've healed."

Is that what he'd decided? That Charlotte had dressed herself up in men's clothing and paraded herself about as Charlie in order to make it easier to prospect for gold? If only it were half so simple. But Noah Kelsey didn't know the first thing about her life.

As for Charlotte Devereaux, no one who possessed all of the facts could dare say that she'd gotten anything less than the full measure of justice she deserved; and maybe now, finally, she would have another chance at living her own life.

Two

Charlotte did her best to put the confrontation with Noah Kelsey out of her thoughts and rest as she had been ordered to do, but in the end, it proved a difficult task. He'd cast a lot of hurtful words, still she had to admit that the good doctor was probably right on one score. Uneasy though it might make her, for the time being at least, it would be best for her to stay right where she was.

Recuperation was not the reason foremost in her thoughts, however, as it had been in Kelsey's, when he'd made the suggestion. No, her foremost thought was saving her own skin. For if anyone aimed to make young Charlie pay for the death of the gambler, Marcus Gideon, then they'd be obliged to find him first.

Before too much more time had passed, the tempting aroma of biscuits and frying bacon wafted into the upstairs room, announcing Rachel Kelsey's presence in the kitchen below. Charlotte squeezed her eyes shut, trying to ignore the persistent, grumbling protest of her stomach, but it was no use. She hadn't had a decent meal in months. Flapjacks, beans, and coffee were her usual fare. There hadn't been the time, nor the wherewithal for anything else in the mountains.

Since the placers had played out, she'd spent hour after weary hour wielding a pick axe to break out chunks of ore down in the drift that she, Ira, and Vernon had been working between them.

Sleep eluded her, and so, giving in to her restlessness, Charlotte rose once more from her sick bed. The pain seemed less intense than before as she gingerly shifted her weight onto her wounded leg. Using the bedpost as a support, she made her way to the trunk that was set before the window. She eased herself down upon it, and pushed aside the lace curtains, propped her elbows on the sill, and drew a breath of fresh, pine-laced air. The town spread out beneath her interested gaze.

In many ways, Cedar Creek was like any of the other languishing mining towns that Charlotte had seen sprinkled through the foothills of the Front Range—made up of a number of rough, log buildings grouped together along a muddy, main street that was just wide enough to turn a team and wagon in, the whole of it sheltered on all sides by rising, red rock slopes, dotted with scrub.

But there were differences as well—signs of care and planning which indicated that progress was taking place here, rather than decay. Yes, there were abandoned mines and scores of rude, makeshift cabins. But a public square had been cleared at the north end of the town, beside the creek itself, and in its midst stood a number of split log benches and a tall pine flagpole, with the Stars and Stripes fluttering in the breeze.

Most of the merchants along the main street had faced their establishments with false clapboard fronts that were set with proper doors and glass-paned windows, and there were painted signboards hanging overhead, which identified the particular specialty of each shop: laundry, meat market, livery and feed. Somehow as she gazed down upon it, Charlotte felt safe and comfortable, as if she were among old friends.

The general store was housed in a brand-new two-story frame building, and even at this early hour, the proprietor, in his shirtsleeves and apron, was busy sweeping the porch. Following his movements, Charlotte was struck by a sense of recognition.

Even from this distance, she could see that the man was broad-shouldered and long-legged. The stray lock of hair that swept across his forehead as he worked was black as soot. And his eyes? His smoky gray eyes suggested a sharp mind and forthright manner. Charlotte knew that, as if for certain. But how could she? There was no way she could possibly have discerned such details from her present vantage point, and if truth be told, her eyesight had never been all that reliable.

She concentrated with all her might, and finally, the heavy fog lifted and her memory began to clear. On the day that her companions had brought her to town, this man, this . . . storekeeper, had wrestled her to the ground, draped her over his shoulder like a sack of potatoes, and then proceeded to carry her to Doctor Kelsey's place at the edge of town.

Charlotte's cheeks flushed with embarrassment at the memory. She looked to the signboard above the store and read the name inscribed upon it—J. Cordell. In the future, she'd have to take pains to avoid running into Mr. Cordell. Things might prove awkward for her, indeed, in the event that he'd gotten too close a look at Charlie.

"Mercy, you oughtn't to be out of bed yet!"

Charlotte's head snapped up, and she turned to see who was talking. A young woman had come into the room and was now placing a breakfast tray upon the bedside table. She was a pretty, little thing, with luminous skin and shining, dark eyes. A thick plait of chestnut-colored hair hung halfway down her back, and the apron tied high over the woman's rounding belly confirmed her identity.

"Mrs. Kelsey?"

The woman nodded, then wiped her hand on her apron and held it out to Charlotte. "Miss . . . Devereaux, is it?"

As Charlotte accepted the woman's soft white hand, she

was immediately struck by the contrast between it and her own, which was sunbrowned and calloused. She hadn't realized how very much she'd changed in the last three years.

"Please," she advised her hostess, "I'd rather you called me Charlotte."

"And I shall be Rachel to you," the young lady replied. "Well, now that we've gotten the formalities out of the way, let's see to it that you're put back into bed where you belong."

Charlotte passively allowed Rachel to escort her back to bed.

"I supposed that you'd be hungry, after two days with no nourishment at all," Rachel told her, arranging the footed breakfast tray she'd brought with her across Charlotte's lap.

Charlotte's eyes widened. Here was the source of the aromas which had tempted her a short time ago. There was a cup of steaming coffee and a plate heaped with food: fluffy biscuits, their tops ever-so-lightly browned; wide, crisp strips of bacon; and fried eggs, resting side-by-side in all their sunny splendor. She hadn't eaten eggs in, well, almost as long as she could remember.

Settling herself in the chair beside the bed, Rachel entreated Charlotte to begin. "Help yourself," she said, "there's plenty more. Noah told me that it's all right for you to eat as much as you like. He says you're far too thin."

Charlotte didn't need to be asked twice. She dove into the meal with hedonistic abandon, blissfully savoring each morsel before consuming the next. So enraptured was she, in fact, that she was hard pressed to follow her hostess's chatty monologue.

"I couldn't help but notice that you were admiring our town," Rachel told her. "It is beginning to shape up, don't you think? When we first arrived, it was nothing more than a tent camp. Noah was sorry that he'd dragged me all the way out here; he even talked about going back home to Pennsylvania. But I saw right off what a beautiful spot it was, and I knew how much he wanted to stay, so I told him that I wouldn't mind. We've been here a little more than a year now. The gentlemen in town all pitched in to help us build this place.

"The only thing I can honestly say that I miss from back home is the ladies; there aren't nearly enough for socializing with out here. This town's chock-full of wild, young men, miners and businessmen alike, all aiming to make their fortune, but I doubt you'd find more than a dozen respectable women in the whole of the county."

"Here in Cedar Creek, we've the Widow Murphy, who runs the boarding house; but she's nearly sixty, and I'm afraid she and I haven't all that much in common. Oh, and there are those girls who live upstairs of the saloons," she said, adopting a hushed tone, "but they're hardly respectable. Noah would never allow me to speak with them, much less socialize. And he's right, of course, though I must say that lately, I've been sorely tempted. Thank heavens, you've come. You're the answer to my prayers."

Charlotte slathered gooseberry jam over the last biscuit and popped it into her mouth. She looked up from her plate to notice that Rachel had been watching her eat. She'd been chowing down with the voracity of a field hand. Swallowing hard, she reached for her napkin and dabbed at the corners of her mouth.

"I'm sorry," she said. "I'm afraid I've been away from civilization for too long. I've eaten so many meals of beans and flapjacks out of a tin pan that I've forgotten what decent table manners are. Thank you for the breakfast, Mrs. Kelsey . . . Rachel."

"Oh, it wasn't anything special."

"It was delicious. And I know more than a little about

cooking myself. I cooked for my father, three meals a day, every day."

Rachel's brows arched higher with this meager revelation. "Where do you come from, Charlotte?" she asked.

Charlotte hesitated. In the mountains, the miners never poked into a person's past. Too many had secrets of their own to keep. But what harm was there in answering the woman's innocent question?

"New Orleans."

Rachel nodded. "I ought to have guessed it was somewhere down South. There's still a hint of a drawl in your voice. Did you leave home because of the war?"

"No."

Questions made Charlotte uneasy, but Rachel didn't seem to take offense at her abbreviated replies.

"Noah was an Army surgeon," Rachel said next. "You're lucky that your friends brought you here. He's had plenty of practice with bullet wounds. He's got a good, steady pair of hands."

Charlotte gazed at the remains of her breakfast. Rachel was clearly proud of her husband. But regardless of his skill as a surgeon, Charlotte thought him entirely too hard-headed.

"I'm grateful to him, of course," she said, "and to you, as well, for sprucing me up and lending me your night-gown."

"It's nothing. I have another one."

Rachel hesitated, and then, as if she'd finally managed to gather up her courage, she asked the one question that Charlotte had been anticipating all along. "Why were you dressed like that? As a man, I mean."

With a weary sigh, Charlotte set aside her napkin, then eased herself back against the pillows. It had been so long since she'd had a confidante. It would be a relief to share her tale with someone at last, to hear someone else agree that she'd been justified in all she'd done. But where was she to start? What was she to say?

"Are you hiding from a cruel relation who's trying to force you to marry against your will?" Rachel posed. Her dark eyes flashed with excitement as she reached across the quilt to take up Charlotte's hand and squeeze it tightly. "Is someone chasing you? It must be something awful; I'm sure of it. Oh, you need only tell me, and I promise that Noah and I will do all that we can to help you."

A pleasant surge of warmth flooded through Charlotte's veins as she realized that Rachel Kelsey was offering not only a sympathetic ear, but friendship as well. For one who'd kept her thoughts her own for so long, it was a tempting offer, indeed.

But then, all at once, Charlotte was reminded of what Dr. Kelsey had told her about his wife's romantic imaginings, and of his warning. He had no intention of helping her beyond his physician's duties; in fact, he didn't want his lovely wife's innocence soiled by any knowledge of the details of Charlotte's sordid life.

Regretfully, Charlotte pulled her hand from Rachel's and allowed her eyes to drift shut. "I'm feeling a bit tired just now," she explained, then added, "too tired to talk, if you don't mind."

"Why, why—yes, of course you are," Rachel stammered, and to her dismay, Charlotte could hear the hurt, plain as day, in the young woman's voice. "Forgive me, I ought to have realized. I'll just take away that tray now, so that you can rest."

Charlotte dared not open her eyes again, for fear the wounded look that Rachel was certain to be wearing would make her change her mind and ignore Dr. Kelsey's warning. *It is better this way,* she told herself, *for even if Rachel Kelsey were to have heard the whole, sorry tale, she'd surely have come to decide that, like the girls who lived upstairs of the saloons, Charlotte Devereaux was not at all fit company.*

Soft heart or soft head? Jack couldn't decide which it was that made him close up the store at noon and—instead of trudging upstairs to prepare his own meager dinner as he did on every other day—walk the half block to Noah Kelsey's to check on the boy he'd carried there a few days ago.

What was he, after all, but another greedy prospector? And this town could surely do with one less of those. But this boy reminded him too much of his brother, young and gangling, with more spirit than sense. Likely that was why Jack felt such a queer sense of responsibility for him.

Maybe a part of him believed that if he could convince this lad that his quest for gold was foolhardy and that he ought to go on back home, it might absolve him of some of his guilt over Matthew's death.

" 'Afternoon, Noah," Jack called out as he drew up before the porch, where his friend sat whittling away absently at a long stick. "The doctoring business must be slow if you've taken to practicing on pine trees."

"My father used to whittle," Kelsey replied to this comment. "He always told me it cleared his mind and helped him think straight. Can't say that I agree with him, though."

Jack brushed the wood curls from the porch step and sat down beside his friend. "Is there something in particular weighing on your mind today?"

Kelsey looked up, and for a moment Jack thought he might be preparing to confide in him. But a frown settled on the doctor's brow, and he shook his head. "Nothing to speak of. It's only, well, a 'general malaise,' I suppose you'd call it."

"That's easy enough to remedy. I'll close the store, and

we'll go up to my cabin up by the lake, like we did last fall, and spend a day or two fishing."

Before anything definite could be decided, there came the tread of footsteps on the planked wood floor, and then Rachel Kelsey appeared in the open doorway. "What's this I hear about someone planning a fishing trip?"

"Don't worry yourself, my dear," Noah assured her. "It's only idle talk."

"Oh, I don't mind the two of you going. I only wish you'd wait till the raspberries are ripe, so that you might bring me back a bucket or two," she explained. "I've got a terrible craving for fresh raspberry cobbler."

Jack allowed his gaze to settle for a moment on his friend's wife, her pretty face flushed with color. He'd always thought that there was something innately beautiful about a woman who was with child. He wasn't covetous exactly, but he could not deny that he sorely envied Noah's good fortune. Good women like Rachel Kelsey were hard to come by, especially in this country.

"We're about to have our dinner, Mr. Cordell," she said to him, and he wondered if she was aware that he'd been staring at her. "Will you join us?"

"No, ma'am," Jack replied. As it was, he'd taken advantage of the Kelseys' hospitality on far too many occasions. "I do thank you for the offer, but I should be getting back to the store. Truth be told, I only came to ask the doc here how that boy I brought over to you the other day is faring."

Noah looked up suddenly, and with that, the blade of his knife slipped, and he cut a deep gouge in the pine stick. Wisely, he set both the knife and the wood aside. Rachel went to him, settled her hands upon his shoulders, and only after that did he seem able to find his tongue.

"That young miner, you mean?"

Jack nodded. "I thought between the two of us, we might be able to talk some sense into him, convince him to go on back home to his family before he gets himself killed out here."

"I'm surprised you'd take an interest in the boy," Noah replied, "but it's too late for that, at any rate. I no sooner patched him up than he went on his way."

"Back to his camp?"

"No, I . . . I think he talked about going on up to Denver for a while."

Jack's eyes narrowed. He could sense that Noah was uncomfortable, but it may only have been that "malaise" he'd been speaking about earlier.

"Now that certainly is peculiar," he observed. "I could swear I saw that bay horse he rode in on in a stall in the livery stable this morning."

"You did?"

Rachel cut in. "Of course, he did," she said, then turned to Jack to explain: "When the boy left, he told Noah that he should keep the horse in payment of his bill. Noah explained that it wasn't necessary, but the boy insisted that he wasn't the sort to be in debt to any man. Isn't that right, Noah?"

Noah seemed too baffled to reply. Then finally, he nodded.

"That's right. He said he didn't want to wait for the stage. He caught a ride with that freighter that came through the other day."

Jack still thought there was something odd in all of this, but he had no chance to consider the matter further, for in her usual energetic fashion, Rachel had already moved on to a new concern.

"Go on inside," she urged her husband, "your dinner will be getting cold. And as for you, Mr. Cordell, you may not have the time to sit down with us, but the least I can do is make you up a plate. A bachelor like yourself could up and die if he eats his own cooking long enough.

Don't bother to argue. I won't have 'no' for an answer.
You wait right here, and I'll bring it out to you."

With that, she turned on her heel and hurried off inside.
Jack grinned at Noah. "I do admire a woman who knows
her own mind."

"Take my advice," Noah replied, a glimmer of amusement playing over his otherwise weary expression, "if you
ever find yourself one, you'd do well to run away, quickly,
in the opposite direction."

Noah got to his feet and proceeded to follow his wife
through the door, past the stairs, and down the long hall
that divided the front of the house between the parlor and
his office and examination room.

Jack hovered in the doorway, feeling very much the
starving bachelor waiting for a handout, but the promise
of a well-cooked meal kept him waiting nonetheless. Rachel returned shortly, bearing a plate that was covered with
a red and white checkered napkin. Jack inhaled deeply—
beef stew—unless he missed his guess.

"I imagine you must have everything moved into the
new store by now," she said, as she handed over the plate.

"Yes, ma'am, and you'll be pleased to hear that I've
just received a shipment of dress goods from Denver and
a stock of satin ribbons as well."

"Satin ribbons? Mr. Cordell, I do believe you're trying
to tempt me."

"Rachel?"

At the sound of an unfamiliar voice—*could it have
been a woman's voice?*—Jack's gaze was drawn over Rachel's shoulder. Behind her, at the head of the stairs, there
appeared a vision.

It was indeed a woman, tall and slender, as gracefully
formed as a willow bough. She was clad from chin to toe
in a white muslin dressing gown. Its pearl buttons were
carelessly unfastened, revealing the embroidered nightgown beneath. She wore a delicate lace nightcap, and a

few rebellious wisps of gold hair had slipped free from
it to curl against her brow.

She wasn't a beauty in the traditional sense. Still, her
face glowed with color, and her features were somewhat
irregular, they also bespoke a quiet strength and patience.
As his eyes lingered over her full, soft lips, Jack found
himself all at once conjuring images of them curved with
laughter and then parting to welcome a kiss. *His* kiss.
God, but he'd been too long without a woman's company.

She came halfway down the stairs before she caught
sight of him, standing behind Rachel on the threshold.
Her blue eyes went wide, and she clutched at the open
edges of her dressing gown, drawing them together. She
drew up short and swayed slightly on her feet. Jack suspected that she'd have turned and run away if she'd been
able.

"Oh!" she exclaimed. "I . . . I didn't realize that you
had a visitor. I thought you were only speaking with your
husband."

Rachel turned and started up the stairs to meet her.
"Whatever are you doing out of bed again?"

"I can manage," the woman insisted. "I'm feeling much
better now. I was restless up there all alone, and so I
thought I'd come down, to see if I could help you somehow. I don't want to be a burden."

Jack was mesmerized. The surprisingly deep timbre of
her voice, combined with the intriguing touch of a Southern drawl, sent an odd ripple of pleasure through him. No
doubt about it, he'd been too long without a woman. By
the time she'd finished speaking, his curiosity was piqued.

"Don't be a ninny," Rachel retorted. "You're hardly a
burden, and you know that Noah has said you oughtn't
to be on your feet yet."

Jack suspected that Rachel had forgotten his presence
entirely. But no matter how awkward the circumstances,
he was determined not to be cheated out of an introduc-

tion. So, he set his dinner plate aside on the hall table, and tactfully as possible, he cleared his throat.

"Excuse me? Ladies?"

When Rachel turned back toward him, she was blushing. "Mercy, Mr. Cordell. I suppose you're wondering . . . well, of course, you are. This is . . . is . . . my cousin, Charlotte Devereaux, from New Orleans."

Noah must have heard the commotion from the kitchen, for he wandered back down the hall, just as his wife was making her introductions. Jack thought that Noah looked more than a trifle green around the gills as he caught sight of the two women perched there by the stairway.

"Charlotte has come to help with the baby," Rachel went on to explain.

"Why, that's just plain unfair, Noah," Jack said, offering Kelsey a wicked grin. "You didn't tell any of us you had company coming. Now there'll be two respectable young ladies in the whole of this town, and you'll have both of them living in your house!"

Rachel went to stand beside her husband, allowing her cousin to complete her descent unaided, and it was only then that Jack realized that the woman's progress was impeded by a pronounced limp.

"I told her she ought to be resting," Rachel said. Then, slanting a glance at Jack, she added, "The poor dear sprained an ankle on the trip out."

"I ought to have dosed her with laudanum," Noah muttered to himself. "That's likely the only way we'll keep her in her sick bed."

But Jack was scarcely listening. He'd advanced to meet Charlotte Devereaux as she hesitated on the bottom stair. The air around her was sweetened with the scent of roses. "Perhaps you ought to take your cousin's advice and rest that ankle, *Missus* Devereaux," he offered.

"It's *Miss*," she corrected, telling him precisely what

he'd been aiming to discover. "And I assure you, sir, I can manage."

Despite her independent tone, those wide, blue eyes of hers remained fixed on the pegged wood floor even as she spoke; and when Jack reached out for her hand, it promptly disappeared within the capacious folds of her dressing gown. With that, a satisfied smile stretched across his lips. *A respectable young woman, both unmarried and modest,* he told himself. Surely, the good Lord had been listening to his prayers.

As soon as Doctor Kelsey escorted Mr. Cordell out of the door, Charlotte collapsed against the newel post, clinging to it for support. She felt dizzy and sick, but not on account of her injury. From the moment she'd caught sight of the storekeeper in the doorway, she'd been filled with the fear that he might recognize her as the young miner he'd carried here only two days ago.

As Doctor Kelsey had explained, if her secret were uncovered, she'd likely be thrown out of town—or maybe worse. And despite her repeated insistence that her injury wasn't serious, she did need time to heal and to think of what she was going to do, before she could leave this place.

She supposed that it really wasn't any wonder that Cordell had not made the connection between the fragile, perfumed invalid, clad in lace and muslin, and the fractious, buckskinned miner who'd wrestled with him in the muddy street. Her years of subterfuge had taught Charlotte that, in this world, people only see what they want to see.

"Let me help you back upstairs," Rachel offered, as she gently caught Charlotte's elbow.

"The parlor," Charlotte suggested instead. "I only need to rest a little while."

After directing her to the horsehair sofa, Rachel helped

her to lift her legs and stretch them out across the seat cushions.

"I am sorry if I've made matters difficult for you," Charlotte said, ignoring the pull of the wound beneath her bandaged thigh. "I'm not accustomed to lying about for all of the day. I couldn't bear it. But I didn't know that you had a guest, or I'd never have come down."

"No need to worry about that." Rachel eased herself into a brocade armchair which, along with the sofa and a pair of mahogany side tables, comprised the entire parlor suite. "I think our little charade was convincing, don't you?"

Oh yes, thoroughly convincing, Charlotte told herself, *even I'd been tempted to believe it.* Faced with Rachel Kelsey's selfless generosity, Charlotte couldn't help but feel guilty at having spurned the woman's offer of friendship when it had been made to her this morning.

"You've done so much for me," she said, "but I haven't earned your trust. I owe you some kind of explanation about myself at least."

Rachel put up her hands. "No. It was wrong of me to question you the way I did. Noah is always telling me I oughtn't to be to sticking my nose in where it doesn't belong. Whatever you've done, Charlotte, I'm sure that you felt you had to do it. We all must make hard choices in this life . . ."

"There was no choice," Charlotte replied to this, "at least, it didn't seem so at the time."

It wasn't hard to discern from her bemused expression that Rachel was battling mightily against her own curiosity, but her better nature won out in the end.

"Well, what's done is done. Maybe now it would be best for you to get on with living and forget all about the past."

Get on with living? While Charlotte might agree with the sentiment, it would be a difficult thing to accomplish.

Her old life had been shattered so completely that there was no hope of ever piecing it back together, even if she wanted to.

She'd finally done what she'd set out to do when she left New Orleans—dispatch Marcus Gideon to hell—but now she was left without the overwhelming need for vengeance. For so long it was all that had given her direction. She felt like a rudderless ship, adrift on uncertain currents. What sort of future could there be for her?

"I have nothing," she said and made the mistake of thinking aloud, "no one, no family . . ."

"You have us," Rachel replied. "You can stay here, if you like. You can be my cousin, just as we've said, and help me with the baby when it comes. I'd like that; I really would, Charlotte. You don't know how lonesome it can be out here."

Charlotte regretted having spoken. Rachel Kelsey was a kindhearted woman, but she couldn't possibly understand the complexity of the situation.

"Your husband won't agree," Charlotte retorted. If her tone was somewhat harsh, it was only because she didn't want Rachel harboring impossible fantasies. "He'll never forget what I've done. Can't you see? To him, I'm no better than those women living over the saloon. He wants to protect you. I can't blame him for that."

But Rachel did not seem disheartened. "You let me deal with Noah," she said, with a gleam in her dark eyes. "I'll convince him. You needn't worry yourself about that. Oh, he may seem cold at first, but he'll get used to having you around."

"I can't impose on you," Charlotte insisted. "I've a bit of gold put aside from my prospecting to pay for my keep while I heal, but once that's gone . . ."

She had intended to say that she'd have to put her buckskins back on and go out and earn her living, but then she remembered Gideon. If the territorial authorities had been informed of his murder, they might already be looking for Charlie. Guilty though she may have been, Charlotte did not relish the prospect of being hung for the murder of a worthless gambler. As she saw it, she had only squared her account with him.

"How am I to get by?" she wondered aloud, only now realizing her dilemma. "I've lived for three years as a man. Working on the riverboats, I could earn thirty-five dollars a month. Even prospecting, I could scrape together enough to survive, but like this . . ." She waved a hand to indicate her frilly, feminine attire. "I'm useless."

"I don't think you've stopped to consider your worth out here on the frontier," Rachel argued. "It isn't the same as back in the States. Women are a precious commodity in towns like Cedar Creek. If you can cook, sew, or take in laundry, your fortune is fairly well-assured."

Charlotte blinked in disbelief. She hadn't even thought about such a possibility. But it wasn't long before the doubts crept in her mind. She shook her head. "After the sort of life I've led . . ."

"No one need know about any of that," Rachel retorted. "And we won't speak of it ever again. As far as the citizens of Cedar Creek are concerned, you are my cousin Charlotte from New Orleans."

"But what about my partners, Ira and Vernon? They'll come back here looking for me . . ."

Rachel smiled. "And when they do, we'll simply tell them that Charlie got tired of the miner's life and went back East."

Charlotte was silent as she considered all that Rachel had proposed, but it took only a glance at her callused hands to remind her that she was likely too rough around the edges to be playing such a role. "Just look at me, Rachel," she entreated. "I'm callused and sunburnt, and I've all but forgotten how to act like a lady. No one will believe . . ."

"Oh, they'll believe it all right . . . because they want to believe. Surely you noticed the . . . admiration in Mr. Cordell's eyes when he saw you just now," Rachel went on to say. "Well, there are plenty of eligible bachelors like him in Cedar Creek, and a decided dearth of respectable women. Once we've smoothed off some of your rough edges, they'll be swarming around you like bees in a clover patch."

What Rachel was endeavoring to impart, in her roundabout way, was that Charlotte would have no trouble at all snagging a husband to take care of her. But she couldn't know that, to Charlotte at least, marriage was not a desirable option. In living her life as Charlie, Charlotte had gotten a taste of what true freedom was, and she wasn't about to give that up, not for any man.

Three

Jack arranged the last of the tins of fragrant India tea on the shelf and stepped down off of the ladder, just as Noah Kelsey came through the front door, jangling the bell.

"I need a bottle of castor oil and three tins of carbolic salve," he said, and flopped down into one of the chairs that was set before the pot-bellied stove in the center of the store. Expelling a weary sigh, he reached up to massage his temples with his fingertips.

"Haven't seen you in awhile," Jack remarked absently as he collected the items from the shelf, and then proceeded to wrap them in brown paper. "From what I've heard, you've been doing a land-office business lately."

Kelsey scowled and shook his head. "It didn't take long for the men of Cedar Creek to discover that there's an eligible female living under my roof. They've been coming into my office with every complaint known to modern medicine, and a few that even I haven't heard of yet. It's been a veritable parade of bunions, blisters, bruises . . . and every last one of them only hoping to catch a glimpse of 'Miz Rachel's purty cousin, Charlotte.' Put a bottle of bicarbonate of soda in with that, will you, Jack? I need to make up some headache powders, and I'm all out."

Jack squared his jaw. He knew well enough what had been going on at the Kelsey's, but it galled him no less to hear it from Noah. Miss Charlotte Devereaux was supposed to have been the answer to *his* prayers, not the object of affection of every man within fifty miles of Cedar Creek.

"The boldest of the lot avoid me entirely," the doctor went on to say. "They march straight up to the kitchen door, offering their gap-toothed smiles and wildflower bouquets. I'd swear every bachelor in the county has crossed my threshold at least once in the past two weeks . . . except for you, now that I come to think on it. Just where've you been, Jack?"

"I'm too old for such shenanigans, and besides, business keeps me too busy for courting," Jack retorted. Of course, it wasn't the truth, but he wasn't about to make himself a part of the circus that had surrounded the Kelsey household since the arrival of Rachel's cousin. "I'm certain with all her many beaux, the lady won't be pining after me."

"Well, if you ask me, you're the wisest man in town. Those lovesick bucks don't know a thing about Charlotte Devereaux. All they see is a pair of bright blue eyes and a well-turned ankle and they're ready to propose marriage."

"Marriage?" Jack echoed. "She hasn't gone and accepted one of them, has she?"

His tone sounded anxious, even to his own ears. Noah glared at him. "I thought you were too busy to care."

"I'm only curious," Jack insisted, as he finished tying up the twine and pushed the doctor's neatly-wrapped package of supplies across the counter. "That's all."

"Well, I'd say that Cousin Charlotte is having far too much fun with things the way they are. Choosing only one beau would spoil the game, now wouldn't it?"

Jack's brow creased, but he hadn't the time to decide just what he thought of Noah's pointed remark, for just then, the bell on the door jangled again, and a stranger came in. He was clean shaven, and his clothing—felt hat, red wool jacket, and canvas trousers—were of good quality, but dusty and trailworn.

"Are you Jack Cordell?" the man inquired.

Jack nodded. "What can I do for you?"

"The fellow over at the livery stable gave me your name. He said you're the head of the town council, and so I figure you're the man I ought to see." He stepped forward and put out his hand. "My name is Jasper Price. I work for Mr. Elias Hathaway. He and a small group of investors intend to put a rail line through from Denver to Santa Fe, and right now, I'm scouting sites."

"Hathaway?" Doctor Kelsey put in. "Doesn't he operate the railroad that runs from Omaha to Kansas City?"

"That he does, sir," Price replied.

Jack eagerly grasped the man's hand and ushered him to the chair beside Noah's. "Sit down, Mr. Price, and tell me what I can do for you."

He could scarcely believe their good fortune. The stage already came through twice a week, but a railroad station here in town would go a lot further toward putting Cedar Creek on the map. It would mean daily mail delivery and travelers coming through; and some of them would stop in town and maybe decide to stay awhile.

"There are dozens of little towns like yours strung out through the foothills," Price began, as he pulled a notepad and pencil stub from his jacket pocket, "mostly built up around mining camps. It's my job to decide which ones are likely to prosper, and well, to be frank, which will be gone as soon as the gold veins play out."

Leaning back against the counter, Jack folded his arms across his chest. "I can assure you, sir, Cedar Creek is here to stay. We have all of the essential businesses: laundry, livery, hardware. The gentleman sitting there beside you is our town doctor, Noah Kelsey. We're about to get our own newspaper, and we've just cleared a square down by the creek for public use."

"How many people are there in Cedar Creek?"

"Close to seventy folk living in town. Wouldn't you say so, Noah?"

Kelsey nodded sagely. "And probably three times that many scattered through the hills."

"Miners?"

"Some of them, yes," Jack admitted, "but . . ."

"And do you have a hotel here in town? Or a restaurant?"

"There's Mrs. Murphy's boarding house, and the Red Bird Saloon serves hot meals."

Price penciled the information onto his pad and then got to his feet. "I thank you, gentlemen. Now I think I'll go and have a look around for myself."

"When will the decision be made on the rail line?" Jack inquired.

"It'll be two months at least, maybe three. I'll need to complete the survey," Price replied, heading for the door. "But I'll stop by on my way back north. I ought to have a better idea of the way things stand by then."

Jack had done his best to contain his excitement while speaking with the man, but as soon as Price was out of the door, it bubbled over. He gave the cast iron wheel of the coffee grinder, sitting atop the counter, a spin, then let out an ear-splitting whoop. "Did you hear that, Noah? A railroad line running right through the middle of town? Do you know what that would mean to us?"

Kelsey pulled himself out of his chair and reached out to retrieve his package. "Don't pin your hopes too high, my friend. We're a mere speck on the map compared to some of the places Price will visit. And you heard the questions he was asking. Why, we don't even have a decent hotel."

"You've counted us out already, haven't you?" Jack accused. He began to pace the pegged wood floor, more than a little irritated with Noah's discouraging attitude.

"Well, I think you're wrong. A person has only to look around to see the improvements we've made to this town.

"Cedar Creek might have started out as a gold camp, but it's more than that now. And if it's a decent hotel that we're lacking, then maybe some of us ought to consider going over to the Widow Murphy's place and fixing things up a bit before Price rides back through on his return trip."

Noah shook his head in amazement. "You are determined, I'll give you that. But I still don't understand why this means so much to you, Jack. It can't be the money. You're already making a more than decent living with things as they are."

Jack had to admit that he'd never bothered to consider the question until now, for it would have entailed a reflection on his past. He'd successfully avoided that pursuit thus far. But now Noah was waiting for an answer.

"I don't know," he said, at last. "I suppose I'd like to live in a place that isn't rough and tumble, a place that feels like home."

Softly humming a tune half-remembered from her childhood, Charlotte pulled open the oven door, carefully withdrew the steaming pie, and carried it to the window ledge to cool. Then she resumed the task of weaving strips of dough into a lattice design atop a second pie. As soon as she finished, she placed that into the oven.

She couldn't remember the last time she'd sashayed about a kitchen in calico skirts, with the sweet scent of baked goods thick in the air, but it struck her now that she had missed it. Life had molded her into a hard-edged individual—too hard, she'd thought, to change. And yet, with each day that passed, she was becoming more comfortable with her new life and her new appearance.

Each morning, she would tuck her scanty curls up into

a dainty, crocheted snood, slip into the faded blue house-dress of Rachel's that they'd altered, as well as they could, to fit, and then she'd go out to meet the day with an enthusiasm that genuinely surprised her. Maybe Rachel was right, maybe she could go back to what she'd been and forget all that had happened in between.

As if summoned by Charlotte's thoughts, Rachel came into the kitchen, her eyes trained on a tattered issue of *Godey's Lady's Book.* "I've found that recipe for whitening hands," she said. "We'll need eau de cologne, lemon juice, and plain brown soap."

Charlotte was busy transferring the dirty utensils from the table to the dishpan. When she did not respond immediately, Rachel looked up, and noticing the floured board and rolling pin, her eyes widened in surprise. "Whatever have you been up to? I thought you were only going to put dinner on."

"I've made pie for dessert. The rhubarb's flourishing in your kitchen garden, and so I thought I'd make use of it."

"First the housecleaning, then the laundry, now the baking. I never expected you to take over all of my chores, Charlotte. You're supposed to be recuperating," Rachel said.

"I've already explained that I intend to earn my keep. I've healed well enough, and it's the least I can do to repay your kindness . . . and Dr. Kelsey's."

For his wife's sake, the doctor had resigned himself to Charlotte's presence. Still, Charlotte felt the chill whenever he came into the room. And although Charlotte had settled into the Kelsey household, adopting the guest room upstairs for her own, she was always aware that it was only a temporary arrangement.

It was late spring now, and Rachel's baby was due in the fall. Once she'd delivered the baby and was on her feet again, Charlotte would have to be on her way.

Rachel set aside the magazine and came to take up

Charlotte's hands in hers, examining them carefully. "You know, I think that, what with the lye soap from the laundry and all of the kitchen work you've done, you won't need my recipe after all."

There came a knock at the back door. The two women exchanged glances, and Rachel's mouth curved into a smile. "You might as well answer," she whispered. "It's no doubt another one of your gentlemen callers."

Charlotte rolled her eyes heavenward. "I'm sorry about this."

It was an apology that had been repeated often of late, but Rachel always seemed more amused than upset by the interruptions. The parlor tables were already filled with bouquets of wilting wildflowers, set about in butter crocks, Mason jars, and whatever other empty containers the two ladies had been able to find.

Almost since the day she'd arrived here, the men of Cedar Creek had been paying Charlotte court. They were diligent and respectful, but she didn't for a moment think it was on account of the abundance of her charms, no matter what her many suitors might avow. She knew well enough what her own failings were. She couldn't take much pride in being sought after when she was the only heifer in the pasture.

Nevertheless, as she opened the door, she fixed a smile on her face and stepped out onto the back porch, where Gunnar Thorssen stood, the burly, red-bearded young man who worked as a blacksmith and ran the local livery along with his brother, Lars.

"A good afternoon to you, Miss Charlotte."

"And to you, Mr. Thorssen."

"I vouldn't vant to take up too much of yer time. I only brought dese posies . . ."

He extended his right hand, which until now had been tucked behind his broad back, and offered her a clutch of pale blue larkspurs.

"I know how much de young ladies like dem."

"Thank you. They're lovely."

It was difficult to maintain a gracious pose after she'd heard the muffled giggle from behind the kitchen door, but somehow Charlotte managed.

"Could dat be a pie I see dere on yer vindow sill?" he asked.

"Yes, it is. It's rhubarb. I made it myself."

"Yerself? *Ja,* I ought to have known dat such a fine voman like you vould be handy in de kitchen. And rhubarb, did you say? Why, it makes my mouth vater just to tink of it."

Charlotte felt sure that Thorssen was angling for a dinner invitation, but pleasant though the young man may have been, she couldn't possibly have offered one. She was only a guest here herself, after all.

She could just imagine how Dr. Kelsey would react to a suitor at the dinner table. He'd already made no secret of the fact that he found the presence of so many overzealous bachelors in his house tiresome, even if more than a few had gained entry with legitimate medical complaints.

"I don't suppose dat you'd be interested in sellin' dat pie of yers?"

Charlotte regarded Mr. Thorssen with startled surprise, but before she could think to form a reply, Rachel ambled out of the kitchen. "Why, Charlotte. I had no idea you had company," she said, without batting an eye. "Good afternoon to you, Mister Thorssen."

"And to you, Mrs. Kelsey."

"Now, what's all this I hear about you wanting to buy our pie?"

"I've a powerful craving, ma'am," he explained, and Charlotte felt a warm blush stain her cheeks at his telling remark, until he went on to clarify. "I haven't had a decent pie since I left my mama's house in Minnesota."

Rachel folded her arms over her chest, adopting a businesslike expression. "How much would you be willing to pay?"

"For a pie? Made by Miss Charlotte's own two hands?" he asked, with an incredulous air. He began to hurriedly rummage through his pockets. "Now, let me see. A dollar, at least—no, vait, two dollars."

"Mercy!" Rachel exclaimed. "If he wants it that bad, Charlotte, I suppose we'll have to let him have it."

Charlotte couldn't believe what she was hearing. "What?" she cried, and then leaned over to whisper into Rachel's ear. "You don't mean to say you're going to sell him the pie I've made for our supper?"

"Why not?" Rachel retorted. "There's another one in the oven, isn't there?"

"Well, yes, but . . ."

"Good, then it's settled."

Before they had an opportunity to change their minds, Thorssen produced the two dollars and presented it to Rachel. In return, she snatched up the pie from the window ledge and handed it over to him.

"Tank you, ladies," he said, in his peculiar accent. "Tank you both."

He stood there for a long while, grinning from ear to ear, with the pie plate balanced on his upturned palms. But then, like a cloud overtaking the sun, an odd, uneasy look settled over him.

"Is there something wrong?" Charlotte prompted.

"No, nothing. I vas only vondering if you might consider, dat is to say . . . I thought if you liked, ve might valk down te de square dis evening and vatch de sun set."

"Oh, Mr. Thorssen," she replied, phrasing her words with care, for she did not want to offend him. "I do thank you for the invitation, but you know my . . . ankle was badly sprained. I've only just recovered, and I don't think I'm ready for such a long walk yet."

"Ja, I understand," he said and cast his eyes downward. "Another time, perhaps."

With that, he turned to walk away. Something in his parting glance warned Charlotte that he hadn't completely given up yet, but as she lingered in the doorway, she was irritated that she should feel guilty for refusing him.

"I wish they wouldn't keep showing up on your kitchen porch," she told Rachel as she turned back inside and set about retrieving the second pie from the oven, "and eyeing me like hungry hounds hankering after table scraps."

Rachel smiled at the analogy. "So long as you're the only marriageable lady within fifty miles, they're not likely to give up. When you've decided upon one of them, though, the rest will let you be."

"But I have already decided. I'm not interested in any of them. I'm sure they're all nice enough fellows, but . . ."

Rachel's delicate brow cinched into a frown. "Don't you want to marry and settle down?"

"I don't want to rely on any man. I have to make my own way in the world," Charlotte said, as she placed her second pie on the window ledge. Her words only seemed to make Rachel more confused, so she took a deep breath and went on to explain. "You see, after my father . . . died I was left with a few meager assets and no means of supporting myself. The war had made rough times for everyone. It was awful to be so helpless. I don't ever intend to feel that way again."

"Poor Charlotte," Rachel mused. "Whatever did you do?"

A frenzied rapping interrupted their conversation. They exchanged knowing glances, and then, expelling a long sigh, Charlotte went to throw open the door. She was met by Henry Sutton, the young man who owned the hardware store. He was breathless and his usually pallid face was flushed from exertion.

"Gunnar Thorssen says that you're selling pies, Miss

Charlotte," he announced, dispensing entirely with any form of a polite greeting, "and so I got myself over here as quick as I could to buy one."

Charlotte shook her head. "I'm sorry, but . . ."

"Come on in, Mr. Sutton," Rachel called out from behind her. "I'm afraid, though, as this is the last one, we'll have to charge you three dollars for it."

Incredulous, Charlotte made an awkward step back to allow Sutton to enter the kitchen, then turned to Rachel, who'd already gone to pluck the pie from the window ledge, her dark eyes alight with mischief.

"Of course, if you think that's too much to pay . . ."

"For a chance to taste Miss Charlotte's rhubarb pie?" Sutton said as he reached for his billfold. "On the contrary, ma'am, I'd call it an honest-to-goodness bargain."

Charlotte watched speechlessly, as Rachel completed the transaction, and then hurried Mr. Sutton on his way. Not until they were alone again, did she finally find her voice. "So now that you've sold off the pies, what are we to do for our dessert?"

"Oh, don't worry yourself about that. We'll have sliced bread with some of my gooseberry jam. Noah won't even miss the pies. He's been away all afternoon anyway, tending to old Mr. Fleming, who sweeps up at the Red Bird Saloon."

Rachel advanced toward her and pressed the money from both of the pies into Charlotte's hand. "There now. Five dollars for an hour's work," she said. "That's certainly making your own way, if you ask me."

Charlotte shook her head. "I can't accept this money. The supplies belonged to you; I only mixed them all together."

"Of course, you'll take it. I insist. Those boys wouldn't have been half so eager for the pies if you hadn't baked them." Rachel hesitated briefly, and then an idea struck her. "You know, I don't think you could count on selling at such a profit every day, but if you were to bake a few pies and maybe a loaf of bread here and there, you could earn a decent living for yourself, if that's really what you want."

"Of course, it is," Charlotte insisted, "but I couldn't consider taking advantage of you that way. You saw what happened here today. There'd be a commotion in your kitchen the whole day long. Doctor Kelsey would be furious, and I've already upset your lives enough."

Rachel wasn't ready to give in yet, though. "There is another alternative," she proposed, after she thought about it for a while. "I'm sure if you made use of that pretty smile of yours, you could convince one of the businessmen in this town to lend you space in his store for a month free of charge, and you could pay him back once you started to make a profit. As I come to think of it, Jack Cordell's old log building is empty now that he's moved into his new quarters."

Charlotte struck a solemn pose as she considered Rachel's proposal. There weren't many options open to her, now that necessity had forced her to put Charlie to rest. She could continue to rely upon the Kelsey's hospitality—knowing that once Rachel's baby was born, she'd have to find another situation—or she could take a gamble now on a venture that might offer her at least some measure off independence.

"I don't plan to accept charity," she informed Rachel when finally she'd decided. "I'll use some of the money we earned today as the first month's rent, and there ought to be enough left in my gold pouch to pay for the supplies to get me started."

Rachel's dark eyes sparkled with excitement. "You'll do it then? You'll speak to Cordell?"

"Why not?" Charlotte said and let go a sigh. "With things as they are, I have nothing to lose."

* * *

Apart from the day several weeks ago when they'd been introduced, Charlotte hadn't encountered Jackson Cordell even once. Taking full advantage of her role as invalid, she'd not gone out of the house at all. Charlotte had not gone shopping with Rachel nor to church services when the circuit-riding preacher came through. She hadn't felt comfortable enough in skirts to parade herself about, and moreover, she feared that her manners had become rusty from disuse.

In spite of her efforts, though, privacy was hard to come by. The townsmen doggedly sought her out. While she scarcely gave them the time of day when they came to call, they must have thought it was merely feminine modesty. They kept on coming back, more determined than ever to win her favor.

Cordell hadn't numbered among her kitchen door suitors, and although Charlotte respected him for his restraint, she had to admit that a part of her was disappointed, and yes, a little curious. Maybe he didn't find her attractive. That wasn't so hard to believe, after all. Or maybe he was promised elsewhere. And why should she care either way?

She did care, so when Rachel offered to help her spruce up a bit before she went to speak to him the next morning, she did not refuse. There was just no telling what sort of foolish things a woman might do if she felt she was being ignored.

And that was how Charlotte came to be standing before the swinging mirror on her bureau, wearing a white cashmere shawl to hide the faded colors and altered-to-fit form of her borrowed blue calico dress; a straw bonnet, trimmed with silk cornflowers and ribbons; and a pair of kid gloves.

"There now. Don't you look lovely!" Rachel cooed as she peered into the mirror over Charlotte's shoulder.

Charlotte wrinkled her nose. She hadn't for a moment believed that these simple touches would transform her into a striking beauty, but secretly she'd hoped for perhaps a little more than the same bland features that met her in the mirror each morning.

"You've done the best that you could," Charlotte said, "but this was a misguided notion. I'm afraid it's true what they say about turning a sow's ear into a silk purse."

"Bah! You've spent too much time in those smelly old buckskins to be any judge of real beauty," Rachel snapped back.

"Well, I'd be good deal more comfortable in those buckskins, if you'd like to know the truth. These bonnet ribbons are about to strangle me."

"Just try and smile, won't you? That would make all the difference in the world."

Charlotte did her best to oblige, but her heart wasn't in it. She curved her mouth until one corner tilted upward, causing her cheek to dimple, but the image in the mirror still looked pained.

"It's no use," she said. "I'm not capable of charming anyone."

"Then think about how much you want this business of your own," Rachel advised, placing her hands on Charlotte's shoulders and urging her toward the door, "and how eager you are to make your own way. Jack Cordell has something you need, and like it or not, you're going to have to be pleasant to him in order to get it. Now go on out there and try, for heaven's sake."

And so, armed with a shopping list and market basket, Charlotte marshaled her courage and marched across town to Jack Cordell's establishment. The tinkling bell on the door announced her arrival, and as she crossed over the threshold, she inhaled the scent of an aromatic blend of coffee beans, pickle brine, and exotic spices. The familiarity of it made her smile in spite of all her anxieties.

The interior of the store was like so many others of its kind she had seen in her lifetime. A long wooden counter stood on either end, and all around, the walls of the high-ceilinged room were fitted with row upon row of shelves. Those on the left contained dry goods: bolts of cloth in mostly somber hues, boxes of shoes, and felt hats stacked one atop the next. On the right were the groceries and kitchenware: tins of soap and canned goods, dishpans and coffee kettles, cheese and chewing tobacco.

She tried not to gape at the merchandise, but it was difficult not to, especially after she spied some of the rarer delicacies: colorful tins of sweet biscuits, hard candies, and chocolates. Charlotte had had a terrible sweet tooth as a child, but it had been a long time since she'd savored a bit of peppermint or a lemon drop. Peering across the counter now with childlike enthusiasm, she considered whether it would be too foolish to dole out some of her savings for a small tin.

In all this time, Jackson Cordell hadn't turned around. He was holed up in a rear corner of the store, sorting letters into a pigeonholed frame. "Have a look around," he called out at last, "and I'll be with you shortly."

Charlotte kept on eyeing the candy counter and found herself wondering if the frivolous young girl who'd so loved candies was still alive somewhere inside of her. It would be best if she wasn't, she decided. Young girls only had their dreams dashed in the end.

She tapped out an impatient rhythm on the floor with one foot while she waited for Cordell, her annoyance increasing. With his back turned, he couldn't possibly have known who had come in, and yet, irrational though it might have been, she could not help but feel that he was again ignoring her.

She took it as a challenge. Ruthlessly, she silenced that part of herself which attempted to warn her of the dangers of playing games, and reaching into the deep, dark well of her memories, she sought out that frivolous, young girl that she'd once been, before circumstance had roughened her up. Once, a lifetime ago, she'd been as poised and practiced as any other young lady. She'd told Rachel that she could not charm a man, but that wasn't exactly true. She may have been long out of practice, but she had not forgotten.

"So, you're the postmaster, too, are you?" she mused aloud, making full use of her deep-pitched, dulcet tones. "Running this store, chairing the town council . . . why, it's no wonder you haven't found the time to stop by and say hello to me."

Cordell's head jerked abruptly, and the packet he'd been holding slipped through his fingers. Half a dozen envelopes spilled onto the floor. A slow smile of satisfaction played over Charlotte's lips. *Ignore me, will he?*

But Cordell was no amateur at this game either. He recovered himself almost at once. With his back still to her, he bent over to retrieve what he'd dropped, then took his time in filing away the remainder of the letters. When finally he deigned to address her, he leaned back against the shelving, arms folded across his clean, white apron. Those smoke gray eyes of his wandered over her in a slow appraisal.

"I'm a man of many talents, Miss Devereaux," he said pointedly. "Now, what is it precisely that I can do to help *you?*"

Charlotte found herself staring at his mouth, flexed with amusement, at the deep hollow of his throat, framed by the open collar of his striped cotton shirt and apron front, at the place where his sleeves were rolled to reveal taut, tanned forearms. The blood pulsing through her veins began to bubble with a pleasing warmth, and a familiar excitement was building in her.

Emboldened now, she advanced on him, settling her basket onto the counter near where he stood. "My, my, my!" Her accent seemed to thicken with each word. "So many things come to mind."

Fanning herself with a gloved hand, she let go a disappointed sigh. "But I suppose we shall have to start with Rachel's shopping list."

She drew the page from her basket and held it out to him, but as he reached to take it from her, she hesitated before releasing it. Their eyes met, and Charlotte felt suddenly aware of the dangerous undercurrents threading between them. Before she'd realized, Cordell's long fingers had edged across the page, making contact with hers, the heat of his skin searing through her glove.

She took a shaky breath, then swallowed hard. Only then did she begin to come to her senses. God help her, she'd actually been flirting with Jack Cordell! And after she'd sworn she'd never play this sort of game again. There was too much danger in it. Hadn't she learned that the hard way? She couldn't win. Women never did.

She took an awkward step backward, shaken to the core. For weeks now she had been made to face a daily procession of gentlemen callers, and not once had she been affected in the least. But one touch from Jack Cordell had turned her knees to jelly.

He seemed cool enough. After scanning Rachel's list, he calmly went about the business of filling the order. As he reached for a can of tomatoes, high on the shelf, the fabric of his shirt stretched taut across his shoulders. Charlotte's eyes lingered over the hard-muscled planes of his back before she caught herself and dragged her gaze down to the floor. Chastened, she stared hard at her pinched toes, now crammed into a too-small pair of Rachel's shoes.

"I'm afraid there've been no letters for you yet from New Orleans," he said, "in case you were wondering."

"I wasn't expecting any." She hoped that she sounded as nonchalant as he, even though the ribbons of Rachel's bonnet were tightening at her throat, and her palms had gone sweaty inside her dainty gloves. "There's no one left to send any."

He placed a box of castile soap and a packet of hairpins in her basket alongside the other items he'd gathered, then regarded her, one dark brow lifting with renewed interest. "So then, you're all alone in the world . . . but for Rachel, that is."

Perverse creature that she was, now that Charlotte had gotten him interested in her at last, she wished for nothing more than for him to ignore her again. When she did not reply to his comment, he pressed on. "I suppose the war must have been hard on a lot of folk down your way."

"I . . . I make it a point not to dwell on the past," she finally managed to say. "It doesn't do anyone any good, after all. We can't change things."

"I hope you don't think I was prying," he told her. "It's part of my job to make conversation with my customers."

He offered her a smile, all the while allowing his eyes to wander over her shamelessly. Charlotte wrapped the cashmere shawl closer around her, in response. She couldn't blame Cordell. It was, after all, she who had started this game. And she ought to have known better, after all that she'd been through.

Hardest of all to take was the fact that she'd lost sight of why she'd come here in the first place, that she'd allowed a man with a charming smile to muddle her thinking. But it wasn't too late to fix things. And she wouldn't let Jack Cordell get under her skin again. She couldn't afford to let that happen.

Four

"There's a reason I've come here today, Mr. Cordell, besides helping Rachel with the shopping, that is. I'd like to offer you a business proposition."

Jack carefully set the bottle of vanilla extract into the basket beside the other goods he'd assembled, and regarded Miss Charlotte Devereaux with a curious stare, certain he must have misunderstood the meaning of her statement.

The woman standing before him now, with feet spread slightly apart and arms folded over her chest, was not the same lissome creature who had dallied with him only a few moments before. Even her voice had changed. The molasses was gone, replaced with a sandpaper harshness.

Though he'd tried to deny it, on more than one occasion, Jack had caught himself imagining what might happen, what he might say, on the day she walked into his store. And he was pleased that she'd finally decided to pay him a visit—even if it had taken her a damnably long time to do so—but he'd never imagined that any one woman could prompt such confusion in him.

"A proposition?"

"I'd like to know if you'd be interested in renting out that old log building of yours next door. You see, I've decided to open a bakery."

"A bakery?"

He was beginning to sound like a witless idiot now, parroting every other word she said.

"Yes. Rachel and I were thinking that, with all of the bachelor gentlemen in these parts, there's a real need. Busy working men can't be expected to bake their own bread and such. Don't you agree?"

At the mention of "bachelor gentlemen," disappointment struck him like a swift kick in the gut. So, that was it. The change in her voice had thrown him off balance, but with this, Jack was reminded of how deftly she'd flirted with him just a short while ago, of what Noah had said only yesterday about how much she enjoyed being the center of attention among the menfolk of Cedar Creek. And now she had devised a way to exploit her popularity still further. *What a cunning vixen she was!*

He shifted his attention to Rachel's shopping list and crossed over behind the opposite counter to fetch a spool of cotton thread, his back safely to Miss Devereaux. He'd heard it told that New Orleans women, with too much French blood running in their veins, made a sport out of beguiling men. And he wasn't surprised that the others in town had fallen under the spell of such a woman; they were young, headstrong, and venturesome.

But Jack Cordell was none of those things. After thirty-six years, life had tempered him into a thoughtful, cautious individual, and so it was doubly hard for him to admit that she'd gotten into his blood, same as the rest of the men.

"Well? What do you think?" she prompted.

The muscles in his jaw went taut as he reached into the box on the shelf, and his fingers curled over a spool of thread. "I think that you've a mind to develop an 'acquaintance' with every bachelor gentleman in these parts," he muttered, beneath his breath.

"I beg your pardon?"

Jack turned to her, fully intending to repeat the remark

aloud, but when he saw her face, brimming with promise, something made him reconsider.

"I was only wondering how you'd gotten the idea to open a bakery, that's all."

"Actually, it happened yesterday afternoon," she said. "I'd baked two pies for supper, and when Mr. Thorssen came to call, he became rather insistent upon buying one. I thought the whole business more than a little peculiar, but Rachel said it would be all right to let him have it. Then, not ten minutes later, Mr. Sutton came by, saying that he'd seen Thorssen's pie and was wondering if he might buy one for himself. Well, we could hardly refuse him."

Jack listened to her tale, wanting to deny that it was jealousy he felt pricking at his insides all the while. Thorssen and Sutton were addle-brained. The both of them panting after her like two sorry hounds in heat.

"That's a . . . charming story," he observed.

Try though he might, he could not prevent the acid from seeping into his tone. The young fools in town might well be guilty of tripping over themselves to compete for Miss Devereaux's affections, but she was far more to blame for contriving to take advantage of them.

"But what practical experience have you?" he asked her next. "After all, two pies do not a business make."

"I've always been handy in the kitchen," she retorted, color rising high in her cheeks at his challenge. "I'm willing to work hard, and what ought to be most important of all to you, Mr. Cordell, I can pay the first month's rent up front."

She sounded rather peckish, but Jack had hardened himself against her. Oh, she might have a talent for leading young men about by the nose, but how would that help her in running herself ragged, day, after day, in stocking supplies, making change, and keeping ledgers?

"Have you discussed this little idea of yours with Noah?"

Her eyes narrowed. "Why on earth should I do that?"

"I only thought that, seeing as he is the gentleman responsible for you, he might like to know what you're up to."

It was the wrong thing to say. Jack realized that before he'd even gotten all the words out. Her spine stiffened, her gloved fingers curled into two tight balls, and those otherwise mild features of hers came to life, brimming with barely-suppressed anger.

"Let's get one thing straight between us from the outset, Mr. Cordell, shall we? I'm well past the age of twenty-one. Noah Kelsey may well be my . . . my cousin's husband, but I can assure you that neither he nor any other man need be responsible for me."

Jack was speechless. He thought he'd been doing her a favor in dissuading her from the poorly-thought-out little plan of hers. He hadn't expected outrage. Had he misjudged her again?

With her eyes flashing blue fire, she came alive. She looked, well, almost beautiful. He hadn't expected it, hadn't expected that she'd have so much spirit. And then, as always, there was that voice of hers. Even taut with anger, it flooded through him like hot chocolate laced with brandy—rich, sweet, and intoxicating.

"I never meant to suggest that you were incompetent," he explained, once he'd managed to gather together his wits, "but we're living in a rough world out here, and an unprotected woman is considered fair game to some men."

Miss Deveraux frowned at him. She began to pace the length of the counter, and as she did, she drew off her gloves, one after the other, tossed them both into her market basket, and then vigorously swiped the palms of her hands on her skirts. Next, she untied the ribbons under

her chin, and removing her bonnet, carelessly cast it in
the basket alongside the gloves.

"Things were no different in New Orleans," she told
him, "especially not once the war had started. Women
were chattel, either their father's or husband's, and those
who had neither were—just as you say—'fair game.'"

The war. Jack hadn't thought of that before. Whatever
she might have been once, the recent war had undoubtedly
had a hand in shaping Charlotte Devereaux into the complicated woman who stood before him now. He couldn't
excuse her manipulative ways, but he thought that, at least,
he understood her a little better now. And he'd have to
take care not to underestimate her again.

She faced off against him, with arms akimbo, the soft
shawl slipping now to reveal her sadly faded calico dress.
"Imagine, just for a moment," she proposed, "that I'm
not a woman. Imagine that I'm a man, albeit one with no
experience in running a business, and that I've come to
you to inquire after renting your building. Would you be
lecturing me then about my shortcomings, Mr. Cordell, or
would you take my money and keep your opinions to
yourself?"

Jack allowed her words to sink in, and then at last, he
threw up his hands. He'd never met a woman so persistent.
"All right. All right, I take your point. I'll rent you the
building, if that's what you want. Go ahead and throw
away your life's savings on this venture; it's no concern
of mine."

Rachel wielded her broom with a vengeance. Not a single speck of dust on the planked wood floor was spared
from her diligent assault. She'd already swept out the
whole of the back room, and now, with a rhythmic swish-
ing of straw bristles, she scooted on past Charlotte, who
was perched on a chair scrubbing down the rough pine

shelving behind the single counter that stretched across the shop.

"I think this will make a fine bakery once we get it cleaned up," she said.

"You'd best not overtax yourself," Charlotte warned. "I can finish that up later."

"Honestly, I'm not tired at all. In fact, I'm rather enjoying myself."

After she'd finished sweeping up, Rachel planted herself in the doorway, and leaning on the broom handle, she surveyed the scene. "Hmmm. We've cleared out the worst of the rubbish; scoured, scrubbed, and polished. It's not half bad. But it could use some frills, I think."

Charlotte looked up from her work in surprise, not sure she'd heard aright. "Frills?"

Rachel nodded. "Everyone will be expecting it, seeing as how this is one of the only businesses in town run by a lady. Maybe some lace curtains on the windows?"

"I couldn't possibly afford lace curtains, Rachel."

"Well then, what if we were to bring some of your flowers from home? Put a vase on the counter and one or two up on the shelves? There's certainly plenty to go around."

"I suppose that wouldn't hurt," Charlotte agreed, and then she looked down in dismay at her clothes. She'd been cleaning out the stovepipe this morning and her apron was grimy with soot. "I'm not as 'frilly' as I ought to be either, am I?"

"Oh, don't you worry about that. Once there's money coming in, you won't have to wear my hand-me-downs any more."

Charlotte shook her head. "I'm not wasting my hard-earned money on fripperies."

"You can buy yourself a new dress, at least, and a pair of shoes that fit. That'll make all the difference in the world."

"Do you think I'll attract enough customers to make a go of it?"

Rachel regarded her in disbelief. "Charlotte, how can you even ask such a question? Every eligible bachelor in town has been lying awake nights trying to devise ways to spend more time with you. To tell the truth, I don't think there'll be room enough in this little shop for all the customers you're going to attract."

Charlotte wasn't so sure, though. Ever since Jack Cordell had questioned her ability to run a business, she couldn't help but wonder for herself. If hard work was all it took, then there was no doubt but that she'd prosper, but she was beginning to see that there were other factors to consider.

"What if—after they do spend some time with me— they come to think I'm peculiar?" she asked. "What if my behavior isn't ladylike enough to suit them?"

"Not ladylike enough?" Rachel cried. "In a town full of men? Believe me, so long as you don't pick your teeth or spit on the floor, they'll think you as refined as the Queen of England."

Charlotte stepped down from her perch and let her dirty rag splash into the pail of wash water at her feet. "I wouldn't care so much what they thought of me if I didn't need for this bakery to be a success," she said. "You *will* help me where you can, won't you? Give me a stern look if you should catch me forgetting myself and doing something that I oughtn't or a sharp word if my tongue gets too salty?"

"You know that I will," Rachel replied, and setting aside her broom, she rushed to wrap her arms around her friend. "Oh Charlotte, I know this is a wonderful opportunity, but I am going to miss you."

Charlotte's throat swelled with emotion. She hadn't expected to ever again feel such fondness for another human being. The way her life had worked out, she'd had to remain detached in order to keep safe her secret. But Rachel had crept in and caught her unaware, treating her from the first moment they met as if they truly had been related by blood.

"Don't be a goose," she chided. "We'll still be living under the same roof, after all."

"But you'll be here all day, and I'll be at home."

"I have to make my own way," Charlotte insisted. "Besides, wasn't all of this your idea to begin with?"

Rachel hugged her tighter and bobbed her head. "Sometimes I can be too clever for my own good. Now I'd better go and get those flowers. We're wasting time standing around here chatting."

Rachel hurried off then, and Charlotte went back to her work. If she finished cleaning up this evening and set in her stores, she might be able to get the oven going and open the bakery first thing tomorrow.

It was while she was wiping down the uppermost row of shelving that she caught sight of a length of leather strap hanging from one of the support beams in a near corner of the room. Likely it was nothing more than a rotting tether from which Cordell had once hung some item of merchandise, but since it had caught her eye, she aimed to remove it.

Shoving her chair against the counter, she climbed from one perch up onto the next, and by standing on tiptoe, she was just able to reach up and grab hold of the strap. She gave it a rough jerk, but it wouldn't come loose, so the next time she pulled a bit harder, and in consequence, was nearly cracked on the head by a hurtling projectile. She stepped back just in time as a flurry of dust rained down and the object hit the counter with a dull thud.

Charlotte clambered down to have a look. There, in the midst of the counter upon which she'd been standing, lay a miner's knapsack, made out of brown leather that was now cracked and worn with age. Curiosity took hold of her, and without giving the matter a second thought, she worked to unfasten the rusting buckle, and then drew back the flap.

She reached inside. Her fingers skimmed over several items, and she drew them out, one-by-one. First came a book. It was an immigrant's guide, she noted as she read the faded lettering on its paperboard cover, one of those which had been written to aid the forty-niners on their trek West.

Folded neatly inside of its front cover was a map. It had been sketched entirely by hand, and its surface was crisscrossed with wavy lines, marked with Xs and peppered with exotic names like Red Dog, Indian Bar, and Spanish Flats. Scribbled on the back side of the page were the names of four men, and a penciled line had been drawn through each.

Joshua Keyes, Thomas Filmore, Hiram Black, Albert Soames. . . . They had probably all been members of a mining company, Charlotte decided. For unless she missed her guess, this was a map of the California gold fields. She'd heard her own prospecting partners speak of more than one of these places while reminiscing about their California days.

Could it be a treasure map, nearly twenty years old? For a brief instant, Charlotte felt the same tingling rush that infused her whenever she'd caught a flash of color in the pan or hacked a promising chunk of ore out of the drift, but the feeling ebbed away almost at once.

Even if this were a treasure map, it would certainly be worthless by now. Thousands of men had already panned and prospected through every inch of the California gold fields, hoping to find their fortune, and more than a few of the unlucky ones had migrated here to Colorado, still hoping.

Also tucked inside the pack were several chunks of blossom rock, wound up in a red calico neckerchief. A closer look told her that it was high grade, gold-bearing ore. *Someone's souvenirs, most likely.* Charlotte knew that prospectors would often hunt through tons of useless rock to find a few rich samples like these, have them assayed, and then use the assay report from them to sell an unwary buyer their otherwise worthless mine.

Once she had removed these rocks, a single item remained. It was of an awkward shape, heavy, and had been carefully wrapped up in a length of blue flannel. Charlotte knew, even as she took it up in her hand, what it was, and sure enough, when she peeled back the fabric, a pearl-handled revolver was revealed, its barrel glinting in the sunlight.

Did the miner's knapsack and its contents belong to Jack Cordell? Charlotte considered it, but somehow had trouble imagining the sober storekeeper ever having need of such a fancy weapon as this. Maybe he'd only been storing it for someone, and after time had passed, he'd forgotten where he'd put it. Or maybe he wasn't aware that it had been up there at all.

She thought about handing it over to Cordell, but something made her hesitate. Considering its awkward resting place up in the rafters, it was a safe bet that whomever had placed it there didn't intend that it should be found. And Charlotte had a great respect for keeping secrets, seeing as how she harbored more than a few of her own.

So, before she could change her mind, she repacked the items, and then, balancing herself upon a crate which she'd arranged atop the counter, and using the broomstick to extend her reach, she endeavored to return the knapsack to its former hiding place.

If only she'd been a few inches taller, she wouldn't have needed to stretch so far. If only she'd been wearing a practical pair of trousers instead of those damned, awkward skirts and petticoats, she wouldn't have had to hitch the fabric up so high in order to brace her knee against the chinking in the log wall, and she wouldn't have looked like a shameless saloon dancer in the midst of a performance when Rachel came in, her arms filled up with vases of wildflowers, and Jack Cordell in tow.

"Charlotte!"

Rachel's shriek was followed by the clanging of metal as Cordell, startled by her outburst, dropped the entire stack of baking pans he'd been carrying.

Charlotte whirled around. The broomstick slipped out of her hand, glanced off the counter, and slammed to the floor. For a long drawn-out moment, she teetered on the edge of the crate, her arms circling backward through the air.

Perched as she was, it was inevitable that she should lose the struggle for balance. Her heart sank as she felt herself begin to fall. Fortunately, though, Cordell had anticipated her dilemma and rushed to position himself beneath her. She dropped squarely into his arms, and instinctively wound hers around his neck.

With her head buried against his chest, she took a shaky breath, very much aware of the awkward silence as a surfeit of sensations flooded through her: the sure, steady beating of his heart next to her cheek, the heady mix of pine soap, bay rum, and strong male scent that permeated the air around him, the long arms clamped firmly as two iron bands behind her back and her knees. . . . *Safe.* The word vibrated through her with a startling intensity. She felt safe in his arms.

As she looked up at him, she noticed the spark of amusement in his eyes. He always seemed to be either chiding her or laughing at her. But hidden within their smoky depths, there was more—there was desire, potent and unmistakable. A shiver slid down Charlotte's spine, and on their own, her fingertips sought the place where his black hair curled against the nape of his neck.

"Thank you," she said, breathless.

Then something else crept into Cordell's gaze. Something Charlotte couldn't quite put a finger on. When finally she recognized the glimmer of mistrust for what it was, disappointment rushed over her.

She'd already decided that he hadn't perceived the connection between her and the young miner, Charlie. If he had, he'd surely have spoken up by now. But nevertheless, Jack Cordell saw something in Charlotte that all of the others had missed, and whatever it was, it made him draw back.

Jack pressed his mouth into a long, hard line, and turned his gaze away from the woman in his arms. But it was no use. He could not escape the heat of her fingertips still resting upon the sensitive skin at the back of his neck, nor ignore the tempting feel of her lithe body pressed against his chest. Each breath he took was sweetened with roses; to him it was her scent now, hers and hers alone. Each thought that came to his mind was prompted by a need that had gone unfulfilled for too long.

Calling upon all his strength, he held himself still and silent. This was torture, nothing less; and yet, in spite of everything, now that he held her quite literally in his arms, he could not make himself release her.

"I . . . I was clearing the cobwebs out of the rafters," she tried to explain.

Across the room, Rachel Kelsey frowned and shook her head. The armload of flower-filled vases clinked together noisily as she settled them down on the counter. "After I just finished sweeping up the floor?" she said. "Charlotte, whatever were you thinking?"

Reacting to her cousin's chastisement, Miss Devereaux turned her head away, and a soft wave of her dusky blond hair brushed beneath Jack's chin. He couldn't stand much more of this.

"You're just lucky you didn't break your fool neck," he heard himself say, his tone sharp with asperity, "scrambling over the furniture like a mountain goat."

With that, she began to writhe against him, unaware that with each sinuous movement that brought their bodies in closer contact, she drove him a step nearer to madness.

"Kindly put me down, Mr. Cordell," she ordered. "I'm perfectly capable of standing on my own two feet."

Reluctantly, oh, so reluctantly, Jack obliged. But he did not fail to get in a parting shot. "It would appear that you're not, or else you wouldn't have wound up in this fix in the first place, would you?"

"I wouldn't have fallen at all," she retorted, smoothing out her skirt with a brisk hand, "if I hadn't been startled by Rachel, screeching like a wild banshee, and the racket of all those tin pans you dropped on the floor."

With a safe distance between them now, Jack pressed his back hard against the chinked log wall and folded his arms tightly over his aproned chest. His brows lifted with bitter amusement as her words sunk in.

"So, you mean to say that all of this is *our* fault?"

"Yes! I mean, no . . . I mean . . ."

Charlotte was nonplussed. Her cheeks flushed hot as she struggled to think of a clever retort. But nothing came to her. Her senses were tingling, her thoughts ajumble, and all on account of Jack Cordell. How dare he hang onto her so possessively? And then berate her as if she were a wayward child? It was almost as if he thought she'd *arranged* to fall off of that crate and into his arms.

Pointedly, she turned her back on him, intending to forget all about the unfortunate incident and get on with her work. She didn't know why in the world she'd reacted to him as she had. She ought to have known better than to give way to her emotions. With all that she'd been through, she ought to have learned by now.

Rachel had already set the vases of wildflowers about the room, retrieved the baking pans that Cordell had brought with him, and was now on her knees, arranging them into a neat stack. Charlotte shook off her uneasiness, determined to concentrate upon the next item on her list of things that needed doing.

She proceeded to drag the battered wooden chair, which she'd been using all day as a ladder, to the open doorframe between the shop and the back room. Next, she reached beneath the counter for the length of calico cloth that she'd purchased to use as a curtain, scooped up the bundle and the hammer and nails resting atop it, and walked toward her chair.

She only managed two steps, however, before she found her progress mysteriously impeded. A backward glance revealed that Cordell had tangled his fist in her apron strings.

"If you're intending to climb on that chair to hang up that curtain, I'd think again. We've had more than enough excitement for one day."

With that, he appropriated her tools, and only then did he release her. "*I'll* hang the curtain," he told her, and then quickly added, "Mind you, not because I think you are an incapable female, but because as your landlord, it's the least I can do."

"Why . . . why . . ." Charlotte blustered, painfully unable to form words that could express the full measure of venom she wanted to convey.

"Why, how kind of you to offer," Rachel finished for her and cast a warning glance in Charlotte's direction.

With baking pans now firmly in hand, she headed off for the back room and called out over her shoulder. "Seeing as how Mr. Cordell is giving you a hand, Charlotte, I'm going to run home and put supper on the stove. You will behave yourself until I get back, won't you?"

Charlotte didn't have to reply. She'd perceived Rachel's warning well enough to know what was expected of her. Once Rachel was gone, though, Charlotte found it decidedly difficult to comply. She stood beside the chair as Cordell nailed the calico curtain across the top of the doorframe, biting her tongue until her patience had all slipped away.

"Don't you have a store to run?" she snapped.

She couldn't say why she felt compelled to provoke him now, when it appeared that he was only trying to help, but nevertheless she did.

"Oh, I think the town can do without me for a few minutes while I finish this up," he replied cheerfully. "Besides, I've asked old man Fleming to keep an eye on things while I carry over your supplies. He spends enough time bent over my checkerboard and warming his feet by my stove to know how to run the place."

"You don't have to deliver my supplies. I can manage on my own."

Cordell climbed down from the chair and met her, eye to eye. "Most of us can manage alone if we have to, Miss Devereaux," he said frankly, "but it's the spirit of cooperation that has made Cedar Creek the sort of town it is."

Charlotte had to admit she found that a tempting notion. She'd grown sorely tired of loneliness. Perhaps that was part of the reason she'd decided to make a stand here, but there was no way she was going to give Jack Cordell the satisfaction of knowing it.

"Cooperation?" she echoed. "Oh, is that why you're here? But aren't you the same man who told me I'd be throwing away my money on this venture?"

Jack winced. She had a sharp wit, no doubt of that. This afternoon wasn't working out quite as he'd expected. He hadn't wanted to argue with her. He'd been hoping that they might reach some kind of reconciliation. But then, maybe it was for the best that they keep their distance from one another.

"That was before I saw how hard you were willing to work," he admitted. "You've done quite a job with this old place. It doesn't look half bad now that it's been scrubbed down and dressed up."

He settled the hammer down onto the counter and made his way toward the door. "I'm sure you'll do well, Miss Devereaux, if you're serious about making a success of this bakery of yours; if you're not just playing games . . ."

Her voice was hushed with disbelief. "Is that what you think I'm doing here?"

Jack cast her a backward glance that made his suspicions more than clear.

"I don't know how you come by your notions about what sort of woman I am, Mr. Cordell, but I can assure you that frivolity is a luxury I've scarcely been able to afford."

With this she turned her hands palm up and thrust them toward him. "Do these look like the hands of a woman with the time to play games?"

For a moment, Jack stood his ground, refusing to turn back and take a closer look, afraid of what he might see. But in the end, curiosity won out, and he complied.

It was a pity to see the slender hands spread before him, both palms scored with lines, heels, and rises discolored and hardened by calluses. These were not the hands of a lady, nor even a poor woman charged with the heavy burden of daily household chores. They were the work-scarred hands of one who labored for a living.

Jack was stunned. *What trials had she been forced to endure after the war had turned her world upside down?* he wondered. And if she was the manipulative vixen that he'd supposed her to be, then why hadn't she used those skills to arrange an easier life for herself?

Miss Devereaux must have been able to read the dismay on his face, for she paled visibly, as though realizing that she'd gone too far . . . revealed too much. Curling her fingers, she drew back her hands and thrust them into the folds of her skirt.

She sought to turn away, but Jack caught her by the arm. "I'm sorry," he said. "You're right. I have treated you unfairly. But if you're willing, I'd like to call a truce in this little battle of ours."

Jack purposefully put out his hand to her. She stared at it hard, and then, finally, offered her own. He clasped it firmly, imparting his strength to her through his touch, willing her not to be ashamed.

"There now. That's better," he told her. "We'll begin again . . . as friends this time."

Five

"I hereby call this meeting to order," Jack announced, and then solemnly struck his gavel twice on the countertop.

The half-dozen members of Cedar Creek's town council, who'd been lounging informally in the chairs that Jack provided for the convenience of his customers, straightened in their seats, offering at least a semblance of decorum. Nate Phillips, the newspaper editor, stood with his shoulder propped against the door jamb, pencil poised over his pad as he prepared to make notes.

"Most of you are aware of the visit paid me last week by Mr. Jasper Price, who is a surveyor for the railroad," Jack went on to say. "Now I think you'll agree that we would all benefit if Cedar Creek were to become a railway stop, and as Mr. Price will be paying us a call again in the next month or so, I'd like to entertain ideas as to how we can convince him that our town deserves consideration."

Hollis Lloyd, the burly young butcher who owned the meat market, leaned forward in his chair. "Do you think he'd accept a bank draft? If we was all to pitch in, we could . . ."

"Bribery isn't quite what I had in mind," Jack replied patiently. Lloyd wasn't unscrupulous by nature, only somewhat dull-witted. "I was thinking more along the lines of making some improvements to the town. You know, spruce things up a bit."

"You mean, say, if we were to paint our storefronts?" Henry Sutton put in.

"That would be one suggestion, yes," Jack agreed.

Elliot Baird, the dandified barber, got to his feet and hooked his thumbs into the armholes of his gold brocade vest. "You've already told us that Price seemed disappointed to learn that we hadn't a proper hotel. What can we do about that?"

"Well, I was thinking that if we all worked together, we might put a better face on the Widow Murphy's place," Jack proposed, "maybe a fresh coat of paint and a new sign out front."

Lars and Gunnar Thorssen bobbed their heads vigorously. *"Ja,"* Lars said, "an' ve could replace dem porch steps and maybe fix dem broken shutters."

"An' if ve vere to do de verk on Saturday, everyone could participate," his brother added. "Ve could make a regular holiday out of it."

Although he was not technically a part of the proceedings, the newspaperman, Phillips, couldn't help but put in an idea of his own. "You know, more than anything else, I think Mister Price wants to see a thriving community," he said, tugging thoughtfully on his dark beard. "The more people, the better. I've sent some recent issues of the *Chronicle* up to a number of my friends in Denver with the hope that my printed observations will encourage new folk to settle here. We've a lot to recommend us: plentiful water, beauteous scenery, abundant timber."

Jack was pleased to see that Phillips had already begun to think of himself as a part of things, for the *Cedar Creek Chronicle* was an integral building block in Jack's designs for the town.

"We should give some thought to advertising our Fourth of July celebration," Phillips continued. "I could print up handbills. If you promise folk a rip-roaring celebration, people for miles around will come. And while they're here, they'll take a look around, and maybe some of them will decide to stay."

"That does make sense," Jack agreed. "All in favor of engaging Mr. Phillips to print up handbills announcing our Fourth of July celebration signify by saying 'aye.' "

There was a chorus of "ayes" all around.

Jack leaned back against his shelves and addressed the assembled council. "While we're on the subject, how are the plans for the entertainment progressing?"

Elliot Baird got to his feet once more and struck a pose. "I've engaged Henderson's Theatrical Troupe from Denver to come down. They've performed Shakespeare and the like, and there's a variety bill, too."

"That's all well and good," Hollis Lloyd put in, "but will there be any females? With things as they is around here, we was all sort of hopin' . . ."

Baird rolled his watery blue eyes. "Miss Lila Henderson is a celebrated stage actress," he said. "Her presence alone is well worth the money we'll pay. But for these men with more pedestrian tastes, there'll be at least half a dozen young beauties to dance and sing, as well as a magician, a strongman, and two trained dogs. Will that be enough to satisfy you, my friend?"

Hollis bobbed his head in reply, offering a broad grin that exposed a row of even white teeth.

Gustav Stern, the dour German who ran the assay office, was responsible for taking the minutes of the meeting. Thus far, he'd been busily scribbling in his notebook, but now he lifted his heavy frame out of his chair, signaling to all that he intended to speak. A long silence ensued.

"What do you have to say about all this, Gus?" Jack prompted.

"I was just thinking. What if we were to sponsor some games of skill—a sharpshooting contest, perhaps, or a horse race? That would attract people, wouldn't it?"

"You wouldn't be planning on running that black mare of yours in this horse race, would you?" Henry Sutton inquired. "Everybody knows she can outrun anything else on four legs in this county."

"It's a good idea, though," Jack said. "We could charge an entrance fee and offer a cash purse to the winner."

"I'd be willin' to provide a prize for the sharpshootin' contest," Hollis Lloyd proposed. "Say a smoked ham or some such."

Jack strode out from behind the counter and came to stand before the assembled council. "Are we all in favor of providing contests at our celebration?" Another chorus of "ayes" filled the air. "Make a note of that, Gus, and our thanks to Hollis, who has graciously offered to provide the prize for the sharpshooting contest. Now is there anything else?"

"What about food?" Henry Sutton asked. "Should we ask Arthur Rollins to help out?"

"The . . . saloonkeeper?" Elliot Baird sputtered.

"Well, the Red Bird is the closest we got to a restaurant in town."

Gunnar Thorssen lifted a meaty hand in the air. "How about Miss Charlotte?" he suggested. "She's von damn fine cook, if you ask me."

"But would she do it?"

"I'd be more than willin' to go an' ask her," Hollis Lloyd put in.

"Oh, don't trouble yourself about it, my friend," Baird countered. "I can handle that."

Henry Sutton stepped into the fray. "No need for you boys to argue. I was planning on stopping by her shop later on anyhow to pick up a loaf of bread for myself."

"But I'll be dere dis afternoon to repair dat broken hinge on her back door," Lars Thorssen told them all. "It vould be an easy enough thing for me to ask her."

Jack followed these exchanges and shook his head,

dumbfounded. Ever since Charlotte Devereaux had opened her shop last week, he'd wakened each morning at sunrise to the sweet aroma of baking bread wafting up from next door into his rooms above the store, reminding him that she was already up and hard at work.

In spite of the fact that that aroma filled the air, even now, he'd managed to keep her out of his thoughts throughout the town meeting. But now, here she was again, center stage, as the whole town council squabbled over who would have the honor of requesting her help.

Grumbling, Jack snatched up his gavel and rapped it impatiently on the counter. "Gentlemen. In order to prevent bloodshed, I'm taking it upon myself, as your chairman, to put the question to Miss Devereaux. Now that we've settled that matter, is there any other business that needs our attention? No? Good. Well then, we've all work to get to, and I need to open the store for the day, so let's adjourn. Shall we?"

Charlotte may have been bone weary, dusted over from head to foot with flour, and elbow deep in steaming dishwater, scrubbing out mixing bowls and baking pans; but to her, this was heaven. She shut her eyes, threw back her head and breathed deeply of the sweet spring breeze that swept past the opened rear door of her bake shop; and as she did so, she thanked God for her good fortune.

She'd been in business precisely one week as of today, and from the first hour, there had been a steady stream of townsmen in and out of her store, just as Rachel had predicted. She had to admit she'd been surprised at her success. It almost seemed too easy. Oh, she may have been working hard, but she was making an honest living without need of subterfuge. Charlotte was making her own way, and that was what pleased her most of all.

When the bell on the shop door jangled, Charlotte lifted

her head, then responded at once, wiping her hands on
her apron as she swept through the calico curtain.

Hollis Lloyd, the butcher, was waiting for her on the opposite side of the counter. His broad face was flush with
color, his brown hair wind-tossed. But even so, Charlotte
could tell that he'd made a concerted effort with his appearance, for he'd taken off his bloodstained apron and buttoned
up the collar of his shirt. In fact, it fit so snug about his
massive neck that she feared he must be strangling.

"Good afternoon, Miss Charlotte," he said, meeting her
with a wide smile that showed off his teeth.

"What can I get for you this afternoon, Mr. Lloyd?"

"I'll have a loaf of your bread and half a dozen of
them currant buns."

Charlotte tore a long piece of brown wrapping paper
off the roll on her counter and went about filling the order. "It's a lovely afternoon," she said. "Isn't it?"

Lloyd nodded. "I'd say we're in for a warm spell. I was
huntin' up in the mountains the other day, and I noticed
the blue gentians had already come to flower. I'll bet you
didn't think a fella like me would know about such things,
did you?"

"I must say I am surprised," Charlotte admitted as she
wrapped his selections in the paper and tied it all up with
twine.

Lloyd leaned across the counter, his dark eyes seeking
hers. "There's a lot of things about me that would surprise
you."

Charlotte managed to smile, but nevertheless, she
breathed a sigh of relief as she heard the bell on the door
sound again. She still hadn't learned to gracefully handle
the romantic overtures she'd been receiving from these
overeager gentlemen, and so she preferred to deal with
them in groups, rather than one at a time. It was safer
that way.

When she looked up to see Jack Cordell standing there,

though, his tall, broad-shouldered frame filling up the open door, a tremor of disquiet coursed through her. Alone or in company, Cordell was more dangerous than the rest. Charlotte couldn't explain why precisely, but she seemed to lose her temper and her senses whenever he came near.

They'd called a truce, she reminded herself, and both of them had honored it throughout the week. Of course, they'd scarcely crossed paths in all that time, but there was no need for her to be uneasy. He'd said they were going to begin again, after all, and as friends this time. But did he mean it?

Cordell and Lloyd exchanged greetings as Charlotte finished tying up Lloyd's parcel, and then she handed it over the counter to him.

"How much do I owe you?" he inquired, his eyes never leaving her face.

"That'll be seventy cents, Mr. Lloyd."

He counted out the coins and gave them over, and only by drawing back sharply was Charlotte able to avoid his heavy handclasp. She dropped the money into her apron pocket, then tucked her hands safely behind her back.

"You know, Miss Charlotte," he said earnestly, "I'd be pleased to take you up and show you them gentians some time, if you'd like. It's a real purty sight."

Charlotte found herself wondering if Jack Cordell was listening to this exchange, from his place across the room, as she struggled for a reply that would not disappoint Mr. Lloyd too much.

"Why, Mr. Lloyd. You're very kind."

"So you'll come?"

"Oh, it would be very nice, I'm sure, but I couldn't take the time away from the shop. You understand, don't you?"

He hesitated as her explanation sunk in, then shrugged his massive shoulders. "I suppose I'll just have to stop in here again tomorrow if I want to see you. You will bake another one of those boiled cider pies for me, won't you?"

"I will, if you like."

He seemed satisfied with this and turned at last to leave. "Good afternoon to you then, Miss Charlotte. And to you, too, Jack."

Only after Hollis Lloyd had gone out of the door did Charlotte turn her attention, at last, to Cordell. He was standing at the opposite end of the counter, his heavy brow puckered in a frown, and while his eyes were fixed upon the loaves of bread that remained in the tray, she sensed somehow that they were not the cause of his consternation.

"Has your stomach won out at last?" she prompted him. "I despaired of ever seeing you walk into my shop, Mister Cordell."

"With all of the comings and goings around here, I'm surprised that you were able to notice my absence at all," he replied, with more than a little sharpness in his tone.

"Business *has* been brisk. I've been fortunate so far."

Charlotte could sense the disquiet bubbling in him, just beneath the surface. Did he resent the easy time she was having after he'd warned her of how hard it would be? Or was there something else?

"What can I do for you?" she inquired, for he still did not seem inclined to speak.

"Actually, I'm here in an official capacity. The town council is planning a Fourth of July celebration, and we're in need of someone to organize the refreshments. Your name was suggested, and so I've come to inquire whether you might help out."

Charlotte felt a telling twinge of disappointment. It was silly, she knew, still she couldn't help herself. She ought to have known that the solemn, steady storekeeper would never come calling on her of his own volition. She oughtn't to have cared, one way or the other, but she did.

He'd been keeping his distance ever since she'd shown him her hands. She knew now that it had been a mistake to reveal even that small piece of herself; but at the time, she'd thought that he understood.

"So, you've been *elected* to speak with me," she said pointedly.

"That's not it . . . exactly."

"And I don't suppose that it was you who suggested my name to the council either."

"Well, no, but . . ."

She offered him a lopsided smile and sighed. "No, I didn't think so. It's nice that someone was thinking of me, at any rate. And of course, I'll be glad to help out in any way I can."

With that, Charlotte was overcome by a queer restlessness. She didn't want to stand around talking to Jack Cordell a moment more, and so she turned away sharply. Pacing the length of the counter, she busied herself with condensing her stock and placing the remaining loaves of bread alongside the few currant buns on one tray. Then she gathered up the empty trays with the intention of carrying them back to wash.

When she reached the calico drape that separated the shop from the back room, though, she found Cordell standing there, blocking the way. It was hard to discern the thoughts behind his solemn expression, but a spark had been kindled in the depths of his smoke-colored eyes.

"Charlotte?" His voice was soft, intimate. "Is there anything you need?"

Her foolish heart swelled in her breast at his words and his use of her Christian name. When last they'd met, he'd promised her friendship, and only now did she realize how very much she wanted it.

Fumbling for a reply, she took an awkward step backward and nearly dropped the stack of trays.

". . . for the Fourth of July celebration, I mean," he

amended. "Let me know what your plans are, what supplies you'll be wanting, and if you need any other sort of help, I'll speak to the council."

Oh. Of course. He'd only been speaking about business. Feeling cheated somehow, Charlotte squared her jaw and advanced, bent on pushing past him, if she had to. Cordell stepped out of the way, allowing her to pass, and she swept by the curtain.

When she was safe in the privacy of her back room once more, she cast the stack of trays on the table and returned to the dishpan, thrusting her hands into the still-steaming water. But the pleasure she'd felt in the task only a short while before was gone now, and she scrubbed at a glazed ware mixing bowl with nearly enough vigor to remove the finish.

She heard his footsteps behind her on the pegged wood floor before he spoke. "There is something else I'd like to ask of you, if you wouldn't mind."

Charlotte's hands went still, but she did not turn around.

"It's been my intention, from the first," he began, "to make Cedar Creek into a proper town—not just a supply camp for a bunch of rowdy, roughneck miners, you understand—but a place where folk might settle, build houses, and raise children; a place where a man's neighbor is also his friend."

He was standing just behind her, and without seeing him, Charlotte could nonetheless sense his gaze as it swept across her shoulder and out of the small window to the sparkling waters of the creek and the mountains rising beyond, gilded by the fading daylight.

"We're blessed, you know. A person couldn't ask for a more beautiful spot than this to live out his days."

Awed by the vision that spread out before her, Charlotte had to agree.

"But in order to survive, the town needs advancements, improvements." As he related his thoughts to her, Cordell paced the length of the room and back again. "I want us to build a church, with a tall, white-painted steeple . . . and a schoolhouse. I want to hear the sound of children's laughter in the streets and ladies' gossiping in the corner of my store. I want there to be rows of houses with green window shutters and flower gardens in the yards . . ."

He caught himself, as if not certain whether he'd revealed too much of himself. But it was too late, for Charlotte had already been infected with his enthusiasm; and having looked inside his dreams, she now regarded the man himself with a new interest.

"When you speak of it that way, I can see it all clear as day, as if it were spread out before me."

"A surveyor was here, not long ago," he went on to say, "from the railroad. He's considering us for a stop on a new route from Denver to Santa Fe."

Charlotte felt the excitement welling in her. "A railroad stop? If there were to be travelers stopping daily in town, we'd all prosper."

At this, Cordell drew up short. "We haven't won it yet," he warned, "not by a far sight. We're in competition with dozens of other towns in this territory, and I have to admit we can scarcely provide any of the amenities a traveler needs: a good hot meal, comfortable lodgings . . ."

"What can we do?"

He went to rest himself against the opened back door, and lifting his head to the breeze, he allowed it to ruffle his thick, black hair as he proceeded to explain.

"I was thinking that, for a start, we might all help the Widow Murphy to tidy up her boarding house. I've already spoken to her and she's agreeable. The council's going to enlist volunteers to come out on Saturday to do the carpentry work and painting, and well, I was hoping that you would . . ."

"Help tidy up inside?"

"Yes, that, but we're also going to have one hungry

crew once they've finished, so we'll need a dinner prepared. Mrs. Murphy has taken it upon herself, but I know she'd appreciate anything you could do."

"I'll go to her this evening and offer my help."

"Thank you."

He met her then with that damned, devastating smile of his, and Charlotte felt the hot flush of color as it spread to her cheeks. A queer panic was rising in her. He'd finished his business. She'd given him the answers he wanted to hear. Why couldn't he just go now and leave her alone?

"I see that Lars has been here to fix that door hinge," he remarked, as if he intended to linger awhile yet and make polite conversation.

Purposefully, Charlotte picked up a towel, reached for one of the bowls she'd just washed, and focused on wiping it dry. "Yes, he came earlier," she replied, then hesitated. "But how did you know . . ."

Cordell flicked away an imaginary speck from his clean, white apron. "You ought to have discovered by now that your every move is of utmost interest to the young bucks in this town."

"Yourself included?" she retorted, before she could stop herself.

He chose not to answer the question. But when he spoke again, his voice was softer and not nearly so self-assured. "Why didn't you tell me about the hinge, Charlotte? I'd have seen to it. After all, I'm your landlord."

"I didn't want to bother you over such a small thing," she explained. "Besides, Mr. Thorssen is the blacksmith. It was an easy enough task for him . . ."

"Aren't you a lucky woman to have all these men so eager to help you out?"

Charlotte crossed the room, and lifting up the bowl she'd just dried, returned it to its place on the shelf. She couldn't be sure if it was sarcasm she detected in Cordell's tone or not. But he was smiling at her all the while.

"Lars Thorssen *and* his brother, Gunnar," he continued, "Henry Sutton, Elliot Baird . . . oh, and we mustn't forget Hollis Lloyd. Whatever *do* you see in a boy like that?"

"What do you mean?"

"Come now, there must have been something special about the lad that encouraged you to flutter your eyelashes at him like that. Why, he fairly drooled on the counter all the while he was offering to take you up to see the wildflowers."

So he had been listening. He might have been teasing her, with all that he'd said. She was almost certain that he was, except for the stern set to his jaw.

"I was only being polite," she insisted.

"That's not the impression our young butcher received. He's smitten, truly and thoroughly. Don't be surprised if you wake to find a beef roast on your doorstep tomorrow morning as a token of his affections."

Charlotte went back to the dishpan, sinking her hands in the water, and even as she busied herself with scraping and scrubbing kitchen utensils, her thoughts were on what Cordell had said. Teasing or not, his implication was that she was making use of her feminine wiles to manipulate the men of Cedar Creek.

But it wasn't so. She knew, better than anyone, the dangers in playing such games. A long time ago, she'd paid an awful price, and never would she consciously try . . .

Oh, but what if it were not a conscious thing? What if these men perceived some hidden message in the words that she chose or the way that she moved, and all the while, she was not even aware? No, she couldn't think of that.

"Why, poor lovestruck Hollis is probably writing home even now, telling his family all about the wonderful woman he plans to marry."

"I haven't led him to believe anything of the sort," Charlotte shot back as she struggled for calm. "If you're trying to bait me, it won't work. I've done nothing wrong."

He came up behind her then, so close that, as he bent over her, she could feel his breath warm the back of her neck.

"That's not what I want," he told her, "not at all."

Charlotte inhaled sharply as his right hand settled possessively over her hip and then, with an aching slowness, began to slide, following an invisible trail upward from the narrowing of her waist to her ribcage, his fingertips barely skimming the underside of her breast.

A peculiar warmth rushed through her. She'd only felt this way once before, after drinking too much whiskey.

A soft moan escaped her. "Oh . . . Jack, no."

"But don't you see, Charlotte? You need a man who can appreciate you for all your fine qualities, not a headstrong young bull like Hollis Lloyd, who'd trample you beneath his feet without even realizing. You need an older man, an experienced man, one who knows what a woman needs."

Dizziness overwhelmed her and as her head lagged back, his lips brushed her hair. Never before had a man touched her this way, with such subtle purpose, never had she felt so shameful, yet so vibrantly alive. Closing her eyes, she struggled to focus her thoughts.

"And since you've already made it clear . . . that you don't approve of . . . of the suitors who've come my way so far," she posed, oddly breathless, "where do you suppose I might find such a man?"

She waited an uncomfortably long time for his reply, not daring to move. What she heard next, though, was not the answer she'd expected, only the labored rasp of his breathing as he bent to press a warm kiss on the nape of her neck.

"Closer than you think," he whispered against her ear at last.

A shiver coursed through her, and as she pulled a tremulous breath, Charlotte found herself deeply regretting the sound of his retreating footsteps as he left her, standing there alone.

Six

Saturday promised to be a glorious spring day—bright and clear—no hint at all of chill in the breeze that swept down from the mountains. It would have been the perfect weather, in fact, for fishing, but Jack had already made other, more pressing plans. The future of his town was at stake.

As soon as the sun had made its appearance in the eastern sky, he'd joined the other townsmen at the Widow Murphy's place, and now, hours later, he found himself alternately nailing down wobbling boards on the picket fence that surrounded the dooryard and supervising his companions as they went about making repairs on the house.

From his vantage point, he could see Hollis Lloyd, sitting perched on the peak of the roof, half a dozen nails sticking out of his mouth as he hammered away, tacking down loose shingles. The Thorssen brothers were busy with the front porch, Gunnar sawing boards to replace the rotted steps, which Lars was in the process of tearing up. Gus Stern, the assayer, was in charge of putting up the newly-painted sign, which read "Rooms to Let," and re-hanging the shutter which had broken free from its hinges. Most of the rest of the volunteers were busy whitewashing the clapboard siding.

Dr. Kelsey also wielded a whitewash brush, high on a ladder up under the second story eaves. He was too busy and too far out of reach to tend to the extraordinary number of bashed thumbs, barked shins, and other minor cuts and scrapes which this project was engendering. At least, that's what each victim would claim as, clasping a wounded extremity, he headed for the kitchen. And what could cause a town full of otherwise careful, capable workingmen to inflict such damage upon themselves? What, indeed!

"Hellfire! That smarts, it does. I'm sure I got me a wood sliver in my palm when I leaned up against that post," Henry Sutton exclaimed as he let go of his brush and watched it slip back into the whitewash bucket.

"Shall I call down Doctor Kelsey?" Gus Stern asked him.

"Naw, there's no need to bother him. I think I'll just go on into the kitchen and see if one of the ladies might lend me a sewing needle so's I can dig it out."

Jack let go a rude snort and dropped his hammer. It landed in the dust, nearly missing his right foot. Now this was becoming just plain ridiculous! At any given moment so far this morning, he could have found at least one of his fellow workers loitering in the kitchen, seeking succor from the ladies or—to put a finer point on the matter—from one lady in particular.

When his anger had risen to such a pitch that he felt compelled to put an end to this foolishness, Jack strode across the dooryard and up the kitchen steps, halting on the threshold.

It was an inviting place, he had to admit, with the mingled aromas of fried chicken, biscuits, and custard pie wafting on the air. The Widow Murphy was busy within the kitchen, bent over her stove, and Rachel Kelsey, mixing up batter in a great wooden bowl.

As for Sutton, he'd seated himself in a chair nearby, afflicted palm upturned. The calculating lad had affected the look of a hapless schoolboy; and sure enough, Charlotte was hovering over him like Florence Nightingale, her sewing needle poised and ready for action.

"Here now, give me your hand."

"Oh, it's really nothing, Miss Charlotte," he protested. "I never meant to take up your time on such a trifling thing as this."

"Nonsense. The sliver has to come out or it will become infected."

Cautiously, tentatively, as if it hadn't been his aim all along, the little weasel uncurled his fingers and allowed her to take up his hand so she might minister to him. And while Charlotte's eyes were fixed on his palm, Sutton's were roaming, far too familiarly for Jack's liking, over her face, her lips, her throat . . . and then lower.

She shook her head. "I'm afraid I can't find . . ."

"Just to the left there. Don't you see it?"

Jack couldn't stand by and watch this charade for a single minute more. "Here now, Henry," he bellowed as he strode into the room, "that'll be just about enough of that!"

Sutton sprang to his feet at once, guilty at having been caught in the act. "Well, I'll be," he said, flexing his hand. "I do believe it's gone. It must've worked itself out. I'll just be getting back to work now."

He ducked around the work table and was out of the door before Jack had the chance to react.

"Whatever was that all about?" Rachel remarked, staring after him.

Mrs. Murphy shook her head. "If ye be askin' me, dearie, I'd say some of them boys has been out in the sun a mite too long."

Charlotte went to return Mrs. Murphy's sewing needle to her work basket, which was tucked away on a shelf in the far corner of the room. She was aware, all the while, that Jack's eyes, sharp and cold as hardened steel, were focused solely on her. But she hadn't the vaguest idea what had upset him.

"If you'll excuse us, ladies," he said, and crossing to the place where Charlotte stood, he caught her hand up roughly in his, "Miss Devereaux and I need to have a little chat."

Charlotte didn't know what to think, but nevertheless allowed him to lead her down the hall into the parlor. Only after he'd shut the door firmly behind them, did she voice her protest.

"I don't know what's gotten into you, Jack. It was only a sliver of wood, for heaven's sake."

"This time it's a sliver. And what about next time? Blisters? Bruises? Bunions? Don't you understand, Charlotte? There's work to be done, and these men are contriving to spend all of their time in the kitchen with you."

Now she understood. Jack was having trouble keeping a tight rein on his work crew, and so he'd decided to put the blame on her.

"Can't *you* keep them out?" she retorted, advancing on him. "It's not as if I'm inviting them in, you know. We've work to do in here as well, and they're getting underfoot."

Jack took a step backward in reply, nonplussed. But Charlotte knew better than to believe that he'd let it go at that. After he'd had a moment to gather his thoughts, he came at her anew.

"Just the same, it's your fault they keep coming in."

"*My* fault? What have I done?"

"Well, if you wouldn't keep playing at nurse, smiling at them that way and encouraging them . . ."

Charlotte folded her arms over her apron front and glared at him. "What do you mean, smiling at them 'that way'?"

"You know very well what I mean—when your mouth crinkles up and your cheeks dimple and your eyes get all sparkly. I've never once seen you smile at *me* that way."

"At you?" she echoed in astonishment. Before when he'd taken this tack, she'd thought that he was only making sport at her expense, but now as she thought on it, she began to suspect something entirely different. "Why, Jack Cordell, I do believe you're jealous."

"Wha . . . what?" he sputtered. "Me? Jealous? Don't be ridiculous." With that, he narrowed his eyes and leveled an accusing finger at her. "You know what I think? I think that all this attention has gone to your head."

On that note, he took his exit. But protest though he might, Charlotte knew that she hadn't been mistaken. Something stirred deep in her heart. Whether he was ready to admit it or not, the serious-minded storekeeper *had* taken notice of her, and because of that, the smile that she wore for the remainder of the afternoon was even more brilliant than the one he'd accused her of flaunting all morning.

The gentlemen ate their dinner at noon, then worked till nearly sunset; and when they were finished, the town of Cedar Creek had good reason to be proud, for the Widow Murphy's boarding house looked as fine as any comparable establishment one might happen upon in Denver, Omaha, or Kansas City.

Afterward, instead of sinking, bone weary, into their respective beds, as might be expected, the indefatigable townsmen got together and suggested a celebration dance to be held that evening in the town square.

For her part, Charlotte thought it was a fine notion. She was ready for excitement of some sort. So she urged Rachel and Mrs. Murphy to help her load two crocks of lemonade, the remainder of the custard pies, and all the attendant utensils into the bed of the Thorssen brothers' wagon, and ferried the whole lot down to the square.

The gentlemen had all gone off to wash up. Gus Stern

was the first to return and had seated himself not far away, on one of the split log benches, where he was busily tuning up his fiddle.

The obvious never occurred to Charlotte until she and Rachel walked down to inspect the square of rustic dance floor, lit up by lanterns that were hanging atop poles, which the gentlemen had erected in each of its four corners.

"There aren't enough ladies to go around," she remarked when it finally struck her. "We'll be expected to take turns, I suppose."

"Mercy! I couldn't possibly dance," Rachel replied, "not in my condition. What would folks say? I'm just going to rest myself by the wagon and serve up the refreshments."

"Well then, Mrs. Murphy and I . . ."

Rachel shook her head. "She'll likely tire out after the first reel. She's been on her feet all day, and she's not as young as she once was, you know."

"Surely I won't be expected to dance with everyone," Charlotte protested. "Will I?"

"Never mind about that," Rachel said, as she reached to hook her arm in Charlotte's and drew her closer beside her. "Now that we're alone at last, you've got to tell me why Jack Cordell took you aside this morning. I've been wondering about it the whole day long. What did he say?"

There was an excited gleam in Rachel's eyes. Charlotte hadn't wanted to make anything out of it, but Rachel's enthusiasm was contagious, and she simply couldn't help herself. An amused smile twisted on her lips.

"Oh, Charlotte, has he taken an interest in you? I was beginning to think he'd shied away, because of all the competition. I know he can be deadly serious at times, but I think maybe the two of you . . ."

"Actually, he took me aside to remark on the number of men who'd come to me requesting first aid," Charlotte explained, "and to tell me that I was preventing them from doing their work."

Rachel's mouth dropped open. "Isn't that just like a man? They carry on like silly schoolchildren and when things don't go as they'd planned, they blame us for it. I hope you told him a thing or two."

"Oh, I believe I've left him with more than a little to think about."

Without warning, the gentlemen descended, and before she knew it, Charlotte found herself surrounded, with at least a dozen, insistent voices buzzing in her ear.

"Miss Charlotte, I'd like to request . . ."

"May I have the honor, Miss Charlotte . . . ?"

Miss Charlotte, do you think . . ."

"Hold up now, friend, I was here first."

"What do you mean by pushing me out of the way? Why, I ought to . . ."

Charlotte stood there in shock, not knowing how to reply nor to whom, until Rachel broke through the crowd and raised up her hands to quiet them.

"Gentlemen, gentlemen, a little decorum please," she said evenly. "If you trample Miss Devereaux, she'll hardly be in a condition to dance with any of you. Now I'd suggest that you all compose yourselves. Take a step backward and form a line."

There was grumbling in the ranks, but most of them obliged, and Charlotte sighed a breath in relief as the press of bodies receded and space opened up around her.

It was only then that she spotted Jack, advancing on the square in the company of Dr. Kelsey. He'd washed up and changed into a clean, striped shirt, dark vest and trousers. His thick, black hair was still damp and combed neatly back off his brow. Why had she never noticed before how much taller he was than the rest? And how much broader his shoulders were?

As he and Kelsey drew nearer, they ceased conversing

and turned to regard the commotion before them with wide-eyed surprise.

"Here now! What's going on?" Kelsey called out and shouldered through the assemblage to take up a position beside his wife.

"They all want to dance with Charlotte," Rachel explained. "They're only having a little trouble deciding who goes first, that's all."

"Dancing?" he retorted. "Is that what all this is about? Oh, now if that isn't just the most ridiculous thing I've ever heard! An entire townful of grown men behaving like a bunch of spoilt children."

"Easy enough for you to say, doc," Hollis Lloyd piped up, "seein' as how you got two pretty ladies living up at your house."

The assemblage was rattled by a spate of raucous laughter, but Kelsey did not seem at all amused.

In spite of all of the chaos around her, Charlotte's eyes were drawn to the back of the crowd, where Jack Cordell stood observing the scene before him, his expression mirroring his vexation. Probably, even now, he was blaming her for this entire overblown incident.

Rachel, meanwhile, reached out to lay a reassuring hand upon her husband's shoulder. "Don't worry," she told him. "I'll have all of this worked out shortly. Be a dear, Noah, and go and tear off a piece of that brown paper that's covering up the baked goods in the wagon, and bring it here, would you?"

Shaking his head, the put-upon physician muttered an incomprehensible phrase and then went off to do his wife's bidding.

"Now, I'm sure there's a pencil in my apron pocket," Rachel continued. "Yes, here it is. We'll just make up a dance card; that ought to satisfy everyone."

"A dance card?" Charlotte queried, as Noah returned bearing a large scrap of heavy brown paper.

Rachel took it up, folded it in half and began to write. "I'll make a list of numbers here after which each gentleman will write down his name," she explained. "Then each need only remember his number to know when it's his turn for a dance."

"And what will the rest do while they're waiting?" Charlotte inquired.

"Oh, don't you worry. They'll manage," Rachel told her, "they always do. They'll start off by adding a little whiskey to their lemonade when we're not looking, and then when they're sufficiently liquored-up, half of them will tie kerchiefs onto their sleeves to signify them as the ladies when they dance. Then afterwards, they'll switch places."

"You mean they'll dance with each other?"

Rachel leaned nearer to whisper. "I understand it's common practice out here. Isn't that what the miners did when you were living up in the mountains?"

Charlotte frowned at this reminder of her past and shook her head. "I don't know. I suppose they must have. But then I wasn't much for socializing. It wouldn't have been wise."

Once all of the interested gentlemen had inscribed their names upon Charlotte's "dance card," Lars Thorssen produced a hammer and nail from his wagon, and tacked the list up on the flag pole. Charlotte regarded the prodigious collection of names with increasing dismay, wondering if she'd even be able to stand on her feet when tomorrow came. Why, the list contained the name of every respectable bachelor in town—every respectable bachelor in town, that is, save one.

After the dancing got underway, Charlotte's chafed feet began to throb in her shoes, which were a castoff pair of Rachel's that were at least a size too small, and the nearly-healed wound in her thigh, which she'd managed to forget till now, began to smart.

She'd already finished a waltz with Mr. Phillips, the

newspaperman, a schottische with Henry Sutton, reels with both of the Thorssen brothers, in turn. She'd danced with so many gentlemen, in fact, that their names and faces had begun to blur together in her memory.

At the end of each dance, she'd taken a moment to catch her breath and told herself that she couldn't possibly manage another step. But then the next young man would push through the crowd, his face alight with promise, and tired as she was, Charlotte would manage a smile and offer him her hand.

They weren't smitten with her beauty, wit, charm, or grace; Charlotte had come to realize that almost as soon as she'd arrived here. They weren't interested in hearing her ideas or her dreams, in knowing the person that dwelt inside.

To them, she was little more than a representation of the things that were lacking in their new lives out West— of the comforts of home and family. They competed for her as they would for any other prize, and this knowledge hardened her against any of their individual overtures, no matter how heartfelt they might have seemed.

The evening was waning; she had to be nearing the bottom of her dance card, Charlotte told herself, as she hobbled off the dance floor and toward the flagpole to consult the posted list.

The dim, yellow lamplight scarcely reached the face of the card, and Charlotte had to narrow her eyes and blink several times before the writing came into focus. What she saw made her blink yet again. The last four remaining names on the list had been crossed off, and beside them, a single name had been inserted.

"Cordell?" she remarked aloud.

"At your service, ma'am," a voice intoned, from not far away.

As Charlotte looked up, Jack performed a deep bow and then extended one hand, offering her a tin cup of lemonade. She took it up, but then hesitated, staring suspiciously into the cup.

"You don't have to worry," he told her. "It's plain lemonade. The boys have only been able to doctor theirs cup-at-a-time since Rachel caught on to their scheme."

Charlotte couldn't tell him that she was acquainted with the taste of liquor and wouldn't at all have minded a splash in her cup, especially after the day she'd had. But she only took a sip and then regarded him curiously.

"I could have sworn that your name was not on my dance card. How did you . . . ?"

"I paid off your last few partners," he revealed with a grin.

"You paid them off?"

"And your company didn't come cheap, I'll have you know."

"So now you expect me to dance the rest of my dances with you?" she deduced, wincing as Gus Stern drew his bow across the fiddle strings to begin the next number.

"Actually, I could see that you were exhausted," Jack replied to this, "and I thought to spare you from having your toes trod upon for the remainder of the evening."

Charlotte had to admit that she was surprised and more than a little pleased. "You did that for me? Honestly? Why, thank you."

"Now, why don't we go and sit down so that you can rest while you drink your lemonade," he suggested.

She considered the offer and then countered with one of her own. "If you wouldn't mind too much, I've something a bit more scandalous in mind."

Jack's eyebrows lifted. Certainly his curiosity was piqued, but he didn't inquire further, only waited for Charlotte to reveal herself.

"I'd like to take off my shoes and stockings," she said at last, "and dangle my poor, trod-upon toes in the cool waters, down by the creek."

He grinned and slipped his arm through hers. "Lead on," he bade her.

It was a moonless night, and the shadows were deeper by the creek, but the sprightly fiddle music carried on the air, blending with the rush and bubble of the waters over the rocks.

Charlotte sank down onto the grassy creek bank, and as Jack settled himself beside her, she unlaced her boots and drew them off, then turned her back to him as she rolled down her stockings and shed them, as well. Hitching up her skirts, she eased her bruised and aching feet into the icy waters and let go a deep, contented sigh.

She glanced back over her shoulder and caught sight of Rachel, perched on a bench beside the wagon and keeping a close eye on the crock of lemonade. She may well have claimed to be content serving refreshments, but from this vantage point, Charlotte noticed some regret in her expression, and her toes, which she'd tucked discreetly under the bench, were tapping in time with the music.

Nearby, the gentlemen were hopping and high-stepping as they danced with each other. Several patrons of the Red Bird and Silver Dollar Saloon, miners mostly, had joined in the party now, and several of the saloon girls had followed them out. Here and there across the dusty dance floor, a flash of red taffeta petticoats caught Charlotte's eye, and the sound of shrill, female laughter drifted down on the wind.

She turned back around and flutter-kicked her bare feet in the chilling, rushing waters. "You don't think me too shameless, do you?"

With her attention on Jack now, Charlotte realized that for all the time she'd been watching the dancers, his eyes had been squarely on her.

"After the evening you've just had, I'd say it was the sensible thing to do."

"You know, I would have sworn that you were going

to blame me for all the fuss," she admitted. "I must say, you've surprised me."

Jack stared off into the darkness. "I'm sorry," he said. "You were right in what you said this morning. I suppose I must have been more than a little jealous of all the time you were spending with the others."

Charlotte became still and inhaled an uneven breath. Jack's frank admission had caught her off guard, and before she'd realized, words began to tumble out of her mouth to cover her disquiet.

"I don't much like it, you know—being the center of attention. I'd rather walk about unnoticed, blend into the crowd. That's how I'm accustomed to living. All of these men competing for my favor, why, it's just plain foolishness. I'm not swayed by idle flattery. There's a mirror on the bureau by my bed. I see my reflection every day. I know my own worth. I'm not a young girl anymore, and I've never been a ravishing beauty."

Jack sidled closer, reaching out to touch a wisp of her hair, which had slipped from her crocheted snood and lay curled against her cheek. He let it slide between his thumb and forefinger, as if to savor its softness, before tucking it back in place.

"You're far too hard on yourself, Charlotte. You're an attractive woman, with a lot of fine qualities. You're kind and generous and hard-working and determined."

"But you hardly know me," she protested. "How can you know all of that?"

"Ah, but I do know. I know that—in spite of your own troubles, whatever they may be—you've come out here to help your cousin Rachel. I know that you've put up with the antics of a town full of love-starved bachelors and treated them with patience and good humor. I know that you've had the courage to make a place for yourself here, to start a business."

He was very close now, only a whisper away in the

darkness. Limned in shadows, his features seemed more rugged and forbidding than ever: the heavy, black brows; the angled blades of his cheekbones; the sharply-defined jaw. But his eyes were lit by sparks of silver light, and his mouth was now curving into a mischievous smile.

His hand found hers, resting in the grass, and covered it. The pressure of his fingers and the heat of his skin sent a pleasant, bubbling rush through Charlotte's veins. There was danger here in the darkness, quite possibly more than she could manage.

Her mouth had gone dry, and so, with her free hand, she reached for the cup of lemonade, which she'd set down beside her. She took a long drink and then sought to focus Jack's thoughts in another direction.

"Do you suppose we've a better chance of impressing that surveyor for the railroad, now that we've fixed up the Widow Murphy's place?"

Jack considered the question solemnly. "I'd like to say it'll be enough, but I have to be honest. There's a good deal more that still needs doing."

"Like mending and polishing . . . and building that church with the white-painted steeple?"

"It's going to happen, Charlotte," he insisted. "One way or another, we're going to build ourselves a town of which we all can be proud."

"I've written letters to the Methodists and the Baptists in Saint Louis," he continued. "Surely one or the other will send us a preacher, as soon as they're able. The council's already set aside a plot of land for the church across the creek, over there on the high ground."

He extended an arm, his finger pointing out the direction in the darkness. "That way, on Sunday when the congregation's singing hymns, the music will carry all through the valley."

With this, Jack caught himself and fell silent. "But I must be boring you with all my plans."

"Not at all," she replied. "I enjoy hearing you weave together these dreams of yours. It's been so long since I've had any of my own."

Charlotte hadn't planned to make this revelation, but it slipped out, nevertheless. For the past three years, she'd done little more than exist, every thought and action spurred by the overpowering need for revenge and survival. In all of that time, she hadn't once dared to dream. But sitting here now in the darkness, with Jack Cordell's strong hand clasping hers and a sky full of stars overhead, she found her thoughts filling up with *his* dreams.

She threw back her head, shut her eyes, and inhaled deeply. The chilling night air was laced with pine. "Tell me more of what you've planned for Cedar Creek," she urged him.

"The city hall is going to be made of bricks. We'll have them shipped down from Denver. There'll be a room for the council members, so we won't have to hold our meetings around the stove in my store, and an office for the sheriff we're going to hire. It'll be his job to weed out the riff-raff and keep our rowdy miner friends in check."

Edging nearer, Jack loosed Charlotte's hand. A thrill coursed through her as his hard fingertips drifted up her arm and across the bridge of her shoulders.

"Don't you think you've heard enough for now?" he asked softly.

There was an urgency threaded through his words now, and a purpose to his touch. Charlotte shivered. Had she been leading him on, she asked herself? No, she was sure that she hadn't. She didn't need to get caught up in anything complicated. And yet, when he touched her, the blood began to thrum in her veins, and more than anything, she wanted . . . she wanted . . .

She was afraid of Jack Cordell at that moment, afraid of what might happen if she were to let herself go. She focused on the cup in her hand, sipped again at her lemonade, and then drew her feet from the water and tucked them up under her skirts.

"Do you really believe in all you've said?" she asked him, ignoring the question he'd posed and the portent behind it.

Jack hesitated a moment, as if to focus his thoughts, then lifted his head confidently. "Of course, I do. I'm so sure of it, in fact, that I've just posted a letter back home to Ohio, asking Leah to come out and join me. I'd never have sent for her otherwise."

The tin cup slipped from Charlotte's hand and rattled noisily as it rolled across the grass. "I'm sorry. That was clumsy of me," she managed to say as she concentrated on brushing the droplets of sticky, sweet lemonade from her calico skirts.

A long, awkward moment passed in silence, and all the while, Charlotte sought to deny the warm flush in her cheeks and the queer wetness burning in her eyes. It couldn't be tears; she was too hardened for that. She'd wrung her body dry of childish tears when she'd buried her father. But still, she turned away, fearing that her distress might be visible to Jack, even in the shadows of a moonless night.

She struggled to draw a cleansing breath, but her chest would not expand. It was as if she were wearing a tightly-laced corset. *Leah, did he say? Such a pretty name. And he'd sent for her to come and join him? But, of course, that was why he hadn't been behaving like the others. He'd had a sweetheart back at home all along.*

Charlotte squeezed her eyes shut. When had she grown so fond of Jack Cordell that it should hurt so much to hear this news? There'd certainly been no agreement between them, no understanding. When he hadn't been ignoring her entirely, he'd spent most of the time baiting her. How could she have been so foolish? He had never been romancing her. Oh, he may have developed some affection for her; he may have been seeking friendship, but nothing more than that.

It wasn't enough that a knife had been thrust into her heart. Charlotte felt the need to prove her toughness by twisting the blade.

"This sweetheart of yours," she began, "Leah. That was her name, wasn't it? Tell me about her."

She had scarcely got the words out before Jack gripped her shoulders and turned her to him. Charlotte cast her gaze downward, but he caught her chin between his fingers and made her look at him.

"She's my sister," he admitted. "She's sixteen years old, and I'm the only family she's got. She's been living at school since my mother died. I only said it the way I did to make you jealous. It was shameful of me, I know, but it's so damned hard to tell what you're feeling . . ."

Charlotte couldn't lie to him now, not when he'd been so honest with her. "I'm afraid, Jack."

"You don't have to be. I'd never hurt you, Charlotte. You do believe me, don't you?"

She had no chance to reply. With a violent shudder, he cast aside gentlemanly restraint and swept her up against him, his mouth capturing hers. Charlotte came vibrantly alive at his touch, the heat of his lips, the urgent cadence of his breathing in her ear.

Instinctively, her hands spread in an upward arc over his muscled back, her fingers fanning out possessively across the skin-warmed fabric of his vest. She couldn't have imagined it would feel so good to hold him, to be this close.

Her heart gave a leap as she felt the brush of his lips on hers once more. The next kiss was deeper, wild and potent. It left her giddy, trembling, and wanting more.

But Jack Cordell was a gentleman. He stilled all at once, as if to marshal his strength, and then eased away from her and pulled a calming breath as he fixed his silver-gray eyes on her.

"You know that mirror of yours?" he said, when finally he'd recovered himself, "the one on your bureau? I'd toss it out if I were you. It can't be worth much if you can't see in it all that I do when I look in your eyes."

Charlotte smiled at him and then lifted her gaze to the star-strewn heavens. Experience had taught her to give thanks for each moment of happiness, and this certainly qualified as that. But experience had taught her, as well, that such moments were never long-lived, and indeed, this proved to be the case. As her attention shifted to the lights of the dance floor, she caught sight of Noah Kelsey, standing not far away, with his hands clenched into two fists at his sides.

He'd been watching them. Charlotte knew that even before she caught his accusing glare, and her joy was swept away in an instant as it struck her that Doctor Kelsey considered her an unworthy companion for his friend. He had promised to keep her secrets, but now, if forced to choose between the promise he'd made to her and his loyalty to Jack, there was no telling what he might do.

Seven

By mid-morning on the Fourth of July, the summer's heat was already intense. From his place on the makeshift stage in the center of the town square, Jack stood staring out at the milling crowd. A bead of perspiration formed behind his left ear, then slanted downward across his jaw as he began to read from the crumpled page of notes he'd prepared and now held clutched in his hand. His voice cracked. Slipping a finger between his collar and throat, he tugged to loosen the knot of his silk tie, wishing now that this "honor" had fallen upon someone else.

He felt sorely out of place in his Sunday suit, with its vest, tie, and somber black frock coat, when every other man in the crowded square seemed to be clad for comfort in dungarees and rolled-up sleeves. But like the buildings on Main Street, which had been festooned with red, white, and blue bunting for the occasion, he supposed it was important that the chairman of the town council, too, should take on a more substantial air for the holiday.

From behind the curtain where Jack stood, there came the dull thud of hammers and the scraping of wood on wood. Miss Henderson's theatrical troupe had arrived late last night; and so they were, even now, making last minute adjustments to the stage, which had been erected on the grassy square. The troupe's manager shouted an order and several voices called back in reply.

Jack did his best to ignore the interruption and went

on with his remarks. He thanked the many newcomers for joining in Cedar Creek's celebration, putting forth the hope that they might be tempted to settle here. Indeed, as he looked out over the crowd, he couldn't help but be pleased with the turnout, for it seemed as if Nate Phillips's handbills had attracted every man, woman, and child for miles around.

With as much solemnity as he could manage, Jack began the obligatory reading of the Declaration of Independence, but his mind was not on the words. In fact, he had to struggle with himself all the while in order to stifle a grin.

He'd recognized more than one of the voices back behind the curtain. His fellow townsmen were there helping out, only too eager for a chance to get closer to the beauteous Miss Lila and her dancing girls. And why should this fact please him so?

Because maybe, just maybe, with his competition occupied elsewhere, he'd at long last be able to have Charlotte to himself. Try as he might, he'd not been able to arrange a moment alone with her lately. Each time he walked into the bakery, intending to strike up a private conversation, another potential suitor would arrive, thereby spoiling the mood. And the same situation seemed to occur whenever she came into his store. They were able to exchange but a few, polite words before one of their well-meaning neighbors would intrude.

Nevertheless, Charlotte Devereaux filled up Jack's thoughts, waking and sleeping. He longed to know once more the simple intimacy they'd shared that evening by the creek. He wanted to hold her in his arms, to touch her, to kiss her again. And if he were lucky tonight, if they were able to lose themselves in this assemblage of strangers, he would.

His eyes sought her out, even as he finished his speech and the audience was offering him their applause. It didn't take long to spot the lavender and white Scotch gingham. Although Charlotte didn't know it, he'd sold the length of the expensive fabric to her at a loss, just so he could see her in a dress that wasn't one of Rachel's made-over hand-me-downs. As he looked on her now, he decided that the investment had been well worth it.

She was standing on the fringes of the crowd, her cousin close by her side. Her luminous blue eyes were fixed on him, and she was clapping her hands together with, what seemed to Jack at least, more fervency than any of the others.

Never in his life had a woman looked more beautiful to him than Charlotte did at that moment, standing there with the hot summer wind billowing out her skirts and tugging at the ribbons of her simple straw hat. But how could it be? She'd said herself that she wasn't a fresh, young girl anymore. From the first, he'd thought of her as an interesting woman: strong, patient, spirited, but never beautiful.

She'd changed since she'd come here, he told himself. Her face, now scrupulously shaded from the sun by the broad brim of her straw hat, was rosy from the heat, but not nearly so weathered as it had been. And as to her form, it was impossible not to notice that she was filling out nicely. When first Jack had seen her on the Kelseys' staircase, she'd been far too thin, but there was a much more pleasing contrast now between the trim waist and the curves above and beneath it.

Of course, that must be it, he decided. It was an easier explanation for him to accept than to admit that a man in love observed the world through different eyes.

Eager to reach her, Jack stepped down from the platform, brushing past more than one friend slapping him on the back to congratulate him on a job well done. The throng of people in the square proved a nuisance to him now, for they stood between him and Charlotte, and obscured her from his view.

He caught sight of her at last, standing with Rachel beside the pen that Hollis Lloyd had erected to hold the wild turkey the young man had snared and then decided to donate as the prize in the sharpshooting contest.

"Well now, isn't he a pretty sight?" Charlotte remarked.

For a brief moment as he drew up behind them, Jack thought she meant him, all dressed up in his Sunday suit, but then he realized that both she and Rachel were still staring at the bird.

"He'd make a fine Christmas dinner," Rachel agreed, "but he'd have to be fattened up some first."

"Christmas? Would we have to wait that long? I've a special fondness for roast turkey. My mouth is watering already."

Rachel shrugged her shoulders and pointed to the painted sign that was nailed to the pen, informing passersby how they might win the bird for themselves. "Doesn't matter anyhow. He's not ours to cook. Unless one of us plans on winning the sharpshooting contest."

Charlotte paused, as if to consider, then began to tap out a rapid tattoo in the dust with one foot. "Hmmmm. What would you say my chances are?"

Rachel paled. "Charlotte, no! I was only joking. You couldn't possibly consider such a thing."

"I *can* handle a pistol, you know."

"Yes, I'm sure that you can, but . . ."

"But I want this turkey," Charlotte persisted, "and unless you've a better idea on how I can get it . . ."

"This is a contest for the men," Rachel explained patiently, trying to reason with her. "They like to compete with one another and prove their skill. How will it look if you come along and try to show them up?"

Charlotte didn't seem to be listening, though. She shook her head. "It's too late. I've made up my mind."

With her small hands fisted and planted firmly on her hips, her elbows jutting out, she was the picture of an implacable female. Observing her, Jack grinned. This would certainly be an event worth watching. Charlotte had claimed that she could handle a pistol, and with all her pluck, he thought she just might have a chance of winning that turkey, after all.

"So, you're planning to enter the sharpshooting contest, are you?" he said, revealing his presence behind them at last.

He warmed at the smile Charlotte offered when she saw him. "I am, sir," she replied, and boldly reached out to straighten his tie as if she had every right to do so. "Would you care to join us at the table when we serve this turkey for our Christmas dinner?"

"Christmas, you say? I must admit that this is the earliest invitation I've ever received for a holiday dinner but, of course, I accept."

"Oh, won't you try and talk her out of this, Jack?" Rachel pleaded.

"I don't see that it will do any harm for her to try if, as she says, she can handle a firearm," he said. "I'll admit that I've never heard of ladies entering such a contest, but I don't believe there's any rule says they can't if they want to do so."

Poor Rachel, heavy with child, seemed to be wilting with the heat. Leaning on one of the upright posts of the pen, she swiped a hand across her sweat-dampened brow, then bent nearer her cousin.

"Noah won't like it," she said, so softly that Jack could scarcely hear her.

Charlotte's eyes narrowed, and Jack would have sworn he could feel her irritation crackling on the air.

"Noah hasn't approved of anything I've done since I got here," she shot back irritably, "and I'm sick to death of trying to please him. Now, I'm going to fetch my pistol and go down to the livery. They've already set up the target in the corral beside the barn, and they'll be getting started soon. Come along or not, as you like."

With that, she turned on her heel and stalked off.

"But your pistol's locked in Noah's desk drawer," Rachel called after her.

Charlotte paused for an instant as the words sank in, but then she started off again, without turning back.

Rachel turned to Jack, conjuring up a crooked smile. "Ever since the war, Noah can't abide firearms of any type," she offered in the way of an explanation. "I suppose because he spent so much time in trying to repair the damage they cause."

Jack laid a reassuring hand on her arm. "I can understand his feeling that way," he said.

There were so many questions he wanted to ask her. *Why did Noah seem more solemn and distant of late than he'd ever been? And Charlotte so uneasy? And what could have happened in Charlotte's life to make her feel the need to carry a pistol of her own?*

"Has there been trouble at home?" he finally ventured to guess. "Between Noah and Charlotte?"

Rachel's cheeks colored and she fanned herself with her hand. "It's the heat that's making them both restless," she insisted. "That's all it is."

Despite Rachel's confident reply, Jack was sure that there was more to this than any of them were letting on; but there wasn't time for sorting it out now. Offering Rachel his arm, he escorted her at a leisurely pace to Thorssen's Livery on the edge of town.

By the time they arrived, a crowd had formed. Hollis Lloyd and both of the Thorssen brothers were perched on the uppermost boards of the corral fence, and the competitors were assembled within its dusty confines. Charlotte stood among them, and surprisingly enough, they all seemed to have accepted her presence with good humor.

Someone even put forth the suggestion that she have the honor of shooting first. She refused, though, preferring to wait her turn in line like the rest.

Jack was aware at once of the sober expression Charlotte had adopted. As she filled the chambers of her revolver, she didn't once turn around to seek out a familiar face in the crowd. It was almost as if she didn't care whether or not her friends had come to watch. This was serious business to her. *But what was it, precisely,* Jack asked himself, *that she was trying to prove?*

One by one, the gentlemen took their turns, firing six shots at the paper target which had been tacked upon a bale of hay at the opposite end of the corral. Gus Stern, who'd taken charge of the event, collected the target after each contestant had made his shots, then replaced it with a fresh one for the next man in line.

And finally, the "next man in line" was Charlotte. It was a peculiar sight—the willowy lady in lavender gingham drawing a heavy pistol from within the folds of her skirts. But she wasn't a novice; that much was apparent to Jack at once. Taking careful aim, she leveled the barrel, gripping hard on her wrist to steady it, then drew back the hammer and calmly pulled the trigger.

The shot went wide, just nipping the outside ring of the target.

"That was a right good try, Miss Charlotte," Lloyd called out. "A little more to the left ought to do it."

"*Ja,* you jest take yer time," Lars Thorssen advised her. "Ve ain't in no hurry."

Charlotte got off two more shots in quick succession, but both buried themselves in the hay bale a good twelve inches below the paper bull's eye.

Her hand was trembling now, and beneath the brim of her hat, her face had gone a trifle pale. All of the confidence in the world didn't seem to be helping her, Jack realized, and he wished that there were something he could do.

With this, he left Rachel's side, shouldering his way through the crowd. Maybe if he got close enough to offer her a word or two of encouragement . . .

He'd just made a space for himself along the fence row when he heard the crack of another shot. A cheer went up from the crowd, and Jack's eyes were drawn to the target, where a neat hole had been made, square in the center of the black-painted bull's eye.

"Damned if she didn't get it that time," Hollis shouted.

"Try 'er again, Miss Charlotte," someone else called out.

Her back straightened this time as she took her stance, and she lifted her chin a notch higher. Jack could see the confidence welling in her anew. But from his new vantage point, he noticed something else as well—the gun in her hand. It was a Colt pistol, with a long barrel, a chased cylinder, and a pearl-handled grip, inlaid with tarnish-blackened silver.

A cold chill cut through him, in spite of the heat. What were the odds of another gun like that showing up in this town? *It had to be . . . Of course, it was.* But how had Charlotte come by it?

At that moment, with his eyes fixed on the tableau before him—the pearl-handled Colt clutched in Charlotte's small hand—Jack fully believed in a vengeful God. Perhaps the time had come at last for him to pay for his sins. But why now, after all this time? Hadn't he already made reparation enough for the wrongs that he'd done? Hadn't he lived a blameless life for more than ten years?

The sharp report of yet another pistol shot jarred him from his thoughts. Charlotte was trying her best, but this ball fell short of its mark, kicking up a cloud of dust. There'd be no showing up the gentlemen for her today.

Her abilities, in this case at least, simply could not match her boundless determination.

Jack's worries about his own fate receded as he watched Charlotte narrow her eyes against the sun's glare, shutting first one and then the other, in turn, in an effort to better her aim. But it must have been as apparent to her by now as it was to him that, nearsighted as she was, she would never do well at this endeavor. The prize turkey that she'd wanted so much would go to someone else.

Indeed, he was sure that she realized it, for her slender shoulders slumped, and the last shot rang out, almost as an afterthought, veering wide to strike a rusty, old feed bucket in the far corner of the corral.

Charlotte set the pistol down on a nearby barrelhead. The stench of gunpowder in the air threatened to choke her, and swallowing hard, she fought down the bile that rose in her throat, and wiped her sweaty palms on her skirts. Only then did it strike her what a colossal fool she'd made of herself, quarreling with Rachel, insisting on entering this sharpshooting contest, and all on account of a silly bird.

But, no, it wasn't the turkey, she began to realize. She'd been feeling more and more helpless with each day that passed, waiting for Noah to betray her to Jack. She'd entered this contest secretly hoping that it might help her to regain some of the strength she'd felt when she'd dressed as a man, to prove to herself that she wasn't so helpless, after all. Instead, she'd only confirmed her worst fears.

As she turned back on the crowd who'd assembled to watch her, she hoped she'd managed to conceal the shock. But the onlookers were hardly aware of her distress at all. Laughing and joking good-naturedly, they offered her a scattering of applause.

"One hit in the bull's eye," Gus Stern said as he strode back from the hay bale and handed her the paper target, "that's quite an accomplishment for a lady."

"You bet," Hollis Lloyd chimed in. "But if I'd a known you wanted that turkey so bad, I'd have entered the contest myself to win it for you. Wait a minute, maybe it's not too late. What do you say, Gus? Set up another target for me."

Henry Sutton reached to swipe back the strings of pale hair that had fallen across his eyes and scowled. "But *I* was plannin' on makin' it a present for her if *I* won."

"*Ja,* and I vouldn't haf no use fer dat turkey-bird myself," Gunnar Thorrsen put in.

Charlotte's cheek flushed crimson as she crumpled the paper target in her fist. Well, Rachel would be pleased with this outcome at least. Although Charlotte might not have intended it, she'd managed to increase her popularity among Cedar Creek's bachelor population, and succeeded in making every man who'd entered this contest feel just a little bit taller, a little more manly.

Lloyd had jumped down from his perch and was attempting to borrow Henry Sutton's Navy Colt to make his shots when suddenly Jack burst through the gate. His tie had gone askew again, but his jaw was set in a hard line as he stripped off his black frock coat and slung it over the fence.

"Save your ammunition, Lloyd," he said, and retrieving the pearl-handled pistol from the barrelhead, where Charlotte had left it, he reached into the cartridge box that was also lying there and deftly proceeded to fill all six chambers.

Charlotte watched, in silent fascination, as Jack addressed the target and adjusted his stance. She'd never seen such grim purpose in his steel-gray eyes, never thought him capable of handling a weapon with such ease.

No sooner had Gus Stern stepped out of the way than Jack squeezed off all six shots, rapid-fire. And when the smoke cleared, a tight ring of holes was revealed, all within the black bull's eye.

"God almighty, Jack!" Hollis Lloyd exclaimed. "Why didn't you never tell us you was a crack shot?"

When Jack turned back on them, Charlotte did not miss the beads of sweat standing out on his temples, nor the abject pallor in his face. For an instant, he seemed like a stranger, scarcely human. He had the look of a rough-hewn marble statue standing there. It might have been only the effect of the oppressive heat, but Charlotte didn't think so.

All at once, he shook it off, strode over to her and placed the pistol in her hands. And when he winked at her and grinned, she came to doubt the vision that she thought she'd seen.

"It was just pure, dumb luck," he insisted and shrugged his shoulders as he faced his fellow townfolk. "Miss Charlotte's invited me for Christmas dinner, and I knew she had her heart set on serving that turkey."

"Well, I wouldn't have believed it if I hadn't seen it for myself," Henry Sutton muttered.

"You don't see shootin' like that every day, that's for sure," someone else piped in.

But it was Nate Phillips, editor of the local newspaper, whose well-considered remark stuck in Charlotte's mind for a long time afterward.

"And you don't get that good without one hell of a lot of practice."

It was easy for Charlotte to lose herself in the afternoon's hard work. While the townsmen were busy frying the catfish, which they'd spent the past three days catching, and had kept penned up in a weir in the creek till this morning, Charlotte, aided by Rachel and the Widow Murphy, spent her time in frying up corn pone and then serving the pies she'd been baking all week.

And after everyone had eaten their fill and cheered for

Gus Stern's mare as she thundered down the main street of town to win the horse race, they arranged themselves before the lantern-lit stage in the square to enjoy the evening's entertainment, which was to be provided by Miss Lila Henderson's Theatrical Troupe.

Charlotte fully intended to join Rachel who, along with her husband, had appropriated one of the split-log benches that had been set up in rows near the stage. But as she began to wind her way through the clusters of people, a firm hand clamped down on her shoulder, and she turned to see Jack, standing close beside her.

He looked a bit more comfortable now, for he'd shed his jacket and tie, and rolled the sleeves of his fancy linen shirt to the elbow. But he still seemed the most dignified man in the square in his black silk waistcoat and trousers, even if they were dusty from the day's activities.

"You don't have to sit all the way up front," he said, "the view's just as good from back here. I've brought a blanket that we can spread out up on the red rocks, by the creek. It's cooler up there, and you won't have to slap at the mosquitoes that those lanterns are drawing."

Charlotte smiled and slipped her arm through his. "Well, lead on. You've convinced me."

Frankly, it didn't matter to Charlotte whether they had a good view of the stage or not. She'd rather spend time with Jack anyway than watch a pair of trained dogs perform or a bevy of painted, dancing girls kick up their shapely legs.

Besides, there was a peculiar sense of urgency building within her. There was no predicting how long it would be before Noah came to Jack with the secrets of her past, and once that had happened, Charlotte was certain that Jack wouldn't be half so eager to share his blanket, or anything else, with her.

But for now at least, he was unaware of her sinful past. Together, they quit the crowd, scrambling over the tumble of rocks beside the creek. He chose a place for them and spread the woolen plaid over a flat outcropping of sandstone. And as they both settled onto it, Miss Fannie Garrett was introduced and launched into a breathy rendition of a sweet Scottish ballad.

Charlotte followed the words for a while, then turned her attention to her companion, his ruggedly handsome profile silhouetted against the fading amber sky.

"I haven't thanked you properly yet for winning me that turkey," she said.

Playfully, he winked at her, and one corner of his mouth crooked upward. "Oh, don't worry. There's plenty of time for that."

A blush warmed Charlotte's cheeks. How odd that Jack Cordell should be able to make her feel like a shy young maid, in spite of all she'd been through.

"That was certainly some remarkable shooting," she said next.

"There's no telling what a man is capable of, given the proper motivation," he replied. "I was thinking of that Christmas dinner you promised me, all the while; and of you, sitting there across the table."

Charlotte was afraid to meet his eyes, but somehow she felt them, fixed on her, just the same. This was what she'd wanted—wasn't it?—to have Jack's full attention, to know that he cared for her? Then why did she feel the panic rising in her like a floodtide?

As her thoughts turned in another direction, to her own behavior this afternoon, she shook her head. "I'm afraid I acted like a spoilt child today, quarreling with Rachel and insisting that I could win that contest. And then the only time I did hit the target, it was quite by accident."

"I think you could be a fine shot," he told her.

"Do you really?"

He grinned. "With a pair of spectacles and the proper

technique. Really, though, you don't have to have keen eyesight, just an ability to sense your target."

Try though she might, Charlotte found herself unable to give in to his lighthearted mood. "I'll have to apologize to Rachel for being so peckish. She's been so good to me."

"It's difficult, I'd imagine, to live in someone else's house, even if they are family," he observed, and before she knew it, he had edged his hand across the blanket and laced his fingers through hers. "A woman like you needs a home, and a husband, of her own."

Charlotte paled and was swept by an unsettling wave of vertigo. He was speaking of marriage. It never occurred to her that he'd be considering that. But it ought to have, she realized, as his grip on her hand tightened. A man as serious as Jack Cordell wouldn't toy with a woman.

Up on the stage, Miss Garrett had completed her song. A spate of polite applause followed, and then she took her leave, making way for a banjo player, a fiddler, and a trio of dancers wearing emerald taffeta skirts. No sooner had the bow scraped across the fiddle than the ladies kicked up their heels and the crowd began to whoop and holler.

Dusk was closing in fast, and Charlotte felt as if the boisterous entertainment in the square were a world away. Apparently, Jack hadn't much interest in the performance either. Taking advantage of the noise and the encroaching darkness, he sidled up close beside her and reached to catch up her face in his hands.

Charlotte drew a sharp breath. The summer air was still and warm, and full of Jack's scent, that starkly male blend of bay rum and pine soap. With her face held fast in the curve of his palms, she had no choice but to look into his eyes, luminous as polished silver in the half-light, and to allow him to look into hers.

She prayed he would not see her fears mirrored there, nor all that she'd been hiding. But he was only looking

for her consent, it seemed, and despite the turmoil in her
thoughts, he must have found it there, for his eyelids
drifted shut, and he bent nearer, pressing his lips to hers.

She ought to stop him, Charlotte told herself, even as
the thrill of contact coursed through her. It wasn't fair.
Whatever this was between them couldn't last, not once
he knew the truth about her. *And then, oh, then the hurt
would be so much worse.*

She lifted her hands, pressing them, with palms flat,
against the front of his smooth silk vest, very much aware
of the hard sheath of his muscled chest beneath. But when
she felt the strong, steady pulse of his heartbeat against
her fingertips, she couldn't seem to push him away.

Before she knew it, Jack had swept one hand back, long
fingers tangling in the weave of her snood as he cradled
her head. His tongue was an insistent whisper of velvet
tracing the seam of her lips, parting them to probe deep
within her mouth.

The ragged pull of his breath in her ear ought to have
served as a warning that they had gone too far. But there
was no escape from his diligent assault, and God help
her, Charlotte sought none.

All her good intentions were cast aside now amidst the
flurry of new and potent sensations, wrought beneath
Jack's knowing hand—intimate caresses, featherlight fingertips wandering the soft underside of her jaw and the
sensitive flesh of her arched throat, and then lower still.

Charlotte wore no corset; she hadn't in years. He'd
probably think her a rustic, or worse. But to her surprise,
just now she didn't care, and he didn't seem to mind as
he cupped the swell of one breast through the lavender
and white gingham, with only a thin chemise beneath, his
thumb making soft, lazy circles that raised a taut nipple
and sent a shudder of pleasure through her.

She had never been touched this way before, never
guessed that a man's hand could be so gentle, and yet

cause such turmoil within her. A soft thrumming began to vibrate through her as if a thousand, tiny butterflies had been let loose inside her body all at once.

Jack clutched at her shoulders, and easing her back onto the blanket, he lowered himself onto her, burying his face against her neck.

He groaned deeply, as if she were somehow causing him pain. "Oh, Charlotte. You don't know how long I've waited . . . how much I've wanted . . ."

The terror came to her first as an ominous prickling over her skin, and then suddenly, she could not seem to draw a breath. With the weight of his body on hers, the startling evidence of his need pressing hard against her thigh, Charlotte was aware of the full extent of his power for the first time. Lying here beneath him, she was at his mercy.

Painful memories that she'd thought long buried sprang to life anew like noxious weeds, twining their way into her consciousness, choking out Jack's gentle whispers. Soon she could hear only the echoes of the past—a cold voice boasting, her own feeble cries. Then came the nightmare visions, flashes of hurt and humiliation that would not be shut out, not even when she closed her eyes.

Worst of all was the overwhelming sense of helplessness. In her dreams late at night, Charlotte had been made to relive her shame again and again. Over the years, she'd hardened herself against those memories; but now, at Jack's touch, they had invaded her waking life. God help her, would she never be free?

Jack wasn't certain when first he felt the change in her. He'd dreamt of this for so long that from the moment his lips had touched hers, he'd been caught up in a sensual maelstrom of tasting and touching. Her mouth was as rich and sweet as heated honey, her hair fragrant with the scent of roses, her skin warm and pliant beneath his fingertips.

She had been willing at first; he couldn't have imagined

it. She'd softened, unfolding for him like the petals of a flower to the morning sun, but then, in one shattering instant, she'd gone cold.

"Please," she begged, frantically gulping air as she writhed beneath him. "Please, don't."

Startled, Jack drew back, and Charlotte sat up, staring off at the square below and hugging her knees as she curled her slender body into a tight ball. She was trembling so visibly, he could see it, even in the darkness. He wanted to touch her again, to soothe her, but he dared not.

Hot shame flooded through him. He'd assumed, because of her age and that aura of experience she emanated, that she knew something of lovemaking. But apparently his assumption had been wrong. He'd gone too far. He'd frightened her.

"Forgive me, Charlotte," he said, and straightening his back, he drew a quavering breath. "I had no right to take such liberties. I don't want you to be afraid of me. I never wanted that."

She did not look at him, but when she spoke, her words were soft and tinged with sadness, almost apologetic. "Oh, Jack. You can't understand . . ."

"But I do," he told her. "You're a respectable woman. I ought to have had better control. I haven't any excuse to give, except that it's a warm summer's night, the crickets are chirping, you're a beautiful woman, and we're up here alone. Sometimes a man's . . . needs can overwhelm him."

A long silence ensued, with Jack's guilty admission hanging on the air.

"Have you ever felt as if you were living on borrowed time?" Charlotte wondered aloud, as if she hadn't heard any of what he'd said to her. "That, at any moment your whole world might come crumbling down around you?"

Jack frowned. She was a puzzling creature, no doubt

of that. But all this idle talk was getting them nowhere. Without thinking, he put out his hand and lay it upon her shoulder. She stilled at his touch, but did not pull away.

"Surely you've guessed how I feel about you, Charlotte," he ventured, "what I want for us?"

She let go a weary sigh. "I'm not the woman you think I am."

"I know that. But I've apologized for taking liberties. Won't you forgive me?"

"Forgive . . . you?" Those pale blue eyes of hers went wide, and she shook her head. "You still don't understand. Listen to me, Jack. I'm not fit for marriage, not to anyone, not anymore. You don't want a woman like me, you couldn't . . ."

"I know what I want," he insisted and gathered her up in his arms.

She struggled to free herself, to get to her feet, but Jack held her fast, determined to soothe her. He didn't half understand what she'd been telling him, but if only she'd be still, he was sure he could convince her of his feelings. If only she'd be still . . .

"Let me go," she pleaded, thrashing against him, like a fragile bird, bent on fleeing its cage. "Please!"

In the end, he had no choice but to oblige her. She slipped from his arms, and he watched, helpless, as she stumbled to her feet and rushed off, clambering down the rocks and disappearing into the darkness.

When the shock of her leaving had worn off, Jack rose up, calmly folded his blanket over his arm, and scrambled down from his perch. As he went to cross the square where Miss Lila Henderson herself was in the midst of a dramatic recitation, Noah stepped out of the shadows and followed him out into the deserted street.

"Weren't you enjoying the performance?" he asked.

Still numb, Jack shook his head and kept on walking. "It's been a long day. I think I'll go home and turn in."

"Jack?"

Until now, Jack had assumed that it was only coincidence that had brought both him and Noah out here in the street, while the attention of the rest of the town was engaged by the theatrical troupe. But now he turned back toward his friend, with brows raised, as he waited for him to explain himself.

Noah cast his eyes downward, shuffling his feet in the dust, then reached into his pocket and drew out a handkerchief with which he swiped the sweat from the back of his neck. He was apparently having some trouble finding the right words.

"You aren't . . . serious about her, are you?" he posed at last.

Ah, now Jack understood. Noah must have seen him with Charlotte and come to his own conclusions. "If you mean, 'Am I dallying with Charlotte?', I think you ought to know better than to ask."

"That's not what I mean at all. I don't want . . . That is to say, I'd hate to see you settle for someone you weren't sure of, just because the pickings are slim around here."

Jack didn't feel much like arguing, after his odd encounter with Charlotte, but Noah's peculiar comment rankled him.

"Who says I'm not sure? Charlotte is a good woman. She's strong and independent, and she cares about people. A man couldn't want better than that."

"A man like you could do a lot better," Noah shot back.

The color drained from Jack's face. It was a queer sensation. Noah Kelsey might have been his closest friend, but Jack couldn't have expected him to take his side against his own family.

"What are you saying, Noah? Charlotte's your kin, for God's sake. She's Rachel's cousin."

Noah hesitated, then mopped his forehead with his

handkerchief, as if to give him time to organize his thoughts. And then he nodded vigorously.

"Yes, and so we ought to know her better than anyone else here. Just trust me, Jack. She isn't the right woman for you."

"I don't know what would make you say such a thing," Jack replied, "unless the truth of it is that you don't think *I'm* the right man for her."

"What? Oh, now don't be ridiculous. You're the best man I know . . . salt of the earth . . . pillar of the community. But if you let that woman into your life, I can promise you, you'll come to regret it."

"I know that the bachelors have been swarming thick as flies around your place since Charlotte got here, but that's no reason to blame her."

Jack shook his head. It was late, and he was tired and confused. He didn't know precisely what Noah's problem was, but he didn't want to listen to another minute of his ramblings, especially not after Charlotte had run off on him like she had.

Noah reached to lay a hand on Jack's arm. "I don't want to see you hurt, and you will be, sooner or later. Can't you see it, Jack? Charlotte Devereaux is no lady."

Jack threw off his friend's hand, then grasped him roughly by the shirtfront, casting him a baleful glare.

"You're pushing this too far, Noah. If any other man in this town had said such a thing about Charlotte, I'd not hesitate to knock him on his self-righteous ass. Now I'm going home and I'm going to forget all that you've said tonight. I suggest that you do the same."

And with that, he released his grip. As Noah stumbled backward, Jack turned and walked away.

Apparently, this rift between Noah and Charlotte ran deeper than he could have anticipated. He ought to have guessed it this afternoon, though, when he'd witnessed Rachel's frustration. Still, whatever the argument had been between them, Jack couldn't see how Noah could speak out so strongly against her. There must be something more to this. What was it that everyone was trying to warn him of tonight?

"She doesn't intend to stay, you know," Noah called after him, in a parting shot. "Once the baby is born and Rachel is on her feet again, she'll be gone, and then where will you be? Think about it, Jack."

Jack didn't have to be told. He suspected that for a long time thereafter, he'd be thinking of nothing else.

Eight

The last time that Charlotte had burst into a darkened room, thrown herself onto her bed, and buried her face in her pillow, she'd been scarcely more than twelve years old. She would have thought she was too hardened for such childish behavior now. But then nothing could have prepared her for the hurt she'd seen in Jack's eyes when she'd run from him.

She was to blame for it, there was no denying that; but she'd have hurt him more if she let this go on any longer. Of course, her own pain was no less than she deserved for believing that she might be allowed any measure of happiness after all that she'd done. But Jack was a good man; he deserved better. He deserved a sweet, unspoilt girl for his wife, and that was something that Charlotte could never be.

For the first time in a long while, she wished that she could have wept. It would have a blessed release, but despite the ache inside, no tears would come to her eyes.

The situation with Jack had gone too far. *If I couldn't bring myself to admit the truth to him,* she told herself, *then I must never, never allow myself to be alone with him again.* Let him believe that she was fickle, hard, and heartless. Let him believe that she had never really cared for him. Maybe it was better that way.

Charlotte hadn't time to consider the matter further, though, for just then she heard Rachel and Noah come into the house. She sat there, hoping that Rachel wouldn't call out for her, that she wouldn't want to come up, sit on the bed, and talk over the day as she so often did.

She listened for the familiar sound of footsteps creaking on the stairs, but she didn't hear it. She only heard Rachel and Noah conversing in the kitchen below, and while she didn't mean to eavesdrop, it was hard to ignore the voices.

"It's quiet. I guess Charlotte hasn't come in yet," she heard Rachel say. "I haven't seen her in the last few hours. I wonder where she's gotten off to."

The rattling of a glass chimney told her that someone was lighting the lamp that hung over the kitchen table, and then Rachel exclaimed: "Oh, Noah, you don't suppose that she and Jack have gone off somewhere . . . to be alone?"

Charlotte couldn't miss the excitement threading through her friend's words. Ever the romantic, Rachel was dreaming of a happy ending for her; but in this case, Charlotte knew that there was precious little hope for one.

"You're going to have to stop playing matchmaker," Noah warned his wife, impatience sharpening his tone. "Charlotte Devereaux is not the poor, unfortunate gentle-woman you've made her out to be."

"She's my friend, and that's all that matters. I'm sure that life has kicked her around a bit . . ." At this, Rachel hesitated for a long moment. ". . . even if she never speaks of it, and that's all the more reason we should want to see her settled and happy."

But Noah would have none of it. "What do we know about her, really? She was brought into our home, filthy and wounded, and dressed in miner's clothes. She'd cut off her hair, for God's sake, and her hands were as callused as a man's. That pistol of hers had been fired recently, and all of the chambers were empty. How are we to know what awful crimes she's guilty of committing?"

"Oh, but . . ."

Noah cut his wife off before she could continue. "All *I* know," he said next, "is that the sort of woman so greedy that she would unsex herself in order to prospect for gold, a woman so vicious as to resort to gunplay to settle her differences, is in no way respectable, certainly not responsible, and not half good enough for Jack Cordell. I ought to have turned her out as soon as her wound was healed."

Charlotte sat stock still on the edge of her bed in the darkened room, allowing Doctor Kelsey's harsh words to sink in. His reasoning might not be one hundred percent accurate, but his conclusions were valid.

Rachel, though, wasn't ready to admit defeat. "How can you say such a thing?" she chided her husband. "We're supposed to be Christians. Charlotte has done all that she could in the time that she's been here to prove herself a true friend. And she's made things easier for me, helping out around here with the cooking, laundry, and cleaning."

"Earning her keep, you mean."

"Now that was just plain unfair," Rachel shot back. "I swear I don't understand what's gotten into you lately."

"I don't expect you to understand. You're my wife; I've tried to shield you from the harsher realities of life. But even you ought to understand that there are only two types of women in this world: the respectable sort that a man takes for his wife, and the other, more mercenary sort, whom he may dally with for a time but wouldn't think of giving his name. . . ."

Upstairs in her darkened room, Charlotte shook her head. What Doctor Kelsey meant was that those were the only two types that men would allow women to be.

". . . Even Jack will come to understand that," he went on to say, "once he cools down and takes the time to think about it."

"What do you mean by that?" Rachel asked, her voice ending on a wild note. "Oh, Noah. You and Jack haven't quarreled, have you? You haven't said anything to him about Charlotte. You couldn't be that cruel."

"He has a right to know what he's getting tangled up in, and since she doesn't seem inclined to tell him . . ."

Charlotte could make out Rachel's light tread on the kitchen floorboards as she frantically paced across the room and back again.

"What did you say to him, exactly?"

"Only what I felt absolutely certain of," Noah replied, "that she's not the right woman for him, that she's not good enough."

As the blood drained away from Charlotte's face, she took an unsteady breath and squeezed her eyes shut. She knew that this was bound to happen, sooner or later.

"Noah, how could you?"

"Jack Cordell is my friend. I owe him the truth, whether or not he wants to hear it."

Noah must have reached out for his wife then, or attempted to lay his hand on her arm, for Rachel shouted at him. "Don't you dare touch me."

With that, her voice went brittle. She was positively breathless with anger. "I . . . don't know if I can ever forgive you for this. Until now, I wouldn't have believed you capable of such a thing . . . I just don't know how I can go on loving a man who is so . . . hard and heartless."

"Calm down now," Noah entreated her. "You're only making yourself hysterical."

"I mean it, Noah. Don't touch me!"

Charlotte felt the guilt, heavy as a weighted chain around her neck. Because of her, Jack and Noah, who'd always been the best of friends, were quarreling. Because of her, a chasm now yawned wide between Rachel and her husband. Much as Charlotte might have wanted to run downstairs to her friend and offer her comfort, she knew her interference would only make matters worse. No, given all that had transpired tonight, she knew what she had to do.

Making as little noise as possible, she slipped out of the lavender gingham dress and laid it carefully on the bed. She'd been so proud of that dress. She and Rachel had sat, shoulder-to-shoulder, in the parlor stitching on it every afternoon for two weeks, hoping to get it finished in time for the Fourth of July celebration.

It was the only dress she owned that fit properly, the only one of her very own that she'd had in years, and she had been so sure that once she put it on, she'd feel like every other woman. She'd hoped finally to be able to put away her memories of Charlie, the miners, Marcus Gideon, and all the rest of her past, but it hadn't happened that way. She would never be able to divorce herself from her past, she saw that now; and so the dress might just as well be left behind with all her other broken dreams.

Guilt pricked at her like a sharp needle. She had promised Rachel that she'd help her when the baby came, but Rachel would have to understand. She couldn't stay in Cedar Creek any longer, not with things as they were. She ought to have known from the beginning that she couldn't fit in.

Charlotte looked at the mended blue calico dress, hanging from the peg on the back of her door, but then thought better of it. Sliding out the bureau drawer, she withdrew the worn buckskins that she'd managed to keep Rachel from resigning to the dustbin. Maybe she'd suspected, even then, that she would need them again.

The fringed shirt and leggings had once felt comfortable as a second skin to her, but now as she shrugged them on, the material stretched taut across her bosom and her hips. Apparently, she'd filled out some since she'd come to live in town.

She freed her hair from its crocheted net, then ran her fingers through it and observed her reflection in the swinging mirror. She'd been able to wash her hair regularly since she'd come here. In consequence, it floated about her head in shining curls that were a bit too long and bouncy to be mistaken for a boy's. Taking up her clasp knife from the bureau top, she cut a long piece of rawhide fringe from her shirt and then pulled the whole back into a tight little queue. The disguise was complete once she'd jammed her battered felt hat on her head.

Rachel had done what she could to scrub the worst of the trail dust out of the garments, but there was nothing she could do about the neat, round bullet hole in the right thigh of the leggings, nor the mottled pattern of dark brown bloodstains. It was left as a vivid reminder of all that she'd been through.

Finally, dragging out the worn leather saddlebag that she'd carried with her all the way from New Orleans, Charlotte took a moment to pack up her meager belongings.

All she needed now was to fetch her pistol out of Noah's desk drawer, and then, with Noah and Rachel still bickering in the kitchen, and everyone else occupied with the celebration in the square, she could gather together a few supplies from the bakery, collect her horse from the livery and disappear into the night before anyone was the wiser.

For half an hour now, Jack had been pacing about his rooms in quiet frustration; his encounter with Noah replaying over and over again in his head, fueling his anger. He couldn't imagine what had prompted his friend to rail out against Charlotte, as he had. But it didn't matter; there could be no excuse for purveying such a pack of out-and-out lies.

The truth of it was that Jack was just as angry with himself for not saying more in Charlotte's defense. He didn't believe any of what Noah had said, or at least that was what he kept telling himself. However, he couldn't deny the niggling voice that had begun to pose uncomfortable questions in his head.

What did he know about Charlotte, really? They'd never spoken about their pasts, but then that had been his choice just as much as hers. And why would Noah lie to him about this? He'd always been one of the most rigidly truthful men that Jack knew. But what would make Noah so eager to discourage a relationship between Charlotte and Jack? Not simple friendship, surely. What reason would he have to swear so vehemently that she was no lady, unless—unless, he had some knowledge of that himself.

Jack sank down into the damask parlor chair as the realization struck him, full force. It wouldn't be the first time such a thing had happened—two healthy young people living under the same roof, the man's wife with child and unable or unwilling to satisfy his needs, so he turns to her cousin. The woman, feeling flattered and perhaps more than a little obligated since he has taken her in and provided for her, can hardly refuse.

It was frightening just how clear it all seemed to Jack. Noah had taken Charlotte as his mistress, and so he was warning Jack off. Even Charlotte herself, when she had run from him this evening, had insisted that he wouldn't want a woman like her. Is that what she'd meant?

Repulsed as he was by the thought, Jack couldn't make himself hold Charlotte to blame for any of this. Though he didn't know the details, he knew that she'd suffered a great deal in her life. She'd come here with scarcely any belongings of her own. Her clothes were mostly Rachel's hand-me-downs, altered to fit. He'd heard the ring of steel in her voice whenever she'd been challenged, seen the cracked, yellow calluses on her hands. Charlotte Devereaux would do whatever she had to do. She was a survivor. Jack felt certain he could forgive her. But for Noah Kelsey, there was no excuse.

Jack sprang from his chair and was out the door, down the stairs, and heading for the Kelsey homestead before he'd even realized what he was doing. He had no idea of what he was going to say. All along the way, he was fighting back the urge to thrash his friend, but one way or another, he was going to make Noah face up to what he'd done.

He saw from the windows that there were lamps lit within, but he barely had time to mount the porch steps before Noah rushed out of the house as though he'd been expecting him. One look at his friend's ashen face, though, told Jack that something alarming had transpired.

"What is it?" he asked, all his own concerns evaporating at once. "What's wrong?"

"It's Rachel," Noah replied. His voice seemed steady enough, but there was a wild look in his eye that Jack had never seen before. "She's gone into labor, but it's not her time yet."

"Then, for heaven's sake, man, what are you doing out here?"

"I've already done all that I can for her: put her to bed, given her morphine. It's important that she stay calm, but she won't. She been calling out frantically for Charlotte. You know how fond she is of the girl."

"And where *is* Charlotte?" Jack asked, trepidation causing the hairs on the back of his neck to stand on end.

"I . . . I don't know. She's gone . . . disappeared. I went up to her room to find all the bureau drawers standing open and empty. Rachel and I were arguing earlier, about what I'd told you. Charlotte must have heard us, packed her things and run off."

Jack ought to have suspected that this evening's events were leading to such a climax. "She can't have gotten far at this time of night. I'll find her and bring her back," he said. His suspicions and his anger were set aside for the moment, and he slapped Noah reassuringly on the back.

"You go on back inside now, and do what you can for your wife."

As he turned to do as Jack had bade him, Noah shook his head. "This is all my fault. If I hadn't been so bull-headed, if I hadn't worked Rachel up into such a state, she'd not be lying in that bed now, trying so desperately to cling to our child's life."

Noah's anguished words reverberated in Jack's head as he made his way toward Charlotte's bakery, the first place he aimed to check. If, indeed, the man was guilty of all that Jack suspected, then he was certainly being made to pay the price tonight.

It was now close to midnight. Without the sun blazing overhead, the summer's heat had lost some of its vigor, but the night air was heavy and still. Sweat trickled down Jack's face and collected beneath his jaw, until he swiped it away with his shirtsleeve.

The theatrical troupe had finished its public performance, and so only a few folk remained in the square. There came the occasional pop-pop sound of firecrackers exploding in the street, centered mainly around the pair of saloons on the south end of town. Apparently, the remaining revelers, along with Miss Henderson's entertainers, had adjourned there, for there were voices singing on-key amidst the raucous laughter, and the tinny piano in Arthur Rollins's Red Bird Saloon had never been played with such gusto.

As he drew near the bakery and saw the yellow gleam of lamplight from within, Jack blew out a relieved breath. Just as he'd suspected. Charlotte had taken refuge here. But his relief was short-lived as, only a moment later, he noticed a buckskin-clad figure pass before the window. It wasn't Charlotte, after all. It must be a thief, taking advantage of the commotion in town to cover his crime.

But why the bakery? Charlotte did a healthy business, but she wouldn't be foolish enough to leave cash money lying around. It would have been smarter to break into Jack's mercantile or Henry Sutton's hardware store across the street; at least they had merchandise worth stealing.

As he thought again, Jack considered that it might not be money that this intruder was after. If he had seen Charlotte go into the bakery alone . . .

Concern for her spurred him into action. He kicked open the door and rushed in, knocking the man off his feet before he even knew what had hit him. As they rolled together across the floor, with Jack attempting to hold his own against the buckskin-clad arms and legs flailing wildly about him, it occurred to him that he'd been in this position before.

There was only the one lamp lit up on the counter, and the room was too thick with shadows for Jack to clearly see his face, but still Jack knew with an uncanny certainty that this was the young miner, Charlie, the fellow whose friends had brought him into town after he'd been wounded. Apparently, despite what the boy had told Noah, he hadn't gone up to Denver after all.

"Leave off, damn you!" Jack demanded.

He threw his big body over the boy's, effectively pinning him against the floor. It took tremendous effort, but eventually he'd managed to catch up both Charlie's arms, and fixing them at his sides, he drew back to face his opponent.

His eyes had already adjusted somewhat to the dimness, but nevertheless he could not comprehend what he saw. It must have been a trick of the light, he told himself. He blinked. He blinked again.

"Charlotte?"

Using the full weight of her body, she pushed up against him. Still stunned, Jack rolled off. Charlotte reached to pick up the felt hat that she'd lost in the melee, and got to her feet, swiping the dust from her clothes with a careless hand. He could see quite clearly now that the right thigh of her fawn-colored breeches bore a bullethole and evidence of bloodstains.

Jack propped his back against the counter, drew his long legs up, and pressed his forehead to his knees. He had to struggle to fight down the nausea that welled within him.

His mind was still reeling, but in that moment, a flash of memory came to him. When Charlotte had first arrived here, she'd walked with a limp. Rachel had said that she'd sprained her ankle, but apparently that hadn't been the truth. He looked into her eyes—pale blue eyes—and he remembered how he'd once compared them to his brother's. Why hadn't he seen it before?

"Yes," she said harshly and slapped the hat, which she gripped tight in her hand, hard against her thigh. Jack flinched. The gesture was almost . . . masculine. "I can see you're starting to realize."

"It *was* you then. But, but how—?"

He was fumbling for words, and unable, for the life of him, to form the deluge of questions that flooded his mind into anything coherent.

"Why?"

Charlotte squared her jaw and regarded him dispassionately. "Why dress like this? Because it's by far the safest way for a woman alone in the world. Because I don't have to feel afraid. I can travel where I want without worrying every time I close my eyes that I may wake up to find some brute breathing down my neck and tearing at my clothes.

"Dressed like this, I'm treated as an equal. I can be independent, hold a job, support myself. I don't have to rely upon the whims of a man for my daily bread. So you see, there are a thousand good reasons."

"But what about your family?" Jack protested. "Surely they would protect you, care for you."

"My family?" she echoed. "Rachel, you mean, and

Noah? Haven't you guessed by now? I'm no more Rachel Kelsey's cousin than you are. I have no family, not any more."

She fixed her eyes on the hat in her hands as her fingers worried the fraying brim. "Rachel and Noah took me in. They were kind to me when I needed kindness, and now I've paid them back by setting them against one another, by turning their lives upside down."

"So this is what Noah meant when he . . ."

"Tried to warn you off?" she finished for him. "Yes. He knew all along that someone who's lived the sort of life I have could never make a proper wife for you."

"But he had no right to presume . . ."

Looking up, Charlotte boldly met his eyes. Her jaw was set, her glare intense, her lips pressed into one long, thin line. Every angle in her face was sharp and unrevealing. There was nothing at all to betray her feelings. Nothing, that is, save the merest glaze of unshed tears in those pale blue eyes of hers.

"Noah is a good man, Jack, a good friend. He was only trying to protect you. I can't blame him for that. I've lied to everyone, since I came here. You don't know me—not who I am, nor what I've done. But you don't have to worry, any of you. Things will get back to normal once I've gone."

Shaking her head, she went to the counter, shoved her supplies in her saddlebags and buckled the flaps.

Jack swallowed hard, leaned his head back against the counter and cast his gaze upward at the beamed ceiling, gray and hazy in the shadows. His whole world was crumbling around his ears, and he couldn't even find the strength to get up off of the floor.

Charlotte tossed the weathered saddlebag across her shoulder. "You can keep the supplies and equipment," she told him, gesturing toward the back room, "maybe you'll find someone more deserving of this place."

An intense mix of shock and surprise had kept him paralyzed for all this time; but as those feelings wore off, they were swiftly replaced by anger. She'd been planning to run out on him, without even a word in explanation. Jack shot to his feet and placed himself between Charlotte and the door.

"So if I hadn't come here tonight, I'd have simply woke up tomorrow morning to find you gone, wouldn't have I? And what did you expect me to think about that?"

"I expected you'd hate me for a while, and then eventually forget. Better that than for me to go on pretending to be something that I couldn't be."

"Couldn't?" he echoed, his tone steeped in bitterness. Just now he wanted to hurt her as much as he was hurting. "Or *wouldn't?* Oh, yes, you must have had a good laugh," he continued, "letting me romance you, listening while I poured out my heart, when all the while you had no intention of giving up your precious freedom."

She flinched as if he'd struck her. "It wasn't like that, Jack. I wanted this, more than you could know. But we can't, any of us, simply forget the harm we've done and fashion a new life for ourselves; I can see that now. The old one has a queer way of turning up when we least expect it. Maybe that's the penance we're made to pay for our sins."

Jack didn't believe that. He didn't want to believe it. "You're wrong," he insisted. "The past is dead and buried. I don't care what Noah thinks. Whatever you've done, Charlotte, we can put it behind us. Start fresh."

For the first time since he'd come here, Jack saw Charlotte soften. Buoyed by this, he took a step closer and reached out to her, but she countered with a nervous step backward and put up her hand to stop him.

"Please, don't, Jack." Squeezing her eyes closed, she shut him out in an effort to fortify herself. "You may say that now, but you haven't thought this through, and I've already decided. I'm leaving."

His love wasn't enough to keep her here. It was a painful realization for Jack, but he accepted it with silent resignation. Perhaps it was easier for him because he knew that no matter what she'd said, she wouldn't be leaving Cedar Creek tonight. He held the trump card, after all.

"You can't leave," he told her. "Rachel's gone into labor. Didn't you know? That's the reason I came looking for you in the first place."

Charlotte paled. "But it's not her time."

"Noah is afraid that if he can't calm her down, and she delivers now, the baby will die. She's been calling out for you all the while."

Jack hadn't meant to make it sound as if all of this was somehow her fault—or maybe he had—but either way, he wasn't given the opportunity to amend the statement. As soon as the words were out, Charlotte's saddlebag slipped from her shoulder and slammed to the floor, and she swept past him, rushing off into the night.

Nine

Charlotte stood in Rachel's kitchen, washing up the dishes from the noon meal, and shut her eyes in an attempt to ignore the steam that rose up from the wash water, compounding the heat that had settled in the valley on this oppressive August afternoon.

"Don't forget to remind Noah to pick up a skein of white knitting wool from the general store," Rachel called out to her. "I can't make another stitch on this baby's blanket until I get more wool."

The bedroom Rachel shared with Noah was set beside the kitchen, making it all too easy to communicate, even when Charlotte was busy with her chores.

"Unless you'd like to go out and get it for me," she posed next.

Charlotte hadn't been to the general store in more than a month, and Rachel knew it well. Charlotte didn't want to have to face Jack again. He'd come into the bakery once or twice, and tried to speak with her, but she'd managed to put him off. What was the use in talking? It wouldn't change anything.

"I'll be too busy for that," she called back, without bothering to hide her irritation, "but I'll be sure to remind Noah for you."

It was an uncharitable thought, she knew, but somehow Charlotte suspected that Rachel was secretly enjoying her role as invalid, managing the household from her feather pillow and summer quilt bedecked bedstead, like a general issuing battlefield orders for his footsoldiers from the comfort of his command tent.

After that first frightening night, Rachel's condition had grown no worse, but because of Noah's fears for her, he'd scarcely allowed her to leave her bed in more than a month now, except for the most necessary ablutions; and so he and Charlotte had been taking turns playing at the role of a nursemaid.

They had silently called a truce between them, giving each other a wide berth and communicating in as few words as possible, as they followed a regular routine. Noah took the morning shift, allowing Charlotte time at her shop to do her baking and serve her customers.

While at the bakery, Charlotte would also prepare the noon meal, and then carry it back to the Kelsey household in a basket after she'd closed up shop. This would leave Noah the entire afternoon to receive patients in his office or make visits to those unable to leave their homes.

There was some comfort for Charlotte in the routine. By engaging in the same familiar activities day-after-day, she could almost forget how much things had changed. And they had changed.

Rachel had still not forgiven her husband for what he'd said to Jack about Charlotte. She treated him coolly, and consequently Noah, consumed by a painful mix of worry and regret, moped about the house for most of the time wearing a hangdog look.

With regard to Charlotte, even though no one had told Rachel that she had intended to leave Cedar Creek, Rachel evidently knew enough to guess why her friend had been missing for so long on the night she'd been calling out for her.

More than once in the past few weeks, Rachel had mentioned to Charlotte how thankful she was to have her with her, how she didn't know how she would manage without her. And Rachel seemed calmer in her presence. If Charlotte were even more than a few minutes late in returning from the bakery, she would come in to find Rachel tossing nervously beneath the bedclothes and chiding her for her tardiness.

Charlotte would have been more concerned about all of this if she hadn't known her friend well enough to know that these were merely attempts to strengthen the emotional chain between them, and thereby ensure that Charlotte wouldn't try and run off again.

Rachel needn't have worried, though, for Charlotte had no intention of leaving until her friend had delivered a healthy child and was on her feet again. She owed Rachel more of a debt than she could ever repay, and she would be grateful to her always for encouraging her to settle in Cedar Creek, even if things hadn't worked out as she would have liked.

Rachel had, after all, offered her friendship and helped her contrive a way to support herself. Charlotte had known more moments of happiness here than she had in all of the years since she'd left her home in New Orleans, and that was certainly more than she deserved.

A knock on the front door jarred her from her thoughts. It was probably one of Noah's patients. Since word had gotten out that there was a doctor in Cedar Creek, people often came from miles around seeking treatment.

Charlotte wiped her hands on her apron as she strode through the hall, but drew up short when, through the screen door, she saw Jack standing there. He offered a crooked smile when he saw her. His black hair was brushed back off his forehead, his face flush from the heat, and he had a brightly-colored tin of hard candies tucked in the crook of his arm.

For a brief instant, Charlotte thought that she must be dreaming . . . or delirious from the heat. Jack Cordell on the doorstep, smiling and bearing gifts? Her heart beat a little faster; she couldn't help that, but gathering together all of the strength she had in her, she met him with an expression that, she hoped, would reveal none of the regret that she was feeling, regret for what might have been.

"I haven't seen much of Noah lately," he began, "and so I've come to see for myself how Rachel is faring." With that, he held out the tin of candies before him. "Oh, and I've brought these for . . ."

Charlotte cut him off before he could finish. Pushing open the screen door, she scooped up the tin. "Come in," she bade him. "Noah is in his office. You can talk to him about Rachel, and meanwhile, I'll see that she gets these."

Jack lingered briefly on the porch, as if this wasn't at all what he'd had in mind; but then, finally accepting that she'd left him no choice, he followed her in.

Without offering him a word, Charlotte ushered him into Noah's office, then hurried down the hall to Rachel's room, where she hesitated on the threshold.

"Jack's come to see how you're faring," she said.

"Jack?" One of Rachel's brows crooked upward, and Charlotte could see, by the intrigued expression on her face, that her brain was hard at work. "Jack Cordell, did you say? Your Jack?"

Charlotte scowled. "Yes . . . no. I mean, yes, it's him, and no, he's not 'my' Jack."

"There's no need to snap at me. I only asked a simple question. And what's that you've got behind your back?"

Charlotte came to stand before the bed and handed over the tin. "He's brought these for you."

"For me? But you're the one with the sweet tooth. Don't worry, though. I'll share. Now bring me my white cotton shawl, will you? The one with the embroidered roses on it."

Hearing this, Charlotte paled. "Your shawl? In this heat? Do you have the chills? Shall I call Noah?"

"No, of course not. But I can't very well receive a visitor wearing only my nightgown, now can I?"

"Visitor? Do you mean to say that you want me to bring Jack in here to see you?"

"Why not? It was kind of him to inquire after me, and besides I'm nearly bored to tears, lying in this bed, day after day. I haven't had a visitor since Mrs. Murphy stopped by last week."

"But Noah will tell him how you're doing. You need your rest."

"I'm feeling fine," Rachel insisted. "Besides, I'd like to speak to him myself."

Trepidation prickled, like gooseflesh, over Charlotte's skin as she drew the cotton shawl from the back of the chair where it rested, and handed it over to her friend. Rachel hadn't spoken to Jack since the night he and Noah had argued, and she very much feared that if given the opportunity, she might be tempted to bring up the whole sordid subject again.

"Please, Rachel," she ventured finally, "don't meddle on my behalf, if that's what you're contemplating. Believe me when I tell you that whatever there might have been between Jack and I is over and done with."

Rachel scowled, fixing a gimlet eye on her. "Don't tell me that you don't care for him, Charlotte Devereaux, because I know well enough that you do."

"What *I* feel doesn't matter," Charlotte retorted, and then feeling weary, let her head lag. "Please, please, just leave it alone."

"You haven't been able to forget what Noah said, have you?" Receiving no reply, Rachel breathed a heavy sigh. "Heaven knows my husband is an otherwise educated man, but he doesn't know a thing about judging character. You're a good person, Charlotte. I know that, and Jack does, too. He'd tell you so himself, if you'd just let him."

But Charlotte wasn't listening. "Noah is right this time,

Rachel, can't you see that? I spent three years passing myself off as a man. I've been places, seen things that no respectable lady ought to see, done things that . . . I'm not . . . an innocent anymore."

"But you only wanted your freedom, that's all," Rachel argued. "You weren't living in sin with any of those miners. You told me that much. I know you must have had a good reason for everything that you've done."

Charlotte shook her head. She hadn't wanted to have this discussion, hadn't wanted to see the disappointment in Rachel's eyes when finally she told her the whole truth. But maybe it was time.

"You didn't know me before," she said. "There was a time when I was as silly, vain, and frivolous as any other young girl . . . and as foolish, God knows. I'm not the person you think I am. I've brought only pain and sorrow to anyone who's ever cared for me. Just look at the trouble I've caused between you and Noah."

"How could you hold yourself to blame for that? It's Noah who's acting like a bull-headed half-wit. I must say, I'd never have expected it of him."

"That's not all of it. Trouble has always followed in my wake. My mother died giving me life, did you know that? And it's solely because of me that my father was murdered."

A long silence ensued as Rachel allowed Charlotte's words to sink in.

"Murdered?" she whispered at last.

Charlotte nodded. "He died defending my honor. I'll wager you didn't know that either. And the funny thing about it is that by that time, I hadn't a shred of honor left in me."

"I don't believe that."

"Well, you ought to. And that's hardly the worst of it. I shot a man to death on the night before my friends brought me down here so Noah could patch me up. And it wasn't an accident nor self-defense either, if that's what you're thinking.

"I had a purpose all right when I was haunting those mining camps, masquerading in men's clothes. I wanted a man dead. I didn't care about anything else, and so I hunted him down like the animal that he was, and I killed him. And if you were to ask me today if I regretted what I'd done, I'd have to deny it."

Now came the wide-eyed disbelief that Charlotte had anticipated all along. The color drained away from Rachel's cheeks. She hunched her shoulders, drawing her shawl tighter. Her brow furrowed as she considered all that she'd heard, and it was hard to miss the disquiet that had begun to churn within her, for it was written plain on her face.

"Oh, Charlotte. You don't mean that."

"I do."

There wasn't any satisfaction for Charlotte in this. But as much as she'd valued Rachel's friendship, it wasn't fair to go on allowing Rachel to defend her, or to let her believe that Charlotte was something that she wasn't.

"You needn't feel sorry for me," she said next. "I've danced with the devil, and now it's time to pay the price. I don't deserve happiness, and I certainly don't deserve a man like Jack Cordell."

Charlotte's gaze drifted to the floor. Convincing as her words had been, she was too ashamed just now to meet her friend's eyes. "I'll understand if you want me to leave."

She was sure that, following the first, awkward moment of silence, Rachel would accept her offer. What ordinary person would feel comfortable with an admitted murderer living under their roof? But that wasn't what happened, not at all.

"Leave?" Rachel echoed. "Why, don't be a ninny. We

don't put our family out, where I come from. Good times and bad, we stand together."

Regarding her friend, Charlotte blinked in astonishment. With all that she'd been told, Rachel was still willing to accept her as family, even though there was, in truth, no common blood between them. Charlotte's heart swelled with affection. How truly fortunate she was to have found such a friend.

As for Rachel, she'd already returned to the subject at hand. "Now go and fetch Jack in here, so I can thank him properly for coming to see me," she bade. "And don't worry. I'll behave myself. I promise."

In spite of all they'd just discussed, Charlotte sensed that Rachel still harbored intentions of matchmaking—or match mending, in this case—for there was a sparkle of mischief in Rachel's pretty, brown eyes that Charlotte recognized only too well.

". . . and I'm hopeful that, if she stays calm and keeps to her bed for the next month or so, she'll be able to carry the baby to term."

Jack took in Noah's words, nodded thoughtfully and leaned forward in his chair. "If there's anything you need," he offered, "anything that I can do, please let me know."

For the first time since Jack had arrived, Noah got to his feet and came around to perch himself on the edge of his desktop, cutting down the distance between them.

"Thank you, Jack." Tugging at the ends of his moustache, Noah did his best to smile. "I'm glad you came. I was afraid that after all I'd said about Charlotte . . ."

"I said I'd forget all about that, and I meant it," Jack replied, then seized upon the opportunity to get a few things off his chest. The words came tumbling out of his mouth one after another. "Of course, if you ask me, you've jumped to a lot of conclusions, without much hard evidence. But you wouldn't be the first to be guilty of that offense. Do you know what I thought, after you'd said what you did about Charlotte? I thought that maybe you were trying to dissuade me from seeing her because you and she . . ."

Jack regarded his friend with a knowing glance, one dark brow arched high.

"Charlotte . . . and me?" Noah repeated, incredulous. "But how could you ever believe . . ."

"Look at the evidence," Jack continued, "such as it is. She's living in your house and grateful to you for all that you've done for her. Rachel's not been well lately. You're a healthy man, a man with needs. What's so hard to believe? Especially when you've done your damnedest to dissuade any man that comes near her."

Noah's face went pale. "That's not what I was trying to do. God help me, as if I don't have trouble enough with one woman . . ."

"Of course, those of us who know you well are willing to give you the benefit of the doubt. Too bad you're not willing to do the same for Charlotte."

"All right," Noah said, nodding vigorously. "I take your point."

"For my part, I'd like to know the whole story before I make up my mind what to think about Miss Charlotte Devereaux," Jack continued. "But she won't even talk to me. All she said, when I came upon her that night in the bakery, was that she wasn't right for me, and then she spouted something about being independent and how it was 'safer' for a woman alone to dress as a man. With only that to go on, I'm not any nearer to understanding her than I was on the first day we met."

"You were the one who carried her into my office," Noah replied to this. "You know as much as I do. That pair of miners brought her down from Six Mile. They said she'd been living there, and they called her Charlie. But they didn't suspect that she was a woman, I can tell you that much. She had a gunshot wound in her leg. It was nothing serious, but her own pistol was empty. Those miners never said anything, but I suspect there'd been a gun-fight of some sort."

"And that's all you know? She's never spoken about her life before she came here, not even to Rachel?"

Noah folded his arms over his chest. "Frankly, I don't think it's anything she wants to talk about," he said. "She's already put you off, Jack. Maybe you'd be better off if you just left things as they are."

"Is that what you'd do, if you cared for her? I don't understand why you're so set against her. She's a slip of a woman who's never done any of us any real harm. You're a better man than that. I know you are."

"We have no idea what sort of secrets the woman is harboring. As you've pointed out, she's living in my house, Jack, and Rachel's grown far too fond of her. You saw how distraught it made her when she thought Charlotte had left us. Well, I have Rachel's welfare to think of, and our child's, and it's not a responsibility that I take lightly."

"You must know that Charlotte would never do any-thing to harm Rachel. She didn't have to come back to stay with her when Rachel needed her. She could have left that night, like she'd planned to, but she didn't. She dropped everything and ran to her friend. Doesn't that count for something?"

"You sound as if you don't care, one way or the other, what she's done."

"Maybe you're right, Noah. Maybe if you love some-one, it doesn't matter."

If I had any sense at all, Charlotte told herself as she made her way down the hall, *I'd have refused Rachel's request.* But what was the use? One way or another, Rachel always seemed to get what she wanted from those around her, as if it were inevitable.

No sooner had she appeared in the doorway of Noah's office than the voices within stilled, and Noah and Jack turned their attention to Charlotte.

"Rachel wants to see you," she told Jack.

His face went flush, as if he were embarrassed at the thought of visiting a lady in her bedchamber, and he stammered out a reply. "Oh, I never meant . . . I . . . That is, I wouldn't want to bother her."

Charlotte couldn't help the smile that teased the corner of her mouth as she watched him. He was such an honorable, upright gentleman. Likely it was that which had attracted her to him in the first place and also—she realized with a painful dismay—precisely what made him the wrong man for a woman like herself.

"You might as well go," Noah said, expelling a weary sigh. "She's sick to death of talking to Charlotte and me. If she doesn't find other amusements somehow, I think she may get up from that bed and try and make a break for it. Then heaven help us all."

Jack got to his feet and crossed the room toward Charlotte, but she turned away before he'd reached her and started back down the hall. She didn't want to see his face, didn't want him to see hers. Let him trail at her heels like an obedient puppy. Let him think she was cold and cruel and . . .

They'd only taken half a dozen steps, though, when Jack caught her arm and spun her around to face him.

"Stop treating me as though I were a stranger," he said, his voice a rough whisper. His chest heaved as he pulled in an uneven breath. "You know that it's you I've come to see. Can't we talk, Charlotte?"

Staring into those eyes of his while pretending not to feel anything was, by far, the hardest thing that Charlotte had ever done. But she managed nevertheless, because it was for the best; because setting him free was the one gift she had to give him.

"Don't keep Rachel too long," she said, all the while struggling to keep her words even, her expression distant. "She may seem healthy enough, but she needs her rest."

With that, she turned away, swallowed hard, and continued down the hall, shoving her hands into the folds of her apron so that he could not see how badly they were trembling.

When they reached the bedroom at last, Rachel met them with a satisfied air, her head held high. With two feather pillows supporting her back and her embroidered shawl thrown over her shoulders, she looked as regal as a queen who'd deigned to grant an audience to one of her faithful subjects.

Charlotte was certain that this did not bode well for her, and as she stepped aside to allow Jack to walk past, she crossed her arms tightly over her chest to quell a tremor of apprehension.

"It's good to see you, Mr. Cordell," Rachel said as he drew up beside her. "Thank you so much for the candy and the well wishes. I'm glad to know that I've not been forgotten while I'm whiling away the days here in my bed."

"Oh, no one's forgotten you, ma'am," he replied. "I can assure you of that."

Charlotte had taken up a place in the doorway and now felt Rachel's gaze on her. Sensing that she was about to be dismissed, Charlotte slanted her friend a warning glance to indicate that she had no intention whatsoever of leaving her alone with Jack.

But Rachel was not so easily dissuaded. "Come closer, Mr. Cordell," she invited, "so we won't have to shout across the room."

"I don't want to tire you," Jack replied to this. "Charlotte has explained how important it is for you to get your rest."

Charlotte didn't have to look; she could feel Rachel's stare cut through her.

"I only wanted to tell you what I've already told Noah," he continued, "if there's anything that I can do for you, if there's anything you need, you have only to ask."

Charlotte rolled her eyes heavenward. As if Rachel didn't already have them all dancing to her tune, Jack was offering her still more power. And of course, Rachel didn't waste any time in using it.

"Well, now that you come to mention it," she began, "there is one little thing. Lately, I have had this terrible craving for raspberry cobbler."

"Cobbler?" Jack echoed, then shook his head. "Why, I'm afraid I'm not much of a cook."

Rachel giggled like a schoolgirl. "No, silly, of course, you're not. But I know that Charlotte wouldn't mind baking one for me . . . that is to say, she wouldn't mind at all, *if* we had raspberries."

Jack's face lit up as her meaning dawned on him. "There is that wild raspberry patch not far from my cabin, up near the lake."

"There now, you see," Rachel told him, "I knew you could help. I don't suppose you'd mind taking Charlotte up there this afternoon? Just to show her where this patch of yours is so that she could pick some berries to make my cobbler? I'd be truly grateful."

Jack cast a meaningful glance in Charlotte's direction, then turned back to Rachel with an evil grin. Whether or not she'd realized it, she'd given him precisely the opportunity he'd been looking for.

"How could I possibly refuse such a gracious request?"

How, indeed! For her part, though, Charlotte did not intend to get roped in so easily. "I've far too much work to do," she piped in. "I couldn't possibly go today. Who'll make supper? Who'll look after you?"

"We'll have something cold for supper," Rachel retorted. "It's too hot to cook today anyway. And as for me, I'm not an infant, who needs constant watching. Noah will be here, if I need anything. Besides, it might do us good to have a little more time alone."

Charlotte could have argued with her all afternoon long, found plenty of other excuses to keep her from catering to this whim of Rachel's, except for that last remark. But how could she possibly refuse her friend the opportunity to spend a little time alone with her husband, to perhaps repair the damage to their relationship that Charlotte's own presence in their household had wrought?

Once again, Charlotte had been bested.

Ten

Jack dragged himself out of the raspberry patch, vigorously shaking his leg to disentangle the thorny brambles that had attached themselves to his trousers. Setting aside his half-filled tin pail, he settled himself on a flat rock, drew a handkerchief from his pocket and mopped his brow.

The waning sun had set the afternoon sky aflame in brilliant ribbons of orange and gold, but there was no breeze at all to stir the summer air, and the heat was nigh unbearable. Nothing could have convinced him to ride all the way up here on such a day and scramble around, hunting for raspberries in a wild patch of thorn bushes; nothing that is, except the prospect of spending some time with Charlotte.

But he might as well have been alone up here for all the attention she paid him. She hadn't said more than a dozen words to him all afternoon. She'd neatly parried each and every one of his questions with a simple "yes" or "no" or else pretended that she hadn't heard what he'd said. It was enough to make a man ask himself why he should care at all.

Reaching toward the water pail he'd brought from the well, Jack lifted out the dipper and took a long, cool drink. And then he saw her, out of the corner of one eye, scowling fiercely as she tugged at her skirts, atangle in the brambles, artlessly revealing a fringe of worn cambric petticoat in the process, and the pair of slim ankles beneath it, and he knew.

He'd never met a woman like Charlotte Devereaux before, a woman so vibrantly alive, a woman who could share his dreams and bring a sense of purpose into this hollow life of his—no matter what she'd been before, no matter what she'd done.

The blue calico dress had molded itself to her slender form. Her face was dewy and flushed from the heat, her lips were soft, full, and stained a rich, dark red from the berries she'd apparently been sampling as she worked.

Her pail was nearly full, he noticed. All afternoon, she'd endeavored tirelessly in the brambles, in order to avoid conversation with him, but just now as he watched her, she paused to press a plump, red berry between her lips, then proceeded to lick the sweet juice from each of her fingertips.

Jack shifted uncomfortably in his seat, ashamed of the wild imaginings that were flitting through his brain; imaginings of Charlotte, naked and pliant beneath him, her soft moans like sweet music in his ear, those full, red lips parted and waiting for his kiss.

There was no denying it; he wanted her so badly that he could scarcely think straight. But how could he ever hope to touch her the way that he longed to, to feel her lips on his again, when she wouldn't even speak to him.

With a sharp flick of his wrist, Jack cast the ladle back into the water pail, then rose up, and giving vent to his frustration, started back along the winding path that led back to the cabin. He had to put a distance between them, before he went and did something foolish.

His agitation eased somewhat once he was alone and back on familiar ground, standing before the split rail fence where the horses were penned. His old black horse and Charlotte's bay mare had taken refuge from the heat in the shade of the shed that he'd once used as a stable, and after pausing a moment to check on them, Jack continued on up to the cabin.

He'd built the place with his own two hands; lived here for more than half a year before he gave up being a hermit, and got up the nerve to go down and start up his store in Cedar Creek. It was comfortable enough, with an upstairs loft for sleeping, a cast iron woodstove, a planked wood floor, and a glass-paned window that framed a bird's eye view of the valley below and the scattering of buildings and houses that made up the little town of Cedar Creek.

Propping his shoulder against one of the lodgepole pine logs that served as porch posts, he turned his gaze out over the countryside. From this height, everything below looked small and somehow insignificant: the buildings seemed to be just a collection of painted, toy blocks strewn through the valley; the stands of red rock boulders mere pebbles; the creek little more than a golden thread, glinting in the waning daylight.

Jack stood there for what seemed like a long time, growing more and more restless and out-of-sorts. He'd have to face the facts. Charlotte didn't care for him as he did for her, or else she couldn't have made up her mind to leave as soon as Rachel's baby was born.

That was why she was ignoring him so thoroughly. She didn't want him to foster any false hopes. But it was too late for that. Once, he might have been able to look down upon the town below and see endless possibilities, but now he saw only how empty it would be without her.

"You can see the whole town from up here."

Charlotte's voice was hushed with astonishment. She'd caught him off guard. He hadn't heard her approach, maybe because he hadn't expected that she'd follow him. He didn't turn back on her, though, he only went on staring out over the valley floor.

"When I first came here," he told her, "I'd been living

alone for a long time. I wasn't quite ready to move into a town full of people, so I built this place. I could see all the goings-on from up here, and yet still keep myself apart."

She came nearer. He could hear her shoes scuffing up gravel on the dusty path. "I can't picture you living here, all alone," she said, "and you're so much a part of Cedar Creek, I just can't imagine it without you."

Jack swore silently, squeezed his eyes shut, and pressed his forehead against the weathered surface of the pine post. He wanted to turn around, grab her by the shoulders and shake her hard. Then maybe she'd realize something of what he was going through. He couldn't seem to imagine Cedar Creek at all anymore without Charlotte as a part of it.

"It does look pretty from up here," she observed, "like a perfect, painted picture you could hang upon the wall."

Jack spun around to her, aiming an accusing glare. "Then how can you possibly think of leaving?" he said, before he could stop himself.

She'd been carrying both their berry pails, and after a thoughtful pause, she set them up on the porch and rose up to meet him, eye to eye.

"I'm sorry, Jack. You're a good man; I never wanted to hurt you. I ought never have let things go on. I ought to have told you the truth from the start."

"What truth?" he shot back. "That you were an innocent, young girl, whose whole life was turned upside down by the war? That you found a way to escape, to have a little more freedom, to enjoy life by pretending to be something that you weren't? Well, if you think that this truth of yours makes one bit of difference in the way I feel about you, then you must have an awfully low opinion of me.

"We've all done things that we're sorry about afterward. People learn from their mistakes, Charlotte. People change.

I have to believe that in the end, we're judged on the sum of what we've accomplished, not just on individual mistakes, no matter how awful they might seem."

Charlotte swallowed hard. Her face had lost some of its color. A bead of sweat trickled down her temple and slid across her cheek. She lifted her chin in a confident gesture, but when she spoke, her voice was unsteady.

"I think we've picked enough berries for today, don't you?"

Turning sharply on her heel, she headed down toward the corral. Jack followed. If she thought she was going put him off this time, she was sorely mistaken.

He watched patiently as she unlatched the gate, let herself in and whistled for her horse. Like a trained pet, the bay mare sidled up beside her. Charlotte stroked her muzzle, then reached for a leather knapsack that was suspended by its strap from the saddlehorn.

Jack felt a prickling of uneasiness as he looked at it, and reaching out with both hands, clasped the top rail of the fence with a white-knuckled grip.

What a fool he'd been! He'd been so successful in training himself to get on with life, to never look back, that he hadn't even considered the obvious. All this time, he'd thought that Charlotte had put a distance between them because she was ashamed of *her* past. He'd never imagined that somehow she might have discovered something about *his* past. Suddenly, all that he'd said to her only a few minutes before sounded pitifully self-serving.

Charlotte approached him, and meeting him across the fence, she held out the knapsack to him. "I didn't steal it," she told him. "I found it in the bakery, while I was cleaning. It was up in the rafters. I knew that it must be yours the minute I saw you handle that gun.

"I never would have used it that day, except Noah had mine locked in his desk. I didn't figure it would hurt

anything. Anyway, it's in here, along with everything else.
I've even cleaned it and reloaded it for you."

Jack wouldn't take the knapsack. He wouldn't touch it.
Charlotte shrugged, slung the strap over the fencepost, and
left it hanging there between them.

Was she trying to tell him, without saying it outright,
that she knew what he'd done? That no matter how unsa-
vory her own sins might be, she could never link herself
with a cold-blooded killer?

Shaken, he turned away and managed a few, shambling
steps before settling himself on an overturned tree trunk
to bury his face in his hands. And as he sat there, the
words that Charlotte had said to him, after he'd come upon
her in her disguise that night in the bakery, echoed in his
head: "We can't, any of us, simply forget the harm we've
done and fashion a new life for ourselves . . . the old
one has a queer way of turning up when we least expect
it. Maybe that's the penance we're made to pay for our
sins."

What if she was right?

"I've said I was sorry," Charlotte called out from behind him, "and I've put everything back, just as it was.
You can look for yourself, if you like. Jack? . . . Jack!"

But ignoring the insistent note in her voice, Jack only
sat there, unsure of what he ought to do next. Confess
his sins? Deny them? Offer her an excuse? What possible
excuse could there be for cold, calculated murder, four
times over?

His thoughts consumed him to an overwhelming degree,
but his instincts had been too well-honed not to sense the
danger or to hear the sharp click of a pistol hammer being
drawn back.

Jack's head snapped up, and he saw Charlotte standing
just off to his right, with the pearl-handled Colt in her
hand.

"Good Lord, Charlotte! What are you doing?"

"Don't move," she said, a forced calm behind her words. "There's a rattlesnake in the brush, there beside you. I saw it move just after you sat down."

She waved the pistol barrel in a trembling arc that swept over the thicket of sage close by on Jack's left. Sure enough, as he slanted a glance in that direction, he caught sight of a coil of mottled brown snake half-concealed beneath the gray-green branches.

Panic surged through him. He wasn't sure which frightened him more: the prospect of being bitten by a snake or being shot by Charlotte in her attempt to kill the creature. With her aim, she'd be just as likely to hit him.

She squeezed her left eye shut and leveled the barrel. "Charlotte, no. Don't try it!" he shouted, too late.

The ball whizzed past his ear, too close for comfort, and then sheared off a section of branches, dropping a flurry of bark and fragrant sage needles upon the unsuspecting snake. It twitched convulsively, then began to uncoil, affording Jack a better look.

He didn't wait for Charlotte to take a second shot. Rising up, he threw himself at her, and they both tumbled into the dry, matted grass, his hand pinning her wrist, along with the pistol, over her head.

She lay stock still beneath him, her blue eyes pale as the morning sky and wide with fright. The sound of their labored breathing filled his ears.

He summoned a smile, wanting to soothe her. "I can see that I'm going to have to teach you to shoot straight, if only for my own protection.

"It was only a gopher snake," he told her next, stroking her cheek with the back of his free hand. "Not a rattler. You needn't worry. They're not poisonous."

At this, she released her grip on the pistol, and it fell harmlessly onto the grass.

"I'm sorry," she whispered, still oddly breathless. "I

ought to have looked closer before I reacted. But when I saw it there, so close to you, I thought that . . . that . . ."

"That I might be in danger," he finished for her. "And you cared enough to intervene?"

She frowned at him. "Of course, I did."

"So, in spite of . . . everything, in spite of doing your best these past few weeks to prove otherwise, you *do* still care for me."

She tried to turn away, but reaching up, Jack cradled her face gently between his two hands and made her look at him. "Please, Charlotte," he whispered. "I need to know."

Maybe she hadn't learned about his past after all, he told himself, feeling new hope stir to life within him. Or maybe, just as he'd said, if you love someone, nothing else matters.

Finally, ever so slightly, Charlotte nodded.

"Say it," he urged her. "I want to hear you say it."

"I do . . . I care for you, Jack. But that doesn't change anything."

"Oh, but it does. It changes everything."

By all rights, Jack ought to have raised himself up then and released her, but she was so close, her mouth so tempting, and he knew he might never get this chance again. Leaning closer, he kissed her.

Her lips were soft and full, and just as he'd expected, sweetened with a tang of raspberry. Each intake of breath brought their bodies in closer contact, and Jack ached to strip away his clothing and hers, so that he could feel the delicious swell of her breasts sliding against his bare chest.

He'd wanted her, wanted this for too long. As the moments ticked past, it became more of a trial to ignore the painful pressure of his arousal, to resist fumbling through the layers of her skirts and insinuating himself between the soft thighs trapped beneath him.

But he had to be careful not to spook her. As he'd learned that night on the Fourth of July, Charlotte was an innocent, and as high strung as one of those wild mustangs Lars Thorssen kept trying to capture for himself out at Echo Canyon. One wrong move, and she'd tear off, quick as lightning.

Besides, much as his body might be crying out for release, Jack was not looking for a heated coupling in the grass. Charlotte was too important to him for that. When the time came, he wanted to make love to her all night long, just the two of them in some quiet, comfortable spot; he wanted to introduce her to all the pleasures that a man and woman could share. But not here, not like this. What he wanted for now was to kindle a slow-burning fire within her that would keep her from running away again.

Charlotte lay, quiet and still, beneath him. He couldn't say that she was melting with his kisses, but then neither did she make a move to escape him. All of this was new to her, he reminded himself. She was testing the waters, allowing him the chance to guide her.

Eagerly, Jack gave himself over to the effort, teasing her lips apart with his tongue, while his fingertips skimmed with deft purpose over her face, her slender throat, her shoulders, aiming to explore every rise and hollow.

All the while, Charlotte's eyes were closed. She scarcely breathed. Ere long, though, she began to tremble, and it did not take him long to realize that it was fear, not pleasure, that she was experiencing. When he loosened her mouth, she whimpered, and the pitiful sound of it made him feel like a brute.

"I'm sorry, Jack," she cried, then made a desperate gasp for breath as if she were drowning. "I . . . can't. I just can't."

His ardor ebbed away at once. Regret pierced his heart

like a hot knife. He drew back, and steeling himself, he got to his feet and held out a hand to her.

"It's late," he told her. "We ought to be getting back."

He was hurt and angry and frustrated. It was apparent by the stiffness in his frame and the careful, measured breaths he took. Charlotte wouldn't have blamed him at all if he thought she was a lunatic. In this regard, at least, she was crazy.

She'd made a dreadful mistake in admitting her feelings, in allowing him even a glimmer of hope. She ought to have learned, after her disastrous response to his intimacies on the night of the Fourth of July celebration, that no matter how much she might want to, she was incapable of giving him what he needed from her.

How she wished it could be otherwise. A part of her longed to give in to the tantalizing thrill that she felt at his touch, to learn what it meant to be made love to. For all that she had endured, she'd never experienced that.

But as gentle as his kisses were, tender though his caresses may have been, each time Jack reached out to her, Charlotte saw, in her mind's eye, the ominous glint of a gold ring, a ring fashioned out of a ten dollar gold piece, and her nightmares came alive again.

Consumed by guilt, she silently allowed him to help her to her feet, then ventured to ask him a favor. "I'd like to wash up before we go. I'm grimy with dust and sweat, and my hands are stained with berry juice."

"There's soap and a basin for washing on the table in the cabin. The water barrel is in the corner. Go on in, and help yourself. In the meanwhile, I'll pack the berry pails and ready the horses."

The chill in his tone was hard to take, much as she deserved it. Charlotte swallowed hard, and without looking back at him, she started up the path. This was for the best, she told herself. If he thought she was cold and unfeeling, maybe he wouldn't harbor hopes for things that could never be.

When she reached the cabin, she crossed the porch and threw open the door. Inside, it was still and hot, twilight deepening the shadows that had collected in the corners of the room.

The wash basin was just where he'd said it would be. Charlotte filled it from the water barrel, then carried it back to the table and proceeded to scrub away the dust that had clung to her sticky hands. Next, she splashed some of the tepid water on her face and neck, then daubed it away with the huckaback towel she found hanging over a chair back.

Feeling a bit more refreshed, she gave in to her curiosity and had a look around the room, taking careful note of the arrangement of the simple furnishings: the table and a pair of chairs, the painted cupboard, and a dry sink. In the far corner was a ladder that led, presumably, to the loft where the bed must be. Everything was well-scrubbed and orderly, just as she would have expected of a house belonging to Jack.

There were few of his personal belongings; apparently he'd brought them down with him when he moved to town. But a pair of snowshoes hung upon the wall, several bamboo fishing rods were propped up beside the cupboard, and on the shelf above the sink, she found a small, square shaving mirror.

She reached for it, and when she noticed her own reflection staring back at her, she was struck by the shaded circles beneath her eyes, the pallor in her face. It might have been only the intensity of the summer's heat or the fact that she was weary after such a long day, but Charlotte didn't think so. No, the woman she saw in the mirror wasn't overheated nor exhausted, she was haunted.

She stood there for a long time, studying the reflection, seeing in it a stranger, until one of the last slender rays of daylight stole in the window and flared into a blinding gold blaze when the glass in her hand caught and reflected it. Charlotte set the mirror back on the shelf and drew back, as if she'd been burned.

What was happening to her? Would she keep seeing that damned gold ring of his in every flash of sunlight, for the rest of her life? Would she carry the loathsome memories of her violation with her forever?

Why, oh why, couldn't she forget? Marcus Gideon was dead. She'd seen to that herself, hadn't she? She'd got her right and proper vengeance for his cold-blooded murder of her father and for . . . what he'd done to her. She didn't need to be afraid anymore.

For a time, she thought she'd gotten control of her life, banished the horrors to the deepest recesses of her mind, where they'd only been able to surface in dreams. But since Jack had gotten close to her, she seemed to have lost control. The demons again enjoyed full reign.

"Charlotte? The horses are packed and ready."

She turned to see Jack standing in the doorway, the fading sunset behind him casting his tall frame into sharp silhouette. She had to blink several times before his features came into focus. The hurt had gone out of his expression, she noticed then to her relief, and his tone seemed, well, almost apologetic.

From behind his back, he drew a bouquet of wildflowers: larkspurs, gentians, and blue and white columbines. Their sweet fragrance swept over her like a perfumed cloud as he extended his arm and held them out to her.

"It's for you. I'd have made a bigger bouquet, but these were all I could find. Sometimes, the meadow by the lake is full of them. The weather's been too hot and dry lately though, I guess."

Charlotte took them from him, hoping she didn't look too surprised by his gesture. She opened her mouth to thank him, but he cut her off before she could form the words.

"No, don't say anything. I want you to hear me out first."

He began to scuff the toe of one boot against the floorboards, his eyes fixed on the spot. "Now, I don't doubt that, given the independent life you've led, you've seen the worst in men, and that's what's made you leery of us. But when I . . . touched you just now, I never meant to take advantage of you, nor to hurt you. I want you to know that."

Charlotte shut her eyes, ashamed. "I *do* know," she insisted. "But I . . ."

He held up a hand to silence her. "I'm a patient man, Charlotte, and a persistent one. I'm not giving up on you, no matter what. If you need some time to sort out all these new feelings, well, I can understand that, and so I won't touch you that way again, not until you ask me to. You have my word on that."

She didn't deserve the regard of such a man. No matter how odd her behavior, Jack could always be counted on to give her the benefit of the doubt. After all she'd put him through, she owed him the truth, but somehow when she looked into his eyes, the words wouldn't come.

It was easier to turn away in silence, pretending to study the view from out of the cabin window while she swallowed the lump that rose in her throat and threatened to choke her.

"Thank you," she managed to say at last, her fingers closing tightly over the clustered flower stems of the fragrant bouquet he'd given her.

Outside the window, the heavens were awash in fading sunset hues of apricot and pink. They'd have to be getting back soon, Charlotte told herself. They'd stayed too long already. And then, all at once, she noticed a peculiar

smudge of gray in the paling sky—smoke rising up in a
spiralling column from the valley floor, far below.

"Oh, my God!" she exclaimed, the words hushed with
disbelief.

"What is it, Charlotte?"

As he came up beside her, she clasped his arm tightly
with her free hand and nodded in the direction of what
she'd seen.

"Fire!"

Eleven

It had been a scorching, hot summer with scarcely any rain. Trees and brush were as dry as tinder. Near to a hundred souls living in a little town made out of log, pine board, and canvas; all of them cooking their meals on hearths and woodstoves, lighting their nights with candles and oil lamps. Something like this was bound to happen, Charlotte told herself, sooner or later.

But an acceptance of the inevitable didn't help to dull her fears. Her friends were in danger; their world was at stake. She couldn't catch her breath as she gave the mare her heel and tightened her grip on the reins, trying to keep pace with Jack as he maneuvered the black horse along the steep mountain path that seemed to wind back upon itself again and again.

Darkness had settled in now in earnest, and Charlotte couldn't see more than a few feet in front of her. Both she and Jack were too tense to speak, and she only kept sight of him by focusing her eyes on the back of his light-colored shirt, a pale blur in the shadowy blackness just ahead. This hadn't seemed so treacherous a journey on the ride up, in the midst of a lazy, sun-dappled afternoon. But now, her heart took a painful leap each time one of the horses' hooves shifted, showering the slope below with a scree of dancing pebbles.

It seemed hours before they finally reached the valley floor and were able to direct their mounts at a faster pace toward the ominous, red glow, standing out like a beacon against the night sky. By the time they reached the abandoned mines on the outskirts of town, the smoke was roiling thick and black, and the horses balked.

The Red Bird and Silver Dollar Saloons, not far ahead on opposite sides of the street were wholly engulfed, two stories of searing yellow flame, bracketing the street like the very gates of hell.

Charlotte's mare wouldn't budge, and though she couldn't well blame her, she gave her a sharp kick nevertheless and snapped the reins hard. They had to get through to the other side of town, if they were to see that Rachel was safe, as well as the bakery and Jack's store. Jack was having problems handling his horse, as well. Try as he might to urge him on, the big black horse only wheeled and snorted. Frustrated, Jack swore.

Charlotte called out to him, unsure of what move to make next, and he shouted back in reply. "We'll have to take them around the worst of the fire. Follow me."

He cut back behind the livery. It was not yet afire, but anticipating the danger, the Thorssens had thrown open the stable doors to set the animals free, all except for two draft horses that were yoked to a wagon. Lars was up on the seat with the reins, controlling the pair, while Gunnar hurried to fill the wagon bed with their tools and supplies.

As she and Jack skirted the perimeter of the town, Charlotte could see that a few of the flimsier miners' shacks had caught fire from flying sparks, but for the most part, the blaze was restricted to the main street. Buildings were in flames, up and down the row.

In the dusty streets on either hand, folk were running and shouting out directions. Henry Sutton had brought every pail to be had from the hardware store and organized some of the men into a bucket brigade. They'd appropriated a wagon to ferry themselves and the water buckets to and from the creek, but it seemed a hopeless task. The wind had kicked up, setting loose a shower of sparks, and the sound of it combined with the high-pitched roar of the firestorm, striking Charlotte's ears in a mournful whine.

Jack and Charlotte directed their horses to the safety of the town square, where folk had heaped as many of their personal belongings as they could salvage. Some of them were only standing there, watching the conflagration, dumbstruck.

"Damn it, Jack," the barber, Elliot Baird, called out, when he saw them. "Where've the two of you been? We're losing everything here!"

In the light of the fire, Charlotte saw Jack's face harden. He dismounted, and as she did likewise, he handed her his reins. "Take the horses back to the Kelsey's place," he ordered. "It's far enough away so you'll be safe there."

Charlotte opened her mouth to argue, but thought better of it at once. Besides, Jack wasn't waiting for her agreement; he had already run off toward the Chronicle building, where Nate Phillips and Hollis Lloyd were struggling to carry out the printing press before the roof collapsed.

The horses allowed themselves to be led willingly away from the blaze, and when Charlotte reached the Kelsey house at last, she tied both pairs of reins up on the railing, then ran up to throw her arms around Rachel, who was sitting, ashen-faced, in a rocking chair on the porch, her dressing gown pulled close around her.

"Thank God, you've come back," she said and returning the hug, squeezed Charlotte hard. "I was worried about you."

"I'm fine," Charlotte assured her, "but you ought to be in bed."

"How can I just lie there while the whole town is about to be destroyed?"

Charlotte tried to think up some hopeful response, but

just now, she couldn't think of one. "Where's Noah?" she asked instead.

"Gone off to help. Though I don't know what any of them will be able to do. Just look at those flames. You can see them over the rooftops. Should we pack up our things? Will it get this far, do you think?"

Rachel was looking up at her, wide-eyed. She was worried—who wouldn't be?—about the very real prospect of losing her home and all her belongings, of having to give birth to her child on a blanket in a tent or worse.

Charlotte pulled a deep breath and summoned her most confident air. "Jack doesn't think so. Besides, the wind is blowing in the opposite direction. We ought to be safe here."

"It started in one of the saloons, I think," Rachel explained. "We saw the smoke about suppertime. Probably an overturned lantern from a bar fight that got out of hand. It wouldn't be the first time."

Standing there beside Rachel's chair, Charlotte was mesmerized by the horrifying scene unfolding before her. Billowing clouds of black smoke, orange tongues of flame lapping at the night sky. She could feel the heat, even from here, radiating out in shimmering waves.

A part of her was terrified and she was perfectly content to remain ensconced on this porch at Rachel's side even though, at this very moment, her bakery might be burning to the ground. What did she have to lose, after all, but a few bowls and baking pans? And those could be easily replaced, couldn't they?

But when she remembered the panic-stricken faces of the townsfolk as they ran helter-skelter through the streets, their arms loaded down with whatever few possessions they could gather together; when she thought of Jack's store full of merchandise, so vital to the day-to-day life of a town like this; and more than that, when she thought of Jack's dreams going up in smoke along with the pine boards and canvas, she knew she had to do something.

She crossed to the opposite side of the porch, and then turned back to her friend. "I'm going to go down and see what I can do to help," she said.

At this, Rachel paled. "Charlotte, no."

"I have to do something; I have to. This town is Jack's dream, his whole life. I can't just let it go without a fight. You do understand, don't you?"

Rachel cast her a sidelong glance, but after a long moment's contemplation, she let go a heavy sigh and nodded.

Charlotte had already stepped down off the porch, not wanting to waste another minute. "Don't worry. If the fire changes direction, I'll be back here before you know it."

Lifting her skirts, she raced down to the center of town, stopping only when she reached the square to catch her breath. Around her, she could see that things had gone from bad to worse. The saloons were nothing but smoking timbers and piles of ash now, along with the livery, laundry, and Hollis Lloyd's meat market. Flames were leaping up through the roof of the hardware and assay office.

"This is a sad business, eh?"

Charlotte looked over her shoulder to see Gus Stern, resting himself on two trunks, nearly filled to bursting with belongings. He was coatless, his shirt grimy with soot, and in his hands, he was holding a small wooden box.

"Were you able to get everything out?" she asked him.

"Everything? No. No, time for that. The family Bible's lost, I think, and most of my clothes. But I managed to pack up most of my equipment, and this."

He held up the box, and Charlotte raised a brow, curious. "It's the telegraph key," he explained. "Our lifeline to the rest of the world. We'll need it to let them know what's happened here tonight, just as soon as the smoke clears, and we can restring the wires."

Charlotte was glad that someone was giving a thought to tomorrow, but for herself, she couldn't look that far ahead. There was important work yet to be done tonight.

"Have you seen Jack?" she asked Stern.

"He was down at the boarding house, last I saw, helping the Widow Murphy to get out."

"You mean that he hasn't come back to salvage anything from the store?"

"Well now, I can't rightly say . . ."

With that, Charlotte sprinted off, keeping to the center of the street, where the heat was less intense. She drew up short as, for the first time, she saw the log building that had been her bakery. It seemed wholly intact from without, but the roof must have been breached, for as she looked in the windows, she could see that the interior was already ablaze.

Jack's building next door seemed untouched thus far, but she knew it was only a matter of time. The fire was advancing, swift and sure. Still, she had to try. With two anxious strides, she'd crossed the boardwalk, and twisting the knob, attempted to push open the door, only to find it locked. Without even thinking, she wrapped her fist several times in the fabric of her apron, then smashed it through one of the panes of glass and reached in to unlatch the lock.

Once inside, she scanned the floor-to-ceiling shelves and the counters, piled high with goods, and panic began to rise in her. There wasn't time to salvage everything. What would be most important?

First she reached for a stack of wool blankets, unfolding one of them on the floor. Then she proceeded to toss goods, pell-mell, into the center of it. Dishpans, coffee boilers, bottles of medicine, bars of soap. When she'd gathered a large enough pile, she drew up the corners of the blanket and proceeded to drag the bundle out of the door and into the street. And then she hurried back inside.

Charlotte only managed two such forays before the acrid stench of smoke began to seep through the store's walls and fill her lungs, and she heard the snap and hiss of flames devouring Jack's apartment overhead. The support timbers above creaked and shuddered ominously. There was time yet, though, she told herself. Into another blanket, she sent tumbling rows of canned goods and atop this, men's shirts and shoes, hats and stockings.

Panting breathlessly, she dragged the heavy bundle out onto the boardwalk, and only then did she think of the sacks of flour, coffee, and cornmeal lined up on the floor at the rear of the store. Surely they'd need those staples most of all. Without hesitation, she hurried back inside.

Swiping the sweat from his brow with the back of his hand, Jack stood in the town square, watching helplessly, through the cloud of dust and smoke, as Cedar Creek collapsed and burned around him.

"Is everyone out, do you think?" he called to Noah.

The doctor was busy nearby tending the wounded, who'd been laid out on the grass. A pair of Arthur Rollins's saloon girls had gotten singed in the melee, nothing too serious from what Jack could see, and old man Fleming had broken an arm as he'd battered through a back door of the Red Bird to make his escape.

"God knows," Noah replied. "It's hard to tell, with all the commotion. But you've done enough, Jack. You ought to go and see about your own place, before it's too late.

"With everything burning, we'll need as much of your stock as you can salvage. I'll send Henry Sutton, with some of the boys and the wagon, to help out, as soon as they come by. They're not going to stop this conflagration with only their few buckets of creek water."

Jack agreed with his reasoning and struck off at once for the store. He looked straight ahead as he ran, loathe to see the extent of the destruction that had already been wreaked upon his town. What would he do now? What would they all do?

He was still some distance away when he caught sight of Charlotte, struggling to tug a blanketload of goods out of his store. He ought to have known that she wouldn't stay put. No, she had to be right there in the thick of things, handling matters herself.

Apparently, she and Noah had been thinking along the same lines. She had already made a substantial pile of goods in the center of the street. But from his position, Jack could see that that wouldn't be good enough. The flames were already dancing high up into the night sky on both sides of the street, and tossing hungry sparks in all directions. They'd have to move those goods farther away, to the square or even beyond, in order to prevent them from being consumed.

The heat was growing more intense by the minute. It curled the hair on the back of Jack's neck and stung the skin on his face and hands. He coughed as his lungs filled with searing, ash-filled air, but he kept on running, then cast a quick look behind him, hoping that Sutton and the rest would get here quick with the wagon.

When he turned back around, an explosion rocked the ground beneath his feet, showering shattered glass over everything as the burgeoning heat of the blaze blew out all of the windows in his upstairs rooms. It was too late to do anything more, he realized. In only a matter of minutes, the business he'd worked so hard to build was going to collapse upon itself in a pile of flaming timber.

He looked back for Charlotte who, only a moment before, had been depositing her burden in the street, but she was gone. An eerie groan issued from the building as flames attacked the support beams. Jack's heart stopped for an instant as it struck him that she must have gone back inside.

"Charlotte, no!" he shouted, barreling after her.

Halting breathlessly in the open doorway, he saw her. Heedless of the blaze that had burst through the ceiling above her head, she was attempting to drag a hundred pound sack of flour across the floor.

With his head low, Jack lunged forward and hooked an arm around her waist. He tried to pull her away, but her fingers were locked on that flour sack in a death grip.

"Let go!" he shouted. "Let go, do you hear?"

"But we'll need this, Jack. The town's got to have enough to get by; can't you see? I know how it is to have nothing. I won't live like that, not ever again!"

Grasping her face in his hands, Jack forced her to look at him. Her breath was coming in ragged sobs, her eyes wild with fright.

"You don't have to worry, Charlotte," he soothed. "Everything will be all right. I'll take care of you. I promise. But we have to get out of here . . . *now.*"

Like an obedient child, she nodded and slowly uncoiled her fingers. Jack threw an arm across her shoulders and led her away.

They almost made it. They were only two steps from the door, in fact, when a portion of the ceiling above their heads collapsed, sending charred sections of pine board and flaming debris raining down upon them. Charlotte screamed.

Jack did his best to shield her, until a splintered section of timber caught him hard in the temple, knocking him flat on his back. There came a blinding flash of light. The pain shot through his head, and then he couldn't seem to move at all.

With his last conscious thought, Jack sent a swift but heartfelt prayer heavenward: "Lord, I deserve my fate, there's no denying that. But please, if You truly be merciful and forgiving, please keep Charlotte safe."

* * *

"Hail Mary, full of grace, the Lord is with thee . . ."
Sitting in Noah's surgery, with Jack's hand clasped tightly
in hers, Charlotte fervently repeated every prayer the nuns
had ever taught her.

The mantel clock in the parlor chimed out: three in the
morning. She had refused to stir from his side in all this
time, afraid that he was dying, afraid she'd never get the
chance to talk to him again, to tell him how she truly
felt.

He lay so awfully pale and still. He hadn't awakened
once since Henry Sutton and Hollis Lloyd had carried him
from the ruins of the store. He'd scarcely flinched as Noah
cleaned, stitched, and dressed the jagged gash that had
been laid open from the crest of his temple to his right
ear.

It was a pity to look on him now, with his eye bruised
purple and swollen shut, and his head swathed in bandages. And then, too, there were the splints and wrappings
protecting his shattered left leg.

It hadn't been a pretty sight, when Noah first tore away
Jack's bloodied shreds of trouser to reveal splintered
bones, cutting through the skin. Jack had lost a frightening
amount of blood, but out of necessity, Charlotte had swallowed her fears and done just as Doctor Kelsey instructed.
It was she who had applied pressure to stem the flow until
he could stitch up the damage the falling debris had done;
and she who'd stood by, offering her silent prayers while
he patiently reset Jack's broken bones. And so afterward,
he'd let her stay—as if he'd had any choice in the matter.

The fires had nearly all burnt themselves out by now,
and the bitter stench of smoke and ash seeped through
the open window into the surgery, which was nothing
more than a tiny room that lay between Noah's office and
the Kelsey kitchen.

Charlotte paid no mind to her surroundings, though, nor
to her own disheveled condition—her soot-blackened face;

her hair singed in spots; the poor, old blue calico dress bloodstained and ripped beyond repair. No, her thoughts were all on Jack and on willing him to recover.

"Please, Jack. Please come back. You said you were persistent. You promised not to give up on me. Don't you remember?"

He didn't stir. Charlotte knew he couldn't hear her. Their only connection now was a handclasp, and so she squeezed his fingers as hard as she was able.

"Please . . ."

"You ought to get some rest."

Charlotte started in surprise as the familiar voice cut through the stillness. She hadn't even heard Rachel approach.

"I'm not leaving him alone."

"He won't be," her friend assured her. "I'll stay here with him. I'm not tired. I've been doing nothing *but* resting for the past month."

Charlotte was glassy-eyed and numb, and much as she might wish to deny it, weary to the bone. Still, she hesitated.

"What good will you do him if he does wake and you're senseless from lack of sleep? Please, Charlotte. I'm worried about you. At least let Noah take a look at those burns on your back."

"They're nothing," she insisted, "nothing at all. Jack got the worst of it. He pushed me out of harm's way."

"Just the same, I want you to let Noah put some salve and a bandage on them. I've left a clean nightgown in the office for you, and I've hung my pink-striped challis on your door peg for tomorrow. You know, the one with the fitted waist. I wouldn't be able to wear it for some time anyway. It might be a few inches too short for you, but it'll do for now, and when we get the chance, we can always take down the hem."

Rachel's chatter sounded like an incoherent buzz to

Charlotte's already-muddled brain. She shook her head to clear it. "I . . . I can't accept any more of your dresses."

"I don't see as how you have any choice. That one you're wearing is going straight into the dustbin, just as soon as you've taken it off. Go on now, off with you. Noah's waiting."

Reluctantly, Charlotte unlaced her fingers from Jack's and rose to do as she was bade. "You will call me if there's any change, won't you?" she asked. "Or if he wakes?"

"You know that I will."

Rachel drew nearer and gave Charlotte a reassuring hug, then caught up her face in her hands. "You poor dear. All that you've been through, and you haven't shed a single tear all night, have you?"

"I can't," Charlotte replied, the words taut with emotion. "There aren't any tears left in me anymore."

Rachel shook her head. "I don't believe that, not for a moment. It isn't healthy, Charlotte, this way you have of keeping everything inside. I wish you would cry. It would do you a world of good."

Secretly, Charlotte wondered if that might be so, but no sooner had she considered it than she heard a voice in her head, the voice that had given her direction in those awful days after her rape and her father's murder. It reminded her that tears were a sign of weakness, and the vultures of this world preyed on weakness. She couldn't risk it.

Noah was waiting for her in his office, just as Rachel had said he would be. With hands clasped behind his back, he was pacing, with slow deliberation, before the darkened windows. When he saw her, he stopped short, the lamplight illuminating his deeply ridged brow. His demeanor did nothing to relieve her. He was worried.

"Will Jack be all right?" she had to ask.

For an instant, Noah's glance met hers, then slid away.

"We'll have to wait and see. Thankfully, he's young and strong, but his body has undergone quite a shock. He'll need time to heal."

Charlotte nodded.

"Now, let's have a look at those burns," he urged gently. "Can you take off your dress?"

"I think so."

She began by loosing the buttons that fastened the front of her bodice, but as she reached to shrug the fabric off, a sharp breath caught in her throat. She winced as a searing pain shot through her, from shoulder blade to shoulder blade.

In a few strides, Noah was beside her, stilling her arms as he surveyed the burns on her back. "Don't move," he told her. "I didn't realize it was as serious as this. With all that's happened, I never stopped to ask. You must have been in pain all night."

Of course, she'd been in pain. Her body fairly quivered with it, her knees trembled and threatened to buckle on account of it, her clenched jaws ached with it. But it was impossible to separate the simple pain of her injury from the agony that she was suffering as a result of seeing Jack, broken and bleeding, on that surgery cot.

Noah went to fetch a wooden stool, then helped her to sit and bade her to keep her back as straight as possible. "The skin has blistered," he explained, "and shreds of burnt cloth are adhering to the blisters."

Charlotte shut her eyes, none too eager to envision the picture he'd just drawn with his words. Behind her, she heard him pouring water into the tin basin that he kept on a nearby shelf. She opened up one eye to see him place the basin on his desk. He lay several clean cloths nearby, and then arranged a pair of tweezers and scissors so that they'd be close at hand.

Next came a rattling of bottles as he reached into the tall, glass medicine cabinet, and before Charlotte knew it, he was pouring something slick and cool across her shoulder blades.

"It's only sweet oil," he told her. "It will loosen the skin so that I can remove the cloth from the wounds."

She tried to focus her thoughts elsewhere as Noah dipped one of the clean cloths into the water, squeezed out the excess and then daubed it against her tender skin. As he probed the blistered flesh with the tweezers, she felt the fire all over again, and her head began to swim.

"Grip your knees hard with your hands," he told her, sensing her distress, "and take deep breaths."

"It's my fault, you know," she said, her mind drifting inevitably back to Jack. "If he hadn't gone into the store after me, he wouldn't be lying in there now, fighting for his life."

Noah did not reply, only kept diligently to his work, loosening the shreds of cloth from Charlotte's blistered back and carefully cutting them away with the scissors.

"But then you knew all along that I'd hurt him, one way or another, didn't you?" Her voice was strained, her words punctuated with rasping breaths as she struggled with the pain. "What was it you said to Rachel that night about me? '. . . a hard woman . . . scarcely respectable . . . and not half good enough for Jack Cordell.' Well, you were right, you know, on each and every count."

Silence again, and then a long, slow exhalation, and a loud clang as Noah cast the scissors down on the desk, and they struck the side of the basin. At last, his cool, hard fingers peeled away what remained of the sleeves and bodice of the blue calico and her muslin chemise, and as the fabric fell away, Charlotte modestly crossed her arms over her breasts.

"I wasn't . . ." he said, when it seemed he could stand the silence no more. "I was wrong. I've never been more wrong about anything in my life."

With this, he came to stand before her, heedless of her

deshabille. "I ought to have known that if the two people
I care most for in this world, my wife and my best friend,
both believed in you, then I could, too. It finally struck
me tonight, as I watched you standing there at Jack's side,
pale and frightened, but doing whatever I asked of you. I
saw then that, if you could, you'd gladly trade your life
for his."

"I would. I wish . . . God, how I wish I could."

Noah squared his jaw. "You won't have to. You're going
to be fine, the both of you, if I have anything to do with
it."

With his energy renewed, he strode back to the glass
cabinet where he kept his medicines, promptly returned
with a tin of salve and a roll of bandages, and went to
work.

Meanwhile, Charlotte's mouth flexed, then crooked upward. It was the first time she'd been able to summon a
single pleasant thought all night. This had been a long
time in coming for her—winning the respect of Noah Kelsey—and it was a victory that she did not take lightly.

When he'd finished bandaging her up, Charlotte put on
the nightgown Rachel had left for her and went out on
the porch, forcing herself to witness the final scene of
this night's tragedy.

The flames had burnt themselves out some time ago,
leaving behind an eerie pall of smoke, the ruddy glow of
embers and the charred skeletal remains of the business
district. There was nothing left of the Cedar Creek they'd
known now, except for the Kelsey house and a handful of
ramshackle miners' shacks that had been fortunate enough
to escape the inferno.

Something caught Charlotte's eye then, a pale flash of
color against the ruddy, broken soil beside the porch steps.
Drawn to the spot, she bent down, and picked up a single,
faded bloom from the bouquet that Jack had given her up

at the cabin earlier tonight. She must have dropped it in all of the confusion.

Sinking down onto the steps, she rolled the slender stem between her fingertips, and the head of the dainty, blue columbine nodded lazily in reply. *It is a shame,* she told herself, *that what had started out as such a pretty bouquet was now only a heap of scattered blossoms lying broken in the dust.*

Twelve

Jack awoke with a start, his consciousness pierced by the memory of Charlotte's scream and the world collapsing in flames around them. But she was safe. He knew that she was safe. He'd heard her voice, cutting through the haze of pain and the thick fog of insensibility that held him prisoner. He'd felt her slender fingers entwined with his, her grip fierce and firm, as if she meant to impart to him some of her own considerable strength.

As he became aware of his body, an intense, new wave of pain swept through him, robbing him of breath, leaving him panting and weak. If he hadn't known better, he'd have wondered if he hadn't been trampled by an entire herd of stampeding buffalo. His head throbbed with violent intensity, and every muscle in his arms and legs was cramped and sore. His left leg especially felt leaden, and when he tried to move it, a sudden, sharp twist of agony made him promptly reconsider. Heaven help him, but he was in pitiful shape!

He couldn't just lie here, though. He'd have to pull himself together—even if it hurt a bit—and get up and get moving. There was work to do. He'd have to survey the damage the fire had caused and gather the council, so that together they could decide on a course of action. There'd be clean-up to see to, of course, and rebuilding, but before they could consider any of that, they'd have to work together to make certain that every one of their neighbors had a roof—of one kind or another—over his head.

It must be morning by now, he told himself, and sure enough, when he gingerly raised his eyelids, the bright light of day came near to blinding him. He blinked, ignoring the ache from the swelling on the right side of his face, but the kaleidoscope swirl of brilliant color didn't clear, only shifted and sparkled in a new, but no less blurry pattern.

Apprehension rose in him. His heart drummed furiously in his chest as he blinked again, then strove to focus, but to no avail. All at once, he realized how helpless he was, and as panic seized him, he raised himself up. He couldn't see, didn't know where he was, or if he was even alone.

"Charlotte?" he called out, remembering that at some point in his nightmare, he'd heard her voice, felt her hand in his.

"Jack?"

His heart dropped. The voice wasn't hers, it was Noah's. A dark figure moved into his line of sight. To his damaged eyes, it seemed nothing more than an indistinct shadow, hovering against a field of liquid color. He felt a pair of firm hands clamp down on his shoulders and ease him back down on the cot.

"Thank God," Noah exclaimed. "We've all been worried sick about you. You'd best lie still, for a while, though. You're pretty well banged up."

Jack reached out, hoping to connect with the shifting image of Noah's arm. He exhaled slowly as his fingers found their target, closing over shirtsleeve and his friend's well-muscled forearm. Until now, he might have believed this was all part of his nightmare, but Noah's arm was solid and real beneath his hand.

"Charlotte?" he asked him then. "I thought she was here with me. Is she . . . ?"

"She's fine. She's just outside. I can call her, if you like."

Jack drew back, shaking his head. "No, not just yet. You and I need to talk first. What's happened to me?"

"The bones in your lower left leg were broken. I've set them as best I can, and fashioned a splint, but they'll need time to knit."

Jack lifted a hand to his brow, fingering the bandage there. "And this?"

"A nasty gash. Don't worry, though. I think it'll make a rather rakish scar, once it's healed."

"And how long before my vision clears up?"

The silence was not at all reassuring.

"You can't see?" Noah queried. "Not anything at all?"

Jack could tell, by the tone of his friend's voice, that this particular development was one that Noah hadn't anticipated.

"I can see colors and blurred shapes, mostly," he told him. "You look like a dark shadow, and you're surrounded by a halo of light. That must be the window, over there behind you."

"Yes, you're right."

"You weren't expecting this, were you?"

"To be honest, there's been no damage to the eyes themselves, at least none that I can see. Oh, the tissue beneath the right brow is swollen from the trauma, but not seriously so. It must've been the concussion then, from the falling timber that caused that gash."

"So when will I be able to see again?" Jack asked him outright. "Clearly, I mean, as I did before."

Again came that ominous silence, and then came the sound of Noah's footsteps as he began to pace. Soon, his shadow blended into the blur of light, and Jack deduced his friend had gone to stand before the window.

"There's no telling that, I'm afraid," Noah said. "It may only be a consequence of the swelling, from the trauma, as I've said, in which case things could begin to clear up in a few days."

Jack let go an impatient sigh. "Well, I don't have a few days to waste," he retorted, "so I guess I'll just have to make do with things as they are."

Before Noah could protest, Jack raised the upper half of his body, reached to get a firm grasp on the bandaged splints protecting his leg, then swung the whole thing over the edge of the cot and sat up, taking deep breaths until the pain had subsided somewhat, and the spinning in his head had ceased.

"And just what do you think you're doing?" Noah shouted as he strode back to stand before him.

"I think I'm getting out of this bed. I have to see how much damage the fire did last night. There's a lot of work to be done."

"Last night?" Noah echoed. "Jack, you've been lying on that cot, drifting in and out of consciousness, for the past three days. There were times when we thought sure you were dying. You can't just get up now and go on your way, as if nothing is the matter."

Three days? Jack held himself very still. His empty stomach heaved a bit as he fought off the awful sense of disorientation. He'd been lying here, useless and unaware, for three days while the people of Cedar Creek dealt with their tragedy.

He squared his jaw. "All the more reason to get to work at once," he said. "Now, either lend a hand or get out of the way."

Jack gripped the iron bedframe with both hands. He wasn't certain he had the strength to get to his feet on his own, but he was damned sure going to make the effort.

Finally, Noah seemed to sense that he had no choice in the matter. He settled a hand on Jack's shoulder. "Wait a minute. If you're truly determined to try this, then I think I have something that will help."

His shadowy form receded, then reappeared after a short interval, and he pressed something smooth into each of Jack's hands. Close up, Jack could feel and just barely see, through the blur, thick, wooden staffs from which the bark had been shaved away.

"They're crutches," Noah explained. "You see, I've finally found something worthwhile to do with my whittling. They ought to serve the purpose, don't you think? I've fashioned a crosspiece here at the top and padded it with strips of cloth."

Using Noah's extended arm for support, Jack lifted himself up and positioned the crosspieces under his arms. It was difficult at first to set a balance between his undamaged leg and the makeshift crutches, but once he'd established the pattern, he managed a few steps before turning back to his friend. "So you thought I was dying, eh?"

"Well, now that I come to think on it, maybe I did suspect that it would take considerably more than a building falling on your head to do you in," Noah admitted.

Jack grinned at this, then winced when the action caused a painful pull of stitches.

Cautiously balancing himself on the crutches while he squinted and swiveled his head, he did his best to determine his surroundings. This was Noah's surgery. Yes, things were still more than a little blurry, but better than he'd first thought. He could just make out the shape of the bed, the chair, and a break in the far wall that was most likely the doorway.

Feeling encouraged, he headed in that direction, and very nearly made it through, except for a collision between crutch and door jamb that came close to toppling him. With a shoulder propped against the wall, he paused to draw a calming breath, then steadied himself before turning back toward his friend.

"Are you sure you don't want to lie down for a while?"

Noah asked. "You can always get up and try a few more steps later."

Jack only shook his head. "I have to speak to Charlotte," he said. "This has waited too long already."

"Then I'd suggest you let me help you put on a pair of trousers before you go hobbling about the house. You wouldn't want to embarrass the ladies."

For the first time, Jack glanced down at his attire and saw that he was wearing only one of Noah's nightshirts.

"Oh, all right," he agreed. "But after I've let you help me dress, I am going to speak to Charlotte—that is, if you'll at least have the decency to point me in the right direction."

Charlotte picked through the blackened items that she had collected in a grimy blanket and spread out on the front porch, chose one, then carried it to the wash basin, which she'd set up on the upturned end of an empty rain barrel.

Following a thorough scrubbing, the slightly battered coffee kettle gave up its thick coating of ash, and she placed it with the rest of the salvaged treasures she'd set up on the wide, porch rail: a pair of tin cups, a brass cuspidor, several axe heads, and a cast iron frying pan.

She was bent over the basin, in the midst of washing up a stack of tin plates that had been nearly welded together from the fire's heat, when she heard the squeal of hinges as the screen door opened. She looked up to see Jack standing there, his tall frame filling up the doorway, and her heart swelled and fluttered in her breast.

He was wearing a blue cotton shirt and the pair of Noah's trousers that she had taken a scissors to, at Noah's request, cutting off one leg at the knee in order to accommodate the splints.

For a moment, Charlotte was able to forget the bruises

and the bandages, the pallor behind the beard-stubbled face. He was alive, and he was standing, albeit with the help of Noah's homemade crutches; and he was smiling at her.

She ran to him, but drew up short, suddenly afraid to touch him, for fear she'd disturb his balance. "You oughtn't to be out of bed yet," she chided, nervously wringing her hands. "Does Noah know you're doing this? Oh, for pity's sake, Jack, do sit down. You look as if you're about to faint."

He maneuvered himself across the porch, and only then did Charlotte reach out to take his crutches as he stretched out his bandaged leg and eased himself into the rocking chair.

"Now, what's all this?" he asked, narrowing his eyes as he surveyed the collection of miscellaneous goods she'd arranged along the porch rail.

"I . . . I thought you'd need stock to reopen the store," she explained, her gaze fixed on her shoes. She couldn't seem to face him somehow. All that she'd been doing these past few days seemed so presumptuous now, as she endeavored to explain it.

She took up one of the tin cups, turning it over and over in her hand. "You see, I've found some things in the rubble that the fire hasn't destroyed. Most of them are fine, after I wash them up."

With that, she held the cup out to him. He reached out to take it, but oddly, his hand overshot the distance, and when she let go, the cup bounced off his knee and clattered onto the porch floor.

Charlotte didn't bother to retrieve it. Her thoughts were all on Jack, her apprehensions rising by the minute. Something was wrong.

Kneeling down before him, she looked up into his eyes, those same gray eyes that had always seemed sharp enough to pierce through to her soul, and she realized.

Something *had* changed. Even though he was regarding her at close range, his eyes seemed dull and distant, and he was blinking rapidly as if he sought to clear his vision.

"Jack?"

"You did all this for me?"

He was staring out at the collection she'd balanced on the porch rail, entirely ignoring the question in her voice; and so, with no other choice, she asked him outright.

"You can't see, can you?"

"I can," he retorted, "well, a little. Everything looks rather like a watercolor painting, with the colors all running together."

Charlotte caught her breath, then laid her head upon his knee. In the last few days, she'd come to accept that he'd been gravely wounded, and that if he recovered, he would probably bear the scars of this fire forever, but she'd never expected anything like this.

"Oh, Jack."

Lifting his hand from its resting place on the arm of the chair, he reached out and began to stroke her hair. "It's nothing to worry about, really. Noah says it's a result of the concussion. Once the swelling goes down, things will get back to normal."

But even with his confident assurance hanging in the air, Charlotte still felt uneasy.

"And you needn't have worried yourself about the store, either," he went on. "I'll be able to manage. The building was insured, and I've a little money put aside. It's in the bank in Denver. All I need do is send them a wire . . ."

"I couldn't just sit there, thinking about all we'd lost," she insisted. "I couldn't bear another day of waiting by your bedside. I had to *do* something."

"I know, I know," he replied. Catching her face up in his hands, he made her look into his eyes. Changed as they were, she still caught a hint of a spark deep within, and it gave her hope. "You're a survivor, Charlotte. That's one of the things I've admired about you from the beginning. But before we can think about rebuilding, before we can do anything else, there's one thing we need to discuss, you and I."

Her throat ached, so thick was it with unshed tears. She wanted to apologize to him, but how could she find the words? It was her fault he was in this fix, her fault entirely. If she hadn't tarried so long in the store that night, worrying about a silly sack of flour . . .

"Charlotte?"

"What is it?"

"You've got to marry me, Charlotte."

She drew back from him, shaking her head. "Oh, but Jack . . ."

"Hush now," he bade her. "Just listen. I know I'm not offering you much of a bargain. You're still young and strong, and God knows, the most amazing woman I've ever seen, and I'm a crippled, half-blind wreck, with slim prospects, at best." He hesitated briefly, then pulled a long, calming breath. "But nevertheless, because of the fire, everyone in this town was in the streets the other night. They saw us ride in together . . ."

"You mean that they'll think . . . Why, that's just plain ridiculous, we never . . ."

Jack cut her off, continuing as if he hadn't even heard her protest. "With all that's happened, they've probably not had the chance to think about it yet, but they will, sooner or later, and when they do, the gentlemen of Cedar Creek will never look at you in the same way again. You know it, and I know it. It's my fault, and for that, I'm truly sorry."

Reaching out with surprising acuity, he gripped her hand hard. "Marriage is all that I have to offer you right now, that and a share of my worldly possessions, meager though they may be. But I haven't given up on this town,

Charlotte. There'll be more for you some day soon, I promise."

Dully, she got to her feet and stepped backward, until her hand had slipped from his. Crossing to the opposite edge of the porch, she clung to the railing and stared out over the ruins of the town.

Jack hadn't once mentioned love in his proposal. But then she had gone to great lengths to deny her own feelings where he was concerned, even though there was no denying that she cared for him.

Silly fool, the hard, familiar voice within her chided, *dreaming of love and marriage, after all you've been through. He feels responsible for you. It's nothing more than that.*

In the end, it didn't matter, though. None of it. Not what she'd been before, not what she'd done, nor what had prompted his proposal. For, despite all his bravado, Charlotte knew that Jack would need her now, more than he ever had, and that was enough to make up her mind.

Turning back on him, she smiled. "Yes, Jack. I will marry you."

Jack made the announcement at once to the Kelseys, who seemed pleased by the news but not in the least surprised, and then to the Widow Murphy, who'd been given refuge in the doctor's home when the fire had destroyed her boarding house. For the past few days, she'd been sleeping on the parlor sofa and helping out in the kitchen.

Despite his injuries, Jack seemed to have lost none of his enthusiasm. After learning from Noah that more than a few of the townsmen were talking of moving elsewhere, rather than rebuilding, he promptly ordered Noah and Charlotte out to gather everyone together for a town meeting. In scarcely more than an hour, the weary and disheartened men all stood assembled before the Kelseys' porch.

Jack came out of the house and haltingly made his way

to the railing on his crutches. Charlotte took up her place beside him, and Noah also stepped up, on the opposite side.

"Don't either of you mention a word about my sight," he cautioned them in a whisper, not wanting these people to think him at all disabled.

And then he drew himself up to address his friends. "Gentlemen. I've asked you all here this afternoon because I know what you're feeling. We've lost a lot."

"Don't sugar coat it, Jack," Hollis Lloyd put in. "We've lost damn-near everything."

"Yes, well, that may seem so now, but I can tell you, we've plenty here still worth fighting for. The only way we've lost is if we give up.

"Don't forget we're expecting that railroad surveyor to come back through in a month or two. We've already got the ideal location here. If we can rebuild the town, a better town than before, with all the sort of things the surveyor was looking to see, we'll be a sure bet for that railroad stop.

"Once we've got that, there'll be travelers coming through every day. They'll need food, entertainment, and lodging for the night. Some of them will decide to stay on, and those of us who are ready to accommodate them will make a fine profit, you just wait and see."

Charlotte stood there, awed at how Jack was able to fashion such grand possibilities out of such a dismal situation. Even she, cynically-minded as she was, felt a stirring of hope within her at his words.

Jack wasn't just a dreamer, she told herself; it was much more than that. He was a dream weaver, a man with a gift for making his dreams so real to others that they believed in them, too. And once all doubts were swept aside, those dreams could become reality.

His enthusiasm for Cedar Creek's rebirth was infectious. More than a few of their neighbors were nodding in agreement, their eyes bright as they contemplated this new future. Of course, not everyone was so easy to convince.

"It's all well and good to think big," the barber, Elliot Baird, countered, "but some of us got away from that fire with hardly more than the clothes on our backs. How are we supposed to survive in the meanwhile?"

"We can do it," Jack insisted, "if we all work together. Thanks to Charlotte's quick thinking and all of your help the other night, there's a wagonload of supplies from my store out back. I'm going to ask Noah to see to it that every man gets what he needs to make a start."

"That's mighty considerate of you, Jack," Gus Stern said.

"It's the least I can do to help put this town back on its feet. Now I know that, like me, some of you fellows have prospered here, and no doubt managed to put away a tidy sum for yourselves. And I know that I wasn't the only one who bought up a policy when that insurance salesman came through here last year. You, Henry, Lars, and Gunnar, you'll all certainly be able to put together enough to start fresh."

Gunnar nodded, pulling thoughtfully on his ruddy beard. *"Ja,* ve'll stay. Lars and me already fixed de corral, an' tracked down most of de horses and mules. An' jest as soon as Gus gets dat telegraph machine to vorkin', ve'll vire up to de sawmill in Denver to send lumber to rebuild de stable."

"And we'll all be there to help you when it comes," Jack assured him. "That's how we'll get through this, just as I've said, by working together."

Elliot Baird shook his head, disdainfully brushing the soot that still clung to his fancy green frock coat. "Things will never be the same," he said. "The mining's about bottomed-out around these parts. Bill Spence has already decided not to rebuild the Silver Dollar. He's packed up his wagon, taken his girls and gone out to Idaho Springs.

As for me, I'll stay until the stage comes through on Tuesday, then I think I'm going to try my luck in Black Hawk or Central City, or somewhere thereabouts."

"You do what you have to, my friend," Jack replied, undaunted. "But the rest of us are bound and determined to stay on here."

He didn't ask for a vote to confirm it, but no one spoke up to dispute him. With that, he turned to Charlotte, and throwing his weight onto one crutch, he freed the opposite arm and slipped it through hers.

"This is as good a time as any to make our announcement, don't you think?"

She nodded, and a queer little thrill ran through her as reality struck. No matter what the reasoning behind it, she had promised to become Jack's wife, for better or worse, till death do them part, and soon everyone in town would know it.

She could have sworn that his chest puffed out just a bit as he turned back to face his friends.

"Charlotte and I are going to be married just as soon as the preacher comes through," he told them; and although a long moment of silence followed thereafter, Charlotte thought, as she looked out over the collection of familiar faces, that none of them seemed truly surprised. Was she the only one who hadn't seen that a match between her and Jack was inevitable?

One by one, they came forward, offering broad grins along with their best wishes, cuffing Jack on the shoulder and casting him sly little winks, the meaning of which Charlotte knew only too well.

Until now, she hadn't thought at all about that aspect of things, hadn't stopped to consider precisely what a marriage to Jack would entail. She'd only thought of caring for him, of helping him because he needed her. But once they'd taken those marriage vows, he would certainly have the right to expect her to love him and be loved by him . . . in every sense of the word.

Trepidation swept through her like a chilling wind, and she shuddered in its wake. She hadn't forgotten what had happened the last time Jack had tried to touch her. She'd learned then that the awful nightmares hadn't gone away, likely they never would. But she couldn't tell him the truth, couldn't bear for him to know her shame.

Standing there beside him, Charlotte forced a smile, but she couldn't help but ask herself: *Have I made a promise that, in the end, I won't be able to keep?*

Thirteen

Jack stood facing the swinging glass on the bureau in Noah and Rachel's bedroom, his fingers fumbling with the knot of his black silk tie. Even when his vision hadn't been impaired, he'd never been able to fasten the thing just right. But now, he was utterly hopeless. He'd have to call for Noah to help him, like he had with his suspenders and his shirt studs. It wouldn't do at all for him to stand up before his bride, the preacher, and the whole damn town looking like a drunken sailor.

Although his own clothes had all been lost in the fire, Noah had seen to it that he'd have a proper suit for to-day—well, a clean shirt and black frock coat, at least. For trousers, Jack had no choice but to wear the pair that had been cut off at the knee to accommodate his bandaged leg. And so long as he didn't take too deep a breath nor flex his arms, he figured that Noah's coat would probably serve him well enough.

"Pssssst?"

The hissing sounded as though it were coming from the window, and taking up his crutches, Jack ambled over to investigate. When he got close enough, he could make out a blurred, pale blond head peeping through the opened window between Rachel's lace curtains. Unable to identify the intruder, he simply stood there, waiting for him to make his business known.

"I've got the ring, Jack."

The voice belonged to Henry Sutton.

"Then why on earth didn't you come in by the front door, Henry?"

"Aw, everybody's so busy, getting things ready for the wedding and all, I didn't want to bother. I picked up the mailbag from the stage like you asked me to and sorted everything out, and well, here's the box from that jeweler friend of yours in Denver. Got here just in time, didn't it?"

"Thank heavens for that. I'd hate to have had no ring to give Charlotte on her wedding day."

Jack extended his hand, palm up, and Henry placed the ring box in it. Curling his fingers over the package, Jack breathed a sigh of relief, then leaned over and set it on the bureau.

"I thought you'd want to see this as well," Henry said and began to wave something before him, in an excited fashion.

Jack could just make out a flash of white. Leaning forward on his crutches, he reached out and grabbed for it. Fortunately, he didn't miss.

It was an envelope, he determined, turning it over in his hand. No doubt it contained a letter, an important letter, if he were to judge by the young man's enthusiasm. Jack wouldn't be able to read it himself, but he didn't want Henry to know that.

"It's from that surveyor fella, Jasper Price."

Jack had never imagined that a time would come when he'd be thankful for Henry Sutton's inquisitive nature, but lo and behold, it had.

"I wasn't prying, you understand," he went on to say. "I only happened to see his name on the envelope. Do you think he's writing to let you know about that railway station they're planning to build in town?"

Jack stared hard at the envelope in his hand, but the swimming lines of ink came no closer to being legible.

So, he tucked the envelope into his inside jacket pocket and regarded his young friend soberly.

"Whatever it is, it can wait a little while longer," he told him. "Today's my wedding day, Henry, and that's all I've got time to think about just now."

The blond blur nodded, at least Jack thought it was a nod. "Sure thing, Jack. I understand. Best of luck to you. I'll see you later on."

It seemed that Henry had no sooner disappeared than had Noah burst back through the door. "Are you ready yet? The Reverend Morrison has just arrived, and Rachel will have my head on a platter if everything doesn't go off on time, just as planned."

Jack raised a hand and beckoned to him from across the room. "Help me with this tie, will you?"

He felt like a child, standing there while his friend folded the ends of his tie one over the other, fashioning a proper knot. It was demeaning as hell, being unable to do even the simplest tasks for himself. But he'd be back to normal soon enough, and then he'd be able to concentrate all his efforts on rebuilding the store and the town, and making a comfortable life for Charlotte.

The thought of them living together as man and wife caused Jack's heart to swell so full he thought it might burst. He'd wanted nothing more than this for months, and despite the way it had all come about, he knew they'd be happy. He loved her more than anything, and she . . . ? She cared for him. Hadn't she told him so?

Noah had offered to let them move into his home after the wedding, but Jack had politely refused the invitation. The Kelseys had already taken in Mrs. Murphy, who'd lost everything in the fire. It wouldn't do to have too many houseguests underfoot. Besides, Jack had reminded him, he had a place of his own, his cabin up by the lake. It was a bit rustic, but comfortable enough, and there was no reason at all why he and Charlotte couldn't set up housekeeping there, until they'd built a place for themselves in town.

A part of his eagerness to move out to the cabin, he had to admit, was fueled by a selfish desire to have her all to himself. They needed the time alone. In spite of her age and her experience in so many other matters, he'd already learned that Charlotte was untutored when it came to lovemaking. It was a discovery with which any prospective husband would be pleased, but then she was also wildly skittish, and Jack sensed he'd have to take special care with her.

He'd come to decide that her skittishness must have been because of what she'd suffered during the war. He'd heard the stories of besieged Southern cities, of women made to work hard as field hands to keep hearth and home together. Of course, he had no way of knowing just what Charlotte had been through, for she'd never said a word about it, and somehow, he had never found the courage to ask.

He had seen what she looked like when she first came here, though: so painfully thin, her skin sunbrowned, and those callused hands. Whatever it was that she'd suffered, it had driven her to deny her sex and take up life as a man. Jack thought he'd caught a glimpse of her fears on the night of the fire, when she'd clung so desperately to that sack of flour.

She was a war victim, just as surely as any of the scarred veterans, lacking limbs, who occasionally happened into his store on their way up to the mines. And Jack would need time if he were to win her trust and love, and introduce her to the pleasures of the marriage bed. But he was a patient man.

One thing, especially, had given him hope about their future together. When he'd proposed to Charlotte, he'd expected an argument, and yet she'd scarcely given him one.

Maybe, he thought, *she was healing already. Maybe the hardest part is over.*

She was wearing the lavender gingham dress. Even with his poor eyesight, Jack could make out that much. Standing before the preacher, he waited patiently for Charlotte to make her way through the divided ranks of friends and neighbors, who'd crowded into the parlor, and take her place beside him. Gus Stern provided the music, sawing out the Bridal March on the old, beat-up fiddle he'd managed to save from the fire. At that moment, Jack wished wholeheartedly that he could see more of his bride than a formless figure made up of splashes of color surrounded by a halo of light.

As she twined her arm through his, he caught a whiff of her hair, scented with rosewater, and of the fragrant bouquet of wildflowers she carried. He had to swallow hard to dislodge the lump that had formed in his throat. Even with all that he'd lost these past few weeks, standing here just now he thought himself the luckiest man on earth.

"Dearly beloved, we are gathered here today, in the sight of God and this assembled company, to witness the union of this man and this woman . . . ."

Charlotte listened carefully to the Reverend Morrison's words, and when it came her turn to speak, she managed to repeat her vows clearly and without any trace of a nervous tremor in her voice.

It wasn't that she had conquered her apprehensions about the steps she was taking; on the contrary, she was just as fearful about the night to come as she had been when Jack had first proposed. But she did care for him— at least as much as she'd ever been able to care for anyone. And Jack needed her; she'd reminded herself of that more than once. She'd never been a coward. She would see this through somehow.

When he placed the polished gold band on her finger and kissed her, in front of the reverend and everybody, she blushed as readily as any new bride would have and was surprised by just how right it all felt. Maybe now, with God's blessings on their union, the demon nightmares might be kept at bay.

After the ceremony was over, the guests retired outdoors to the several long, makeshift tables, which had been assembled for the occasion. Toasts for health and happiness were offered and drunk, and the meal, which Charlotte herself had helped to prepare, was quickly dispatched by the ravenous bachelors. When things had finally settled down a bit and most of the guests were sprawled comfortably about the yard, Jack caught Charlotte by the elbow and squired her inside the house, into Noah's office for a private word.

He bade her sit down, and then closed the door behind them. Curious as she was about this summons, as she watched Jack maneuver across the room on his crutches and then settle himself on one corner of Noah's desktop, she could only think how handsome her husband was, in spite of his injuries. Observing him in profile, from this angle, one could scarcely notice that the opposite side of his face was marred by garish purple bruises and that awful, jagged scar.

Without warning, he leaned forward, grasped her shoulders and kissed her. It was not a chaste kiss, by any means, but rather a long, slow, deep kiss that left a ringing in her ears and her heart tripping double-time when finally he released her.

"Wh-what was that for?" she asked, breathlessly.

"This is the first we've been alone all day," he answered, with a grin. "Can't a man kiss his wife, if he wants to?"

Charlotte's cheeks burned as a tingling of arousal swept

through her. It would take time to get used to this new closeness between them. But Jack was her husband now, and today he'd promised, before God and everyone, to love and cherish her forever. She would block out the nightmares. She'd manage . . . somehow.

Noah's black broadcloth frock coat, with a clutch of blue columbine pinned to the lapel, pulled taut across the shoulders as Jack reached into an inside pocket and withdrew an envelope.

At first, Charlotte thought that he would place it in her hands, but he hesitated, holding the paper between his thumb and forefinger instead. A sober look came over him all at once.

"You aren't sorry that you married me. Are you, Charlotte?"

Had he sensed the hesitation in her? Guessed somehow what she'd been thinking?

"What a question to ask on our wedding day," she replied, offering him her mock-chiding air. "Give me a year or two, at least, to see how difficult you are to live with, and then ask me again."

Jack pursed his lips together, seemingly satisfied with that, and then extending his arm, he gave over the precious envelope.

"This came in the mail today," he told her, "from the railroad surveyor. I couldn't read it myself, of course, but so much is riding on the outcome, I have to know. Will you read it to me. Please, Charlotte?"

"Yes, of course, I will," she said, realizing now as she tore open the envelope, the gravity of the paper she held in her hand.

Before beginning to read aloud, though, she took a moment to scan the page, and afterward, she was glad she did.

> *Dear Mr. Cordell,*
> *I regret to inform you that, due to the present un-*

favorable financial climate, Mr. Hathaway and his investors have been unable to secure the necessary capital to fund construction of the proposed rail line from Denver to Santa Fe. If, at any time in the future, conditions should permit a re-evaluation of this project, we will most assuredly contact you.

Respectfully,
Jasper E. Price

Charlotte let go a shaky breath.

"Well," Jack prompted, "what does it say?"

How could she tell him, when his hopes were pinned so high? When he'd all but promised the townsfolk that this railroad would be the means of their salvation?

"Give me a minute. I'm not so good a reader, you know," she lied.

Her mind reeled as she sought a solution to this dilemma. If the people were to learn that there was no possibility of the railroad coming through, they'd likely decide to move elsewhere, just as Elliot Baird had done, and that saloon owner and several others had done since. If too many of them left, there'd be no reason to rebuild the store, the newspaper office, or the boarding house.

Charlotte couldn't let that happen, not only for Jack's sake, but for her own as well. Something had happened to her in the months that she'd lived here. Jack had planted the seeds, by showing her the beauty of this place and filling her head with all of his wonderful plans. But those seeds had taken firm root, and Cedar Creek had become her dream now, as much as it was his.

"It . . . it says that they've had to postpone their decision," she told him, with as much conviction as she could muster, "that it'll be another two months at least."

Jack's brow furrowed, and he reached up to tug on his chin. "Well, that's not exactly bad news for us, is it? It'll give us more time to rebuild."

"Yes," Charlotte agreed. "Yes, I suppose it will at that."

He held out a hand, no doubt expecting her to give him back the letter, but instead, she cautiously tucked it into her waistband.

"I'll take care of it for you," she told him. "You needn't worry yourself."

She'd had to do it. What choice was left to her? She'd already begun to sense a change in Jack since the fire, hints of his frustration with his new lot as. . . . What was it he had so cruelly called himself? A half-blind cripple? Charlotte genuinely feared what would happen to him, without his dream to guide him. Nevertheless, it struck her as an unfortunate omen, indeed, that the foundations of their marriage were to be built upon a lie.

After everyone had finished their supper and had some time to rest, Gus and his fiddle were once more called upon to provide the music, so that each gentleman might have an opportunity to dance with the bride. One after another, each of them took his turn except, of course, for the unfortunate groom, whose injuries prevented him from participating in the fun.

Jack was relegated to observing the proceedings from the front porch steps. He wanted to be magnanimous, but each time the swirl of lavender passed before his dulled eyes, it struck him that he'd never had the chance to dance with Charlotte himself, never held her close against him, fitting his hand into the slender hollow of her back as he whirled her across the floor.

Although he couldn't read her expression, couldn't even see her face, Jack could hear the music of her laughter as it drifted across the yard, and with the sound of it, jealousy pricked at his insides. Who was it making her laugh this time? Gunnar Thorssen, with his soft-spoken simplicity? Or the suave, city-mannered Nate Phillips? Or was it his pale, lank friend, Henry Sutton, and his affable charm?

Frustrated, he tried to turn his thoughts elsewhere, reminding himself of the good news he'd only just received in Jasper Price's letter. It was a blessing, no less, for the citizens of Cedar Creek that the decision about the rail station had been put off. With another two months to rebuild, they could make their town into everything the surveyor had been hoping to see. Yes, it was good news, indeed.

"Have a drink with me, Jack. Maybe then I won't feel so bad 'cause you're takin' her home tonight instead of me."

Hollis Lloyd settled down on the step beside him, and Jack heard the chink of glass as Lloyd poured them each a drop from the bottle he held in his hand. Jack nearly refused, but then, thinking better of it, extended his hand. Hollis gave over the glass, and curling his fingers around it, Jack raised it to his lips and let the liquor slide down his throat, all in one swallow.

A warm burn radiated outward from the pit of his stomach, soothing the prickling of disquiet he'd begun to feel inside. He didn't ordinarily drink whiskey, but maybe a few stiff drinks were just what he needed right now. He held out his glass and Lloyd promptly refilled it.

"You're one lucky son-of-a-bitch, Jack Cordell, that's all I can say."

Jack turned to him and offered a lazy smile. "Why, thank you kindly, Hollis. I like to think so."

"All of us been sniffin' around her skirts for months, and she don't pay us no never mind at all, but you up and get yourself brained by a falling building, and all of a sudden, it's true love."

Jack sipped at his whiskey in thoughtful silence, not quite sure what to make of the young man's remark.

"Women are like that, though," Lloyd continued. "I had me two sisters, when I was growin' up on the farm back in Illinois, and I can't count the times they came into the house, carrying some wounded animal tucked up in their aprons—bird, rabbit, didn't matter what kind. Women got a soft spot in 'em for any creature that's hurtin'. So, if you take my advice, old friend, you'll keep that leg of yours bandaged up just as long as humanly possible."

What was it Lloyd was trying to say? That Charlotte had only agreed to marry him because she thought of him as some kind of wounded creature? That she'd felt sorry for him?

The sweet ring of her laughter cut through Jack's thoughts, as she whirled past in the arms of yet another partner. Lifting his glass, he tossed back the remainder of his whiskey and let it burn the length of his throat. Well, if that's what he was thinking, then Hollis Lloyd was just plain crazy.

Before she knew it, it was time to go. After a borrowed buckboard had been loaded up with the supplies they'd need for the cabin, Charlotte went in to say her goodbyes to Rachel who, despite all the excitement, was already tucked away in bed.

"I'm glad to see you resting," Charlotte said, as she came to stand beside her.

"I didn't have a choice in the matter. I never thought when we took in poor Mrs. Murphy that she'd turn out to be such a martinet."

"She's only concerned about you and the baby."

"Yes, I know."

With that, Rachel caught up Charlotte's hand, and drawing her down, embraced her. When she spoke again, her voice was choked with tears. "I'm going to miss you."

"I won't be far away," Charlotte assured her. "I wouldn't leave you at all, if I didn't know that you had Mrs. Murphy here to help."

"Don't be silly. You've got a husband of your own now, and a pretty little cabin, up there by the lake, with your very own raspberry patch."

Charlotte grinned. "I should think you'd be sick of raspberries, after all you've eaten."

"You won't get to liking it too much up there in the mountains with Jack?" Rachel wanted to know. "So much that you won't come back down to Cedar Creek."

"Now who's being silly? You know how Jack feels about this town. He's already made plans to come down tomorrow and get to work hauling away rubble from the fire."

"But what about your honeymoon?"

At this, Charlotte bit her lips, and her eyes slanted away, avoiding Rachel's. She couldn't help herself.

"Charlotte? You're not afraid of what's to come, are you? The way you've always spoken, I thought you'd had some experience . . . Oh, I know we've never discussed such things, but if you'd like to . . ."

Charlotte shook her head, too vigorously perhaps. This was something she couldn't talk about, not even to Rachel.

"Well, you needn't worry about Jack. He's a good man. You couldn't have made a better catch. But if he's planning to drag you back down here tomorrow morning to work, I think you ought to send him in here to see me right now, so that I can give him a serious talking-to. Why, you'll not even have been married twenty-four hours, for heaven's sake."

"He's worried about the town, Rachel," Charlotte said in defense of her husband, "and frankly, so am I."

Rachel offered her an indulgent smile. "But there's nothing to worry about, is there? We'll be fine, once everything is rebuilt, and we get that railroad station. Isn't that what Jack's said? It'll all be new and better than before."

Clutching a handful of skirt in each fist, Charlotte went to the window and pretended to look out on some of the wedding guests, lounging in the yard.

"I wish I could believe that. But what if . . ." She

paused to gather her courage before she turned back on her friend, "what if we don't get it?"

Rachel's brow arched high. "Jack seemed so sure. You haven't heard anything, have you?"

"No," Charlotte lied. "No, of course not. But still, I can't help but wonder what might happen . . ."

"Things would be a good deal more difficult, in that case," Rachel replied, matter-of-factly. "Some of the men would say there'd be no reason to rebuild."

"But Cedar Creek is such a beautiful place, and there's plenty of game, fresh water, and timber close at hand. It's a perfect spot to build a home. Isn't that enough?"

"For some it might be, I suppose. But most of the men who've built this town aren't simple homesteaders. They followed the miners here. It's people and money that make a town like this prosper. Without customers, Jack can't run his store. There'd been no need for a newspaper, nor Lars and Gunnar's livery, nor Henry Sutton's hardware either."

"You mean to say there isn't anything else that would entice everyone to stay?"

Rachel thought about it for a long time. "It was the gold that brought them here in the first place," she said at last. "Nothing short of a new strike would bring in enough folk to make the living worthwhile."

Charlotte considered her friend's words in thoughtful silence. Sooner or later, Jack and the townsmen would discover that there was to be no railroad. Once that happened, there'd be nothing more to keep them here. Cedar Creek would die, sure as so many other mining camps scattered through the foothills had. But what could she do?

The distress must have been visible on her face, for Rachel regarded her with new concern. "You aren't having second thoughts, are you, Charlotte? About marrying Jack, I mean."

Odd. This wasn't the first time today that someone had

asked her that question. "Second thoughts?" she echoed. "No, of course not."

"Good. For a moment, you seemed so solemn and silent, that I couldn't help but wonder . . . After all, it wasn't so long ago that you stood in this very room and insisted to me that it was over between the two of you."

"Everything's changed now," Charlotte replied. "Jack needs me. What sort of person would I be if I abandoned him, as he is? Besides, it's entirely my fault that he got hurt. He nearly paid with his life for my carelessness."

Her voice drifted off. She wasn't telling Rachel the whole truth. But how could she admit that she cared for Jack too much to let him go? That she was making up all of these excuses in order to have what she wanted out of life, even though she didn't deserve it?

"Taking care of him is the least I can do."

Jack drew up short before the half-closed door, the grin he'd been wearing frozen upon his face. The tip of one crutch wavered in mid-air. He didn't use it to push open the door as he'd planned, only stood there, the blood draining away from his face as he listened to the last of Charlotte's revealing remarks.

He ought to have guessed, when she'd changed her demeanor so abruptly after the fire, that she was only feeling sorry for him. Hadn't Hollis Lloyd said the very same thing to him, just a short while ago? He wouldn't believe it, though. The devil take him for a witless, lovesick fool! He ought to have known.

Forgetting himself, he took a sharp step backward and very nearly lost his balance. But Mrs. Murphy, who was bustling about the kitchen behind him, noticed his dilemma and rushed up behind him, thrusting a meaty shoulder square into his back to keep him from toppling backward.

"Best be careful now," she remarked, once she'd helped him to regain his footing, "else you'll be breakin' yer other leg, and then what kind of honeymoon will it be for ye?"

What kind of honeymoon, indeed, he wondered, when the woman he had married had more intention of serving as a nursemaid than a wife?

Just what did Charlotte see when she looked at him anyway? Jack knew that he was awkward and unsteady, his face bruised and scarred, but looking at life through a blurred haze, he hadn't yet been able to see for himself precisely how much the accident had changed him.

What if he was hideous? No one had said a word to him about his appearance, and he had never thought to ask. But what if every one of his friends here today were shaking their heads in sympathy for poor, sweet Charlotte, attaching herself for life to a helpless, hulking cripple?

Fourteen

The sun had slipped low on the horizon when Charlotte came out into the yard to find Jack, aided by his friends, in the midst of an awkward ascent into the buckboard. His good leg was already perched upon the frame; he'd gotten a firm grip on the wagon seat; and as he attempted to heave himself upward, Noah helped support the splinted leg and Hollis Lloyd offered a hearty shove from behind.

"Steady," Noah urged. "Here we go now."

"Don't lean backwards; you'll throw off your balance."

Jack looked over his shoulder, scowling at Lloyd. "I'm not leaning," he insisted. "Just stand back, the both of you. I can manage on my own."

"Like hell you can. We step away, and you'll topple backwards and hit the ground like a felled tree. But then if what you're aiming for is to spend your honeymoon night in Noah's infirmary . . ."

"What I'm aiming for," Jack shot back, a wicked gleam in his eye, "is to heal up quick, so I can use this leg of mine to kick your sorry ass halfway down the canyon."

With that, he swung his bandaged leg around and dropped into the wagon seat. Noah handed up the crutches, and Jack stowed them beneath his feet.

"There now," Noah said, eager to smooth things over. "You're all set."

All of this might have been a comical affair, if Charlotte had suspected that Jack's threat to Hollis Lloyd had been made entirely in jest. They'd always been polite friends at least, but then lately there had been times when Jack had seemed, well, almost unreasonably jealous of Hollis's innocent attentions to her.

"*Ja,* dat's fine fer now," Gunnar Thorssen called out, waving about his half-emptied whiskey glass, "but how's he supposed to get back down ven dey get to de cabin?"

Charlotte hitched up her skirts and swept across the yard. "Don't you worry; we'll manage," she replied, and then hoisted herself up into the buckboard without even waiting for one of the gentlemen to lend her a hand.

Only then did she notice that Jack had taken up the reins. He must have known he couldn't manage. Or hadn't he even stopped to think?

"Jack, you can't possibly . . ."

She caught herself just in time, remembering how important it was to him that his friends not discover the damage that had been done to his sight.

She had to give him credit; he'd managed to keep them from learning his secret thus far. But she knew it wasn't simple pride that motivated him. He was worried that if his neighbors detected any sign of weakness in him at all, it might affect their decision to stand with him and rebuild the town. And he was probably right.

She laid a gentle hand on his arm. "You're tired," she said, not forcefully, but loud enough for all to hear, "and your leg must be paining you. Why don't you sit back and rest, and let me have the reins?"

As if he'd only been waiting for her to ask, Jack handed them over, but he kept on staring straight ahead, his gray eyes dull and unrevealing.

Charlotte didn't wait around to see if her act had convinced their friends. She flicked the reins, the horse lifted his head, and with everyone cheering them, the newlyweds started off.

They'd hadn't gone more than a quarter mile, though,

before she began to suspect that something was amiss. Beside her, Jack sat, stiff and silent, and the air around him peculiarly redolent of whiskey. Jack had never imbibed, so far as she knew. But then given the occasion, she supposed he might have had a glass or two along with the rest to be social.

What bothered her most was that he didn't speak, not a single word. He wasn't the sullen type, and it left her wondering what might be wrong. Yes, he had seemed frustrated when he'd been the only man unable to dance with her, but he'd taken the news about the railroad in stride, at least as much as she'd told him. A pang of fear vibrated through her chest. What if he'd discovered the truth? No, he couldn't have. The letter was still tucked safely in her waistband. But if not that, then what?

Charlotte didn't have to wait long to find out. Dusk had settled in by the time they reached the cabin. This was the worst time of the day for Jack, she knew, when there was not enough sunlight and no lamps yet lit. For all practical purposes, he was blind at dusk.

She tied off the reins, then prepared to help him alight, but before she'd realized it, he'd scrambled down from the wagon seat on his own and begun to unharness the horse from the buckboard.

It soon became apparent, though, that he'd be unable to manage the buckles, while balancing on his crutches. Beneath his breath, Jack swore, and sensing his distress, the horse began to step nervously. Charlotte jumped down and came to his aid.

"Go and rest yourself on the porch," she said, taking the straps from his hand. "I'll see to the horse."

"Then I'll carry in the bags," he insisted.

He swung himself around, and by using one crutch to feel out the way, he maneuvered himself around to the back of the buckboard, where their supplies had been lashed.

While Charlotte unharnessed the horse, she kept a close eye on Jack, who now proceeded to tuck a carpetbag up under one arm and hook the opposite elbow through the handles of a market basket, all the while steadying himself on his crutches.

"Will you be able to carry all that and still find your way, do you think?" she called out to him.

In response, Jack drew up to his full height, his mouth pressed into a tight line, a muscle knotting in his jaw. "I'm injured, that's all. I'm not a child, who needs to be led around by the hand. I think I can manage this much, at least."

Stung by his sharp retort, Charlotte turned her attentions back on the horse, leading him into the corral before fastening the gate behind him. *It was in the nature of a man to want to take charge of things and to want to be in control,* she reminded herself. It must be a difficult position Jack now found himself in, helpless and dependent as he was. She'd have to try harder to remember that.

By the time Charlotte had finished with the horse, Jack had already gone up the path to the cabin. She was honestly surprised to see that he'd made it so far without calamity, given his awkward pose, but just when she'd begun to feel foolish about her concern, the items in the basket Jack was carrying must have shifted, throwing off his balance. In mounting the stairs, one shoulder slammed against the porch post, and he toppled sideways.

"Jack!"

Charlotte lifted her skirts and ran to him. Her heart was pounding in her ears, her breath coming in shallow gasps. By the time she reached him, he was sprawled out on the porch, surrounded by the tins, sacks, and bottles that had rolled out of the market basket.

Kneeling at his side, she helped him to ease into a sitting position, and when she noticed an abrasion on the back of his hand, she drew the handkerchief from her sleeve, wet it with the tip of her tongue, and began to dab away the blood.

"Oh, Lord! Are you all right? I was afraid of something like this. You oughtn't to have tried to carry anything. You haven't fallen on your bad leg, have you?"

She reached down, and her fingers fluttered nervously over his bandages. Thankfully, nothing seemed amiss.

"Damn it, Charlotte!" he growled, swatting away her hands. "Stop fussing over me. I'm fine."

With that, he sought out his crutches, and hoisting himself up, lumbered into the cabin. After she'd retrieved the carpetbag, gathered up the items on the porch, and replaced them in the basket, Charlotte followed him inside.

The daylight was nearly gone now, and it was difficult, even for her, to see much of anything within the shadowy cabin. She set down her burden at the door, then headed for the matchbox on the wall beside the stove. After some fumbling about, she finally managed to light the lantern that hung over the center of the table.

When the soft yellow glow had edged its way across the room, she saw Jack standing before the window and staring dully out into the darkness. Advancing on him, she swallowed her fears and reached out to wind her arms around his waist, then lay her head against his chest.

"I'm sorry, Jack. I know how hard this must be for you, having to depend on others . . . on me. But there isn't any shame in it. I've always thought that that's what marriage was all about, each partner drawing strength from the other. Besides, everything will be back to normal soon."

Instinctively, Charlotte's arms tightened around him. She hadn't just been trying to salvage his pride with her words. The truth was that she was drawing strength from him, even now. She couldn't explain it but, even after all she'd been through, she felt safe here with him, his heart beating close against her ear. His chest expanded as he drew a long, unsteady breath. For a moment, it seemed he might speak, but he did not.

"I know that in the past I've seemed temperamental," she went on to say, "that I've made things difficult for you, but I took a vow this afternoon, and I want you to know that I intend to abide by it . . . to be your wife in every sense of the word."

Only now did she turn her eyes up to meet his, and the unexpected chill she saw in them made her shiver, even with the summer's heat.

"I think we ought to get one thing clear between us from the outset," he replied at last, taking an awkward step back out of her arms. "This marriage is a comfortable arrangement for both of us. You'll have a home of your own at last and some of that freedom you're always talking about. And me? Well, I'll have three square meals a day and someone to pick me up when I fall down."

Charlotte had never heard him speak so bitterly. But then his pride had been damaged, what else could she expect?

"Oh, but Jack, I . . ."

"You needn't feel you're taking advantage of me. It's an honest bargain. I'm sure to thrive under your excellent care. But given the circumstances, it would be selfish of me to ask any more than that."

Charlotte stood there, twisting her hands in her skirts. What did he mean, exactly? That all along he'd intended for theirs to be a marriage "in name only"? Maybe he had only proposed marriage to save her reputation, she speculated, maybe he had only felt sorry for her, just as she'd imagined. But no, he couldn't have been thinking of that when he'd kissed her this afternoon in Noah's office.

Some change had come over him in the past few hours, of that much Charlotte was certain. She ought to have argued with him right then and there to try and get at the truth, but she didn't. She hadn't the strength, burdened as she was with demons of her own. And she was ashamed to acknowledge that a part of her was thankful. With no conscious effort at all, a sigh of relief escaped her.

Soft as it was, Jack heard the sound. She knew that he had, for just after, he met her with a wistful smile.

"I'm hardly in any condition right now to perform my conjugal duties, at any rate," he admitted. "I can't even climb the ladder to get into the loft. So, if you would just be good enough to throw a few blankets together and fix me a spot down here, we can both get some sleep. We've a lot of work to do tomorrow."

Lying in the loft bed alone that night, Charlotte felt a sharp stab of regret at her meek acceptance of what Jack had called their "honest bargain." It might have been over by now. She might have been lying here in Jack's arms, his wife in more than name. She might have been laughing at her foolish fears by now, but instead she was alone.

And she had other worries on her mind as well. It was only a matter of time before Jack and the other townsfolk discovered that there was to be no railroad running through their town. Before that happened, she had to think of something else that would make them want to stay.

Rachel had told her that only another gold strike nearby could accomplish that. But Charlotte knew, from her own experience, that the placer deposits around these parts had played out several years ago.

There was gold here all right, but it was bound up in quartz ore, and only if it promised to prove profitable enough would an investor be willing to reopen the old stamp mill that stood just out of town. The stamps could then crush the ore and free the precious metal from the worthless rock.

News of any gold find had a way of kindling enthusiasm in people, she told herself, of drawing hopeful souls from miles around. A strike, even a modest one, might prompt someone into reopening the stamp mill or building a new one, and that would be enough to keep the town alive. But what were the odds of there being a gold strike in Cedar Creek any time soon?

The stench of smoke clung to the rubble. Balancing himself carefully, Jack bent down, scooped up yet another chunk of charred timber and tossed it over into the wagon. He'd been at it more than two hours now, piece at a time, fighting with frustration all the while.

Sweat streamed in rivulets down his face. His head ached. His bandaged leg was throbbing, and his muscles bunched in protest with each move he made. He'd thought that if he gave it his all, he'd be able to have the property cleared by supper time, but then he hadn't counted on his injuries proving such an impediment, his body rebelling at every turn. Here it was nearly noon, and he'd scarcely made a difference.

Still, he was spurred on by the rasp of saws and clattering of hammers that echoed from down the street. The Thorssen brothers were already in the midst of rebuilding, and maybe if some of the others saw that he was, too, they'd stop mourning over what they'd lost and get to work themselves.

"What in heaven's name do you think you're doing out here? Are you crazy?"

Jack couldn't help but wonder about that himself, as he considered Noah's question. But in the end, he chose not to voice his own doubts. There was no need to help Noah with his argument.

"Just doing what needs to be done," he said, turning toward the sound of his friend's voice.

Noah stood near the wagon: a stark, stiff column of black fringed by a brilliant aura of sunlight.

"I cannot believe that after less than twenty-four hours

of marriage, you'd leave your bride all alone, and come out here to clear away rubble."

"That's how much you know," Jack shot back. "Charlotte is here, too."

The figure wavered as Noah tossed his head from side to side. "Here? Where? I don't see her."

"Well, she *was* here," he explained, "but she kept on complaining that I was going to hurt myself, so I sent her off to find Gus and asked her to have him wire instructions to my bank in Denver."

"She's right, you know. If you don't give those bones in your leg time to mend properly, you could well be limping for the rest of your life."

Jack shook his head. "I'd expect you to say that, Noah. You're a cautious individual. Physicians need to be. But I'm a businessman, and I need to rebuild my store."

"Why can't you wait a few weeks? Give your body time to heal? Unless your vision improves soon, you won't be able to run things, even if you do rebuild. How do you expect to read the labels on your merchandise, keep your ledgers, make change?"

"But surely whatever is wrong will have cleared up by then."

The silence which followed did not help to comfort him.

"We don't know that. I've told you, Jack, I don't even know what's caused the damage. I can't say for certain if you'll ever see clearly again or not. And even if the problem is only some kind of swelling in your brain, as I suspect, you can be damned sure that all of this exertion won't speed the healing process. Keep on as you are and you're liable to wind up completely blind."

Jack dragged himself to the wagon, tossed in the armload of debris he'd been carrying, then leaned heavily against the box. Drawing a handkerchief out of his pocket, he wiped the sweat from the back of his neck.

Noah was right, of course. He'd never claimed that

Jack's sight would improve. But Jack hadn't been able to accept the possibility that he'd never be the man he once was, and so he simply hadn't listened. He'd tried to pretend to the whole town that there was nothing at all wrong with his eyesight. If he could convince them, he'd thought, then maybe somehow that would make things all right. But it hadn't.

"What do you expect me to do, Noah?" Jack posed, more weary now than ever. "Set myself up on the street corner with my cane and tin cup and beg for change? Let Charlotte support me? Oh, I don't doubt she'd make a fine job of it. Do you know that by the time I woke this morning, she'd already baked a dozen loaves of bread? She brought them down this morning and sold the lot of them, right here in the middle of the street."

"I'm only saying that you should take a little time to get your strength back," Noah replied. "Practice at training your eyes to focus on objects. That might help, and in the meanwhile, you might consider what skills you do have to rely upon."

"Skills?"

"You're a clever fellow. There must be plenty you can do."

For his part, Jack didn't believe it, but nevertheless Noah had made him think. He wasn't wholly without means. He had this property, and a little money set aside. Maybe rebuilding the store wasn't the wisest course, after all. If his impaired vision were to prove permanent, and he'd have to accept that it might be, then he'd have to find some other venture to support Charlotte and himself, something he could manage on his own, even without his sight.

He'd be damned if he was going to let Charlotte support them both.

* * *

Charlotte found Gus Stern set up in an old, abandoned miner's shack on the north end of town. It was just a temporary arrangement, he'd explained, until his place on the main street could be rebuilt.

"I take it then you're not thinking of leaving us," Charlotte said, as she followed him inside.

"No, I'll be kept busy right here. There'll be plenty of folks needing to send telegrams for a while, and the miners from Six Mile will keep on coming down to have me assay their ore."

Gus took up his stool, and unfolding the page containing Jack's telegram and spreading it out before him, he addressed the telegraph key, which he'd set up atop a rickety, wooden crate, and began to tap out the code.

While she waited for him to finish transmitting the message, Charlotte considered the best way to begin a conversation. After all, she hadn't let Jack talk her into coming here simply to see his telegram sent.

For all of last night and most of this morning, her thoughts had been occupied with the town's dilemma. If she'd paused long enough to consider it, she might have had to admit that her obsession with the subject allowed her to ignore the other, more painful, questions in her life. But she wouldn't allow her mind to stray that far. If, indeed, the only way to prompt folk to settle in Cedar Creek was with a gold strike, then she needed to discern whether or not it was a realistic possibility.

Charlotte knew more than a little about prospecting for gold, but by the time she had come to the Colorado territory, Cedar Creek's heyday was already over. Was there more gold to be found here? How thorough had the first wave of prospectors been in their efforts? The remnants of prospects holes dotting the landscape seemed to indicate that the ground had been well worked over, but she had to know for sure, and Gus Stern, who was the local assayer, would be the logical person to ask if she wanted answers to her questions.

"Why didn't the Cedar Creek mines pan out?" she asked, in her most casual air when the rhythmic clacking of the telegraph key had ceased at last. "Wasn't there any more gold?"

"Oh, there's gold enough all right, but what's left is locked up tight in quartz. It's got to be processed in order to separate gold from gangue. Oh, I don't expect a young lady like you to understand the scientific principles involved. All you need to know is that, for right now, it's just too expensive to get the gold out.

"The mines around here might be able to make a go of it," he added, after careful thought, "if someone were to put up the money to reopen the stamp mill. But there isn't much chance of that happening, with things as they are. No one wants any part of a dying town."

Charlotte winced at his words. "Is that what we are?"

Gus didn't bother to reply, but she knew his answer all the same.

"But what if there was a new strike?" she prompted.

"Well now, that would be different. Just take a look at Central City and Blackhawk, they got fellas as far away as New York City investing in their mines and mills. Once the fever's been touched off, there's no telling what can happen."

Charlotte had heard what she'd come here to, and after Gus had answered a few more of her innocently-framed questions, she left his little shack with a better idea of what needed to be done. There was no getting around it. In order to save Cedar Creek, she would simply have to conjure a gold strike.

It could be done. Her old friend, Vernon Taylor, the miner from Six Mile Canyon, had told her once about a fellow up in Gilpin, who'd been trying for months to dispose of his near worthless mine, until he hit upon an idea. . . .

She had enough gold dust to invest in the scheme. More than a few of her bakery customers had used that medium of exchange, but what she really needed was a few rich pieces of blossom rock.

Deep in thought, with her head hung low, Charlotte was scarcely aware of the stage as it thundered past, then drew up, not far away, amid the charred remains of Cedar Creek's business district. But she shook off her reverie in time to recall that there'd be a mailbag on this morning's stage, and her husband was the postmaster.

Lifting her skirts, she hurried down to the meet the driver, a wizened, old jehu who was looking about for signs of life.

"Has everybody up and left?" he posed, as soon as he saw her. "I expected they would, after what's happened."

"No," Charlotte replied. "We're scattered about, here and there, until we can rebuild things."

"And where might I find Jack Cordell?" he asked, as he tied off the reins and jumped down from his high perch.

"He's down the street a ways, talking to Doctor Kelsey, it looks like. But you can leave the mailbag with me, if you like. I'm his wife."

The old man's eyes narrowed as he took stock of Charlotte, and still more creases formed in the leathery face. "So, you're the new bride, are ye? Hard way to start a marriage, I'd say."

"Oh, we'll manage," she told him, sounding far more confident than she felt.

"Well, my best wishes to ye, missus."

With that, he winked at her and handed over the worn leather saddlebag. Charlotte thanked him, tossed the bag over her shoulder, and turned to walk away. But she hadn't gone far before he called out to her.

"Miz Cordell, wait. I've a passenger for ye, too."

Surprised, Charlotte stopped in her tracks, then turned around just as the old man opened the stage door and reached in to help a young lady alight.

She extended a gloved hand, and as she stepped out, Charlotte noticed the blue traveling suit, of fashionable Eastern cut. She threw back the veil of her bonnet as soon as her tiny, booted feet touched the ground and looked up, expectantly.

Charlotte knew who she was the moment she set eyes on her. There was a similarity in the features, and she had the same thick, black hair sweeping across a wide forehead, the same luminous, gray eyes.

"Leah?"

With all that had happened lately, Charlotte had almost forgotten what Jack had told her about sending for his sister. He must have forgotten about it himself, else he'd surely have wired her to delay her arrival. Cedar Creek, as she was—a crumbling, burnt-out wreck—was fine for the band of toughened settlers, who were aiming to rebuild her, but certainly not a welcoming sight for a young lady used to the comfortable confines of a Cincinnati young ladies' academy.

Apparently, Leah Cordell felt the same, for as Charlotte came forward to greet her, the girl took a good look around her, pulled a handkerchief from her sleeve and dissolved in tears.

Fifteen

It was no wonder that Leah had a hard time adjusting to life out West. She'd spent the last six of her sixteen years sequestered at the Brierson Young Ladies' Academy of Cincinnati, Ohio, where—according to the missives that Jack had received from its estimable headmistress—she had learned all of the finer arts of being a lady: of pouring tea, painting watercolor landscapes, and playing the pianoforte. And then, poor child, to come to this.

Leah hadn't even been born yet when Jack had left home to find his fortune. He'd taken on responsibility for her after their parents died, though; paid for her schooling; corresponded with her so she wouldn't feel as if she'd been abandoned; and overall, he tried to do what was best for her. When he'd written inviting her out to join him, he'd envisioned the circumstances of their first meeting much differently, but then fate always seemed to have a way of twisting things around.

Charlotte was patient and kind, and did her best to make the transition from civilization to wilderness as painless as possible for her new sister-in-law. She shared her loft bed with Leah and assured her, over and over again, that no matter what the Eastern newspapers said, there was really very little chance of attack by hostile Indians, bears, or mountain lions. She offered the girl equal parts of mothering and friendship, and Jack was grateful to Charlotte for that.

In the weeks since Leah's arrival, he'd done a lot of thinking. He had two women to support now, a sister and a wife, and his rapid recovery was more important than ever. In consequence, he'd been careful to do precisely as Noah had instructed him, keeping out of Cedar Creek and thereby out of mischief, resting himself at the cabin instead, fishing and taking short walks each day for exercise and training his eyes in order to make the best use of what little sight was left to him. This forced indolence was difficult for him to endure. But his mind was working all the time, weighing his options, making plans for the future.

It was Charlotte who kept him informed on what was happening in town. She made a trip down each morning, to sell her bread. It chafed him to realize that she was raking in profits, while he lay idle, but then he had promised her her freedom, hadn't he? He couldn't very well complain.

Besides, the further apart they remained, the less likely he was to weaken his resolve and make a fool of himself. More than once as he'd sat across the supper table from her, reflecting on the soft, silhouetted curve of her cheek and the glint of firelight on her hair—all that he could see of her—he'd had to remind himself that she was his nursemaid, nothing more than that. Charlotte hadn't married him out of love, but rather because she'd felt responsible for his injuries, because she pitied him. Given that reality, it was better to keep the distance between them.

The afternoon sun had begun to slant in the cabin windows, affecting Jack's vision worse than ever with its irritating orange glare and heating the room to an intolerable degree. He had already had his exercise and had been resting on his cot, but he ventured outside again anyway, scanning the blurred landscape for a bright patch of yellow, which was the color of his sister Leah's dress.

For the first few days, she'd scarcely left the cabin at

all, and even now, she never strayed far—still afraid of Indians, Jack supposed.

Eventually, he spotted her in the clearing down by the corral. She was perched among the rocks, and as he maneuvered down the path, drawing closer, he noticed a squarish splash of white blending with the yellow of her skirts.

Resting himself on his crutches, he paused to listen, and to his surprise, he made out a sound, which he recognized as the scratching of pencil lead on paper. Leah was sketching.

"It's not so bad up here, is it?" he asked her.

"The mountains are beautiful," she admitted, "and the scenery's always changing. I could sit right here and make a dozen different pictures, then come back tomorrow and make a dozen more."

Jack wondered about his sister. He'd already begun to learn that Leah was a gentle and sensitive soul, but he hadn't a clue as to what she looked like. While she had been speaking just now, he thought he'd heard a note of his mother's voice in hers. Did she resemble her, too? Or did she take after their father, as Jack himself did?

Thinking about his own appearance made him frown. He'd been torturing himself lately with the thought that the bruises and scars on his face must have made him into a monster. All this time spent up here with only Charlotte and Leah didn't help his confidence, nor did the pity he imagined he heard in Charlotte's voice each time she spoke to him.

He limped over and settled himself beside her. "I need to ask you a question," he said to Leah, all at once, "and I want you to tell me the truth. You've an artist's eye, and well, I haven't been able to see myself in the mirror since the accident. Am I horribly disfigured?"

To his surprise, she laughed. It wasn't a mocking laugh, though. The sound was light and infectious. "You men are vain creatures, aren't you? Mrs. Brierson always told us so."

Jack felt her fingertips touch the mottled bruises on his face, then trace along the long, twisted rope of flesh that was his scar.

"It's not so awful," she said. "As a matter of fact, I think it's rather dashing. You look like you might be a brave pirate, who's been wounded by a cutlass while defending his ship, or a brooding European nobleman. They all have dueling scars, you know."

He leaned nearer to her, so that he might whisper in her ear. "You've been reading dime novels, haven't you? I doubt that Mrs. Brierson would approve."

There came a long silence. Clearly, he'd discovered her secret.

"It's all right," he told her. "You've made me feel much better. From now on, whenever I'm feeling sorry for myself, I shall imagine that I'm a European nobleman, brooding in his castle."

That made her laugh again, but Jack's thoughts had already turned serious. "You may go on reading your adventure stories, if you like, Leah. I wouldn't take your dreams away from you," he said, and then paused a long moment before he continued. "I am sorry to have brought you out to such a rustic life. I hadn't intended for it to be this way, you know. Cedar Creek was a comfortable town before the fire. I had a store, stocked full of sundries that a young girl like you would appreciate: hard candies, hair ribbons . . ."

"Yes, Charlotte's told me all about it. She says that I ought to be proud of you, that you're the head of the town council, the most important man in Cedar Creek. She said that you helped build the town into what it was before and that you're going to make it even better this time."

Jack's head lagged forward until his chin nearly touched his chest. He felt uncomfortable with Charlotte's praise and her faith in him. He wasn't so sure he could measure up any more.

"She may have been exaggerating a bit, for your sake," he said. "But do you think you'd like to stay here anyway?"

"I'll admit I was a little homesick at first. But then that's only natural, isn't it? Charlotte says I'll adjust. Charlotte says that a home is only what you make of it."

"You like her a lot, don't you?"

Leah's dark curls bobbed. "I've never met a woman like her before. She's different from Mrs. Brierson, my other teachers, and all of the ladies back home. She doesn't have spells or worry about getting her hands dirty or mussing her dress. And she isn't afraid of anything. I hope I can be like her one day."

Jack smiled at the ingenuous remark. "I'm sure she'd be pleased to hear that."

"She's teaching me to make bread, did you know? I got up very early with her this morning and helped her mix the dough. She says that one day soon she'll let me come with her when she goes to town. Won't that be nice?"

Jack caught himself before forming a reply. Here was the other reason why he hadn't complained about rusticating up here in the mountains. If he'd gone down to Cedar Creek, he'd have had to take Leah with him, and well, to be honest, he wasn't eager to do that.

He didn't know precisely how attractive his sister might be; although when he'd questioned Charlotte about it, she'd assured him that she was a lovely, young girl. A lovely girl of sixteen. A girl that age could have her head turned far too easily. And Jack was afraid that Leah would prove too much of a temptation for the lonely young men of Cedar Creek.

Why hadn't he thought of this before he'd sent for her? At the time, he'd only told himself that his sister needed to live at home, not in a school surrounded by strangers. But a lot had transpired since then. He'd seen what had happened when Charlotte first came to town, and he wasn't sure he had the stamina to go through all that again.

But he couldn't keep Leah hidden away up here forever. Sooner or later, they'd all be moving back to town. Suddenly, Jack had developed a greater appreciation for the situation Noah had endured only a few months before. Two women in one household meant too much worry for one man.

Shading her eyes with one hand, Charlotte pulled up on the bay mare's reins with the other, and surveyed the empty lot before her with satisfaction. The job was completed at last.

Every day for the past two weeks, she'd come to town. In the morning, she'd peddled her bread and the remainder of the goods she'd managed to salvage from the wreckage of Jack's store, but her afternoons were spent clearing rubble from the lots where the store and the bakery had been. All of Jack's friends had taken time from their own work to come by and offer their help; and finally, finally, it was finished.

"Good afternoon, Miz Cordell."

Charlotte turned in the saddle to see Hollis Lloyd ride up on his pinto. He'd told her once that he'd bought the sturdy Indian horse from a Ute trader because it was accustomed to mountain trails, and Hollis spent a lot of time hunting in the mountains. In fact, Charlotte decided that he must be heading out on a hunting trip now, for his carbine was tucked into the saddle boot.

"I was going to apologize for not coming out to help you today, but it seems as if you're just about done anyhow," he said, as his horse drew up beside hers.

"Henry Sutton and Mr. Fleming lent a hand to finish up," she explained. "We're ready to rebuild now. How about you, Mr. Lloyd? You're not thinking of packing up and leaving, are you?"

Lloyd shook his head. "Naw, this place is as good as any, far as I'm concerned. As long as I can make a go of it, I'll stay."

"Well, Jack will be glad to hear it. He's been worried that too many folk will be tempted to give up. I almost hate to tell him how many we've lost already."

"How is Jack, by the way?"

"Doctor Kelsey has ordered him to rest up, and he knows it's for the best. But he's champing at the bit. We won't be able to keep him away from Cedar Creek for too much longer."

"Well, you tell him that we're carryin' on in his absence. The Thorssen brothers have arranged for delivery of another load of lumber from Jamieson's sawmill. I'll be starting on my place as soon as I get back."

"Are you off on another hunting expedition?"

"Not exactly. I'm goin' to track the mountain lion that made off with two of the Widow Murphy's laying hens last night. Best to see to it right off, else that old cat'll be thinkin' that Cedar Creek is easy pickin's. And that fat turkey you're boardin' in Miz Kelsey's coop may be next."

"Well then, Mr. Lloyd, I would certainly be grateful to you if you tracked the beast down. There might even be one of my pies in it for you, if you're successful. I don't mean to be robbed of my Christmas dinner."

"Now there's a powerful incentive, if I do say so."

Grinning, Lloyd urged his mount forward and took his leave.

Charlotte studied the rubble and charred remains of the town for a long while before giving her heel to the mare. Reaching over, she patted her saddlebag, to assure herself that everything she would need was inside. She had made the right decision to go ahead with her plan, she told herself. If she waited too much longer, there might not be enough of Cedar Creek left to save.

Scattered to the south along the outskirts of town were prospect holes and piles of worthless chippings; the battered, wooden shaft houses and the headframes that supported hoisting works, now rusting from disuse; and beyond these, the tall, weathered gray building, tucked into the hillside beside the creek, that had once housed the stamp mill. As she rode past, Charlotte narrowed her eyes in order to read the fading letters that had been painted on signboards and headframes to identify each venture: the Ajax, the Evening Star, the Little Dora.

As the trail began to wind uphill, the mines no longer consisted of hoisting works and shafts, but rather tunnels that had been cut into the mountainside. These mines, too, had colorful names that hinted at the enthusiasm their owners must have felt when first they registered their claim: Bonanza, Bullion King, Lucky Strike.

Seeking inspiration, Charlotte cast her gaze here and there about the veritable graveyard of mines, until one particularly sorry tombstone caught her eye. It was a single board, tacking over a yawning, hillside opening, with the words "Last Hope" painted upon it.

Somehow that seemed genuinely appropriate to her. The action she'd contemplated might, indeed, prove to be Cedar Creek's "last hope." Dismounting, she tied her horse's reins to a nearby bush and gathered up the items she'd brought with her from the cabin: lantern, saddlebag, shotgun. She hesitated at the mine's opening for as long as it took to light the lantern, and then she went inside.

Holding it aloft against the shadowy darkness, she studied the rock walls on either hand and the support timbers that framed the tunnel. She was looking for fault lines in the rock or rotting timbers that might signal disaster, but her survey told her that all within seemed sturdy enough.

Hers was not altogether an untrained eye, for Charlotte—or rather young Charlie—had worked for months under the tutelage of two, skilled "old Californians": Vernon Taylor and Ira Jenkins. She noticed, for example, that the rock face bore bands of dingy yellow, but as she had learned early on, yellow wasn't the color of gold-bearing ore, nor was everything that glittered worth investigation either. More likely that would prove to be bits of mica or fool's gold. But upon closer examination, she also spotted rusty streaks, indications of iron compounds, which she'd been taught were the genuine signpost of gold. Nevertheless, the tunnel played out about one hundred and fifty feet into the mountainside. Evidently, the owners had decided that further effort was not worth the investment.

Charlotte set the lantern down at a safe distance to illuminate the chamber, then unbuckled her saddlebag and drew out a small pick and the bandana containing the heavy pieces of blossom rock that she'd taken from Jack's miner's pack. It had seemed to her to be some kind of sign that she ought to put her plan into action when she'd remembered about those samples of his.

He wouldn't miss them, she assured herself, as she eyed a particular promising chunk. He hadn't once touched the pack that she'd brought up to the cabin. She'd long since decided that as he was such a sensible sort, he was probably ashamed of the fact that he'd caught gold fever and gone off to California. To this day, he'd never mentioned the pack to her . . . or that part of his past.

No, he wouldn't miss these souvenir pieces of blossom rock. They weren't worth much on their own, anyway, but if they should be found by the right person, in a promising mine, and then assayed, they might just provide the impetus that Cedar Creek needed for its revival.

Thus decided, Charlotte scattered them across the chamber floor. Next, she drew her rawhide pouch out of the saddlebag, took up Jack's old shotgun, and loaded it with gold dust. Carefully, she chose her angle, took aim and fired at the wall.

The shot was deafening and roared through the tunnel with a force that stunned her. She cringed as she heard loose rocks skittering through the smoky gloom. The support timbers hadn't budged at all, though. They would have had to have been built to withstand the black powder blasting that was vital to hard rock mining. One gunshot would be hardly more than a sneeze by comparison.

Once the air had cleared sufficiently, Charlotte reloaded, using up the last of her gold dust. It was for a worthy cause, she reminded herself, and again, took aim.

The sun had set by the time Jack finally heard the stamp of horse's hooves and the creak of the corral gate that told him that Charlotte had returned at last. From his chair on the porch, he breathed a long, low sigh of relief.

The full moon that was rising now provided light nearly as bright as daylight, but just the same, he had been concerned. Charlotte had never returned so late before. While he'd been waiting, he'd driven himself half crazy with worry. Anything might have happened to her on the trail between here and town. She might have been thrown from her horse and been lying in the dust somewhere, unable to summon help. She might have been accosted by a drunken miner—there were certainly enough of them haunting the back trails in these mountains—or any one of the renegade Cheyenne, who hadn't gone south with the rest of their tribe.

Good Lord, his imagination was becoming nearly as vivid as Leah's. But he could put all those silly notions aside now, for here Charlotte was, coming up the path. His vision was surprisingly clear tonight; it must have been on account of the bright moonlight. He could make out the glint of her gold hair and the willowy frame. She was clad in the pink dress that Rachel had lent her after the fire. There was something dark thrown across her shoulder, a saddlebag, he thought it must be, and she was carrying a lantern and another object in her hand. A staff? An axe handle? No, it was . . . his shotgun.

"Good evening," he said, clambering to his feet and reaching out to one of the upright posts for support as she approached the porch.

"Oh!" She sounded surprised to see him there, and more than a little startled. "I . . . I didn't expect for you to be waiting out here for me."

"It was late," he explained. "I was worried. Is that my shotgun you're carrying?"

"You can see this far? Is your vision improving then?"

"The moonlight's softer on my eyes, I find. But you haven't answered the question, Charlotte."

"I . . . I, uhm, well," she stammered, "when I was coming back from town the other day, I . . . thought that I heard something . . . yes, something in the rocks just above the trail, and then . . . then there came an ear-splitting yowl. The horse was spooked; it took me some time to calm her. I think it might have been a mountain lion."

At that moment, Jack wished that he could see her face. She sounded peculiar somehow, but without reading her expression, he couldn't be sure if it weren't only his perception. His nerves had been awfully jangled by all the waiting and speculating he'd done.

"You know what a terrible shot I am," she continued. "I thought it would be easier to hit something, if I had to, with your shotgun. So I took it along with me. I hope you don't mind. I suppose I ought to have asked."

"No, no. I'm glad that you're being cautious."

With that, Jack settled back down in his chair, remembering the reason he'd come out to wait for her in the first place. "Can we talk for a minute?" he asked.

"Have you had your supper yet?"

Jack shook his head. "I brought home a string of catfish today. Leah's inside now, frying them up. She wants to impress you, I think, with all she's learned."

"Well, I won't bother her then. I'll just put away these things, and afterward, I'll come out, and you and I can have our talk."

She left him alone then, and Jack used the time to go over in his head precisely what he wanted to say. He'd been plotting and planning for weeks, trying to hit upon just the right scheme, a venture that would not only be profitable, but easy for him to manage, even if he should never be restored to the man that he once was. And finally, he believed that he'd found it.

Charlotte swept back out of the cabin, hung her lantern from a nail on one of the posts, and drawing up beside Jack, she set a tin washbasin in his lap. There were several items laid within it, but he wasn't able to focus his eyes well enough to recognize any of them. By running his fingers lightly over each, though, he was able to identify a comb, a pair of scissors, and the fancy metal flask that held his hair oil.

"What's all this?" he asked her.

"Your hair is getting rather shaggy, I'm afraid," she explained, "and since our barber has gone off to seek his fortune elsewhere, it's up to me to tend to it."

Shaking out the towel she'd carried with her, she fastened it around his neck like a cape. "There now," she said. "I'll clip while we talk. You won't mind that, will you?"

Jack looked up at her and grinned, in spite of himself. Charlotte had a way of barreling into a situation like a steam locomotive.

"Well, that depends," he told her.

"Depends? Depends on what?"

"On whether you've any experience at this. You might

nick an earlobe, you know, and I'm not up to dealing with any more bodily injuries just now, no matter how trivial."

"I used to trim my father's hair, as a matter of fact," she retorted. "I've shaved you every morning since the accident, and I haven't cut your throat yet, have I? You mean to say you don't trust me with a simple pair of scissors?"

"Now, don't get testy. I was only teasing."

Jack deduced that she hadn't forgiven him entirely when she asked him to tip his head back and then proceeded to dump the entire contents of the pitcher of water, which she'd brought out, on him.

He came up sputtering. "What'd you do that for?"

Coolly as ever, she began to run the comb through his hair. "It's easier to cut when it's wet," she said. "Didn't you know that?"

Jack cast her a sidelong glance and used the towel to blot away the droplets of water that were scattered across his face. Charlotte ignored his reaction, and taking up the scissors, she set to work, snipping at his hair.

Theirs was an unusual relationship, Jack thought to himself; it ran the gamut from antagonism to amusement. Still, they both seemed to be careful at all times to avoid revealing any hint of their true feelings, and he wondered how much longer they'd be able to keep it up.

Snip, snip.

"Now, what was it you wanted to talk about?"

"I've been thinking about what that railroad fellow said when he came through here a few months back, about the sort of things our town ought to have . . ."

Snip, snip.

"Why should it matter to us what he thinks?" Charlotte asked, sounding oddly defensive.

"Because he's the man who's going to decide whether or not the rail line runs through Cedar Creek," he explained, trying to be patient, "and so long as we've got to rebuild anyway, I thought that I might try something different this time."

Snip, snip.

"But what about the general store? What will people do for all the goods they'll need?"

Jack hesitated before replying, and then expelled a deep breath. She didn't mean to be tiresome. After all, she had no way of knowing where he was heading with this.

"It's been pointed out to me recently that a lame, blind man might have a difficult time running a general store. Besides, Henry Sutton's been talking for a long time about expanding his inventory. There's no reason why he can't stock all the goods we need."

With this, Charlotte's scissors stilled. "And what about you, Jack? What will you do?"

She was worried that he'd lost his interest in Cedar Creek. He could sense it in her tone.

"I'm going to build a hotel."

"Really?"

He nodded. Was he only imagining the enthusiasm in her voice? Or could it be that she cared more than she'd let on?

"I thought that we'd run it together. I'd handle the guests, and you could manage the kitchen. There's be plenty for Leah to do, too. The town will need a good hotel once the railroad comes through."

Her hand fluttered down and settled on his shoulder.

"Oh, Jack."

She was standing close behind him now, and he was vividly aware of her touch. The heat of her fingers seeped through the towel and the fabric of his shirt, and warmed the skin beneath.

Jack felt the need, that he'd been ignoring for too long, begin to well in him anew, and heedless of the consequences, he reached up and laid his hand over hers. She didn't pull away.

"What is it, Charlotte?"

"I . . ."

For a brief, thrilling moment, he thought she would reveal herself, but then all at once, she slipped from his grasp, and snatching the basin from his lap, she tossed her tools into it and turned to leave.

With a deftness that he'd not possessed since the accident, Jack tugged off the towel that had been wrapped around his neck and tossed it aside. Springing to his feet, he reached out, and hooking her by the waist, he dragged her against him.

What happened next, he could not account for. Charlotte felt so frail in his arms, and yet she had the power to overwhelm him completely. He was only aware of the heat of her body, her ragged intake of breath, the soft slide of her breasts against his chest. He inhaled sharply and caught the scent of roses; her scent, and afterward, all was lost.

His lips descended on hers, drinking in her sweetness like a man too long deprived. In an instant, he was reminded of all that he'd been missing. It was a damned fool's bargain that they had made, agreeing to fashion themselves a marriage without passion, and he couldn't for the life of him remember now just what the reasons were behind it.

It pleased him to note that Charlotte did not resist him. Her mouth was warm and pliant beneath his, her arms coiled around his neck. She seemed to be caught up in the strange fever, too. The basin she'd been carrying slipped out of her fingers, but the clang and clatter sounded far off in the distance as its contents spilled out onto the porch and the basin rolled away.

Excitement pulsed through Jack's blood in a heated rush. He hadn't felt so alive in weeks. He wanted to tell her, to put into words all that he was feeling, but he was afraid that if he stopped kissing her, the spell would be broken.

Alas, it was inevitable that the world should intrude upon them.

"Supper's ready!" he heard his sister call from within, and in response, he and Charlotte stilled simultaneously and then drew apart.

Jack counted it as a victory that she did not rush off at once, but instead wandered to the far end of the porch and propped one shoulder against the post. He drew up behind her, not daring to touch her again. The mood had changed now. Everything seemed different.

"I . . . I think it's a good idea, Jack," she said, but for the life of him he could not be certain of whether she meant the hotel they'd been talking about . . . or something else entirely.

Sixteen

Jack must have been eager to put his plans to build a hotel into action because the very next morning, he rose before Charlotte had even a chance to take her bread out of the oven, and after he'd put on a clean, striped shirt with his vest and trousers, he announced that he'd be accompanying her into town.

It was, by far, the most enthusiasm he'd shown since the accident, and that gave her hope, at least. Although she hadn't dared admit it, she'd missed the old Jack, who'd been so easygoing, confident, and sure of his dreams.

Lately, Charlotte had felt obliged to walk around her husband on tiptoe, never sure of his mood from one minute to the next. But last night she'd gotten a glimpse of the man he used to be—oh, much more than a glimpse, if truth be told—and she swore to herself that she'd do anything to have him back again.

Of course, when Leah discovered that her brother had made plans to go to town, she protested against being left behind alone, and so before Charlotte had realized, her daily run into town had turned into a family excursion.

Only a few days before, Jack had fashioned a less cumbersome splint for his leg, and so, when they were ready to leave at last, he lashed his crutches to the saddle and was able to hoist himself up, with only a minimum of assistance from Charlotte.

She'd already put the bread she planned to sell into

sacks, which she proceeded to tie to her saddlehorn, and then, once she'd mounted the bay mare, she gave Leah a hand, settling before her in the saddle. Instructing the girl to hang on tight, she gave the mare her heel, and they were on their way.

For her part, Charlotte wasn't convinced that Jack was ready for riding just yet, but she dared not voice her fears and risk destroying his newfound confidence. She merely took the lead so that he'd have an object to train his damaged eyes upon, then set a deliberate, leisurely pace, and offered up a silent prayer that Jack's horse would prove keen-eyed and sure-footed enough for them both.

The breeze that swept down from the mountains on this particular morning was crisp and laced with the scent of pine. There was a definite chill in the air. It raised goose-flesh on Charlotte's arms and caused her to expel a soft sigh of regret. Much as she'd come to love this country, she still thought that fall came too quickly here. She wasn't ready to face a change in seasons just yet. There was far too much work to be done before the snow came.

Jack's hotel had to be built and the rest of the town's reconstruction completed, and there was the next step in her plans for a gold strike to consider. She'd already set the stage for that. Now, she had only to choose the actor who'd perform the starring role in her little drama, and there wasn't any time to waste.

The Cordells didn't encounter a single soul on the ride into town, excepting the usual number of playful chipmunks scampering over the rocks and a startled jackrabbit that dashed across their path. Jack seemed hardly aware of their surroundings, though, for he spent the entire journey regaling Charlotte and Leah with his plans.

The hotel would be called The Mountain View, he told them. He envisioned it as a modest, two-story clapboard structure, painted white with green shutters and a veranda running its whole length. There'd be ten upstairs guest rooms, and on the main floor: a kitchen, a dining hall, a parlor, and the lobby. They might have to invest in a horsehair sofa and a pair of marble-topped tables for the parlor, in order to give the place some dignity, but otherwise it was to be a down-to-earth establishment.

By the time they neared the town, Jack had painted such a clear picture of the place that Charlotte almost expected to see it standing there on Main Street. But when she looked up, there wasn't any such fanciful structure, nor any signs at all of life in Cedar Creek, except for Hollis Lloyd, who was riding down the dusty street toward them.

"Good morning, Mr. Lloyd," she called out as he approached, her voice a bit louder than it might have been ordinarily. She wanted Jack to have no confusion as to whom she was addressing, though, just in case he couldn't see him well enough for himself.

"Good morning to you, Miz Cordell. And who is that pretty young lady there with you? Why, it must be Jack's sister. We heard you'd come for a visit."

Before either Charlotte or Leah could reply, Jack urged his horse up beside theirs, putting him squarely between Hollis Lloyd and the women.

"Yes, Hollis. This is my *baby* sister, Leah."

Charlotte thought that he'd perhaps put too much emphasis on the word. Leah certainly didn't take it well. She'd let go an irritated little huff and squirmed in her place.

Lloyd offered one of those flashing grins of his, swept the dusty, felt hat from his head and bowed low in the saddle. "I'm right pleased to meet you, Miss Leah."

Leah nodded, shyly averting her eyes. "And I, you, Mr. Lloyd."

Jack squared his jaw and scowled at their exchange, and Charlotte had to press her lips tightly together to stifle a smile. He looked like an overprotective papa. It was apparent that he wasn't pleased by the attention that Hollis Lloyd was paying his sister.

"Have you come across that wildcat yet?" Charlotte asked Lloyd, endeavoring to change the subject.

"No, ma'am. I'm afraid I haven't. But I haven't forgotten that pie you've promised me once I taken care of the problem."

"Wildcat, you say?" Jack put in, not wanting to be left out of the conversation. "Funny thing, Charlotte mentioned a wildcat just last night. She said she thought she'd heard one when she was riding back up to the cabin."

Leah stiffened in her seat, and Charlotte couldn't help but feel responsible for the poor child's distress. Why did she have to mention that wildcat? Until now, Leah had done a fine job of setting aside all the fears her vivid imagination had conjured up, but now they appeared to be rising anew.

"You heard it?" Lloyd echoed. "Whereabouts?"

Charlotte paled. She'd only told Jack that little white lie in order to explain why she'd been carrying his shotgun. But after considerable thought, she realized that the two men were handing her the perfect opportunity to put the next phase of her plan into operation.

"It was up near those abandoned mines in the foothills," she explained carefully, "right near the spot where the trail twists back on itself. Now that you come to mention it, I thought I even caught a glimpse of the creature. Mind you, I'm not sure of it, but I thought I did. Before I could get a closer look, though, he'd disappeared into one of those old, mine tunnels."

Lloyd's interest was piqued. "You don't happen to remember which tunnel that would be, do you? Most of them mines up there have names, you know."

"Well, yes, as a matter of fact, I do remember. I drew up and waited there for a moment, just to be sure that that cat hadn't somehow got up in the rocks ahead of me, and when I looked up over the tunnel where he'd gone in, I saw a signboard painted with the name. 'Last Hope,' I think it was. You don't suppose it's made its den in there, do you?"

Lloyd shrugged. "Could be. I'll go on up directly and check it out."

With this, Leah let go a small whimper.

"Oh, now, you needn't fret any, Miss Leah," Lloyd said and slapped the saddle boot where he kept his trusty carbine. "If that big old cat is up there, I'll see to it he won't be stealin' no more chickens.

He tipped his hat, and then rode off, and casting a backward glance, Charlotte couldn't help but notice how wide and round Leah's pretty, gray eyes got as she watched the burly hunter ride off.

Meanwhile, Jack's scowl deepened, and as if sensing his master's irritation, his mount tossed its head, and stamping restlessly, pawed at the earth. Jerking on the reins, Jack began to mutter to himself.

Charlotte wasn't sure she'd heard the words aright, but they sounded to her very much like a threat: "Just let him try and lay one hand on my sister, and I *will* kick his sorry ass halfway down the canyon."

Considering Jack's distaste for Hollis Lloyd, it might not have been wise for Charlotte to have chosen him to play the pivotal role in her little scheme. But then Lloyd was the perfect sort of man for what she had in mind: hard working and energetic, but also a trifle greedy and not too bright. And she hadn't really had time to think about it, had she? The situation had presented itself, and it had all worked out so perfectly that Charlotte was left to wonder if there weren't a divine hand offering her assistance.

Ah, but would the Almighty approve of salting a gold mine? Charlotte shook off her disquiet, reminding herself that whatever she had done, it was only to save Cedar

Creek. But it was too late for second thoughts now, at any rate. The scheme had already been set in motion. All she had to do now was wait.

Jack slid out of the saddle and retrieved his crutches soon after the horses drew up before the lot where his store had been. He didn't want anyone to witness Charlotte helping him to dismount or leading him around like an invalid. He'd have to manage on his own, after all, if he was going to make a go of this new venture of his.

Charlotte dismounted as well, then reached up to hand Leah the mare's reins. "You go on over to Mrs. Kelsey's," she told her. "You remember, the place we visited on your first day here? They'll be expecting us. Take the bread sacks into the kitchen. Everyone who needs to buy has been coming there. Do you think you can handle the sales for me today?"

Leah's pale eyes sparkled with enthusiasm, the brim of her sunbonnet bobbing as she shook her head. "Yes. Yes, I'll manage. Don't you worry."

"Just ask Mrs. Kelsey or Mrs. Murphy for help, if you need any."

As he watched his sister ride off, Jack thought how grateful he was that Charlotte had taken such pains to see that the girl was settling in comfortably. She'd already taught her to ride, given her beginning instructions on cooking and laundry, and various other, practical skills that Mrs. Brierson's Academy had not deemed important to a lady's upbringing. But as Jack was already learning, his wife had been gifted with infinite patience. After all, she'd put up with him, day after day, hadn't she?

Propping himself on his crutches, he prepared to make a cursory survey of his property. There was still a lot of cleanup work that needed to be done before construction could begin. He'd already proven that he couldn't do the job single-handedly, and he certainly couldn't expect his friends to do it for him.

Lending a neighbor a hand was one thing, but building a hotel was no small undertaking, and they all had to tend to their own interests. He'd have to wire his banker in Denver to hire a crew of carpenters, just as he had when he'd built his store.

Tugging the brim of his hat lower across his eyes, Jack studied the scene more closely. His vision was a bit less blurred when he was able to shut out the glare, but nevertheless, he had to blink more than once to assure himself of the sight that met his eyes. Someone had been at work here. The stands of charred timbers that had stood on this spot only a few weeks ago had been removed and most of the rubble cleared away.

"Nearly everyone helped," Charlotte explained as she came to stand at his elbow, "and I did a little myself, each day. We've been ferrying out rubble from all over town by the wagonload and using it to fill in some of those old prospect holes."

She expected him to be pleased that she had taken his place and done her share of the work, standing shoulder-to-shoulder with the townsmen. God knows, maybe he ought to have been, but all he could think about was how useless it made him feel and how sorry they all must have felt for poor Jack.

Charlotte had gotten too used to playing the man's role, a rebellious voice within him warned. She didn't know what was expected of her anymore. Before he could even react to her revelation, though, she reached for his hand. Turning it over, she drew a leather coin pouch out of her apron pocket and placed it in his upturned palm.

"There's close to one hundred and fifty dollars there," she told him. "It's the profits from my bake shop, and what I've managed to salvage and sell from your store and the bread I've been baking."

Jack straightened his back and squared his jaw. "I've money enough of my own, Charlotte."

"But I want to contribute something toward the building of our hotel. You did mean that we should be partners in this, didn't you?"

He told himself that she meant well, and somehow, he managed to hold his temper and his tongue. It struck him, though, that Charlotte didn't know precisely what sort of a partnership a marriage was meant to be, nor understand the difference between what was expected of a husband and a wife.

It was for him to provide the support, to care for her and keep her safe. Her contribution was not supposed to be monetary. She was supposed to make a home for them and offer him comfort, when he needed it. Yet how much comfort could there be in the practical, passionless partnership that was their marriage?

It mightn't have been that way. Jack had felt that last night when he'd kissed her. She was willing for there to be more between them, even if, as he suspected, she wasn't sure precisely what was entailed. No, he couldn't blame Charlotte. This sorry fix was all his fault. It was he who'd stood there on their wedding night, wrapped up in his wounded pride, and set the boundaries of their relationship.

A part of him had genuinely thought it for the best at the time. It wouldn't have been right to bind her to him for life, if she only meant to be his nursemaid. But if he'd been wrong, if her feelings ran deeper than that, then perhaps he had made a grievous error. He wondered then if it was too late to change things.

He thought about how long it would be before this damned leg of his was mended. Two more weeks? Three? Surely his sight would have begun to improve by then. And at length, he decided. As soon as he could walk to her on his own two feet and see into those brilliant blue eyes of hers, he'd take back all that he said about "bargains" and insist upon a real marriage.

"Jack?" Charlotte prompted him.

Curling his fingers around the heavy, money pouch, he offered her the warmest smile he could muster. "I'm sorry. I suppose I've too much on my mind today. This contribution of yours will help us to make a fine start."

"So we're partners then?"

He met her with a firm nod. "Nothing less."

Nothing less, he'd told her. But maybe, with time and a little luck and a concerted effort on his part, just maybe, something more.

"Charlotte! Charlotte, come quick!"

At the sound of his sister's anxious voice, Jack looked up to see Leah, still astride the bay mare and bouncing in the saddle as she trotted towards them at an awkwardly slow pace. Leah hadn't learned how to manage a gallop yet.

Charlotte lifted her skirts and sprinted down the street to meet her halfway, while Jack could only gather up his crutches and trail along after her.

"What is it? What's wrong?" he heard her ask.

"It's Mrs. Kelsey. She's going to have her baby, and she wants you to come."

Considering the sort of life she'd led, Charlotte hadn't had much experience with babies, or the birthing process. Nevertheless, after a number of hours had passed without a perceptible change in Rachel's condition, Charlotte thought that her friend was being made to suffer for far too long.

When she came out to the kitchen to voice her fears to Noah, though, he assured her that everything was perfectly normal and that eight or even ten hours wouldn't be an unusual wait for the appearance of a first child.

The Widow Murphy, who'd brought three healthy sons of her own into the world, looked up from her place at the dishpan, where she and Leah were scrubbing up the supper dishes, and readily concurred.

Charlotte had to concede to the argument of those of greater authority. Still, by the time the sun had set that evening, she was certain she must have worn her shoe leather clean through what with all the trips she'd made from the chair she'd sat in while she kept Rachel company, to the bedside, then out to the kitchen to express her continuing concern to the others before going back to Rachel once again.

And all the while, she was wishing that there was something more that she could do for her friend besides bathe her fevered brow with a damp cloth, clasp her hand, and offer up meaningless words of comfort.

Not that Rachel wasn't holding up well enough on her own. If she hadn't already earned Charlotte's admiration a long time before, she'd have won it that day. Hour after hour, she endured the pains contorting her swollen body with quiet acceptance—the beads of perspiration strung across her brow and an occasional, breathy moan were the only indications of her distress. She even managed to conjure a smile now and again to assure her friend that she was faring well, under the circumstances.

Periodically, Noah came in to check his wife's condition, but doctor or not, he seemed to Charlotte to be as nervous as any other husband, and preferred to spend most of the waiting time outside, pacing the length of the front porch.

When he finally came into the room to check on Rachel and rolled up his sleeves instead of walking back out again, Charlotte knew the time had come. She made a move to leave, but Noah invited her to stay and help him, if she'd like. Of course, she agreed, and afterward, she was glad that she had.

What she witnessed affected her profoundly and left her with a lump in her throat and hot tears pooling in her eyes. Never before had she felt so sharply what it meant to be a woman, nor realized how sacred was the bond between husband and wife that it should bring about such a miracle.

Benjamin Thomas Kelsey, named for both of his grandfathers, came into the world with a lusty cry. He was round, ruddy, and perfectly-formed in every way, and after his mother had had the chance to look him over, Noah handed him to Charlotte, so that she might wash him up and dress him in the tiny robe and shawl that his mother had so lovingly stitched for him.

Charlotte could not remember ever having held a baby before, but the moment Noah placed him in her arms, it seemed like the most natural thing in the world. His downy head fit neatly into the crook of her elbow, his body settling along the curve of her forearm.

So, while Noah tended his wife, Charlotte carried the baby to the washbasin and placed him in the water, which set off a new round of wailing. She washed him gingerly, handling him as if he were a fragile piece of porcelain, and while she went about her work, her instincts took over and she found herself cooing at him and patting him in order to soothe him.

He was the most beautiful thing Charlotte had ever set eyes on, and happy as she was for Rachel, all the while she tended the babe, her heart was breaking. She'd always thought herself a hardened individual. She wouldn't have expected to feel this way. Until this very moment, in fact, she'd never realized just how much she wanted to share a normal life, a normal marriage with Jack.

But then that wasn't likely to happen. Their marriage was nothing but a sham. Jack didn't love her. How could he, knowing what she'd been before? He had wed her only to save her reputation. An "honest bargain," isn't that what he'd called it? And she had selfishly agreed to his terms because although she was afraid of getting close to him, she cared too much to let him go. It was an impossible dilemma.

After she'd dressed the baby and returned him to Rachel, Charlotte stood back to look upon the pleasing picture that the Kelsey family made, with the child in his mother's arms and the beaming papa looking on, and she realized how wrong she'd been to allow her fears to keep her from trying to make things work with Jack.

It was possible she had already spoiled her chances for any kind of happiness at all with him. She'd pushed him away too many times for him to trust her now. *But then what had happened between us last night had seemed to be a positive step,* a desperate voice inside her argued. Maybe Jack's reluctance to get close to her hadn't been on account of anything she'd done. Maybe now that he was making plans, now that he had his confidence back, there might be hope. . . .

Charlotte was still considering that possibility half an hour later as she sat out on the porch steps in the cool, evening air, waiting for Jack to return. Earlier, he'd called together the members of the council for a meeting to discuss the business of rebuilding, and they'd all gathered at the livery to discuss the work that was already in progress, to exchange ideas and make plans.

"Oh, here you are," Leah said, as she pushed open the screen door and then came to sit beside her. "I wondered where you'd gotten off to."

"Just having a moment's rest," Charlotte explained. "It's been a hectic day."

"Isn't Mrs. Kelsey's baby the sweetest thing you've ever seen?"

A wistful smile curved on Charlotte's lips as she agreed with her sister-in-law.

"And I'll bet you've been sitting out here and thinking how much you'd like one of your own, haven't you?"

Charlotte regarded the girl, her eyes widening in surprise. "Oh, no. That wasn't what I was thinking at all. I . . ."

Her voice trailed off and a blush warmed her cheeks. The truth was that she had, indeed, felt a powerful urge as she'd cradled Rachel's son in her arms. But how could she even begin to think of having children, afraid as she was of intimacy? And besides, she wasn't even sure of Jack's feelings. And with things as they were . . .

Leah seemed to sense the turmoil within her. A frown creased her pale brow. "It's my fault that you and Jack haven't had any time alone," she put in suddenly, "and that you're sharing your bed with me instead of him. Maybe I oughtn't to have come to Colorado. Maybe it would be better if I went back home."

"You mustn't say that." Placing an arm around the girl's slight shoulders, Charlotte drew her closer. "This is your home now, and Jack and I are both happy that you're here with us."

"I know it's hard having me around. I can see the strain I'm causing between the two of you. You scarcely talk to one another, you never touch . . ."

Charlotte looked away quickly, startled by the revelation. She hadn't considered what Leah might think of the situation between her and Jack. She supposed she'd assumed that a child wouldn't pay such things any notice, but as she'd discovered, Leah was much more than a child. She was a perceptive, young woman, who was blaming herself for things that had nothing whatsoever to do with her.

"You mustn't feel responsible for anything that happens between your brother and me," Charlotte told her. "Making a marriage takes a lot of hard work, and there are bound to be some problems along the way. But it's nothing to do with your living with us.

"And as for giving up his bed, you know that Jack can't

climb the ladder into the loft just now anyway. Believe me, there'll be plenty of time for us to start a family of our own. So, I don't want to hear any more talk from you about leaving. You're already a part of our family."

Charlotte gave Leah a hug, then drew back to search the girl's face for a sign that she'd convinced her that all would be well. She certainly hoped that she had. Maybe that would help Charlotte to convince herself.

It wasn't the jangling of harnesses nor the heavy thud of hoofbeats in the dust that made Charlotte lift her head only a few moments later to see the Thorssens' wagon rumbling up the street; it was the sound of at least half a dozen, boisterous male voices, raised in song.

Charlotte spotted several familiar faces, illuminated by the moonlight: Lars and Gunnar, Gus Stern, Henry Sutton, Nate Phillips, and of course, her husband, Jack. The lot of them were grinning like half-wits, and as they approached, she could have sworn she saw the newspaper editor, Mr. Phillips, thrust a half empty whiskey bottle behind his back.

"Good evening, ladies," one of the brothers called as the wagon drew up to the Kelsey house.

"Good evening," Charlotte replied, dusting off her skirts as she got to her feet. "Have you all come by to congratulate the proud papa?"

Jack eased himself down from the wagonbed, propped his crutches up under his arms, and taking a step forward, swayed ominously.

"D'you mean to say the baby's come already?"

He'd been drinking. Unless Charlotte missed her guess, they all had, and she couldn't help but wonder what could cause the entire town council to abandon the important business they'd met to discuss and get themselves so thoroughly soused.

Planting her hands on her hips, she glowered at her husband. "Poor Rachel's been laboring for nearly ten hours, for heaven's sake. You wouldn't have thought it such an easy trick, Jack Cordell, if you'd been the one giving birth."

The wagonload of men found this thought particularly amusing, hooting and guffawing until Charlotte feared that one or more of them was bound to tumble out.

"It's a baby boy," Leah put in, brightly. "He arrived about half an hour ago, and his name is Benjamin Thomas Kelsey."

The men cheered with approval and someone called for Noah to come out and have a drink with them. Meanwhile, Jack turned back to his friends. "Well now, gentlemen, it seems we've yet another reason to celebrate tonight."

"Another reason?" Charlotte echoed, suddenly more confused than ever.

Looking very pleased with himself, Jack gave an exaggerated nod. "Do you remember this morning when you directed Hollis Lloyd to that old mine tunnel to look for that wildcat?" he said. "Well, he didn't find it."

Charlotte cocked a brow and regarded her husband more closely. He wasn't making any sense. Whatever was it he was trying to say? And then slowly, it began to dawn on her.

"What . . . did he find?" she asked, not daring to hope.

Jack leaned forward, his nearly useless eyes gleaming with a feverish excitement. "Gold!"

Seventeen

The rush was on. All it took was a whisper of "gold," and every hopeful prospector within a hundred miles came running. The Pike's Peak gold rush had not lived up to people's expectations, but the hardiest folk hadn't given up hope just yet. As word spread, more and more of them came to think that maybe Cedar Creek would be the place to make their fortune, and so, packing up their meager belongings, they came to see for themselves.

Before the month was out, there were more than five hundred souls crowded into the little valley, exploring old shafts, digging new ones. Cedar Creek went from a burnt-out wreck to a hodge-podge of shanties, canvas tents and hastily-constructed wooden buildings, the air thick with the scent of newly-sawn pine, and alive, dawn till dusk, with the clamor of construction.

Oddly enough, the gold ore that Hollis Lloyd hacked out of the tunnel he'd rechristened the Wildcat Mine hadn't proved as rich as those first few samples. But by then no one seemed to notice, and near the beginning of October, much to the surprise of everyone (and most especially Charlotte), he struck a rich vein of silver, and within only a few short weeks, he'd become a man of means.

Silver. Who would have guessed it? The first prospectors who'd arrived here some six years ago had been so intent on finding gold that they'd only cursed the heavy, black sand that filled their pans, sluices and long toms, casting it aside without ever stopping to realize the fortune that they were overlooking.

And so Cedar Creek became a silver town. Eager representatives from the stamp mills and smelting works in established mining towns arrived soon thereafter, eager to buy up as much rich ore as could be mined, and before too much time had passed, a group of investors came down from Denver and decided it might be worth their while to reopen the old stamp mill that stood just outside of town.

Businessmen followed in the wake of the prospectors, adding to the variety of goods and services available. Before too long, the citizens of Cedar Creek were able to boast of their own grist mill, tinsmith, half a dozen carpenters' shops, two laundries, four saloons, a saw mill . . . and a church, with a tall, white-painted steeple.

In the center of it all stood the Mountain View Hotel, a two-story clapboard building with green shutters and a wide veranda, just the way Jack had said it would be. The first time she stepped over the threshold, Charlotte could scarcely believe her eyes. She'd never imagined anything so grand, even with all her husband's promises.

There was a peculiar mingling of hope and fear within her at the thought that things might change between the two of them once they'd moved into the big, second floor bedroom with the balcony that overlooked Main Street. But on their very first night under their new roof, Jack retired to the adjacent dressing room, where he'd set up a cot for himself.

Confused as she was about their relationship, Charlotte wasn't sure whether she ought to be relieved or disappointed. But in the end, it was disappointment that rushed in to fill the empty place in her heart. She supposed she shouldn't have expected anything else. Jack had never promised her more than a home of her own and the freedom that she'd once told him she so desperately required.

"It'll be better, for now," was all he'd said as he left her.

For now. Those two, small words left her some hope yet.

Eventually, they settled into a routine. Jack took charge of the front desk and engaged old man Fleming to tend to the odd jobs that needed doing. Leah cleaned up after the guests, and with the help of a hired girl that Jack had arranged to help out part-time, Charlotte managed the dining room and kitchen, as well as their new flock of laying hens and a milk cow.

Under Jack's direction, Charlotte also kept the books and saw to the paperwork, gaining more confidence in her business skills with each day that passed.

All of Jack's carefully-laid plans had finally come to fruition. His hotel had been built, and business was brisk. Cedar Creek was a real town now, peopled not only with miners, but with women and children and families. And it had all come about because of Charlotte's outright manipulation of circumstance.

Questionable though her methods may have been, she wasn't sorry that she'd done it. Somehow, though, she had thought that she and Jack would be happy once everything had fallen into place. Unfortunately, nothing had turned out quite as she'd expected. Cedar Creek was no longer the calm, peaceful place that it had been. The town was bustling, dirty, and overrun with strangers, and she and Jack were farther apart than ever. . . .

Charlotte sensed Jack's apprehension about the council meeting that was to be held that night. He'd been distracted and short-tempered all morning. Changes had to be made in the local government; no one could argue with that. With the growth of the town, there were more decisions that needed to be made, more work that needed doing, and so, the members of the town council were gathering to vote to appoint a mayor.

Jack wanted the position. Charlotte knew it, even if he'd never told her so outright. He'd worked hard to help to build this town; it had always been his dream to make it into a thriving community. Even after the fire, he'd never lost faith. It was he who'd convinced everyone to stay on when things looked bleak. He deserved this position, she told herself. He simply had to be appointed. After all that he'd been through, it would provide a much-needed boost to his battered self-esteem.

The council meeting was to be held in her dining room, after the last meal of the day was served, and so Charlotte took special care to straighten the landscape pictures hanging on the wall, polish the sideboard, and wipe down each of the tables. She'd only gotten halfway through that chore, though, when Hollis Lloyd swaggered into the room.

He'd changed since striking it rich. There was a new boldness about him. It no longer seemed to matter that he wasn't as polished nor as educated as some of the other townsmen. In his elegantly-cut black wool frock coat with the velvet collar and heavy links of a solid gold watch chain draped across the bosom of a satin brocade vest, he looked every inch a "bonanza king." And as was evidenced by his attitude, he had come to the conclusion that he no longer had anything of which to be ashamed.

Sweeping the black felt hat with the braided silver band from his head, he sat himself down at the very table where Charlotte was working, eased back in his chair, and flashed her his even-toothed smile.

"Good evenin' to you, Miz Cordell. I'm a mite early, I guess."

"Just make yourself at home," she told him, as if he hadn't already done so. "The others should be here shortly."

With that, Charlotte moved on to the next table, very much aware that Lloyd's eyes were following her as she went. Harmless as she believed him to be, it still made her uneasy. She never seemed to know just what to say to him.

"Have you heard about the house I'm havin' built on that plot of high ground across the creek?" he asked, after a protracted moment of silence. "I hired an architect to come all the way from New York City and make up the plans. It's goin' to be three stories tall and made of red brick, with marble fireplaces and some of them long, fancy windows and carved cornice pieces and everythin'."

"I hope you'll be happy there," she replied, but continued to concentrate on wiping down each of the bottles in the caster on the table where she worked.

"We haven't seen much of you around town since this place opened up," he remarked next. "Jack keeping you busy, is he?"

Charlotte stopped her work long enough to slant him an impatient glance. "You ought to know very well what I've been up to, Mr. Lloyd, seeing as you've come in here every night this week for supper."

She went back to what she'd been doing, but stiffened when she heard first the scraping of wood as he pushed back his chair and the click of his bootheels on the floorboards as he came to stand behind her.

"It's a shame, that's what it is," he said, his deep bass voice softer now, a fine woman like you sweatin' over a hot stove and waiting tables, day after day. Why, if you was my wife, I'd hire someone to wait on you."

Charlotte's cheeks flamed. How was she to reply to this? She didn't want to anger him. Hollis Lloyd was a good customer, after all, and she was convinced that his attentions to her were harmless. Probably, he was only trying to make her regret the fact that she'd not paid him more notice when she had the chance.

"There's no shame in working to earn one's living," she said, after careful consideration.

"No, ma'am," he agreed, and suddenly catching up her elbow in his meaty hand, he leaned closer, "but I'd think you might like somethin' better for yourself. It ain't too late to reconsider the choices you've made, you know. I'm sure Jack would understand, seein' as how he can't give you what I can."

Charlotte held her breath. Her heart was hammering a violent rhythm in her breast, but she told herself to be calm. He meant no harm. He was only teasing. Wasn't he?

She dared not look around to see his face. She decided then that it would probably be best to get herself back into the kitchen, where things were familiar and comfortable and there were chores waiting to be done.

But as she disentangled herself and turned to go, she noticed Jack, standing in the archway that separated the dining room from the lobby. The wooden cane he'd been using since he gave up his crutches was resting against his thigh. He had put on his simple, black broadcloth suit for the occasion, and although he seemed to be concentrating on straightening his tie as he stood there, it was apparent that he had heard every word that Hollis Lloyd had said. A dark look had settled on his brow, and he was working his jaw in the same subtle way he did whenever he was irritated.

Charlotte didn't want to make a scene, not over something so trivial as this, and certainly not tonight, with the council members due to arrive at any moment, and so, turning on her heel, she left Lloyd without another word and pushed her way back through the swinging doors into the kitchen.

Once there, she thrust her hands into the dishpan, and staring into the soapy water, she busied herself with washing up the last few dishes. But all the while, she was listening and waiting, with trepidation trickling like ice cold drips of water down her spine. Thankfully, though, no words at all were exchanged between Jack and Hollis Lloyd, and before too long, the others began to arrive.

The rapping of the gavel on the table told her when Jack was finally ready to call the meeting to order.

"Good evening, gentlemen," she heard him say. "Now that we're all here, we can begin. I think you've all met our new sheriff, Sam Willis."

Charlotte had already been introduced to him, and to her mind, Willis seemed eminently suited for his job. He was not very talkative, a gruff-looking character; all in all, he was of massive build, with a crooked nose and a thick, reddish moustache.

Jack's voice startled her out of her thoughts. "Good. Well then, let's begin, shall we? For the past several years, this council has managed to run Cedar Creek ably enough, but due to the town's recent expansion, it has been proposed that we are in need of an official administration to look after its needs. We've come here tonight to see if we can reach a consensus . . ."

"Excuse me, Jack," Hollis Lloyd put in, "but before we get to that, I want to say that I'd be willin' to donate the funds we'll need to build a town hall. We can't very well have a local government if there's no place to put it. I could have that architect of mine draw up the plans while he's still here in town."

"Dat's mighty generous of you, Hollis," one of the Thorssen brothers replied. Charlotte couldn't say for sure which one. The musical rhythm of their accented voices sounded too much alike for her to tell them apart.

"Yes," Jack agreed. "Thank you, Hollis. I'm sure the townsfolk will be most appreciative."

"Let's not waste any more time on this, shall we?" It was Noah speaking now. "We all know that Jack Cordell ought to be our mayor. If it weren't for him, we'd all have given up on this town long ago. He deserves the job."

Charlotte was pleased to hear a rumbling of agreement from the assembled council, but then before the wave of assent could build in Jack's favor, another voice broke in.

"Excuse me, gentlemen." It was the newspaper editor, Nate Phillips. "This is an important decision we're making here, and while I certainly mean no disrespect to Jack, I think perhaps we ought to consider whether or not he would be, well, physically able to handle the job."

A scraping of wood on wood cut through the silence, telling Charlotte that one of the men had gotten up from his chair. Apparently, it was Noah, for he was the one who spoke next.

"I can address that point," he said. "Jack's leg is nearly healed. In another week or so, he ought to be able to give up that cane of his and start walking on his own two feet."

"That's all well and good," Phillips retorted, "but that wasn't what I meant."

Charlotte barely breathed, her attention riveted on what was going on out in the dining room. She heard only footsteps next, measured footsteps. Their familiar, hesitant cadence told her that it was Jack and that he was pacing back and forth before his friends.

"Just what do you mean, Nate?" he asked at length.

His voice was low, restrained. Charlotte knew how fearful he must be of what was to come. More than anything, she wanted to push through the swinging doors, twine her arm through her husband's, and stand by his side, but she'd already learned how much he hated her mothering. So, instead she only stood there, hands poised above the steaming dishwater as she waited to hear what would happen next.

"None of us likes to pry into a man's personal affairs, Jack, but we can't help but have noticed that since the accident, you're not able to see so well. I've watched you collide with furniture and door jambs more than once myself. You're sand-blind, aren't you?"

Finally, it was out in the open. Charlotte supposed that she must have known all along that some of the townsfolk had guessed Jack's secret, even if she hadn't wanted to believe it. Her heart ached for him. He'd so desperately wanted to keep everyone from finding out. He wasn't the sort of man who could easily suffer pity from his friends. He'd concluded from the first moment—and rightfully so, it now seemed—that if they knew, it would limit his effectiveness as a leader.

"I'm not blind!" he protested. "It's only a temporary condition, due to swelling from the injuries. Isn't that right, Noah? . . . Noah?"

The silence didn't help his case, and the reply that eventually followed did nothing to ease the tension in the room.

"I can't say that for sure."

A note of panic crept into Jack's voice then. "What do you mean?"

"I've tried to tell you, Jack, more than once, but you never seem to want to listen. The swelling's gone down, but your vision, well, it hasn't improved."

When Jack spoke this time, his words came out slow and pained. "So, what you're saying is that I could be stumbling around like this . . . forever?"

It must have been awful for him to have been made to accept the news in front of all his friends. But Noah had said that he'd tried to warn him.

"I don't think that any of this is relevant to the decision we've come here to make tonight," Noah said next, addressing his remarks to the entire council. "It's not Jack's mind that's been affected, nor his judgment. His vision is a bit blurred, that's all. In my opinion, he's still the best man for the job of mayor."

"Nothing against Jack, of course," Gus Stern, who was

ever the cautious individual, put in, "but with things as they are, maybe we ought to at least find out if there are any other potential candidates."

"Now that you mention it, I was going to suggest Hollis Lloyd," Nate Phillips said.

"Me?" Lloyd sounded surprised.

"You're a member of the council and a long-time resident, aren't you?" Phillips replied. "Not to mention a respectable mine owner, with at least a dozen men in your employ, and one of our most prosperous citizens. The folk in town all know your name, even the newcomers."

"Well now, I'd have never thought it . . . that is . . . mayor, did you say? Yes, well, I s'pose I could see myself fulfillin' such an obligation, if I was to be called upon."

A shiver coursed through Charlotte as she realized that Lloyd was actually considering it. Why, he'd even managed to make himself sound like a politician.

At that point, the meeting disintegrated into a chorus of dissenting voices. Jack's gavel was rapped repeatedly on the table as someone attempted to quiet them all down. But it wasn't Jack, but rather Sheriff Willis, who spoke next.

"Gentlemen, gentlemen, if you please," he said. "It may not be my place to offer an opinion here, but nevertheless, I'd like to say my piece. You're scrapping and squabbling like children, and it's clear that you're not likely to come to any sort of agreement soon. Why don't you leave this decision to the citizens of Cedar Creek."

"An election?" Henry Sutton offered. "Is that what you mean?"

"I do."

This proposal seemed to settle the council members down somewhat, and after a vote was taken, it was duly decided that a general election would be held in one month's time to decide the question of who should serve as mayor of Cedar Creek.

For her part, Charlotte thought it perfectly ridiculous to believe that even one of the town's citizens would throw away his vote on a man like Hollis Lloyd. Apparently, though, Jack did not share her confidence, for as soon as the meeting had broken up, he burst through the swinging doors and into the kitchen, a deep frown etched into his brow.

"Jack," Charlotte called out, wiping her hands on her apron as she rushed to meet him. "I heard what's been going on, and I . . ."

He put up a hand to stop her. "I don't need your pity, Charlotte. I know I haven't a chance in hell to be elected, if I'm running against Hollis Lloyd."

"What? Why, you're twice the man he is."

"And just how would you have come to that conclusion, my dear?" he shot back bitterly. "Wasn't he cozying up to you earlier this evening to tell you about all the things that he can give you that I can't?"

The remark caught her like a slap in the face. He had been listening to them. "That was nothing but foolish talk," she retorted, "and you ought to know it."

"But I don't know it." With that, he shook his head. "Maybe Lloyd is right. Maybe you'd be better off with a rich, handsome young stallion like him than with the half-blind, broken down wreck that you've married. Maybe you wouldn't cringe when *he* tried to touch you . . ."

Charlotte's heart dropped to her feet. He hadn't forgotten how she'd pushed him away. He'd been deeply hurt by her rejection; she could see it all too clearly now.

"Oh, Jack. You don't understand . . ."

She extended a hand to him, as she tried to find the words to explain. But he stepped back out of her reach, his expression gone hard. "It doesn't matter. I told you before, I don't need your pity."

With that, he turned, strode to the back door and opened it, letting in the evening chill.

"Where are you going?" she asked.

"That depends on how far a blind man can stumble in the dark."

Jack managed to "stumble" halfway down Main Street to the closest saloon, the Golden Palace, a two-story establishment built of rough-sawn boards, with what he assumed must be its name painted across its front in bold, gilt letters, but appeared to him as only a glittery blur, lit by the light that shone out of the windows of the private rooms over head.

Despite its grandiose name, the interior was smoky, dark, and sparsely furnished. But Jack was thankful for that. It made it easier for him to maneuver once he'd purchased his bottle of whiskey at the bar. With his cane in one hand and juggling bottle and glass in the other, he found himself an empty table from among the half dozen spread across the room, then sat down and poured himself a drink, hoping the liquor would dull the ache he felt inside.

It was bad enough that he'd been made to face his limitations in front of all of his friends tonight, but what had been worse was watching as Hollis Lloyd tried to steal away his wife, and realizing that if Charlotte decided to go, there was nothing, nothing, that he could do about it.

What had he to offer her? A life of scrubbing pans and waiting tables? Of serving as nursemaid to a crippled husband nearly ten years her senior? The truth of it was that Charlotte wasn't his wife at all. They'd taken the vows, lived together under the same roof, but he'd never lain with her, never forged the bond that made a husband and wife one. Maybe if he had . . .

"Good evening."

A stranger pulled up a chair beside him, then drew a deck of cards from out of his jacket pocket and began to riffle them absently. All that Jack could ascertain was that the man was squarely built, with a bearded face, and that he was well dressed. Each time he turned his hand, his gold cuff button would catch the lamp light, then glint and flare, effectively blinding Jack for a moment.

"You interested in a hand of poker, friend?"

"Not from around here, are you?" Jack replied, as he poured himself another drink.

The stranger hesitated, apparently taken aback by the question. "I am now. Just bought this place. I come from New Orleans originally, though."

"Lots of newcomers around here lately. I knew you must be from out of town, else you'd have heard the talk. 'Jack Cordell couldn't tell the Queen of Diamonds from the Ace of Spades. He's sand-blind, poor fellow.' "

"Sorry to hear it." The man pushed back his chair and got to his feet. "But don't you worry, I'll see if I can't arrange some other sort of entertainment for you. I like to keep my customers happy."

Jack took a swig of the second-rate whiskey, threw back his head and let it burn the length of his throat. He hadn't come here looking for entertainment. He'd only wanted to numb himself sufficiently, so he might not lie awake all night, restlessly tossing on his cot and dwelling on the painful embarrassments he'd suffered this evening.

He would never have thought it would come out this way. Optimistic fool that he was, Jack had expected that the council would appoint him as mayor. After all, he'd been in charge of things for years, hadn't he? He'd put all of his energies into building this town, not satisfied until he'd made his dreams into reality. Didn't that mean anything at all to them?

Now he found himself in the position of fighting for the post he'd already earned, and fighting against a man who would like nothing better than to take all that he had.

Hollis Lloyd was hardly qualified to run Cedar Creek,

and Jack was sure that Nate Phillips knew it, even as he'd nominated him for the job. But then Phillips likely had his own agenda for the town, and to see it adopted, he'd need a more malleable man at the helm.

Jack knew well enough that, in the real world, it didn't matter who was the more qualified. A rich man, whose name was known to all, who could afford to do favors for his friends and to build a town hall for the citizens, had a far greater chance of being elected mayor than a beaten-down dreamer. And so he poured himself another drink.

He'd hardly had a chance to swallow it down, though, before the rustle of cheap taffeta caught his attention. A pair of slender hands snaked over his shoulders, edging boldly down his shirtfront, and he felt the press of warm flesh against the back of his neck as a voice whispered in his ear.

"It ain't right for a man to look as lonesome as you do, mister. My name's Alice. Anythin' I can do to help?"

Jack took an unsteady breath and inhaled a cloud of cheap perfume. This must be the entertainment the owner had promised. Without waiting for an invitation, Alice sat down beside him, took the glass from his hand and re-filled it for herself. Slowly, she raised it to her lips, leaning slightly forward as she sipped to afford him a better view of her ample cleavage.

Each movement she made was designed to entice, but the poor girl had no way of knowing that her efforts were wasted. To Jack, she was nothing more than a haze of emerald green, dipping and swaying in the dim lamplight. He almost dismissed her, but when he felt the pressure of her hand as it slid up his thigh, the words caught in his throat.

He hadn't been touched in . . . too long. He hadn't had a woman since before Charlotte came into his life. It was inevitable that his body should betray him. His head was already spinning from the whiskey. Every muscle in his body went rigid with anticipation and an insistent pulse began to pound in his ears.

Alice leaned so near that Jack could feel the heat of her breath against his lips. Beneath the table, her practiced hand sought his arousal and took its measure. She sighed appreciatively.

In an instant, his hand flashed out and tangled in her hair. With hunger nigh unbearable, he lowered his mouth on hers and kissed her. *What was the difference anyway?* he told himself. One woman was the same as the next, to a blind man. He could even pretend that she was Charlotte, if he liked.

Yes, maybe this was what he needed: to sate himself so fully that he'd not lie awake on his cot at night, thinking of Charlotte, and then fall asleep, only to dream of her.

All at once, Alice put her hands up to his chest. Pushing him back, she giggled and drew a ragged breath. "Easy now," she said. "I've got me a room upstairs. Why don't we take this bottle of yours and go on up there?"

Jack thought he had convinced himself. His body certainly didn't need convincing. Inside, he was coiled up, tight as a watchspring, and beads of sweat had broken out in profusion across his brow. But in the end, he only shook his head and pushed her away.

This pitiful, painted girl wasn't his Charlotte. She never could be.

"You take the bottle, Alice," he told her, a hint of apology in his voice. "I've got to go home."

As he made his way out of the smoky saloon and back toward the hotel, Jack's heart hammered hard against his chest in anticipation of what was to come. He felt stronger with each measured step he took. Why hadn't he realized before what he ought to do? How peculiar that it should take an infusion of whiskey to clear the fog out of his brain.

His purpose was fixed. He'd waited too long already to take what was his. But he wasn't going to wait any longer.

Eighteen

"Charlotte?"

The voice, vaguely familiar, beckoned her from the depths of her dreams. Charlotte wasn't alarmed at first. Why should she be? There was nothing threatening in the tone, and she knew this voice, she told herself, as she sought to clear her sleep-clouded mind.

She rolled onto her back and stretched out her arms, flexing the torpid muscles. "Hmmmm?"

His next words tumbled out in a breathless rush, too fast for her still-groggy brain to assimilate. "We've been fooling ourselves to think we could go on this way, ignoring our needs. But I'm willing to admit it now. I need you, Charlotte. I want you."

It was the faint smell of whiskey that set off the warning bells in her head, but by then it was too late. Her eyelids snapped open. All she could see in the darkness was the shadow of a figure bent over her bed. Before she could react, he'd grasped her by the shoulders, captured her mouth with his and lowered his big body on hers, pressing her back into the mattress, his erection pressing hard into the soft flesh of her belly and poised, like a weapon, between them.

Oh, God, no. Not again. She thought she had put the nightmares behind her. They'd plagued her less frequently lately, and so she'd dared to hope . . . But now they were back, and it frightened her to realize how much they'd changed; they were more real than they had ever been.

He tasted of whiskey; the bitterness of it came near to choking her. And then his hands began to move, tracing circles over her body, cupping her breasts through the thin fabric of her nightgown. His touch was gentler than she'd remembered. Ah, but that was only to put her off her guard. He wanted her willing—*Isn't that what he'd said?*—but he'd have her regardless. Panic seized her as her mind raced ahead to the memories of the pain that was to come.

Dragging her mouth free of his, she fought to breathe, gulping in air between sobs.

"Please. Oh, please, Marcus. Please don't," she begged him. "Take me home. I want to go home now."

"What?" he replied, sounding dazed. "What are you saying, Charlotte? You are home. Here with me, where you belong."

No. She'd never belong to Marcus Gideon. No matter that he'd so cruelly branded her, spoiling her for any other man. She'd never be his.

Charlotte whimpered softly as he drew back just enough to toy with the buttons of her nightgown, managing to loosen only a few before his patience eluded him, and he yanked apart the two sections of fabric, popping off the rest.

"Now, look what I've done. I'm sorry," he said. The apology startled her. He'd never apologized in her other dreams. As the flat of his hand slid over her bared skin, he buried his face in her neck and groaned. "Too eager, I guess. But don't worry. I'll buy you a new one. Hellfire, I'll buy you a closet full, if that's what you want."

"Please, oh, please, no," she whispered, knowing how useless it was to resist. Whatever she did, the dream always came out the same.

"Don't be afraid of me, Charlotte. We need this, you and I. We've waited too long as it is."

Too long? He'd scarcely got to know her at all. A walk on the levee, a dinner in the French Quarter, and then he'd expected . . .

When his fingers slipped between her thighs, probing her most private place, Charlotte stiffened. She wanted to wake up now. This was far too real for her liking. She wouldn't endure the pain again, not again.

"No," she cried, then began to writhe beneath him. "Don't touch me! Don't dare touch me!"

She struck at his chest with her balled fists, legs thrashing wildly as her terror increased.

To her surprise, he rolled away. Relieved of his weight, Charlotte gasped for breath, wasting no time in scrambling off the bed. She streaked across the room, and when she'd reached the farthest corner, she collapsed there, and burying her face against the wall, she dissolved in tears.

Jack got to his feet and shook his head, hoping to clear away the whiskey fog. But the bleary picture of his wife, whimpering like a frightened child, curled up on the floor in the corner, the ruined nightgown clutched tightly across her breasts, was all that he needed to sober him.

Bile rose up in his throat, making him want to retch. He swallowed hard. What had he done?

There came a padding of footsteps in the corridor, a murmured exchange of voices and then a knock on the door.

"Jack?" a voice called out. "Charlotte? Is everything all right?"

It was Leah. Jack cast a last look back at Charlotte. She hadn't moved at all. The pitiful sight she made, and the realization that he was responsible for it pierced his heart like a hot knife. Gathering his wits, he went to the door, opened it only a crack and looked out to face his sister, certain that he must look as guilty as he felt.

"Are you both all right?" she asked again.

"It's Charlotte," Jack explained, once he'd managed to summon his voice. "She's . . . had a nightmare. Tell that to the guests for me, will you? Everyone can go back to sleep. And don't worry yourself about it. She'll be all right. I'll give her a sip of brandy before I tuck her back into bed."

Leah nodded. She'd seemed relieved by his explanation and went off to do as he had bade her. He'd forgotten how easy it was to lie. The truth of it was, though, that Jack didn't know whether Charlotte would be all right or not. He shut the door, and pressing his shoulder blades against the panels, he threw back his head and felt the color slowly drain away from his face. What had he done?

There was no forgiveness for him in this. He'd behaved like a mindless, rutting stag, creeping into Charlotte's bed in the middle of the night without warning, trying to force himself on her; and he, stinking drunk into the bargain.

When he opened his eyes at last, Jack was relieved to see that his wife had recovered from her shock. She was standing now, limned in the blue moonlight that spilled in the windows behind her. Was he only imagining it, or could he see the shadowy, soft curves of her slender form beneath the transparent, tattered nightgown? For once he was sorry that his vision was improved by the moonlight. He swore that he could see something of her eyes, too: wide, but oddly distant, and her gold hair, sleep-tossed and gleaming like a halo. She was beautiful, in her frightened disarray, and Jack hated himself for wanting her, even now.

"Can I . . . can I get you a glass of brandy?" he offered haltingly.

In reply, Charlotte crossed her arms tighter over her breasts and shook her head. Her voice was fluid and husky. "No. I'll be all right."

More than anything, he wanted to reach out to comfort

her, but he dared not take one step closer. There was fear yet in the air. He could feel it. He was the enemy now. What he'd done, what he'd tried to do had made him so. How could he have been such a stupid, selfish fool!

She shifted in her place, gaze fixed on the floor at her feet. His presence was causing her pain, he knew. What could he do but leave her?

And so, Jack crossed to the dressing room door, careful to maintain the distance between them. With his hand on the knob, he turned back one last time.

"I . . . I'm sorry," he said.

In the sunny, private sitting room that Jack had had built for her beside the hotel kitchen, Charlotte sat worrying over next week's menu. *Catfish on Tuesday and salt pork and beans on Wednesday, or the other way around? And were there enough apples in the pantry to count on making pies?* She'd have to set in a new supply of sugar and cinnamon—they were nearly out—and coffee, while she was thinking of it.

None of this was of pressing importance, but it helped to keep her mind off of other matters. She hadn't gotten a wink of sleep all night, worrying over what had happened with Jack. It was early afternoon now, and she hadn't seen him all day. He was avoiding her.

She ought to have been furious with him. Last night he'd scared her witless, getting himself drunk and then climbing into her bed uninvited. But then Jack wasn't wholly to blame. He'd only intended to claim what was his by right. How could he know how she would react? He had no hint of the nightmares that haunted her because Charlotte had never managed to find strength enough to confide in him.

She had to tell him now, though, and the sooner the better. She hadn't been able to forget the memory of his face last night, so full of self-loathing. There was no doubt in her mind that Jack felt responsible for her hysteria; he thought himself a monster.

Charlotte would not have him go on believing that it was disgust for him that had made her push him away. She'd tell him the truth, that the woman he'd married was soiled goods and worse, and if he should afterwards decide he didn't want her for his wife, she'd understand. She'd go away. She'd have to. It was only right.

Restless now, she set aside her shopping list and went to take up her nightgown out of the sewing basket. She'd gone back this morning and carefully retrieved all of the missing buttons from the bedclothes and the floor, and now she meant to sew them back on. It was a first step toward fixing the damage that had been done last night.

She'd only just threaded the needle, though, when Jack came into the room and promptly shut the door behind him.

"Noah's arranged for me to speak at a rally this evening at the church," he said, as if nothing at all awkward had passed between them.

Charlotte's eyes remained fixed on the button she was stitching. "The church?" she echoed.

Silence filled the sunny room. Finally, Charlotte lifted her head to see Jack blanch as he noticed the pooled white fabric in her lap and the flash of her needle as she pulled up on the thread. His vision may have been dulled, but he could see well enough to know what she was doing.

All at once, he began to pace, from door to window and then back again, as if the action were a metronome to regulate his thoughts. "Yes, the church. It's the biggest building we've got in town," he explained. "They're expecting a large crowd. But . . . I . . . I can't help thinking what a travesty it will be for me to stand up at that pulpit before God and the whole town, asking them to believe in me, pretending to be worthy, when the truth is . . ."

Charlotte's hands went still in her lap. She squeezed her eyes shut. "Oh, Jack, don't . . ."

"We have to talk about this, Charlotte," he said, and then the words spilled out. "I've come here to tell you that I'm willing to set you free from our marriage, if that's what you want. I'll leave Cedar Creek. I'll give you the hotel. You can't deny that I've made your life nothing but misery."

"It's not true!" she protested, unconsciously curling her fingers until the point of the needle she'd been holding bit into the flesh of her thumb.

"You've sacrificed your freedom because of some misplaced guilt that you feel about what happened to me in the fire," he insisted. "But when I proposed to you, Charlotte, I didn't mean for you to be my nursemaid. Even if I'm never again the man I once was, I'd rather stumble through life alone than to risk hurting you like I did last night."

Charlotte rose up, and everything in her lap—needle, thread, fabric—slipped onto the floor unnoticed. She took several steps toward him, "It wasn't you, Jack. Don't you see? You're my husband. You had every right to expect to share my bed. There's so much that you don't understand about me. That's my fault, I know. I believed that it was best to bury the past. But I see now what a mistake it can be."

Jack lifted an unsteady hand to his brow to knead out the creases that were forming there. "What . . . what are you talking about?"

"Please, just sit down and listen to me, will you?" she entreated, waving a hand toward the chair that she'd recently vacated.

Charlotte hesitated while he did as she bade. Now it was her turn to pace. By concentrating on the sound of her footsteps, on the steady progress that she made across the room, on the familiar view from the sitting room window, she was able to calm herself enough to summon the awful memories.

"I've never spoken to you about my life in New Orleans. But it's well past time that I did," she began. "I told you that mother died when I was born. I lived in a convent school until I was seventeen. When I came home again, I gave myself over to caring for my father—kept house, cooked his meals. By the time I started to think seriously about young men, I was already an old maid of twenty-three, and all of the gentlemen of my acquaintance had gone off to fight in the war.

"I see now what an easy mark I must have been for a flashy, riverboat gambler like Marcus Gideon. I was vain, frivolous, and hungry for excitement. I encouraged him, in spite of all my father's warnings about men of his kind. Gideon could be charming when he wanted to be. He flattered me, and I let him take me to dinner."

"But I don't understand what all this has to do . . ."

Charlotte went on with her story, as if Jack hadn't even spoken. Now that she'd started, she had to tell him everything.

"He arranged for a private dining room, with velvet hangings and crystal chandeliers. He ordered the choicest fare, the finest wine. The dinner was wonderful, but I was too naive to know that he was looking for something more than my company in return. Eventually, it became clear, though, and when I refused his advances, he got angry. He called me a 'little tease' and grabbed me by the hair. I tried to break free, but he slapped me so hard that my teeth rattled."

Jack winced at her words as if he had been the one that was struck. There was no doubt that she had his full attention now.

"I cried out," she continued, "but no one came to help.

The place was too busy, too noisy, and besides, I don't think anyone interfered with what went on in those private rooms. He forced himself on me. I tried as best I could to stop him—I did, you have to believe that, Jack—but I couldn't fight him off forever. He . . . he raped me . . . right there on the velvet chaise that had been so thoughtfully provided by the management."

"My God, Charlotte . . ."

Jack's words were hushed with disbelief. Charlotte heard the chair rattle over the floor as he got to his feet, but she dared not turn to look at him for fear she'd see disgust in his eyes. So, she squared her jaw and went on with her tale.

"Afterward, he tossed a few coins at my head," she said, struggling to keep her voice even, "and left me lying there, like a discarded rag doll. I limped home on my own, clutching together the remnants of my dress."

Jack stood there, speechless, frustration tearing at his insides. He'd always told himself that it was the war that had hardened Charlotte, but he ought to have guessed that she'd suffered something more. Maybe he had guessed, somewhere deep inside him, but he hadn't wanted to deal with it. And lately, he'd been too concerned with his own problems.

Now he understood. Each time he'd touched her, each time he'd made a move that she perceived as threatening, he'd unwittingly forced her to relive her pain.

Charlotte had seemed detached during this whole revelation. He'd never seen her shed a tear in all the time he'd known her. But surely now . . . Blinking, he sought a hint of expression, but what he could make out seemed only a blank stare, and when she spoke again, her voice did not waver.

"It would have been all right," she told him, "if my father hadn't seen me come in, if I'd borne my shame in silence, but fate meant for me to lose everything that night. Unthinking little fool that I was, I fell into Papa's arms, sobbing as I told him the whole, awful truth. Of course, he went after Gideon. What else could he do?

"I don't know what his intentions were, what words were exchanged between them, but I do know the outcome. Marcus Gideon shot him, and my father bled to death on the cold cobblestones of the New Orleans levee."

With this, Jack expelled a harsh breath, as if he'd been struck in the gut. His shoulders slumped, and he clenched his fists so tightly that his fingers went numb. More than anything, he longed to reach out to comfort her, but he dared not.

"I'm sorry, Charlotte," he whispered, "so sorry." The words seemed pathetic and helpless. "But why didn't you tell me any of this before?"

She cast her gaze downward. "He said no man would want me, after I'd been used by him. I was afraid that if you knew . . ."

"Worthless bastard," Jack spat, his lip curling. "They hanged him for your father's murder, I hope."

Charlotte shook her head. "He disappeared before he could be arrested."

"And what did you do?"

"What little money my father had left me soon ran out," she explained. "I was hardly qualified to earn any sort of living back then. I hadn't any friends or family to turn to, and I couldn't ask for charity. Still, desperate as I was, I could think of nothing but finding Marcus Gideon myself somehow and making him pay for all he'd done."

"And so that's when you first got the idea to put on men's clothing?" he surmised.

"I found that I could move about more easily on the levee in disguise. And after what Gideon had done to me, I couldn't bear to have any man look at me as if he might . . . as if he wanted . . .

"I was safe, as a man. Can you understand that? And

then one day while I was loitering about, looking for clues to Gideon's whereabouts, a riverboat captain offered me a job as a cabin boy. The salary seemed a fortune to me, desperate as I was. How could I refuse? So, I went to work on the river and looked for Gideon along the way.

"It was more than a year before I found someone who'd heard news of him. I was told that he'd gone to Colorado, bent on making his fortune off of miners with more gold dust than sense. I didn't even have to think about it; I just followed him."

"Oh, Charlotte, revenge won't ease the pain, nor put things back the way they used to be," he told her.

But she didn't seem to be listening. "By then I'd become hardened. I was comfortable in my life as a man. I made my way by prospecting and working small claims until about six months ago. That's when I came across Gideon, gambling up at Six Mile Canyon."

Jack was incredulous. "You mean to say you found him?"

"I knew that it was him as soon as I saw him," she said. "He wore a ring fashioned out of a ten-dollar gold piece; I saw it, glittering in the lamplight. I'd recognize that ring anywhere. You see, he was wearing it when he . . ." She hesitated for a few, painful seconds before shaking off the memory. "I called him out that night, and I shot him dead."

The satisfaction in her voice was unmistakable. With all he'd heard, Jack couldn't say that he blamed her.

"So you see," she told him, sadness pervading her words, "your wife is a murderer, too."

By now, Jack's mind had begun to raise questions about what she'd said. He remembered the shooting contest and the "rattlesnake" up at the cabin. Charlotte's aim was wild, at best.

"You shot him?" he repeated. "Charlotte, are you sure?"

"It was dark that night," she replied. "There was

gunsmoke in the air. Still, he stood no more than twenty feet away from me, and I fired at him until my gun was empty. It's true I never had a chance to see the body, but he can't have escaped. He's dead. He's got to be."

Jack didn't have the heart to argue with her. True or not, she wanted to believe it.

"I've always known I didn't deserve a man like you, Jack," she told him finally. "It was wrong of me to accept your proposal in the first place. I convinced myself that you needed me, but the truth is that I . . . I love you, and I wanted desperately to know what it felt like to be happy, if only for a little while."

Jack opened his mouth to protest, but Charlotte lifted a hand to stop him. "You don't have to say anything," she said. "I don't blame you for not wanting someone like me for your wife. But I can't let you give up all you've worked so hard for here. You keep the hotel. Leah will help you run things. It's only right that I should be the one to leave. You needn't worry. I'll pack my belongings and be gone in the morning."

Charlotte turned on her heel then and quit the room without giving him an opportunity to argue.

Does she think I am so shallow, so utterly heartless? he wondered, as the numbness that had gripped him for the past several minutes began to subside. Well, if her intent was truly to leave him, then she had make a serious mistake in admitting that she loved him. Jack clung to that knowledge now with all the desperation of a drowning man. She was wrong if she thought this was over, by any means, and her hasty departure didn't stop him from calling out to her in a voice that was loud enough to shake the roof timbers.

"I won't let you go, Charlotte. Do you hear me? I'm not the man you think I am," he admitted at last. "You're not the only one who's been keeping secrets."

Nineteen

It was an easy enough thing to say that you were leaving, but when it came down to packing your belongings and saying goodbye to all your friends; well now, that was something else entirely. Leah had been underfoot for all of the afternoon, washing dishes and helping to prepare the evening meal, and yet still Charlotte couldn't seem to find the words to explain to her what she had planned. *Maybe it would be best to wait until after supper to give her the news,* she reasoned. Why upset her before it was absolutely necessary?

And Charlotte knew that she would be upset. There was no denying that Leah had grown as fond of her as she was of Leah. But there was nothing to be done about it. She had to leave. She and Jack couldn't go on as they had been, especially not after what had happened last night. The admissions she'd made to him this afternoon had only helped to make up her mind. A decent, upstanding man like Jack Cordell deserved better than someone like her.

Apparently, Jack had decided the same. He'd not set foot in Charlotte's kitchen all that day, and was conspicuously absent from the supper table that evening. Leah informed her that he had gone to Noah's so they might work out his speech together, but Charlotte knew it was only an excuse. She couldn't blame him for wanting to avoid her. The twist of pain she felt in her heart, though, when she realized that his opinion of her had changed, made her glad that she would be leaving soon.

All through supper, she tried to find the words to explain to Leah why she had to leave. She didn't feel comfortable relating all the details, but how else could she make the girl understand? In the end, she wound up saying nothing, assuring herself that she'd have decided what approach to take by bedtime. She'd talk to Leah then.

Charlotte couldn't help but wonder if the girl might not have already sensed that something was amiss. She'd seemed unusually pensive for most of the day, and when Charlotte sent her out to Henry Sutton's general store to fetch the cinnamon and nutmeg for her pies, she was gone for an awfully long time; and when she returned, she'd seemed more distant and distracted than ever.

In fact, it was only after they'd finished supper that she'd remembered to tell Charlotte that Jack was expecting them both to meet him at the church to hear his speech. Charlotte hadn't planned on going at all; she'd thought that Jack wouldn't want her there. But now that Leah had said that he was expecting her, she'd have to go. Besides, Rachel would surely be there, and while Charlotte didn't relish the prospect of facing her friend with the news, she knew that she would have to tell her, too, that she was leaving. And although she might not be so eager to admit it under the circumstances, she *wanted* to hear Jack speak. Just one more time, she wanted to watch as he wove a spell on the townsfolk with his words and made his dreams take shape. Just one more time . . .

Charlotte and Leah entered the church, arm in arm, wrapped up in their woolen, winter shawls, their cheeks flush from the cold. Jack was seated beside the pulpit, with Noah at his side. He was pale and shifting in his seat, and Charlotte thought that she had never seen him look so nervous.

There was good reason, she knew. While he and Noah

may well have discussed the remarks he'd make tonight, Jack couldn't read from a prepared speech. He wouldn't have been able to see the words on the page. So, he'd have to try to keep all that he wanted to say straight in his head and hope that it came out all right.

It was important that he make a good impression on the people of Cedar Creek, especially the newcomers, who weren't aware of how much he'd already done for this town. This speech of his would help them to decide whether they could risk electing a man who was nearly blind and still recovering from his injuries to be their mayor.

There were those who had their doubts. Some, like Nate Phillips, had already decided that they'd be better off with an empty-headed blowhard like Hollis Lloyd, who had no experience, but lots of money to throw into his campaign. But Charlotte knew better.

A familiar voice broke into her thoughts then, as Rachel came up to the place where they were standing at the back of the church and caught her by the elbow. "Charlotte, Leah, there you both are at last."

"Where's the baby?" Charlotte asked her. "Didn't you bring him with you? We've been so busy lately, I've scarcely had the chance to see him. I'll bet by now he's grown so big I wouldn't even recognize him."

"Oh, he has. Mrs. Murphy is watching him tonight so I don't have to bring him out in the cold. She's become rather a permanent fixture around our house now. If you ask me, it's because she's grown so fond of little Ben. Every week she makes plans to go and visit her sons up in Blackhawk, but by week's end, she's found some reason or another to change her mind."

"It would appear that she's adopted you," Leah observed.

This made Rachel giggle as she reached to fold her arms around them. "Yes, I suppose you're right. Oh, I'm so glad you both got here at last. We'd begun to wonder if you were coming at all."

"We had to finish up the dishes," Charlotte explained.

"But we wouldn't miss this, not for anything," Leah said next, her gray eyes sparkling. "I'm going to go up and let Jack know we're here and then find us a place to sit before they're all taken."

Charlotte nodded, and there followed a long moment of silence as she and Rachel watched the girl thread her way through the crowd milling in the aisle.

"Such a pretty thing, she is," Rachel said and let go a breathy sigh, "and she seems so happy. Looking at her, I can remember just what it felt like to be young and in love."

At this, Charlotte's brow puckered. "You make it sound as if it were a lifetime ago, but you're scarcely more than a child yourself." She hesitated as the rest of her friend's words sunk in. ". . . and what do you mean by, *in love?* Leah isn't in love. Why, she's hardly had the time to meet any of the young men in town."

"I wouldn't be too sure about that, if I were you. Just look at her. I'd know that look anywhere."

Charlotte opened her mouth to reply, then shifted a glance in Leah's direction and promptly swallowed her words. Come to think on it, the girl did seem different somehow. Hadn't she told herself just this afternoon that Leah seemed peculiarly pensive? She'd have to mention it to Jack, and see if he'd noticed the change. Perhaps she ought to sit the girl down and have a talk with her. But, no, there wouldn't be time for that, not if she were leaving.

"Is something wrong?" Rachel prompted after Charlotte fell silent.

Charlotte pulled a long breath. She knew that the time for honesty had come. There was no use in putting it off.

"Well, there is something I need to tell you," she said. "I'll be leaving in the morning."

"What?"

Before Charlotte could say another word, Rachel caught her by the arm and dragged her out through the big double doors. She ushered her around to a quiet corner of the building, and only then did she release her and face off to demand an explanation.

"Now, what do you mean you're leaving?"

Charlotte turned away, staring off into the darkness. It would be easier to explain, if she didn't have to face her friend. A bitter wind whistled between them, tugging at Charlotte's skirts and fluttering the long fringes of her shawl. Shivering, she clutched the woolen fabric closer about her shoulders.

"I've told Jack everything about my past," she revealed, *"everything.* I can't expect him to want me for a wife now. I ought to have known all along that it wouldn't work."

"Have you even given him a chance to tell you how *he* feels?" Rachel wondered. "You haven't, have you?"

Charlotte turned back on her friend. "What do you expect him to say? That he doesn't mind taking another man's leavings? That it doesn't bother him at all that the woman he's married is a murderer? He's a good man, Rachel. He'd never tell me to go, but I can't live with seeing the disappointment in his eyes, day after day."

"Disappointment? Why, that's just plain foolishness. He's in love with you. I can see that, even if you don't. He'll understand what you've been through, if you just give him the chance."

"But he deserves better."

Just then the church bell began to clang noisily overhead, signaling the start of the evening's events. "Don't think we're finished with this discussion," Rachel shouted, wagging a finger at Charlotte. "You belong here, in this town now, as much as any of the rest of us."

Charlotte only shook her head as the pair of them hurried back inside, and made their way up to the front of the church, where Leah had saved them a seat on the bench. When Charlotte drew near enough for Jack to recognize her, he got to his feet, strode over to the rail and reached out his hands to her, offering her such a brilliant smile that she forgot for a moment all the distress she'd been through these past few days. She had no choice but to go to him.

"I'm glad you've come," he said, taking up both her hands in his. "I don't know if I'd have been able to do this without you here."

As he spoke, his thumbs were tracing circles across the back of her gloved hands, sending ripples of heat to the skin beneath. A lump rose in Charlotte's throat as she considered what he'd said. Did he really mean it? That he needed her here? This certainly didn't sound like a man who was ashamed of his wife. Could she have been wrong to assume that he'd want to be rid of her? She swallowed hard, trying not to think too much. Thinking could only get her in trouble.

"Nonsense. You'll be fine," she assured him. "Just tell them all what's in your heart. Just tell them what you told me about your dreams for this town, and they'll have to see that you're the best man for the job."

Squeezing her fingers tightly in his, Jack drew her close enough so that she could hear his whisper. "We need to talk, Charlotte. You sit right there up front between Leah and Rachel, and when all this is over, you wait for me. Do you hear?"

Even though her heart might wish things could have worked out differently, she knew the time for talking was over. But she didn't want to argue with him, not here, not now. So, she agreed to his request, albeit reluctantly, then settled herself onto the bench beside Leah and waited, along with the others, to hear her husband speak.

Noah rose first to make the introduction. "Fellow citizens of Cedar Creek," he began. "A few of you here tonight know Jack Cordell, but for those of you who don't, I'd like to tell you something about the man I'm proud to call my friend, and explain why I feel he ought to be elected our mayor.

"When Jack first came here six years ago, Cedar Creek was nothing but a handful of canvas tents and a couple of lean-tos got up out of pine boughs. He built a trading post around which this town grew up, and then later, a general store. He organized the first town council, and we, in turn, elected him chairman, a position which he's managed ably ever since.

"Things haven't always gone smoothly. We were left flat busted when the Pike's Peak rush didn't pan out, but we stayed on, mostly because Jack kept insisting that this place was our home. Somehow, he made us believe that things would get better. And then there was the fire a few months back, burned near every building in this town to the ground. That ought to have broken us. It came near to killing Jack Cordell, I can tell you that. But nevertheless, he got himself up out of his sickbed to rally his friends and neighbors with his dreams of better times ahead.

"Now those better times are here at last, and we're preparing to elect a mayor. What better man for the job, I ask you, than the man whose vision created this town? The man but for whom Cedar Creek would likely today be nothing more than a pile of ash and rubble: Jack Cordell."

The applause was heartening. Charlotte told herself that maybe Jack had been wrong. Maybe people would choose the more qualified candidate rather than the most notorious.

At last, Jack stepped up to the pulpit. To Charlotte, he seemed more handsome than he'd ever been, even with the jagged scar that cut across his temple. He towered before them, an impressive figure of a man in his sober black suit. Damaged or not, those gray eyes of his scanned the crowd with surprising acuity. His broad shoulders certainly seemed capable of supporting the burdens of an entire town, and as he lifted his squared jaw to address the assemblage, he appeared to have set aside all of his earlier disquiet.

"We've had some setbacks, there's no denying it," he said, "but look around you, folks. It isn't hard to see that God has smiled on this place. We've much to be thankful for: ample water and timber, the beauty of the mountains all around us, and now a wealth of silver.

"We've come a long way, no doubt of that, but we've still a lot of hard work left to do. With the increase in our population, we need to build a proper schoolhouse. We need to organize a fire company, so that we'll never again be faced with the helplessness of watching our homes and businesses burn. We need to think about petitioning the railroad about that Denver to Santa Fe route they're building, so they'll be sure to give our town due consideration."

Charlotte wriggled uncomfortably in her seat as he mentioned the railroad. With all she'd confessed to Jack this afternoon, she thought she'd told him all her secrets, but apparently she'd forgotten about this one.

"It's vital that we elect an official who will tend to all of these issues," he continued, "one who'll keep a close watch on the future needs of our town. Now, some of you may have heard that I'm suffering a bit of trouble with my eyesight just now, and you may be wondering if I'll be able to handle this job. Let me just say, in answer to that, that a man of vision isn't always the one with the sharpest eyesight. I can promise you all that, if elected, I will look after the needs of Cedar Creek with at least as much zeal as I have always shown, and I will certainly be grateful for your support."

He spoke to them earnestly then, outlining his plans to

one day make Cedar Creek as prosperous and modern a
city as Denver. He spoke of possibilities that few of them
had contemplated: of public utilities and sidewalks; wide,
tree-lined streets; and parks where children might play.
The pictures he painted with his words were bright and
vivid, and once more Charlotte found herself caught up
in her husband's dreams. Oh, what she wouldn't give to
be a part of them!

The applause began before Jack's words had died away.
Charlotte couldn't help but grin. She got to her feet and
clapped her own gloved hands together as vigorously as
she was able. She'd been so sure he'd win them over. Jack
had a gift for swaying crowds, for making others believe
in his dreams.

He held up his hands, to still those assembled, and once
they'd settled back down in their seats, he addressed them
anew. "Before I bid you all goodnight, I would like to
introduce someone who has been of immense help to me,
someone whose faith and encouragement have made it
possible for me to weather the rough times and to find
the strength to start anew."

Charlotte thought it particularly touching that Jack
should publicly acknowledge Noah for all that he had
done for him. She turned and locked eyes with Rachel,
who met her with a broad smile. Next, she turned her
attention on Noah, to catch his reaction to the tribute.
Oddly enough he, too, was smiling at her.

"She's been my partner, my helpmate, my nursemaid,
and if not for her love and support, I would likely not be
standing here before you this evening."

With his words, Charlotte's heart fluttered in her breast
as a thousand confusing thoughts flitted through her brain.
Finally, it struck her. She'd mistaken Jack's intent.

"I'd like you all to meet my wife, Charlotte Cordell."

A blush warmed her cheeks as Jack extended a hand
to her. But she was still so stunned by disbelief that she

only sat there until Rachel jabbed an elbow in her ribs to jar her. "Go on now," she urged. "He's waiting for you."

Still dazed, Charlotte got to her feet and went up to join her husband. As soon as she drew near enough, Jack slipped an arm around her waist, and there in front of God and everybody, he kissed her.

Her lips were tingling when finally he drew back. Shyly, she dropped her gaze to the floor, not wanting anyone else to see how deeply his gesture had touched her. A whole new world had opened up for her now, for there was no doubt in her mind that Jack was saying, in as public a way as possible, that no matter what she'd been or done, he still considered her his wife.

Charlotte could scarcely believe it, but it had to be true. Even after he'd kissed her, Jack wouldn't let her go. He threaded his arm through hers and led her into the crowd to meet some of Cedar Creek's newest residents and make polite conversation. For his part, Jack seemed perfectly able to chat with his neighbors and still cast meaningful glances her way in between, but Charlotte dared not permit her own thoughts to stray too far, for she was determined to make the best impression she possibly could on these people, for Jack's sake.

When finally the crowd had thinned, Charlotte's heart began to beat a little faster. After all she'd told him this afternoon and the way that he'd avoided her afterward, she'd been certain that Jack wanted to be rid of her, but apparently he had only been busy plotting his strategy. In fact, if the subtle smiles and sidelong glances he'd been giving her in the past few minutes were any indication, it would appear that he was determined to sweep all of the remaining impediments that stood between them out of the way. And knowing this made Charlotte nervous as a schoolgirl. Ere long, her heart was racing and her mouth had gone dry.

"Let's go home," Jack said as he drew up behind her,

lifted her shawl up onto her shoulders and then bent to press his lips against the nape of her neck.

Surprised by the contact, Charlotte drew a sharp breath. But before she could manage a reply, Leah scampered up the empty aisle to join them. "Everyone's leaving," she said. "Are we ready to go?"

"You go on ahead," Jack told his sister. "We'll be along in a minute or two."

Leah did as she was bade, hurrying off, and by the time Jack had squired Charlotte out of the big double doors, they were at last alone. The wind had stilled and a soft, steady snow was falling, draping the landscape in a cloak of pristine white.

They walked together, arm-in-arm, without speaking, until they reached the wooden bridge that spanned the creek. Jack led her up to the rail, then peered over at the bubbling waters below. "Do you remember the night I brought you out here so you could soak your feet in the water?" he asked. "The night that every man in town got to dance with you? Every man, that is, except for me."

"It seems a lifetime ago," Charlotte admitted, her eyes fixed on the icy waters as they eddied and churned over the rocks.

Grasping her shoulders, Jack turned her toward him, then slipped his forefinger beneath her chin, coaxing her to look up at him. "I fell in love with you that night, you know. Oh, I was too stubborn to admit it then, even to myself, but it's true. I know because, from that moment on, I never dreamed another dream about Cedar Creek that didn't include you."

Snowflakes, light as feathers, dropped out of the night sky and brushed against Charlotte's face, settling on the bridge of her nose, the tips of her lashes; then melting, they ran like teardrops.

"I never dared have any dreams of my own," she admitted. "But I let my heart fill up with yours. I wanted all of this as badly as you did, and because of it, I . . . I did some things, some things that weren't quite right."

Jack didn't press her to explain. Catching up her hand, he wove his long fingers through hers, and taking up his cane in his free hand, he started off in his stiff-legged gait, tugging her after him. "We'd better get going. It's cold. You'll catch a chill."

"I lied to you about the letter, the one from that railroad surveyor," she said, as she lengthened her strides to match his, and her skirts kicked up a flurry of snow. "He said they'd called off the project because they couldn't find the money to finance the line. But I couldn't bear to tell you that."

Jack's brow creased in a thoughtful frown, but he kept on walking. He nodded. "I suppose I ought to have guessed."

"You aren't angry with me?"

"It hardly matters now. We're sitting on a rich vein of silver; the town is booming all on its own. Sooner or later, the railroads are going to come to us."

"Yes, well, then there's the second thing."

At this, he drew up short in the middle of the street, saying nothing, only waiting. Charlotte wondered what he must be thinking, if he was reconsidering all that he'd said tonight.

"I salted that mine," she revealed at last, "the one that Hollis Lloyd stumbled onto."

"You *what?*"

Wincing, she prepared to meet his wrath. "I . . . I salted the mine. I scattered pieces of that blossom rock you were saving in that old pack of yours all around the tunnel, and then I filled your shotgun with gold dust and peppered the walls with it."

By now they'd reached the hotel. Jack let go of her hand, then reaching out for the upright post, hoisted himself up onto the porch, threw back his head and let go a hysterical laugh. The sound of it echoed through the empty streets. With arms akimbo, he turned back on her. "Do you mean to tell me that if it weren't for you . . ."

Charlotte lowered her head, concentrating on the toes of her boots. "I know it was wrong, Jack, but I was desperate. Everyone was talking about leaving, and I knew if something didn't happen fast . . ."

"But don't you see? If you hadn't gotten that greedy oaf's attention, we wouldn't have found out about the silver, and none of this . . ." He waved a hand wildly up and down the whole of Main Street. "None of this would be here today. I may have dreamt a future for Cedar Creek, Charlotte, but you're the one who made it happen."

"Then you wouldn't rather I went away?" she asked, her voice scarcely more than a whisper.

In reply, Jack set aside his cane, then reached out, hooking her waist with one long arm and dragged her full against him. Her hands splayed against the damp wool of his overcoat, and when she took a breath, it was rich with pine soap, bay rum, and that male scent that was uniquely his own.

"I meant all that I said tonight," he told her. "I couldn't manage without you, and I don't want to try. So let's not have any more talk about leaving."

His hands had found their way beneath her shawl and were sliding possessively up and down the ridge of her spine. Charlotte sighed as the blood in her veins began to bubble with heat, in spite of the winter chill.

"If you're sure that's what you want . . ."

"What I want . . ." Jack bent nearer, until she could feel his breath warm her cheek. "What I want . . . is to dance with you, Charlotte."

Her eyes went wide. "Dance?" she echoed in surprise. "What, right here?"

"Why not? It's our porch, and we're out here all alone."

"But there's no music."

"Yes, there is," he replied, then pressed his forefinger against her lips. "Hush now and listen."

Sure enough, when she did as he'd asked her, Charlotte could make out the faint, tinkling notes of "Buffalo Gals" being played on a piano somewhere. The sound was probably coming from one of the saloons at the other end of town.

Before she'd realized, Jack was nuzzling her earlobe, and his hands had slid down her arms, his fingers circling her wrists, then slipping purposefully beneath her gloves to tease the tender flesh there.

"Please," he urged.

Catching up her hands, he placed one on his shoulder, then clasped the other and lifted it into position. As he guided her through the first few steps, his arm tightened across her back, drawing their bodies so close that her breasts molded against the broad breadth of his chest. Charlotte could feel the steady beat of his heart close to her own, the lean hardness of his thighs pressing against hers, and then something more. . . . Instinct seized her, and she stiffened.

Jack did not step back, though, nor move to release her. He splayed the fingers of the hand he'd had pressed on her back and began to make long, lazy circles that warmed the skin beneath her dress and left it tingling. When he spoke, his voice was soft and soothing in her ear.

"It's only a dance," he told her, "there's nothing to be afraid of."

Swallowing her fears, Charlotte followed his lead. Somehow the rhythm of his dancing seemed more languid and provocative than the sprightly tune played on that far-off piano. Jack's steps were sure and faultless; his limp had all but disappeared. On its own, her head settled onto the wide pillow of his shoulder and the heat of his body seeped into her, relaxing her. If only they could stay here like this forever. . . .

"I've dreamed of dancing with you for so long," he said, his voice hushed and oddly labored. "Did you know that I bought up all your dances that night because I wanted to take you in my arms like this and never let you go? But after I saw how tired you were, I . . . just couldn't ask. And then at our wedding, it was torture, nothing less, to watch you whirl past on the arm of every man but me."

"I'm sorry," she told him, startled at the breathlessness in her own voice. "So much has gone wrong since then. I never ought to have let you push me away, but I had my own reasons for being afraid . . ."

Jack hesitated mid-step. His eyes were silver with reflected moonlight. His lips hovered only inches above hers. The harsh, uneven cadence of their breathing filled the air. Time stopped.

"You don't have to be afraid of me, Charlotte."

"I know."

Those two words seemed to give Jack the permission he'd been seeking. With the floodgates flung open, he eagerly closed the gap between them, his mouth covering hers. Charlotte was seized by a sudden, irresistible surge of excitement. Her lips melted under the firm pressure of his, and she welcomed the moist heat of his tongue.

They were not dancing any longer, yet still Charlotte could feel the pull and sway of powerful rhythms, rhythms she'd never experienced before. They threatened her balance, drumming in her head and weakening her knees, and in consequence, she leaned nearer to Jack for support. When at last their lips parted, she lifted her rheumy eyes to his, offering him, without a word, the trust he had already earned, the trust she ought never to have denied him.

Go slowly. Be gentle. Take care not to frighten her. Don't push. Jack's brain was spitting out warnings so fast he could scarcely absorb them all. Ever since Charlotte had admitted to him that she'd been misused, he'd wondered how he would handle this moment when it came. They'd have to get past this, the both of them, if there was to be any hope for happiness between them.

Damn his poor eyesight! If only he could see more in her eyes than two, blurred, twin pools of blue, he might be able to guess what she was thinking. She wasn't fighting him, that much gave him hope, and she seemed to be content in his arms. But still Jack was terrified that as soon as he made a telling move, she'd look at him and see instead that bastard gambler.

Frustrated, he blew out a harsh breath and pressed his forehead against hers. "It's getting late." He was reluctant to admit defeat, but what else could he do?

Charlotte nodded. "Morning comes awfully early. We ought to be getting to bed."

Jack let her go, then turned to retrieve his cane. He was headed for the door when she caught his arm to stop him. Placing herself square in front of him, she lifted her chin, so that the moonlight fully illuminated her face. Even he couldn't have missed the determined set to her jaw. "I meant *together,*" she said.

Numbed by a potent mix of anticipation and disbelief, Jack followed his wife into the small lobby, past the empty front desk, and up the stairs, his heart drumming so hard against his breastbone all the while that he'd have sworn she must be able to hear it. Charlotte didn't look back even once, though, as she mounted the last stair then headed down the hallway to their room. *Their room.* He repeated the thought once more, pleased by the sound of it.

Once inside, he shrugged off his overcoat and jacket, and cast them aside. Then he bent before the hearth and proceeded to lay a fire in the grate—a slow burning fire that would last them all night long. And when the flames were orange and crackling, he rose up in one fluid move and took a bold step forward. By God, he would not limp tonight. If it took every ounce of his strength, he'd be again the man he once was, the one Charlotte had fallen in love with.

She had already closed the door to shut them in. Jack found her standing there waiting for him, in the center of the room. Carefully focusing his eyes, he noticed that she'd discarded some of her clothes; they lay alongside the pink-striped dress, which was pooled at her feet. Firelight gilded her upswept hair, the soft, sloping shoulders, the slender arms. With her hands poised over the ribbons that fastened her chemise, she made a fetching picture, indeed, albeit a somewhat hazy one. Jack blinked hard several times, hoping against hope that his vision would clear; but of course, it did not.

He approached her slowly, making each step with careful deliberation. He was a mere arm's length away before he noticed that her hand was trembling. Pain twisted his heart as he recalled anew the hollow tone in her voice as she'd related to him all the hurt and humiliation that she'd suffered at the hands of the last man she'd trusted.

"You don't have to do this, Charlotte, if you don't want to," he said, even though his body had already begun to pulse with the want of her. "We have all the time in the world, you know. I'll wait."

She shook her head, and when she spoke, her husky voice vibrated like a shiver through his body. "It's well past time, Jack."

A flick of her wrist drew the ribbons apart. The thin fabric slipped over her shoulders, and once she'd shrugged it off, she stepped, naked, into his arms.

His eyes may have offered only an indistinct rendering of Charlotte's beauty, but the other senses left to him soon made up for the loss. Removing the pins that bound her hair, he let it drift through his hands in a silken-soft tumble of curls. A cloud of lavender and roses enveloped him, and he inhaled until the sweet fragrance filled up his lungs.

With deft purpose, he traced his fingertips over her eyelids, her cheeks, her lips, aiming to remind himself of the features he knew as well as his own, but which he hadn't been able to see clearly since the accident. Her skin was warm and satin smooth, the pulse in her throat fluttering wildly beneath his fingers. His hands dipped lower, his thumbs brushing over taut, pink crests as he cradled her breasts, and a sigh of pleasure broke from her lips. It was like music to him.

He marveled at the narrow span of her waist, the gentle curve of her shoulders, but when he touched several, odd ridges of raised skin on her upper arm, his right hand went suddenly still. His stomach twisted into a knot as the obvious crossed his mind. Had that bastard who'd scarred her so horribly within left his mark on her body as well?

Sensing his disquiet, Charlotte laid a gentle hand over his. "You're not the only one with scars, you know," she said softly.

"My God, Charlotte, he didn't . . ."

She hesitated briefly as she considered the direction of his thoughts. "Gideon? No, it wasn't him. It was the wildcat."

Jack regarded her, blinking in confusion.

"Up at Six Mile," she continued. "Vernon, Ira, and I were working our claim one day, when he dropped right down out of the rocks and took a swipe at me."

And then Jack remembered. Those miners had told him a story about a wildcat when they'd brought Charlotte into Cedar Creek. "That claw necklace you were wearing when you first came to town?" he posed. "You mean to say it's true? That story about how you killed a wildcat?"

She shrugged. "Must've been a lucky shot," she said,

and he could have sworn he saw a smile. "We both know my aim can't be trusted."

At this, Jack smiled, too. He couldn't help himself.

"You don't have to be afraid to touch me," she told him then, her voice hushed but earnest. "In fact, truth is, I find I rather like it. But . . . promise me you won't be alarmed when you get to that bullet hole just above my knee."

A long, thoughtful moment passed before Jack shook his head, and his chest rumbled with barely-suppressed laughter. "Whatever am I going to do with you, Charlotte Cordell?"

She reached up to grasp his face between her two hands. "Love me, Jack. Just love me."

She'd given him permission now, and so gathering her against him, Jack lowered his mouth on hers and drank in her sweetness. Tasting her, touching her, breathing her scent left him lightheaded and aching for more. Every muscle in his body was taut and vibrating with the restraint he'd exercised thus far, but still he held back. He wouldn't spend himself in a heated rush and wind up regretting it afterwards. He kissed her again, deeper this time; and slowly, amazingly, she began to respond.

Reaching up, she unknotted his tie, unfastened the buttons of his vest and then the shirt beneath. Without losing her mouth, Jack managed to work his arms free of his sleeves, then impatiently shed the lot, casting it all onto the floor in a tangled heap. Charlotte drew closer, her long, lithe body melting against his, fingers threading through the mat of hair on his bared chest. Lifting her arms, she coiled them around his neck, innocent of the effect that the slide of her taut breasts across his skin had upon him. His need had begun to press painfully, insistently, against his trousers. There was no more putting it off.

In one swift move, Jack bent to catch her up under the

knees and lifted her into his arms. Carrying her to the bed, he freed one hand to strip back the quilt, then settled her onto the mattress.

"I don't want to hurt you, Charlotte," he said, drawing back. "If I frighten you, if there's anything you don't like, just tell me and I'll stop. I swear it."

Given the effect that she had on him. Jack knew it would be difficult, nigh to impossible, in fact, but he'd manage somehow. This woman meant that much to him.

In response, Charlotte extended her arms. The air filled with the ragged cadence of her breathing, and it pleased him to know that, in spite of all she'd been through, she wanted this, wanted *him*. He shed the remainder of his clothes, then stood for a moment, allowing her to get used to the sight of him.

The chilly night air raised gooseflesh on his body, but waves of heat from the fire in the hearth caressed his back. The feather bed, warm and waiting, heaped with quilts and linens, beckoned to him and Charlotte. But eager as he was for what was to come, he held back just a little while longer to remind himself of his purpose. Looking down toward his wife, her eyes wide and trusting, his heart welled anew with the love he felt for her; and he made a silent vow. This wouldn't be pleasure, just for pleasure's sake. In loving Charlotte tonight, Jack aimed to wipe away her nightmares, to replace them instead with memories of what lovemaking ought to be.

The bedsprings creaked as he lay down beside her. Charlotte's heart was pounding in her throat, and she swallowed hard to silence it. This was what she wanted. She wouldn't allow her nightmares to return and spoil everything. Turning to him, she coiled a hand around his neck, drew him to her and kissed him, open-mouthed, just as he'd done to her. It didn't take long to rekindle the fire within him. Nostrils flaring, he blew out a harsh breath, and ere long his lips were trailing her jawline, branding a path across the sensitive skin of her neck to the hollow of her throat, and then lower still.

Capturing the sensitive peak of one breast, he nipped it with his teeth and then suckled gently. Charlotte cast back her head, her mouth dropping open in amazement as he did the same with the other. Meanwhile, his arms had slipped around her, his hands kneading the soft flesh of her backside. A rush of heat flooded through her veins, making her body quiver with an odd anticipation. Never before had she experienced anything like this.

A soft moan broke from her lips. "Oh, Jack."

Reticence ebbed away, replaced by a hunger for more of the pleasures Jack wrought with his mouth and his hands. She sidled up closer, marveling at the fit of their two bodies and the tingling that coursed through her as she slid along the finely-muscled length of him. Instinctively, he turned full against her, his arousal pressing into her belly. Charlotte caught her breath and froze.

Exhaling long and low, Jack pulled away. "There's nothing to be afraid of," he insisted. His voice seemed oddly strained and breathless. Taking up her hand in his, he drew it down, folding her fingers around his swollen shaft. "It's meant to be this way. It only shows how much I want you . . ."

The words broke off, ending in a strangled groan. Charlotte sensed that this was causing him pain somehow, and there was no denying how very patient he had been. But with curiosity spurring her on, she curled her fingers closer over his flesh, sliding them up the smooth, hard length of him.

Jack squeezed his eyes shut. Beads of sweat broke out across his brow, glittering in the firelight. She'd always believed that the intimate joining of a man and a woman necessarily meant pleasure for the one and pain for the other. But now she was coming to realize that it wasn't so simple, and she wasn't half so powerless as she had imagined.

Jack caught his breath and then her hand. "Charlotte! Please . . . no more."

Obliging, she released him. He pressed his lips to her fingertips, each in turn, then the sensitive hollow of her hand, the throbbing pulse point of her wrist. Before long, his breathing had resumed its normal rate, and with renewed purpose, he turned to her and buried his face in her hair.

"Now let me touch you," he whispered.

Without waiting for a reply, his lips sought hers in a kiss so potent it made Charlotte's blood race and left her giddy and ripe for the intimate caress he intended. As he urged her back onto the mattress, she scarcely noticed that he'd parted her thighs, until after his fingers had insinuated themselves between the soft folds of flesh. Still and breathless, she accepted his touch, trusting him in spite of the vestige of fear that remained. Ere long, she felt a fluttering deep within her belly, where a queer pressure was building, demanding release. The blood in her veins had turned hot and thick as molasses, and shamefully, she found herself pressing closer against his hand, concentrating on each languid stroke of his thumb, wholly caught up in the potent sensations he wrought in her.

Sparks of pleasure flamed, then flickered out with increasing frequency. The ultimate release she was seeking seemed just out of her reach. It was torture, exquisite and all-consuming.

"Please," she hissed, without even stopping to think what it was she was asking of him.

His reply was an assault on a new front, his open mouth grazing the exposed arch of her throat before sweeping down to devour again the swollen peak of one breast. She purred with delight, then shivered as he forged a new trail, his lips slanting across her ribcage, over the taut skin of her belly, then lower still to the cleft of her thighs. She gasped at the wet heat as his tongue touched her intimately, insistently, and then she drove her head backward into the pillow as a new, blinding shower of sparks lit up the world.

"What is it?" Jack teased, lifting his head to reveal a devilish gleam in his eye.

Charlotte's breathing was ragged and shallow. Her fists had been frantically clutching at the bedclothes, but she loosed her fingers now and reached for him. She knew that he was taking his time with her, taking care so that she'd not be hurt. But she wasn't afraid anymore, and it hurt much more now when he left off touching her. He could ease the awful ache she felt inside, if only he wished to.

"Love me now, Jack," she begged him. "I want you to. I do. I won't be afraid."

Jack wanted to believe her. Heaven knew his own need had grown nigh to unmanageable. With the scent of her filling his every breath, the taste of her still on his lips, he ached with desire, trembled with it. As he eased his body up along the silken length of hers, though, he felt her quiver beneath him, and he froze. This is what he'd been afraid of, that when he finally moved to cover her, she'd panic, and withdraw from him in fear as she had so many times before. Crestfallen, he waited to hear her protest in his ear.

Ah, but this time he was mistaken. Charlotte had reacted, not out of fear, but rather anticipation, and that became all too clear to him as she caught his shoulders, and drawing him down to her, spread her velvety thighs. He settled in between them, his arousal sliding along the wet, slick warmth of her. The sensation made his head reel, but nevertheless he repeated the movement, and with each sure stroke, he was rewarded by a small gasp of pleasure against his ear.

Just when he thought he could stand to wait no more, she caught him by surprise, tilting her hips so that his next thrust brought the blunt head of his erection full against her. The warm flesh yielded, and he found himself deliciously enveloped. He let go a deep groan and stilled, his heart pounding in his throat as he looked down into her eyes, wishing he could see more there than a mere shimmer of blue light.

The voice he summoned was hoarse and deep. "Charlotte, are you sure?"

In reply, she slid her legs up, locked them around his waist and drew him in, deeper. Jack had his answer, and so, eagerly he drove into her, filling her up in the ancient rite of possession. She was truly his wife now, he told himself, his and only his. He pressed his mouth into the sleek curve of her shoulder, slowly, surely losing control as she matched him thrust for thrust.

The indrawn breath of surprise, the trembling climax of the slender body joined to his, helped drive Jack over the edge. Stars exploded in his head. The feral groan of ecstasy that rumbled through his chest seemed strangely far away. With all the strength remaining in him, he plunged deep inside her, shuddered, and spent his seed.

At length, Charlotte stirred beneath him, rousing him from pleasant exhaustion. Her trilling sigh was sweet in his ear. He'd wanted her sated, swept away, but as he took up her face in his hands and pressed his lips to her cheeks, he tasted salty tears, and alarm sped through him.

Raising up, he rolled aside, then hooking her with his arm, he drew her to his chest, cradled her gently. "Oh, God, Charlotte. Have I hurt you?"

She'd buried her face against him. Her only reply was a series of ragged sobs that shook her through and through. Stroking her hair, he struggled to find words to soothe her, but none came to him. Never in all the time he'd known her had he seen Charlotte shed a single tear, not even this afternoon when she'd described for him the painful secrets of her past. Life had treated her mercilessly and that had made her hard. Jack had begun to think his wife incapable of any weakness, but now here she was, weeping a veritable flood which flowed unchecked, making hot, wet trails down his bare chest.

And then it struck him. This was a good thing. It meant that, at last, he'd broken down the wall Charlotte had built around herself. She was feeling again. "You aren't hurt, are you?" he asked her, although he sensed he already knew the answer. "Or unhappy?"

"Oh, no, Jack," she assured him, as her arms went round him possessively. "It's only that . . . I never knew, never guessed how wonderful it could be. How can I thank you? You've . . . chased away the demons."

Twenty

Cradling the mixing bowl in the crook of her arm, Charlotte beat the flapjack batter vigorously with her wooden spoon, and then poured it onto the hot griddle. She felt free, wonderfully free this morning. The shadows that for so long had darkened her life had finally fled, and she was eager to face the new day. She wasn't even aware that she'd been humming while she worked until Leah, who'd been arranging the breakfast plates onto a tray for serving, remarked on her mood.

"You're awfully chipper this morning. You must have got a good night's sleep."

"Mhmm," Charlotte replied, stifling a secret smile as her mind filled with vivid memories of last night and of how soundly Jack had still been sleeping when she'd slipped out of bed this morning. After all the uncomfortable nights he'd spent on the dressing room cot, she hadn't had the heart to wake him.

"No more nightmares then?"

At this, Charlotte looked up from her task, eyes wide. However had Leah . . . ?

"You know, you nearly scared me and the guests to death the other night with your screams."

Charlotte exhaled slowly. So that's what she'd meant. Jack had told them that she'd had a nightmare after he'd startled her in her bed. "Well, everyone can rest easy now," she told the girl. "I don't think there'll be anymore nightmares."

Both of them went back to their work, but only a few more minutes had passed before Charlotte remembered the conversation she'd had with Rachel at the church last night about Leah. Confident as she was, she decided to broach the subject.

"You're looking awfully bright-eyed and rosy-cheeked yourself, young lady. Mrs. Kelsey thinks you've got a secret beau. I told her, of course, that you'd hardly the time to meet any of the local boys."

"He's not a boy," Leah insisted, unwittingly revealing herself with her words. "He owns a mine."

Charlotte hiked her brow, interested now. So, Rachel had been right; there was someone. "Half the men in this county own mines, or pieces of them," she said, trying to be patient. "But what they get out of them isn't enough to put bread on the table."

"Oh, he does well enough. I can tell. After all, he dresses like a gentleman. There's no dirt under his fingernails, I've noticed that, and he has the most charming manners."

For a fleeting, frantic moment, Charlotte wondered if Leah mightn't be speaking of Hollis Lloyd. Heavens, wouldn't that be a fix? But no, Lloyd might, indeed, be a well-dressed mine owner, but he couldn't be considered a charming gentleman, not by any stretch of the imagination.

She framed her next question cautiously. "How did you meet this man?"

"Oh, Charlotte, it was the most romantic thing," Leah replied, clearly pleased by her interest. "I'd gone off to run an errand, and I was coming out of Sutton's Mercantile when he stepped out right in front of me and said that he didn't believe he'd ever seen a lovelier young woman in all his life. Can you imagine that?"

An icy shiver coursed through Charlotte. She didn't

have to imagine. That was almost precisely the same approach that she'd fallen prey to in New Orleans all those years ago. The coincidence was unsettling.

"He asked to walk me home."

"But you hadn't even been introduced," Charlotte protested.

"Oh, now, don't you go lecturing me like a maiden aunt. These are modern times. He's escorted me on errands several times since then; we were out on the public street. What's wrong with that? Besides, you ought to be pleased that someone's taken an interest in me. If I get married, then I won't be a burden to you and Jack anymore."

Marriage? How had things gotten so serious, so quickly? Crossing the room in a few, swift strides, Charlotte put her hands on Leah's shoulders and looked into her eyes.

"Haven't Jack and I have told you before?" she said. "You're a part of this family, and you're welcome to stay with us for as long as you like. Now, as far as this smooth-talking gentleman is concerned, Leah, I want you to listen to me. There are a lot of dangerous men in the world, and especially in a boom town like this one. If this *beau* of yours wants to see you again, you bring him here and introduce him to your brother and me. If he won't agree to come, then that ought to tell you that he's not the right sort of man for you. Do you understand?"

Leah's mouth dropped open, and her face went pale. It was apparent by her expression that, at that moment, Charlotte's role had changed, in her eyes, from that of a trusted friend and confidante to that of a meddling parent. Charlotte felt a twinge of sadness to see it, but deep inside, she knew that she was right.

"You've no right to tell me not to see him. You're treating me like a child," the girl snapped, her pretty mouth forming a pout. Wrenching free of Charlotte's grip, she picked up her tray and barreled through the swinging doors into the dining room.

Maybe she oughtn't to have taken it upon herself to speak to her about this, Charlotte told herself in retrospect, maybe she ought to have consulted with Jack first. She was his sister, after all. But she couldn't help it. This was a sore subject with her, a lesson she herself had learned the hard way.

Replaying in her mind her confrontation with the girl made her realize how familiar it all sounded. Her father had cautioned her in much the same way a lifetime ago, and like Leah, she had refused to listen and stormed out of the room, still convinced that she was right.

It was a glorious morning. The air was crisp. The sun was shining brightly overhead, and nature had cast a snowy blanket over the town, making it seem as if Cedar Creek had been freshly whitewashed, stem to stern. Wrapped up as he was in his thoughts, though, Jack scarcely noticed. He ought to have been pleased with himself, preening, thoroughly confident. He'd made a success of his speech to the townsfolk, and more important than that, last night he'd managed to eliminate the last of the misunderstandings between him and Charlotte. Loving her had proven more satisfying than he had ever dreamed possible.

Yet as he trod through the powdery snow down the familiar path to Noah's house, he found himself plagued by an odd uneasiness, a niggling . . . something that hovered just beyond his conscious thoughts. Try as he might, though, he could not put a name to it. He'd felt the first symptoms early this morning, before the dawn's light had stolen in between the shutters and roused Charlotte from his arms. It was a fear—a not so unusual one, perhaps—that if he let her go, the magical spell would be broken, that he'd never again know the joy of her embrace.

Of course, when she'd met him later, smiling and radiant across the breakfast table in their small, private sitting room, nothing between them had changed at all. They'd talked together, and he'd taken her hand. She'd blushed and gone shy and silent with his veiled references to their well-spent night, and his promises for nights still to come. Still, even after he'd been reassured by her manner, the peculiar disquiet hung over him like a pall, preventing him from savoring the happiness he'd found.

Tightening his grip on the head of his walking stick, Jack increased the length of his strides. Maybe once he'd talked to Noah, he'd feel better. Maybe his distress was only due to his frustration at the fact that his eyesight still hadn't improved. Much as he had tried to reconcile himself to the loss, the truth was that it was hell going through life as if his eyes were swathed in gauze veiling, unable to shave himself in the morning without cutting his own throat, unable to read an advertisement in the newspaper, or to look across the breakfast table and simply see the love reflected in his wife's eyes. God, what he wouldn't give to be able to do that!

But as he analyzed his agitation, he decided that it wasn't self-pity he was feeling; it was something far more threatening. Jack drew himself up on the Kelseys' porch, hesitating before the closed door. With brow furrowed, he threw back his head, inhaled the frigid winter air, feeling it burn his lungs, and then gave his thoughts full rein, sifting through the disorganized jumble of sounds and images that were the memories stored in his brain.

A glint of fire flashed suddenly before his eyes, blinding him. Could it have been a cuff button catching the light? Or a ring, perhaps? A ring made out of a ten-dollar gold piece? Next, he distinctly heard the flutter of riffling cards, followed by a male voice, deep and drawling: "I come from New Orleans originally . . ." It struck him that the accent was much the same as Charlotte's, and soon as that thought took shape, he heard her voice proclaim, "I shot him . . . he's dead. He's got to be."

They were all only memories, but potent nonetheless, and they left Jack with a sense of impending disaster, replete with prickling gooseflesh and the acrid taste of fear on his tongue.

Just then, the door swung open, and Noah stood gaping before him. "Jack? I thought I saw you out here, but I didn't hear you knock. Mrs. Murphy's busy in the kitchen, and Rachel's gone over to your place, I think. For heaven's sake, come on inside before you catch your death."

Jack did as he was bade, wiping his boots on the front hall carpet as he allowed his friend to take his overcoat and usher him into his office. "I'm glad you've come. I wanted you to see the campaign posters we've had printed. I've hired some of the local boys, and they've been tacking them up all over town this morning."

Before he could even settle in his chair, Noah had thrust the sheet of paper in his hand. Blinking awkwardly, Jack endeavored to focus his eyes on the swimming black type. He could just barely make out the large block letters of his name. But even so, his thoughts were elsewhere.

Resting himself on the corner of his desk, Noah folded his arms across his chest and only as he looked on Jack, mutely examining the paper, did he realize his mistake. "Oh, God. That was stupid of me. I'm sorry," he said. "It's only that I'm excited about how well you did last night. I'll read it to you, if you like."

Jack shook his head. "Don't bother. I didn't come here about the campaign, Noah. What I want to know is if you've had the chance to write to any of your doctor friends back home in Philadelphia yet. You remember you told me that you'd advise them of my case, and ask if they'd ever treated anything like it."

"Yes, I did, and I have," Noah replied. "But the news isn't good, I'm afraid. I've had letters from fellow physi-

cians that described similar cases—war injuries mostly—
in which varying degrees of blindness had been the result
of a concussion. Most of them concur that that's likely
what's happened in your case. But I'm afraid I can't offer
you any guarantees. Some of these patients have recovered
their sight, some haven't."

This wasn't at all what Jack wanted to hear. "What
about consulting a specialist?"

"In cases such as yours, there isn't much any doctor
can do, not even a specialist. If you take my advice, Jack,
you'll try to adjust to this. I know it won't be easy, but
you're luckier than most. You at least have some vision,
enough to help you get around."

"That's not enough, I'm afraid," he retorted.

"If it's the election you're worried about, last night
ought to have convinced you that your poor eyesight
doesn't matter to most folk."

Slowly, purposefully, Jack crushed the election poster
he'd been holding in his hand into a tight ball, then
dropped his fist down hard onto his knee.

"It isn't the election," he insisted.

Of course, Noah didn't understand. How could he? He
hadn't heard any of Charlotte's story, didn't know what
she'd been through. Jack had only just realized the truth
himself a few moments ago. Marcus Gideon wasn't dead.
Charlotte thought she'd killed him, but with her aim, he
ought to have known . . . And now Gideon was right here
in Cedar Creek. Jack had seen him, talked to him a few
nights ago in the Golden Palace Saloon. He was all but
sure of it.

God damn it, he couldn't afford to be blind and useless
right now! There had to be something he could do. What
if Charlotte should run across him one day on the street?
He didn't want to think what that would do to her. She
was healing, but still fragile yet. What if the bastard
should come into the hotel, see her, recognize her?

He considered speaking to Sam Willis, but he knew that the peace officer could do nothing unless Charlotte were to testify against Marcus Gideon for his crimes in a court of law, and Jack would never subject her to that.

A powerful mix of fear and anger wrenched his gut, and all the old feelings he thought he'd buried for good years ago rose up in him anew. Justice never served the innocent. Justice was more blind than he was. And left unchecked, the evil in men like Marcus Gideon would spread like a pestilence, and more innocents like Charlotte and his brother, Matthew, would be made to suffer. This was something he would have to handle on his own, Jack told himself, something, after all, that he was eminently qualified to handle. If only he could see . . .

Ah, but then maybe it was better that he couldn't, for it made him stop now and think. Hadn't he told Charlotte only yesterday how little satisfaction could be got out of revenge? Hadn't he already learned that lesson for himself? Violence was not the answer. There had to be another way.

Charlotte bent over the basket set in the center of her bed, admiring the peaceful features of her godson, who was sleeping within it. "He's perfect, Rachel."

"You wouldn't say that if you'd seen him half an hour ago, red-faced and squawling for his dinner."

"Well, it's all worked out for the best, hasn't it? He's tired himself out, and you've got a few minutes of peace."

Rachel sighed and settled deeper into the chair beside the windows. "You sound as if you're ready for one of your own, now that you've settled your misunderstandings with Jack."

Charlotte hadn't given much thought to a family of her own. For so long, she'd been tormented by her past; she'd never really believed that she could have a normal life. But last night had taught her that anything was possible.

Unconsciously, one hand stole over her skirts, fingers stretching across her belly. Even now, she might be carrying Jack's child. The thought made her smile.

"I suppose I am ready . . . now," she admitted. "But until it happens, I'll have to hone my mothering skills on Leah. Heaven knows that'll be challenge enough."

Rachel leaned forward in her chair, her dark eyes sparkling. "I *was* right, wasn't I? You've spoken to her, and she does have a beau."

"I wouldn't put it quite that way," Charlotte replied as she went to stare out of the long windows. "She says she's only gone walking a few times with someone. He's older, that's all I know, and he claims to own a mine."

"You didn't ask her for his name?"

Charlotte shook her head. "I told her if she wanted to see him again, she'd have to bring him by to meet Jack and me. She accused me of meddling. Maybe I was a bit too harsh with her, but she's so young, Rachel. She hasn't any idea what could happen to her."

"Have you spoken to Jack about this?"

"He's planning to discuss it with her after dinner tonight. But I don't see that he'll have any more success than I did. Leah's a dreamer, and she wants so badly for her life to be as exciting as those stories she likes to read."

"Do you think she'll try and see him again, even if her brother forbids it?"

"I know what I'd have done at her age," Charlotte replied to this, "what I *did* do, and it doesn't make me any more at ease, I can tell you. I sent her to run some errands a while ago. She's probably out there with her gentleman friend right now, her head so full of pretty dreams that he'll be able to talk her into anything."

"Well, if you're worried about her, why don't you go out and see for yourself? This isn't so big a town that you wouldn't be able to find them. *If* they're only walking, that is."

"I couldn't do that," Charlotte exclaimed. "If she were to see me spying on her, she'd never trust me again, and besides, it might push her into the arms of this admirer of hers, even if that wasn't what she'd intended. I fear I might have done that already."

"Maybe we're worrying over nothing," Rachel posed then. "There are plenty of decent men in this town, who might be attracted to a pretty girl like Leah."

"I wish I could believe that's all it is. But if this man is serious about her, then why hasn't he ever come by the hotel? Why hasn't he done the honest thing and asked Jack's permission to court her?"

Rachel's soft brow creased as she considered all that Charlotte had said, and then she got that mischievous sparkle in her eye. "Well then, your only alternative is to get up a disguise and . . ."

It was apparent as she lifted a hand to cover her open mouth that Rachel regretted her audacious suggestion even before she'd finished making it. Likely she hadn't even realized. But they both knew how adept Charlotte had once been with disguise, and so now Charlotte couldn't prevent herself from considering the possibility.

As Rachel had said, it would be easy enough to find Leah in town, if she and this beau of his were out walking, and if Charlotte were wearing a disguise, she wouldn't need to worry about the girl spotting her. She could see for herself just who this man was that Leah was seeing and that would be the end of it.

"You wouldn't mind keeping an eye on things here for me for a few minutes, would you?" she asked as she went to the bureau and pulled open the bottom drawer.

"Charlotte, no. You're not going to put on those nasty buckskins again."

"It's the only way I'll know for certain that Leah's not

gotten into something she can't handle," she told her as she reached in and pulled out the parcel containing Charlie's clothes.

"Jack won't like it."

"He won't have to know. He's over plotting campaign strategies with Noah, and I'll only be gone half an hour at the most." Having made up her mind, she began to unfasten buttons and wriggle out of her clothes. "Oh, Rachel, I know I am probably worrying over nothing. But don't you see, I have to do this. I know what can happen to a high-spirited girl with more dreams than sense. I won't see Leah hurt that way. Once I'm sure that Leah isn't playing into the hands of some sweet-talking charlatan, I'll step back and let Jack handle the rest. I promise."

Once she'd pulled the fringed shirt over her head and fastened her wide leather belt at her waist, Charlotte gathered up the old felt hat and went to stand before the bureau mirror. The reflection that met her there startled her. It was not at all the Charlie she'd remembered. Especially after she'd removed the pins from her hair, and let it slip down from the topknot to frame her face with curls, she wondered how she'd ever been able to carry off the masquerade. Had she always looked so soft, so harmless? Or had she'd changed so much since she'd come to live in Cedar Creek?

Sweeping back the curls, she bound them into a tight queue with a leather thong, then put on the hat, pulling the wide brim low across her face. Still dissatisfied, she reached into the drawer for her pistol and stuck it in her belt.

Rachel shot her a nervous glance. "What's that for?"

"Don't worry," she assured her as she stepped into the dressing room and took up one of Jack's wool frock coats. "It's only for effect."

The pistol did add a certain roughness to her character. But as she shrugged into the coat and stood there, taking a last look in the mirror, Charlotte realized that, as comfortable as the buckskins had once been to her, they now felt foreign and strange. Yes, she supposed she had changed.

She left the hotel by way of the kitchen door, but as she came around the front of the building, she spotted Jack's campaign posters and had to stop to take a look. There was one on each of the porch pillars and yet another tacked up on the front door. Forgetting for a moment that she had business to tend to, she stepped up on the porch to admire them. Like the others, the sign on the door read "VOTE FOR JACK CORDELL" in bold, black letters, but drawing nearer, Charlotte noticed that there was a handwritten note scrawled across its face. Without thinking, she snatched it up to read, and then remembering that she was in disguise, started off down the street toward the butcher shop where she'd sent Leah.

"There is a reaper whose name is Death, and with his sickle keen, he reaps the bearded grain at a breath and the flowers that grow between."

A shiver coursed through her as she read the words. This was a warning of some type, and clearly an ominous one, with its reference to death. Was it meant to make Jack withdraw his name from the race? Or was it only some sort of mean-spirited prank?

Charlotte had too much on her mind right now. She didn't have time to address any more troubling questions. The best thing to do, she decided, would be to show this to Jack when she got back home, and so folding the page, she tucked it into the pocket of his coat and returned her thoughts to the business at hand—finding Leah.

It was easy enough to lose herself in Cedar Creek at this time of day. There were tangles of horses and mules at the hitching posts, ore wagons rumbling over the ruts of frozen mud in the street, their teamsters shouting warnings to pedestrians as they passed. There seemed to be people everywhere—from the workmen, who were busily constructing yet another saloon opposite Thorssen's Livery, and miners who had come to town for a few supplies or a taste of whiskey and wild life, to neighbors toting heavily-laden market baskets on their arms. Whenever she happened to pass a familiar face, Charlotte dropped her gaze quickly to the boardwalk so that the brim of her hat shaded her face. No sense taking any chances.

She walked past the mercantile, staring in through the windows, but didn't see a sign of Leah. She moved on to the laundry and the butcher's, with no luck at either place. A bitter wind whipped up, slicing through her. Shrugging deeper into Jack's wool coat, she began to wonder if she wasn't a fool for playing hide-and-seek with Leah, and freezing out here in the street. Maybe she'd overreacted to this whole situation. Just because she had had a bad experience, didn't mean that Leah was in any danger. Maybe she ought to just go on home, and let Jack handle this. And then she turned and saw the vivid green of the girl's velvet bonnet.

They were sitting close together on one of the split log benches that were scattered across the windswept town square. It was a public place, and innocent enough, but still as soon as she caught sight of them, Charlotte was seized by a prickling of uneasiness that radiated throughout her body. She couldn't see the man's face from her present vantage point—but the broad shoulders that stretched the dark fabric of his overcoat told her that it was, indeed, a man, and not the gangling youth that a girl of Leah's age ought to be interested in.

Angling for a better view, Charlotte crossed the street and then took up a casual stance, leaning against the rough clapboards that stretched across the side of Gus Stern's newly-built assay office. The man's clothes were those of a gentleman and expertly tailored to his muscular frame. A neatly-trimmed beard, reddish in color, shaded his jaw, but Charlotte could make out little else, for the wide brim of his black felt hat effectively hid his features from view, and so she stood there, trying to match the figure before her with all of the likely gentlemen of her acquaintance.

It wasn't Hollis Lloyd, and that, at least, made her breathe a short sigh of relief. It couldn't have been Henry Sutton; he was thinner than this man, and clean-shaven. Gunnar Thorssen had a beard about that color, but he never dressed so fashionably. Of course, she really hadn't expected it to be someone they knew.

For all this time, Leah had been staring shyly at her gloved hands, neatly folded in her lap, but when at last she lifted her head, Charlotte could see that her pretty face was flush with color, a change effected partly by the November chill and partly because her admirer had just caught up her small hand in his.

As he drew it to his lips, Charlotte caught a flash of gold that caused her heart to lurch painfully and skip a beat. She swiped a fist across her eyes. It had only been a trick of the light, she told herself, seeking to dismiss what she'd seen.

Leah got to her feet then. Picking up the market basket that she'd set on the bench beside her, she said her good-byes, and with obvious reluctance, parted from her friend, heading back down the street toward the hotel. Unaware that he was being watched, the man got up as well, turned and made his way toward Charlotte.

She waited, frozen in her spot and trembling with an old, familiar fear. Try though she might, she hadn't been able to erase the image of his hand as he'd reached out to Leah and the glint of the ring upon it. Was she losing her mind? Was she so afraid for Leah's safety that she'd imagined she'd seen a dead man—her nightmare, her nemesis—sitting there on the bench with the girl?

Stepping up onto the boardwalk that ran in front of the

assay office, Marcus Gideon lingered a moment to light
his cheroot. The matchlight gleamed, reflecting in his feral, amber eyes, and the sickeningly-sweet odor of tobacco
smoke seeped into Charlotte's lungs, threatening to suffo-
cate her. He was no more than a few yards away now,
but he didn't even notice her, standing there beside the
building. Absently, he cast aside the matchstick and continued on his way.

Charlotte's knees buckled, no longer able to support her
weight, and she sank to the ground, burying her head in
her shaking hands. What she wouldn't give to open her
eyes and find that it was only an awful dream, but she
knew that it wasn't. She hadn't killed him, after all.
Gideon had gone off, unscathed, to scavenge through the
mountain mining camps, until word of a gold strike had
brought him to Cedar Creek. And now he was stalking
Leah.

Once Charlotte had dared to imagine herself as hardened and fearless, but at this moment, she was quaking
inside. She wanted nothing more than to run home to
Jack, to throw herself into his arms where she'd be safe
and forget what she'd seen. But would he believe her when
she told him that Marcus Gideon was alive and living
somewhere here in town? She wouldn't have believed it,
not if she hadn't seen it for herself. And if she lost track
of him now, how would she find him again to prove it?

She shuddered, realizing that the only solution was for
her to trail him to his lair, and then, after she'd learned
where he could be found, she would go to Jack. Fear
washed over her in a paralyzing wave, but she shook it
off and swore beneath her breath, chiding herself. There
was more at stake here than her peace of mind. Marcus
Gideon had his eye on Leah. He was playing his evil
games, same as before, only this time it was Jack's sister
who was in danger. Understanding him as well as she did,
Charlotte knew that he wouldn't leave off until he'd had

what he wanted from the girl. But she wasn't going to let that happen.

Scrambling to her feet, she rounded the corner and scanned the bustling scene before her for a glimpse of his retreating figure. She fixed her eyes on each man of about the right height until finally she spotted him not too far ahead, seemingly bound for the opposite end of town. She increased her pace, and with each purposeful step she made, a little more of her fear ebbed away, replaced by a fierce determination. She wasn't going to run away, and she wasn't going to lose this chance. She had to see to it that Gideon stayed away from Leah, and one way or another, she was going to do just that.

Twenty-one

Jack pushed through the swinging doors into the hotel kitchen, and the scene that met his eyes was not at all what he'd expected. He recognized Leah at once by the sunny color of her dress. She was sitting beside the kitchen table, bouncing a baby on her knee, while nearby, someone else stirred the pots that were bubbling on the stovetop. It wasn't the hired girl, nor Charlotte, of that much he was certain. The woman was smaller in stature, and her hair was of a darker tint.

"Rachel?" he guessed.

She turned around, still clutching her wooden spoon, then drew back in surprise. "Jack? Why, we didn't expect to see you back so soon."

"Since when were you drafted to be our cook?" he wondered aloud. "Where's Charlotte?"

"Charlotte?" Rachel echoed, an odd, hesitant note in her voice. "She's . . . well, she's gone out for a few minutes."

"Gone out? Running errands, you mean?"

"She can't be," Leah put in. "I've only just come back from the butcher's, the laundry, and the mercantile . . ."

Jack felt the disquiet begin to bubble in his veins. He didn't like the thought of Charlotte out there on her own, not now that he knew that Marcus Gideon was close at hand. He turned his attention back on Rachel, but could read nothing at all of her expression in the blurred image swimming before his eyes.

"Leah, be a dear and take little Ben into the sitting room for me, will you?" she said next. "I think he'll be ready for a nap, if you'll only rock him a while. You'll find his basket on the table."

Leah did as she was bade, and as soon as she'd quit the room and shut the door behind her, Jack turned back on Rachel. Sensing that she'd dismissed the girl for a reason, he kept his voice low.

"Now, what's going on?" he asked her. "Where's Charlotte?"

Rachel set aside her spoon and wiped her hands on her apron. "I don't know where she is just now. She'd planned to follow Leah. She thought she might find out something more about the man that she's been seeing . . ."

Muttering an oath under his breath, Jack shook his head. "I told her I'd take care of that."

"She only wanted to see for herself," Rachel said in her friend's defense, "to be sure that the girl wasn't getting herself into something that she couldn't handle. But Leah's been back a while now, and there's still no sign of Charlotte. I can't imagine what's keeping her."

Jack knew he ought to remain calm. Pacing the length of the kitchen, he told himself just that. It was late afternoon; the sun hadn't even set. There wasn't any particular danger for his wife in walking the streets of Cedar Creek. And so there was no reason for him to be worried.

"Jack?" Rachel called out then, breaking into his thoughts. "Charlotte wanted to disguise herself, so that Leah wouldn't notice her, and so she . . . she's wearing those buckskins."

With that, he spun on his heel, crossed the room in a few, long strides and pushed his way through the sitting room door. Behind him, Rachel let go a startled little chirp and rushed to follow him. Leah was just as surprised when he drew up before her. She clutched little Ben closer against her bosom.

"Jack? What is it? What's wrong?"

Calm wasn't an option any longer. Dressed in those buckskins, masquerading as a man, Charlotte was free to trail Leah's secret admirer any place in town. Even now, she might be inside a saloon or worse, getting into God only knew what kind of trouble.

With his hands clenched at his sides in two tight fists, he barked an order to his sister. "You're going to tell me the name of that man you've been seeing, young lady. Do you understand me?"

Leah scowled at him. "Charlotte's been talking to you, hasn't she? Well, neither of you has any right to treat me like a child . . ."

"His name!" Jack repeated. Impatience did not come near to describing the turmoil burgeoning within in him. This time Leah seemed to sense the gravity of the request, for she immediately stammered out. "I . . . it's . . . Gideon."

The strangled groan Jack heard escape from his own throat sounded harsh and foreign to his ears. He'd been imagining troubles, yes, but he'd never expected anything like this. The bastard gambler who had raped his wife had now set his sights on Leah. It was more than one man could handle.

"I don't see why you're upset with me. He's a perfect gentleman," Leah protested. "He's a charming gentleman. He's treated me with kindness and respect every time we've met."

Jack's arms shot out, and grasping his sister by the shoulders, he shook her roughly. "You stay away from him, do you hear me?"

The jostling he'd given Leah set the baby in her arms to squawling, and Rachel rushed forward, gathering up her son.

"What is it, Jack?" she asked him. "What's wrong?"

He shook his head, unable to sort through the tangle of

his emotions. He swallowed hard. "Charlotte and this Gideon fellow. They're . . . acquainted.

"I don't think she'd follow him, though," he went on, almost as if to soothe his own jangled nerves. "God knows, she was too afraid of him for that. But if she saw him out there today, if she found out that he was still alive, there's no telling what she might do."

"Jack?" Rachel interrupted again.

"What is it?"

"I don't pretend to half understand all that's going on here, but I think you ought to know. When she left here, Charlotte was wearing a gun."

He'd gone into the Golden Palace Saloon, by way of a side entrance that opened off a drafty alleyway. Charlotte followed, cautiously pushing open the door to peer inside.

Within was a spacious, private office, with a desk and chair in which he'd already settled and made himself comfortable. There was a poker table in the opposite corner of the room—for private games, or so she imagined—and a couple of lithograph landscapes hung on the wall, and a cheap horsehair sofa, strewn with red brocade pillows, to round out the decor.

Across the room stood a second door, which presumably opened into the saloon itself. Just beyond, she could hear the tinny chiming of a piano, the shouts of men laying bets on the roulette wheel and the faro tables, and the rowdy clamor that accompanied any such gathering of drunken males.

To think that Marcus Gideon had not only survived, but prospered, made Charlotte's blood run cold. What sort of world was this, where a man like him was allowed to roam free? To prey, without conscience, upon innocent girls and still make a comfortable life for himself?

A potent mingling of fear and anger welled in her, and

before she'd even realized, her hand had gone to her belt and she'd drawn out her pistol. Raising the barrel, she took careful aim at his uppermost vest button, without speaking a word. It was a minute or more before Gideon looked up and noticed her standing there.

"You!" he exclaimed, as with his shaking hand, he set down the bottle from which he'd just poured himself a drink.

Charlotte had to admit to a certain grim satisfaction at his reaction. "So, you recognize me, do you?"

"You're that crazy boy who tried to kill me up at Six Mile Canyon," he replied, and for the first time, she was aware of a tremor of fear in his voice. "I've still got your God-damned pistol ball in my shoulder."

"Well, I'm afraid that isn't good enough," Charlotte heard herself say, "not by half. Our account won't be squared until you've been made to pay for everything you've done."

Those amber eyes of his flicked nervously beneath half-closed lids, as if he were gauging the distance between himself and the door. "Well now, that's not a problem," he said, and let go a nervous laugh. "I've done quite well here. How much will it take to get you out of my life? One hundred dollars? Two hundred?"

Charlotte exhaled slowly. "You still don't understand, do you?"

With that, she lifted her free hand and drew off the felt hat, shaking her hair loose from its tie. "Now, take a good look," she entreated, as she took a step toward him, "and tell me if this face brings back any memories."

He'd acquired a paunch in the years since New Orleans, and his hair was thinning. She noticed it as he lifted a trembling hand and combed his fingers through it. Beneath the ruddy beard, his face had gone pale. "I'll be damned. You're . . . you're that Devereaux girl, aren't you?"

"I'm surprised you can even remember the name, after

all this time," she said. "Tell me, how many other innocent lives have you ruined since then, Gideon? Surely, mine isn't the only one."

He shook his head. "You can't accuse me of that. We had some fun, that's all it was, and you wanted it as badly as I did."

Regarding him closer, Charlotte was stunned to see that he was serious. Her hand began to shake and her palm, where it wrapped around the pistol's grip, was slick with sweat. "You think I *wanted* to be savaged by you? To have my innocence taken by a man who sought pleasure in my pain? To be left bruised and bleeding and so devoid of self respect that I wished I were dead?"

Her voice ended on a wild note. While she'd been speaking, Gideon's right hand had slipped off the desktop, but Charlotte was not so caught up in her tirade that she'd neglected to keep a close eye on him. In response to his action, she extended the pistol, lifted her thumb and drew back the hammer. He flinched at the loud click that it made, and froze.

"Put both your hands there on the desktop, where I can see them," she told him, "unless you're in a particular hurry to die."

Gideon threw up his hands, and then cautiously got to his feet. "I swear I never meant to hurt you, *cher,*" he said, as he came around the desk. His voice was as she'd remembered it once, smooth as silk and laced with charm. "It would have been pleasant for us both, if only you hadn't fought me."

Vigorously, Charlotte shook her head. He was trying to twist the truth, hoping to confuse her. "And what about that young girl you were with this afternoon? When you've managed to get her alone with you, when you've forced yourself on her, will you tell her the same things? My father tried to warn me once. He said that you'd earned a reputation for despoiling innocents. But I wouldn't listen to him. I wouldn't listen, and now he's dead—murdered by your hand. Or will you deny that, too?"

"I was only defending myself," Gideon insisted, lifting his hands in supplication as he took another step toward her. "It was he who came after me. Please, *cher,* please understand. I had no choice."

There was a note of desperation in his voice and a pleading look in his eye. But Charlotte didn't want to acknowledge either. "I can't let you," she said, steeling herself against him. "I *won't* let you hurt anyone else."

It shouldn't have been hard to kill him. He was, after all, nothing more than a vicious animal, and the world would be well-rid of him. But looking on him now, Charlotte saw only the most pitiful excuse for a human being, and she wasn't afraid of him any more. Killing him wasn't worth the risk of losing the happiness that she'd found. Her arm and the pistol dropped to her side, and she pulled a ragged breath.

At that moment, the inside door that led into the saloon swept open, catching her attention just long enough for Gideon to pounce. In an instant, he'd snatched up her wrist in his merciless grip and twisted it until he'd wrested the gun from her hand. Then, coiling an arm around her waist, he pulled her back against him to use as a shield between him and whomever had burst into the room.

"Jack!" Charlotte cried out when she saw who it was. She thrashed against her captor to free herself.

Jack shoved the door closed behind him. He was breathing hard, as if he'd run all the way from home, and standing there before them, with hands fisted, he seemed fully prepared to do battle. But he drew up short as he recognized that Gideon had slid the barrel of the pistol up against Charlotte's throat. Charlotte stilled as well, worried more at that moment for Jack than for herself.

"Well now," Gideon drawled, his relief apparent, "if it isn't the blind man."

"Let her go, Gideon!" Jack warned.

"I'm afraid I can't do that. She's tried to kill me once already. I can't let that go unpunished. I'll have to teach her a lesson, I think."

With that, he ran the back of the hand that gripped the pistol along the line of Charlotte's jaw. She shuddered at his touch and began to writhe again.

"You have two choices, my friend," the gambler said next. "You can either close the door on your way out to give us some privacy, or you can stand there and listen, if you enjoy that sort of thing."

Jack stood his ground and glowered. "She's my wife," he replied. There was a cold, ominous edge to his voice that Charlotte had never heard before.

As Gideon digested the news, Jack took a threatening step forward. But what could he possibly hope to do— near blind as he was, and unarmed? Charlotte knew that she'd have to do something to aid their cause, and she'd have to do it quickly. With this thought in mind, she ceased her struggles, relaxing in Gideon's grip, and in response, his hold on her eased a bit.

Seizing the opportunity, she twisted around to thrust a knee up into his groin. Exhaling sharply, he doubled over, permitting her to gain enough leverage to break loose. But she'd no sooner stepped free of him, when Jack charged, and he and Gideon tumbled together onto the floor.

Charlotte stood back watching, helpless, as they struggled, exchanging blows. Fueled by rage, Jack managed to roll atop his opponent. He caught up Gideon's hand, smashed it and the pistol he still gripped against the planked wood floor. Gideon would not loose his hold on it, but then neither could he use it.

It wasn't long before the tables turned, though. Gideon was a streetfighter, schooled on the docks of New Orleans, and bloodied though he may have been, he was far from giving up yet. Freeing his arm, he blindsided Jack with a single, ham-fisted blow, and with their positions reversed now, they scrambled across the floor, arms and legs flailing.

Charlotte had kept her distance, while still trying to keep a close eye on the pistol, but when she saw the blood streaming down her husband's face, it distracted her. Before she'd realized it, the pistol had disappeared from view, wedged somewhere between their two bodies. A few seconds later it discharged, and with an anguished cry, she rushed forward to find both men lying still, her pistol on the floor between them.

"Jack!"

Charlotte rushed to kneel beside him, afraid that he'd been wounded. Rolling him over, she took up his bloodied face in her hands. Her heart was pounding so hard in her throat that she could scarcely breathe. His eyes were closed, and he lay ominously still.

Dear God, he couldn't be dead! He couldn't be! Frantically, she ran her hands over his chest, but could find no bullet holes. A deep gash had opened up over his left eye; that seemed to be the sole source of his bleeding. Gathering him up in her arms, she pulled him close, close enough to hear him pull a shallow breath.

Only then did she cast a glance in Gideon's direction and see the massive crimson stain spreading across the front of his vest. It was he who'd been shot. He was dying or was probably dead already. But Charlotte hadn't an ounce of pity to spare for him, nor any inclination toward regret. It was Jack who filled up her thoughts. She had to get him up and out of here.

Already there was a commotion at the inside door. From within the saloon, someone was calling out Gideon's name, and twisting the knob back and forth. The door must have locked when Jack slammed it shut.

Clutching two handfuls of her husband's woolen overcoat, Charlotte jostled him. "Please, Jack," she whispered against his ear. "Please, you've got to get up. We've got to get out of here before someone comes."

Responding to the jostling and his wife's deep, molasses-rich voice, Jack struggled to lift his heavy eyelids. Once he'd succeeded, the world spun around him in a blur of whirling colors; he'd grown all too used to that. But after he'd blinked once or twice, he looked up and to his surprise, he could see her face: the gently arched brow, the full, soft lips. He'd forgotten how soft a shade of blue her eyes were and how radiant the blush upon her cheeks. The image was sharp and clear as could be. It was a miracle!

He couldn't remember just how he'd come to be lying on the floor, but Charlotte seemed so concerned that he allowed her to help him to his feet, throw one of his long arms across her shoulder, and lead him out of the unfamiliar room and into an alleyway, where even the lengthening afternoon shadows could not hamper the clarity of his vision. Somehow, he'd gotten his eyesight back. Then a cold shiver of reality vibrated through him. This must be a dream, he told himself.

Charlotte paused only long enough to pull a kerchief from her pocket and press it firmly against his brow. "Hold that there," she instructed him. "You're bleeding. We've got to get you to Noah's. He'll be able to help."

Jack lifted his free hand and did as she'd asked. Beneath the kerchief, the wound throbbed, and he had to struggle mightily against the vertigo that threatened to fell him. But Charlotte needed him up and moving, and so he put one foot in front of the other, following her lead. She kept in the shadows of the buildings, traversing the narrow alleyways so they might not be spotted. What was it that she was afraid of?

It was a minute or more before the fog began to lift from his brain, and he was able to recall his struggle with Marcus Gideon, their struggle and the gunshot. The memory stopped him cold in his tracks. This was no dream.

"Charlotte," he posed, wary now, "what happened to Gideon?"

"Please, Jack. We've got to hurry," she entreated and urged him onward, tugging at him with the arm she'd thrown around his waist for support. "He's dead. He's gotten what he deserved at last. He won't hurt Leah; he won't hurt any of us any more. But you're bleeding badly. We've got to get you to Noah's, so he can take a look at that cut over your eye."

Jack couldn't say he was sorry to hear the news, but he understood now why Charlotte had kept him off the main streets, why she was fired with such haste. He'd killed Marcus Gideon, and even if it had been only an accident, she was trying to protect him.

His heart sank as his vision began to falter again. Beside him, Charlotte wavered and stretched out of shape, as if she were being reflected through rippling water. His dizziness was growing worse, too, and so he allowed her to help him the rest of the way. They stumbled together up the Kelseys' back porch stairs and barged, without knocking, into the kitchen.

"Is Doctor Kelsey here?" Charlotte asked a startled Mrs. Murphy, who'd turned on them, brandishing her spoon before her like a weapon.

As soon as she recognized them, the woman's arm dropped to her side, and she managed a stiff nod, her eyes wide with curiosity. "He's in his office," she said. "Charlotte? Is that really you, dear?"

Charlotte didn't take the time to reply, and Jack realized just how worried she was for him when, still struggling to support him, she swept into Noah's surgery, eased him into a chair, and cried out in a trembling voice: "Noah, come quick!"

Warm drops of blood had begun to slide out from under the sodden kerchief that Jack held pressed against his temple. Expelling a shaky breath, he settled back and as his sight slowly cleared once more, he focused his eyes on his wife, who'd gone to stand in the doorway. Her soft brow was marred by a frown, her face flooded with color. He found himself mesmerized by the familiar features he'd been deprived of looking at for so long. How easy it was for him now to read the concern in her eyes. No matter what should happen to him because of all of this, he'd count himself a lucky man for being able to see her face just one more time.

"Mrs. Murphy didn't know quite what to make of you, all decked out in those buckskin breeches," he told her, feeling more lighthearted than he had a right to be. It was probable the loss of blood had made him giddy.

Charlotte didn't have time to acknowledge his remark, though, for just then Noah burst in. "Why in heaven's name are you dressed like that?" he asked her, and then he spotted Jack. "Good God, what's happened to you?"

Neither of them replied to his questions. For Jack's part, his attention was wholly fixed on his wife. She seemed so slight and fragile, even clad in those old buckskins and his oversized coat. She pressed her lips tightly together, and her face had gone dangerously pale. He'd never seen her look so frightened, and it was all on his account.

After scrubbing his hands in the basin, Noah drew up beside him. Only then did Jack remove the blood-soaked kerchief from his brow. Deftly probing the wound, the doctor frowned and shook his head. "I know we've all told you that that scar of yours isn't unattractive, but we didn't mean for you to go out and get yourself one to match on the opposite side."

The humor that was meant to put them both at ease went unappreciated. "Will he be able to ride?" Charlotte inquired, clutching at the door frame. "We'll have to go soon."

"Go?" Noah echoed, looking up in astonishment. "How can you think of going anywhere when Jack's nearly split his skull wide open? And I'm still waiting to hear how it happened."

She wouldn't oblige him. With her head lagging, she began to pace. "Maybe no one saw us," she muttered. "Maybe the sheriff will think it's only another dispute among gamblers and not worth pursuing."

Jack watched her fuss and fret, unable to take his eyes off her. There wasn't much likelihood that he'd escaped unseen, he knew that much. He'd gone straight through the saloon on the way to Gideon's office. Every man in the Golden Palace had seen him, and his wasn't a face that went unrecognized in this town, not since he'd begun his campaign for mayor.

When they found out that Gideon was dead, the sheriff would be notified, and they'd know precisely who to come looking for. This time, Jack Cordell would be arrested as a murderer. One could only escape fate for so long.

A single thought cheered him, though. There was nothing at all to tie Charlotte to this episode. She'd been wearing her disguise. No one need know that she played a part in this. Now, if only he could spirit her out of harm's way, before it was too late.

"I've killed a man," he admitted to Noah at last.

Charlotte quit her pacing and drew up short. "That isn't the whole story, Noah," she told him, her voice aquiver. "He didn't intend to. He had no choice. He was trying to protect me."

The two men exchanged glances, and then Noah turned to Charlotte. "Fetch me a pitcher of hot water from Mrs. Murphy in the kitchen, will you?" he asked. "I'll have to clean this wound out properly before I stitch it up."

She hesitated, eyeing them both speculatively. Jack maintained an impassive air until the throbbing in his head worsened, and again the image of his wife began to shift and swim before his eyes. Desperately, he blinked, trying to maintain the focus, but to no avail. Once more his vision went blurry, leaving him as good as blind.

Noah pressed a clean cloth over Jack's brow and then hurried to shut the door, once Charlotte had gone out. "Now, you're going to tell me just what in the hell is going on," he insisted, keeping his voice low.

"Sheriff Willis will be here soon, looking for me," Jack explained. "I don't want Charlotte to be here when he comes."

Jack hoped his friend couldn't hear the disappointment in his voice, but the few brief glimpses of clarity he'd just experienced had been so potent that he felt the torment of his blindness worse than ever now.

Noah reached for a bottle from a nearby work table, uncorked it and poured it over the wound. Jack winced. It stung like hell. Then Noah went back to the table, and when he returned, he was threading a needle. Easing Jack's head back, he smoothed the torn skin together with his thumb and made his first stitch.

"The sheriff?" he echoed. "What's this all about, Jack? I know what you've said, but I can't believe that you'd be capable of killing anyone."

Jack regarded him askance. "You'd be surprised what you don't know about me, friend."

"But if you were only protecting your wife, as she claims . . ."

Without even thinking, Jack reached up and caught his arm. The thread tugged against his skin. "Charlotte wasn't there. She didn't have anything to do with this, and if anyone asks, you haven't seen her all afternoon. Got that? Now, when she comes back in here, I want you to act as if you're prepared to help us make a run for it. Tell her to go home and get out of those buckskins she's wearing. Tell her to bring me a fresh suit of clothes, so these blood-stains won't arouse suspicions. Tell her anything, just get her out of here. Do you understand?"

Jack's sudden move had stilled Noah's hand for a time, but as soon as he released him, he went on, patiently making his stitches.

"I'll do what you've asked me to," he agreed, "but I still don't understand. If Charlotte's a witness to whatever happened . . ."

"I'll get out of this on my own," Jack insisted. "It was self defense . . . this time. But I won't have Charlotte involved. I won't let her suffer a moment's more pain because of a no-account gambler who well-deserved his fate."

Twenty-two

By the time Charlotte had changed her clothes, packed a bundle for Jack, and hurried back to the Kelsey house, they had already shipped him off to jail. Sheriff Willis had come for him while she was gone, just as he and Noah had anticipated. Noah admitted as much when she pressed him, and angry as she was with her husband for deceiving her, Charlotte would have expected nothing less.

Knowing Jack as well as she did, she feared that he might be making an outright confession. He was responsible for Gideon's death, after all. But it was an accident, and if anyone was to blame, it was her. She was the one who'd brought the gun to Gideon's office in the first place. She was the one who'd intended to kill him.

Doubtless Jack was trying to spare her from having to reveal her past with Gideon. He must have believed that if he could convince the sheriff that he'd killed Gideon in self defense, she wouldn't have to be involved at all. But with the life of the man she loved at stake, Charlotte could not be so optimistic. In spite of Noah's objections, she marched down to the jailhouse at once, intending to speak with her husband, to tell him that he didn't have to go to all this trouble to protect her, but Sheriff Willis wouldn't allow it.

"Jack said you'd be along, sooner or later," the lawman explained. "He said that he didn't want you to see him in here like this, that I ought to tell you to go on home and wait for him, and that everything would turn out all right."

"And do you think it will?" she asked him.

At that, Willis tugged thoughtfully on his chin. "Well now, ma'am, I've got to speak to a few more people, gather together the facts, you might say, and have Doc Kelsey take a look at the body. But if it turns out to be just as Jack claims, that he went down to the Golden Palace to warn this gambler fella against dallying with his sister, only to have the man attack him, then I'd say it's a clear case of self defense. You go on home now and don't worry yourself about it."

And so Charlotte had done as he'd suggested, feeling a bit more confident than ever that Jack would be released on the morrow. But it didn't work out that way in the end, for none of them could have bargained on the editorial that Nate Phillips ran in the *Chronicle* the following morning, in a column directly opposite the story detailing Jack's arrest for the murder of saloon owner, Marcus Gideon. Its placement was impossible to ignore:

> *The Grim Reaper in our Midst?*
> *During the height of the California gold rush, as many fanciful legends came out of the mining camps as did nuggets of gold. Working for a newspaper in Sacramento during those years, I became acquainted with more than a few of them: tales of fortunes made overnight, of characters bigger than life. One, in particular, has come to mind of late and should, I think, prove of more than passing interest to the citizens of Cedar Creek.*
> *It is the tale of an outlaw, known by the distinctive firearm he wore on his hip: a long-barreled, Colt pistol with a chased cylinder and a pearl-handled grip, inlaid with silver. I have seen its like only one time since, and curious as it might seem, it was in*

this very town. The outlaw of whom I speak was called the Grim Reaper by his fellow forty-niners because of the peculiar habit he had of appearing in a gold camp, choosing a particular fellow, as if on a whim, and then calling him out. The confrontation invariably ended in death for the poor chosen fellow, for the Reaper was a crack shot.

At least four men that I know of lost their lives in this little game of his, men who, while they might have been considered little more than the dregs of society, surely did not deserve to die on account of it. And how did I come to be acquainted with these facts? Because, my fellow citizens, I was there to witness one of these murders for myself.

Yes, I say murder because that's what it was. The souls that this Grim Reaper singled out to send to their Maker never had a chance. Standing outside of a tent saloon in Spanish Flats, I watched with my own eyes as a poor drunkard by the name of Albert Soames was cold-bloodedly executed by the Reaper, without more than a dozen words ever having been exchanged between the two of them.

But what does this lurid tale have to do with Cedar Creek, you might ask, a boomtown more than ten years and many miles removed from the gold camps of old California? Well, we here are on the verge of making a vital decision with regard to the running of our town, and I believe that it is important that before we do so, we be possessed of all the available facts.

From the time I first came here, I found myself plagued by the nagging of my memory, but only in light of recent events did I realize the cause. I am now prepared to testify, if I should be called upon to do so, that the murderer known as the Grim Reaper is, indeed, here in our midst and apparently up to his old tricks once again. We shall not be deceived.

Charlotte set aside the newspaper. The message she'd found scribbled across one of Jack's campaign posters made sense to her now. It had been a warning to Jack to get out of the race, else Nate Phillips would reveal what he knew of his past. But Jack had never had the chance to see it, and now it was too late.

Phillips's editorial was sure to affect Sheriff Willis's decision to release Jack. A man defending his kin from the attentions of an interloper, well, that was something anyone could understand, but if Phillips was to be believed, Jack had already made a sport out of killing innocent men.

For her part, Charlotte wanted to deny what she'd read, yet found that she could not. Jack had always steered clear of any examination of his past. He'd tried to warn her that she was not the only one with secrets, but she had been so caught up in her own worries, that she hadn't really listened to him. She was sorely ashamed of her selfishness now as she remembered the miner's pack, the pearl-gripped pistol that Jack had handled with such expertise, and the map of the gold fields with names penciled onto the back. There had been four names, she realized as she thought on it, and one of them might well have been Albert Soames.

But no matter the evidence, she would not believe that Jack was the cold-blooded killer Nate Phillips made him out to be. Phillips may not have been lying about the Grim Reaper, still he had his own motives in writing up this story, to be sure. His intention was to destroy Jack's campaign for mayor, nothing less, and Charlotte wasn't about to let him do it. Somehow, she'd have to discover the truth in all of this. She knew, without a doubt, that her husband was an honorable man. For him to have committed murder, four times over, something must have driven him to the very brink. But what?

It would do no good to question Jack; he'd refused to allow her to see him in jail, and besides, he had never been the sort to make excuses for himself. No, she'd have to find another source of information. Not Nate Phillips, surely. He'd already made up his mind that Jack was a monster. But up at Six Mile there were plenty of men who'd been out to California. . . .

Charlotte felt rather like an unusual species of animal as she rode up the familiar, rutted mountain path and past the row of canvas and split log shelters. There was a haze in the morning air from the smoke of the cook fires, and the smell of frying bacon fat and coffee mingled with the ever-present scent of pine. It might have seemed more like she were coming home if the eyes of every grizzled miner and every weary, workworn prospector she passed hadn't been so clearly focused on her as she dismounted and wrapped her wool shawl tighter across her bosom. But as it was, she felt like an outsider, a stranger in this rough community where she'd once been such a familiar member.

Leaving her horse to graze in the clearing, she strode up to the shack that her one-time companions shared.

"Vernon?" she called out, rapping hard upon the door. "Ira? Are you in there?"

"Well, I'll be damned," a voice cried out. "Charlie? Charlie? Is that you, boy?"

The door swung open, and Charlotte found herself staring into Vernon Taylor's wizened face. He drew back, clearly puzzled and then dropped his gaze to the scuffed toes of his boots. "Beg pardon, ma'am. But I thought you was . . . that is to say, I thought I heard . . . What can I do to help you?"

"May I come in?" she asked, very much aware of the curious eyes still fixed upon her back. She didn't intend to conduct her business here on the doorstep, where everyone could hear. "There's a chill in the air this morning, and I'm not as tough as I used to be."

"Oh, my, yes. Do come in."

Vernon stepped aside, allowing her to pass, then motioned her toward the most comfortable seat in the house—a rickety wooden chair that was set beside the squat, black box stove in the corner. Charlotte settled into it and reached out to warm her hands over the cast iron stovetop.

"May I offer you a cup of coffee?" he asked, still confused by her presence.

"Yes, please," she told him. "Where's Ira this morning? Still in his bedroll?" With that, she cast a glance across the room and noticed the pair of empty bunks, piled high with blankets and buffalo robes. "Or has he already gone out hunting rabbits for tonight's supper? No one makes a better rabbit stew than Ira."

As he poured coffee from the pot into a battered tin cup, Vernon regarded her through narrowed eyes, startled by her remark, and then he cocked his head as if concentrating anew on the sound of her voice.

"You still don't recognize me, do you?"

Handing her the cup, Vernon set the pot back on the stove and sat himself down on an upturned crate. "Recognize you? Why, ma'am, I . . ."

"Look closely, Vernon," Charlotte entreated. "It's me . . . Charlie."

"Don't go playing such games, ma'am," he told her. "I may not be as sharp as I once was, it's true, but I should hope that I can still tell the difference between male and female."

Tossing back her shawl, Charlotte drew up the claw necklace she was wearing round her neck and rattled it before him. "There now, you see? You and Ira made this for me after that wildcat pounced on me last spring, and I shot him, right between the eyes. And if you still don't believe me," she persisted, "go on outside and take a look at that bay mare I rode in on, the one grazing in the clearing. It's Charlie's horse; she won't let anyone else ride her. Do you remember? She'll come if I whistle for her."

Charlotte leaned forward to rise, but reaching out a hand to still her, Vernon regarded her earnestly. At last, he believed her. She could see it.

"But why?" he wanted to know. "Why'd you do it, Charlie?"

"It's Charlotte," she corrected, "and well, it seemed the only choice at the time. I was on my own and had to make some kind of living. Then, after I'd had a taste of the freedom that a man enjoys every day of his life, it was hard to give up. Mostly, though, the disguise made it easy to travel on my own. I wanted so badly to have my revenge on the man who'd ruined my life that I chased him half way across the country."

"That there fella you was shootin' at that night you took a ball in the leg?" he guessed.

Charlotte nodded.

"And where have you been for all these months? That doctor in Cedar Creek told us you'd gone back East."

She sipped at her coffee, shaking her head. "I stayed on there, reclaimed my old identity," she said. "Things were better for me. I was able to make a decent living. I made friends, and I got married, Vernon."

"You had friends *here*," he retorted.

"Oh, don't look at me that way. You'd never have let me stay on in this camp if you'd discovered that I was a woman, and if I'd have come here in the first place as I was, a single girl on her own—all of you would have assumed that I was a harlot. You'd never have helped me out, taught me about living out here, trusted me like you did Charlie. With things as they were, I never hurt anyone with my disguise.

"I wouldn't have come back here at all, nor told you

any of this, except that—you see, the truth is, I need your help. While we were prospecting, you and Ira talked a lot to me about the old days in California. I need for you to tell me if, while you were out there, you ever heard talk of an outlaw called 'The Grim Reaper.' "

Vernon nodded. "Wasn't a man in the gold fields hadn't heard of him. Whenever he came into a camp, everybody knew that some poor fella was gonna need burying soon."

"And that's it? That's all you know about it? Not who he was, nor why he might have done what he did."

"Didn't seem to be no rhyme nor reason to it. The way I hear it, it was as if he had him a list, and if your name was on it, well then, your time was up. Don't rightly know myself how many men he killed, but there was no end of stories—a gamblin' tough up in Red Dog, a drunken Irishman at Placerville. . . . Some said he wasn't a real man at all, but one of God's avenging angels sent down to punish the sinners in a lawless land. We all kept a close look out over our shoulders for a long time after he showed up, I can tell you."

A wave of disappointment washed over Charlotte. She had wanted so much to believe that Vernon would provide her with some simple explanation that would serve as a balance against the vicious assertions that Phillips had made in his newspaper. She'd even allowed herself to hope that he might be able to identify the outlaw as someone other than Jack. But instead everything he'd said had only confirmed the worst. With the available evidence to go on and Nate Phillips more than willing to identify Jack as an outlaw who'd already killed several men, there was little doubt but that he'd be put to trial for Gideon's murder.

"I would appreciate it," she said, trying to keep her voice from faltering, "if you could talk to Ira and the other fellows up here who were out in California, and let me know if you discover anything more about this."

Vernon nodded in agreement. "I'll do it, but I don't

understand why something that happened so long ago should be so important to you."

"My husband accidentally killed a man down in Cedar Creek. Now, in order to convince the sheriff that he's capable of cold-blooded murder, they're trying to say that he is this Grim Reaper."

The old man's eyes widened. "And is he?"

Charlotte avoided his gaze. Without answering the question, she finished her coffee and got to her feet. "If you learn anything, you can find me in Cedar Creek at the Mountain View Hotel."

Vernon rose up and put out his hand, but then spying the dirt beneath his fingernails, he drew it back awkwardly. Charlotte knew that he'd never be able to accept her both as a woman and a friend. She ought to have expected it, but with things as they were, it only served to heighten her melancholy.

She didn't ride back to town when she left the camp. She had one more stop yet to make: the cabin where she and Jack had lived after the fire. There, she rummaged through the trunk where she'd hidden Jack's old knapsack, and when she'd found it, she unlatched the buckles and drew out the contents to examine them one last time—the pearl-handled pistol, the immigrant's guide, the maps with its penciled notations—all pieces of Jack's past. Then, having satisfied herself that she hadn't only imagined it, she carried it all out to the lake, filled the weathered knapsack with heavy stones, and cast it into the depths of the frigid, black waters.

Jack wasn't surprised to find that the Silver Slipper dance hall had been converted into a courtroom for his trial. After all, arrangements had to be made quickly when the circuit judge arrived in town, and Cedar Creek had no such public building as of yet. He wasn't surprised either to note that the rows of spectator's benches behind him were filled to capacity. A murder trial promised to provide more excitement than a town like this could count on in a whole year's time.

What did surprise him was that Charlotte was not any-where among the spectators. Even blind as he was, he'd have recognized her, but she wasn't there. The Kelseys had come to lend him support; they were seated directly behind the table where he and his counsel, a keen-eyed young lawyer by the name of William Prescott, sat. More than a few of his old friends were in the gallery, too. They had all come up to offer him words of encourage-ment before the proceedings had gotten started. But as for his wife, she was nowhere to be seen, and he suspected that some of the whispers that he heard all around him were speculations on that fact.

He couldn't blame her, really. Hadn't Charlotte come to the jail nearly every day for a week, asking to see him, only to have him refuse her request? He'd done so partly because he didn't want for her to see him locked up and partly to keep her at a safe distance from this entire affair. But there were other, more selfish reasons that he was reluctant to acknowledge, even to himself. If he had seen her, spoken to her, he mightn't have been able to maintain his resolve to do what was right. And Charlotte had al-ways thought him such an honest, forthright man; he wasn't sure he could bear facing her once she'd been stripped of her illusions. Much as he wanted to see her again, Jack decided that maybe it was better that she hadn't come today.

Of course, Leah wasn't here either, but then he was glad of that. He'd rather not be present when she heard the truth revealed, that her brother was a murderer. She probably hated him already for what he'd done to Gideon, whose spell she had so easily fallen under. He supposed it was no less than his fate—and a fate long overdue—that he should be abandoned by those he loved most.

The proceedings commenced with Edwin Morrow, the stiff-spined, prosecuting attorney, calling forth witnesses who'd been in the Golden Palace Saloon that day. One by one, they came forward to offer testimony, and to Jack's dismay, several of them said they'd seen not one, but *two* men running from Gideon's office on the day of the murder.

After each statement to that effect, Prescott aimed what Jack was sure was a pointed glance in his direction, but Jack only met him with an impassive air, pretending that he hadn't noticed. They'd discussed the matter time and again, with Prescott pacing the length of Jack's cell and reminding him that he needed to know the whole truth in order to help him; and Jack stubbornly insisting that he'd gone alone to Gideon's office. As he regarded his lawyer now, though, Jack was sure the man had never believed him. But that didn't matter, he would not bring Charlotte into this mess.

By the time Nate Phillips had given his testimony, bearing witness to all that he'd printed in his newspaper, and insisting that the defendant was an outlaw who had already murdered before, Jack's prospects for acquittal looked grim. He knew he deserved to hang, if not for Gideon's murder, then most certainly for the others he'd committed, but inside himself, he was far from resigned. In fact, he found himself railing against the perversity of fate.

Justice might have been meted out to him in any number of ways, since the day he'd first strapped on that pearl-handled pistol. He might have been shot by one of the men he'd called out as the Grim Reaper. He might have been thrown by his horse, struck by lightning, felled by mountain fever, snakebit. . . . He might have died in the fire that scarred him, for God's sake, but he hadn't. No,

he'd been allowed to make a life in this beautiful spot, to
help build a town, to prosper, to fall in love, to know
more pleasure and happiness than he'd ever dreamed it
possible for one man to have—and now all of it was going
to be taken away.

Charlotte pulled the worn buckskins out of the bottom
drawer of her bureau and slipped them on one last time.
In the note that he'd sent down from camp, Vernon had
told her that he'd found an old Californian who was willing to swear that the Grim Reaper was much older than
Jack Cordell could have been at the time, and he'd promised that the man would be here for the trial.

As much as she knew Vernon's friend must be mistaken,
Charlotte had waited for him to come all last night and
this morning, but he'd never arrived. She couldn't wait
any longer. The trial had already started, and without anyone else to speak on Jack's behalf, she knew that she was
his only hope of avoiding the hangman. She would have
to be there to testify by the time Mr. Prescott began to
call his witnesses.

She and Jack's lawyer had made these plans several
days ago, after she'd gone to see Prescott and explained
that she could not allow her husband to go on protecting
her if it meant he might be convicted of cold-blooded
murder. This "Grim Reaper" nonsense had gone too far,
she'd told him. It was all only speculation, aimed to throw
more suspicion on Jack's motives. Couldn't everyone see
that? There was no real proof of his guilt in that regard.

Finally, she made her admission. She herself knew the
truth about Jack's confrontation with Gideon because she
had been in his office on the day of the murder, and no
matter what Jack had intended, she was going to testify
on his behalf, if she had to. Of course, they hadn't told

Jack any of this. There was no need to upset him, nor to allow him time to circumvent their plan.

Charlotte had just cinched the belt around her waist and reached for her old felt hat when she heard a frantic knocking. Her heart lifted as she wondered if Vernon's friend had arrived at last. But then all at once, the door burst open, and Leah rushed in, ashen-faced, clutching a piece of paper in her hand, and Charlotte's hopes crumbled.

"I think you ought to see this," she said.

Looking up, Leah blinked in surprise, then took a quick step backward as she spied what appeared to be a stranger standing before her.

For her part, Charlotte was equally surprised to find Leah still at the hotel. The girl had been moody and sullen since she'd heard the news that that her brother had killed her "beau," and even after Charlotte had explained how dangerous a man Marcus Gideon was, Leah hadn't seemed to be convinced. Still, Charlotte had thought she'd persuaded her to go to the trial this morning, along with everyone else.

"Charlotte?" Leah asked, her voice hushed. "Is that . . . you? Why are you dressed that way?"

Charlotte dropped her head, fingering the brim of the hat in her hand. "You might as well know the truth. I was there when Gideon was killed. That second man the sheriff has been looking for? The one that was with your brother? It wasn't a man, it was me. I went there dressed like this."

"But why?"

"That's a long story, too long for me to tell you just now. All you need know is that I saw everything that happened. Jack has been trying to protect me, but I can't let him keep on doing that. I'm going to testify. But you ought to be there already; the trial will have started. Your brother will think we've abandoned him."

"I was angry," the girl explained, dropping her pretty,

pointed chin untill it almost touched her chest. "That's why I didn't go along with everyone else. I know what you've told me about Marcus Gideon, but after I'd read what they'd written about Jack in the newspapers, I . . . I just didn't know what to think any more. And then I remembered the letters.

"After my mother died, I kept some of her things: her favorite silk shawl, our family Bible. Inside, she'd tucked away some of her letters, including those that Jack had written to her after he and my brother Matthew went off to California. I'd never opened them before, never thought about them till all of this happened. I read through them just now, hoping to find out more about the kind of man my brother is, and well . . . you have a look for yourself."

She extended her hand. Charlotte took up the page she proffered and swiftly scanned the lines. They were written in Jack's hand:

Mother,

I have never been charged with so painful a task as writing this letter to you, but it must be done. On Friday last, Matthew was murdered in cold blood outside of a gambling saloon in the mining camp at Rich Bar.

As I have mentioned before in my letters, this prospecting has proven to be rougher business than we'd first supposed, and something for which Matthew was hardly suited. More often than not of late, he preferred to try his luck with a deck of cards, rather than a gold pan. I daresay he was not wholly unsuccessful, but it was this gambling skill which eventually cost him his life, when a man from whom he had won a great deal of money sought revenge against him.

This man and a trio of his worthless friends cornered Matthew outside the saloon, stole his winnings,

*and then, ignoring his cries for mercy, they beat him
to death. I regret to say that I was not there when
he needed me; I was out working our claim, dreaming of fortune, even as my brother lay dying. Mother,
I know full well that I bear the responsibility for Matthew's death, as it was me who brought him to this
bloody, lawless land, and I swear to you that somehow I will find the men responsible for this and make
them pay, each and every one.*

Your loving son, Jack.

Charlotte's eyes lingered over the words. Here on the
page, in Jack's own hand, was the explanation for which
she'd been searching, the motivation that could turn an
honorable man into a killer. The Grim Reaper hadn't wandered through the California gold fields choosing random
victims, he'd gone after particular men with a very spe-
cific purpose in mind—to see justice done on behalf of
his brother.

Now Charlotte understood why he'd tried to sway her
against hunting down her tormentor, before he'd realized
how far it had already gone. What was it he'd said? "Revenge won't ease the pain, nor put things back the way
they used to be." He'd been speaking from experience.

"I never knew how my brother Matthew died," Leah
told her. "It all happened before I was born. But this
means that Jack killed those men, just as the newspaper
says. Doesn't it?"

Charlotte thought carefully for a moment. "There's no
way for us to know that for sure," she said, as confidently
as she could. "One thing may have nothing to do with
the other."

Smoothing the girl's dark hair with one hand, she fur-
tively tucked the other, which was still holding the letter,
behind her back. "Now I want you to put on your bonnet

and shawl, and go down to that dance hall they're using as a courtroom. Jack needs to see you there."

"And what about you?"

"Don't worry about me. I'll be along in a little while."

Once she was certain that Leah had left the hotel, Charlotte sat down to read Jack's letter one more time, and then she went downstairs and thrust it in the stove. She had no right to do it, no right at all; but as she stared into the firebox, watching the edges of the paper brown and curl before the flames consumed it at last, she took comfort in the knowledge that there was no longer anything more than hearsay to connect her husband to the Grim Reaper.

Now there was only the matter of Gideon's murder to clear up. Jack would hardly be pleased with what she was about to do, but Charlotte had no other choice. She could not stand by and see him hanged for murder, only to spare her reputation. And besides, she'd come to suspect that Jack was doing nothing to aid his own case because he harbored some deep-seated belief that he ought to be punished. Charlotte didn't believe that, though; and if it meant that she must expose her secrets before all of Cedar Creek, then so be it. If it meant that Jack would be too ashamed to claim her as his wife after she'd dressed herself up like a mangy prospector and admitted to the whole town what she'd been through, then . . . so be it. Even if it meant she'd lose him, she had no choice. She loved him too much to let him die.

The trial wasn't going well at all. Even old Judge Bailey had propped his head on his hand, seeming to have lost patience with Mr. Prescott's endless string of witnesses. One after another, they had attested to the strength of the defendant's character, but not a single one was able to shed any light on the matter at hand.

It was almost as if his lawyer was stalling for time, Jack mused, as Prescott rearranged his notes and then got to his feet once more. He seemed a little more confident as he spoke this time, though. "Your honor, I should like to call as my next witness . . ."

The color drained away all at once from Jack's face as an ominous thought took shape. He swung around in his chair. But no, she wasn't sitting beside Leah or Rachel. She wasn't anywhere in the courtroom, so far as he could see.

"Mrs. Charlotte Cordell."

Too late, Jack realized his mistake. His heart slammed against his breastbone as he saw her step forward. It was her. He knew it instinctively, though his sorry eyes could not confirm it from this distance. She was clad in her buckskins, her hair tucked up into that old, felt hat. On her way up to take the chair that was set beside Judge Bailey's table, she drew close enough for Jack to see a smile that was meant to reassure him. But no sooner had she sat down than he noticed her worrying that soft bottom lip of hers between her teeth . . .

He shot to his feet and faced off against his lawyer. "No! God damn it, Prescott, I won't let you do this to her!"

The young man caught his arm. "Sit down, Jack," he retorted, his voice low, but threaded with steel. "You'll not do yourself any good by losing your temper. Your wife will be fine. She's made up her mind to do this."

What choice did he have now but to let her speak? Feeling as helpless as he ever had, Jack settled back down into his chair, kneading his throbbing temples with the tips of his fingers. At that moment, he was glad of his blindness. At least he wouldn't have to watch as his wife faced certain humiliation before the entire town.

He hadn't told anyone, not even Noah, that the blow he'd suffered in his struggle with Gideon had briefly cleared his vision. It hadn't seemed prudent at the time, and now, if he were to be found guilty and sentenced to hang, it wouldn't make a difference anyway.

Charlotte reached up and tugged off her hat, and when her gold curls tumbled out, even those who'd been confused at first realized what they were seeing played out before them. What had started as a discordant murmur at the back of the room swelled to an unruly mingling of voices. Everyone was speculating aloud, even those sitting in the jury box. Judge Bailey scooped up his gavel and then slammed its head down hard on the table.

"Here now!" he told them all. "I will have order before we continue."

With that, he turned his attention to Charlotte, and his bushy, white brows angled disapprovingly. "Young woman, I expect a good explanation as to why you have upset my courtroom with this . . . this masquerade."

Mr. Prescott stepped forward. "If I may, your honor. I asked Mrs. Cordell to dress this way to illustrate a point. We have already heard more than one witness testify that there was another man in the company of my client on the day that Marcus Gideon died. I maintain that the truth of the matter is that that *man* was his wife."

Another rumble of whispering swept across the room.

"Is this true?" the judge asked Charlotte directly.

"Yes, sir, your honor," she told him.

The old judge smiled. "Well, now we're getting somewhere. Sheriff Willis, come on up here and swear in Mrs. Cordell, will you?"

Once the formalities had been taken care of, Prescott drew up near Charlotte and addressed her in a gentle tone. "Mrs. Cordell, I think everyone here would be interested to know what you were doing in Marcus Gideon's office on the day in question, and why you felt you had to put on this disguise."

Jack tried desperately to focus his gaze on Charlotte. He could see that she was paler than usual, clearly daunted by her surroundings, but drawing upon the reserve of courage she'd proved she'd possessed so many times before, she hosted her chin and gave her reply.

"It all started out because Jack's sister, Leah, was being pursued by a stranger. She's a young girl, only sixteen, and so, of course, she was flattered by the attention. But I came to suspect that this man might not be entirely honorable. I questioned her and . . . we argued."

She hesitated for a moment, her gaze drifting over to the place where Leah sat, almost as if, in spite of all that she herself was going through, she were trying to offer the girl reassurance.

"She wouldn't confide in me, but as Jack and I are responsible for her, I felt compelled to find out for myself just who this man was. I decided to follow her the next time she went out. I knew that if she saw me spying on her, it would destroy whatever trust we'd built between us, but I was too worried for her not to interfere, and so, I concocted this disguise."

"So, you followed your sister-in-law, in disguise, as she went out on her daily errands, and you learned that the man who'd been pursuing her was Marcus Gideon, and that his intentions were—just as you'd suspected—not at all honorable."

Mr. Morrow voiced his objection. "Your honor, counsel seeks to impugn the reputation of a dead man, yet he has offered no proof . . ."

Judge Bailey held up a hand. "Thank you, Mr. Morrow, for your astute observation, but I'm afraid I have to agree with the witness's assessment that a man who is the owner of a local saloon and bawdy house is not likely to have honorable intentions when it comes to a young girl who is less than half his age. I have daughters of my own, you know. You may continue, Mr. Prescott."

Prescott began to pace a small stretch of floor before

the judge's table. "So, Mrs. Cordell, what did you do next?"

"I followed Marcus Gideon back to his office. I wanted to warn him to stay away from Leah."

"Did he listen to you?"

Charlotte shook her head. "When Jack questioned Leah and discovered where I'd gone, he came after me. He was afraid for my safety, and rightly so, it seemed, because when he burst through the office door, Gideon grabbed me, held a gun to my throat and started making vile threats. I managed to break free, but by then, Jack was angry. He threw himself at Gideon, and while the two of them were struggling on the floor, the gun went off. It was an accident. I saw it myself."

"And what did you do then?"

"Gideon was dead, but Jack had been badly beaten. He was bleeding, and I knew he needed a doctor. So I helped him to his feet and got him to Noah's house just as fast as I could."

"And that's why the witnesses claimed to have seen two men running from the scene that day?"

Charlotte nodded.

"Thank you for coming forward, Mrs. Cordell," Prescott said, looking pleased with himself as he returned to take up his seat beside Jack. "You've helped to clear things up for us."

Jack breathed a long sigh of relief and whispered thanks to his attorney. The young man had somehow managed to get at the truth without causing Charlotte any embarrassment; Jack wouldn't have believed it if he hadn't seen it for himself. The jury couldn't convict him, given this testimony. Why, even the judge seemed to be satisfied that Gideon's death had been an accident. For the first time, Jack dared to hope that he might get through this after all, that he and Charlotte might put all their tragedies behind them and start anew.

But he soon discovered how premature his relief had been. With a predator's gleam in his eye that even Jack could see, Edwin Morrow got to his feet and approached Charlotte. Jack's heart sank; he hadn't counted on the cross-examination.

"Are you aware, Mrs. Cordell, that in putting on this *disguise,* as you call it, you are violating the law?"

His tone was sharp. He must have thought to alarm her, but he had no idea of the sort of woman with whom he was dealing. As Jack had learned for himself long ago, Charlotte was at her best when cornered. She was not at all troubled by his remark. "And do you intend to prosecute me for this terrible offense, Mr. Morrow?"

"I only seek to make you aware of the gravity of your actions, ma'am. A man is dead because of this little masquerade of yours. I should think you'd feel some remorse . . ."

"I'm afraid you ask too much, sir. Marcus Gideon was a man who well-deserved to die."

Jack caught his breath. Charlotte had said more than she ought to; if she wasn't careful . . .

"For bothering your sister-in-law, you mean?" Morrow retorted. "I fear that our streets would be veritably littered with dead bodies if every man who looked at a pretty girl were to suffer such a fate."

In spite of the tension in the room, the silence was broken by a smattering of uneasy laughter at his remark. "Or was it more than that?" he asked next. "Was it, perhaps, that *you* had a personal acquaintance with Mr. Gideon yourself, and when your husband found out about it, he decided to confront the man . . ."

Anger surged through Jack like quickfire. He'd have been on his feet in an instant, if Prescott's hand had not clamped down hard on his shoulder as he, himself, rose up to argue. "I must object, your honor. This is pure speculation. Counsel has no right to cast such vile aspersions on the character of the witness."

But Morrow seemed to have already decided upon his strategy. He did not back down. "Your honor, a woman who would brazenly enter a court of law wearing trousers, who sees fit to flaunt her contempt for the laws of God and man in assuming the role of her betters ought not to expect the decent folk of this town to believe that she could not, just as easily, violate the laws of adultery and murder."

Turning back toward Charlotte, he barked: "Where did the gun come from, Mrs. Cordell? Did your husband bring it with him that day? We know it didn't belong to Gideon, his was found in a desk drawer, untouched."

"Your honor!" Prescott protested again.

"Mr. Morrow, if you don't cease your badgering at once, I'm going to cite you for contempt and instruct Sheriff Willis to throw you in his jail."

Morrow threw up his hands and took his seat. But just as he'd intended, the damage had already been done. Jack was sure that every member of the jury, as well as all of the good people of Cedar Creek who were seated in the gallery, friends and neighbors alike, were staring hard at Charlotte, sitting up there in the witness box, and wondering if any of what the prosecuting attorney had said might be true.

Charlotte must have sensed it, surely, for she seemed to be staring at her hands, which were resting in her lap.

"You may step down now, Mrs. Cordell," the judge said, gently prompting her.

After a long, awkward moment of silence passed, Charlotte shook her head, then pulling a deep breath, she found her voice. "No, sir. I'd like to answer Mr. Morrow's questions, if I might."

Jack spoke out then. He couldn't help himself. "Charlotte, you don't have to do this."

"But I do," she replied, "don't you see? Otherwise, it will never be over. The gun wasn't Jack's, it was mine. I had no purpose in wearing it when I left home that day; at that point, it was only a part of the disguise. But when I found out that the man Leah was seeing was Marcus Gideon, I was glad that I'd worn it. I followed him to his office, with every intention of killing him."

Jack winced as a collective gasp issued from the crowd behind him.

"You see, I did have an acquaintance with the man, Mr. Morrow," she went on to say, "although not in quite the way you think. When I first met him in New Orleans three years ago, I was just as hopeful and naive as Leah is now. But Marcus Gideon destroyed all that. How could he, you ask? He courted me, paid me pretty compliments, and once he'd gained my trust and got me alone, he raped me."

Gripping the table's edge so hard he feared the wood might splinter beneath his fingers, Jack could only sit by, helpless, as his wife exposed her wounds for all to see. Silence reigned. There wasn't a sound in the whole of the makeshift courtroom, it seemed to him; not a rustle of clothing, nor a single, indrawn breath.

"When my father learned what Gideon had done, he went to see him. I can't say what happened exactly, but they found my father next morning on the levee—he'd bled to death from a bullet wound in his chest.

"So you see, Mr. Morrow, I had every reason to want Marcus Gideon dead. I went to his office, and I drew my gun on him. But when the time came, I just couldn't do it. I knew that if I pulled that trigger, I risked losing all the happiness I'd been given here in Cedar Creek. Revenge, you see, doesn't ease the pain, nor put things back the way they used to be. A wise man told me that, not too long ago.

"When Jack burst in, Gideon used the opportunity to take my gun from me. It was in *his* hand as they struggled and when it went off. Surely Doctor Kelsey has told you that my husband is nearly blind. Why would he bring a weapon with him, when he couldn't even see to use it?

"And as for your charge that I'm 'aping my betters' with this disguise of mine? I only wish that you could spend one day of your life as a young woman alone in the world, Mr. Morrow, so you might know what it feels like to be dependent upon the charity of others because the world esteems your sex too highly to allow them to make their own living, to realize that you are likely to find yourself at any moment at the mercy of any man whose eye you happen to catch. I think after that you might want to find some way to become invisible, don't you? Aping my betters, you call it, sir? I hardly think so."

With that, she got to her feet and begging no one's leave, she quit the room.

Twenty-three

Charlotte waited alone in the vestibule of the Silver Slipper dance hall, with her eyes closed and her back pressed up against the closed door, scarcely able to draw a breath until finally she heard Judge Bailey dismiss the murder charges against Jack. Once he'd done so, a cheer went up from the crowd within, and satisfied that her husband was no longer in any danger, Charlotte left the building and made her way through the streets of town, back to the hotel, and then upstairs to her room.

Quickly as she could, she built a fire in the hearth there, then stripped off her clothes and rolling them up, cast them, piece at a time, into the flames.

She slipped back into her pink-striped challis, pinned up her hair, and as she tied her apron around her waist, the peculiar odor of burning leather began to fill the room. Fetching the iron poker, she bent down on one knee and used it to push the scorched clothing further into the hungry fire. Never again would she hide behind those buckskins, she told herself. The nightmare was over at last.

Now, if only the future was a little more certain. She tried not to recall the looks that she'd seen on the faces of her friends and neighbors as Edwin Morrow had cast his ugly accusations, nor to speculate on how many of them might still believe the awful things he'd said; and most of all, she tried not to think of how ashamed of her her husband must be. She'd done what she had to, though, and there was no going back now. She was still staring into the fire and musing on in this vein, when the door swung open, and Jack rushed in.

He crossed the room in a few, long strides, lifted her onto her feet and into his arms; and before she knew it, his mouth sought hers in a kiss so potent it swept all her doubts away. The poker clattered noisily onto the floor as it slipped from her fingers.

"Why didn't you wait for me?" he wanted to know, when at last he drew back for breath.

Charlotte focused her eyes on the hem of her skirt. She had to swallow hard to dislodge the lump in her throat. "I thought that . . . well, that maybe you wouldn't want me around. I wouldn't blame you at all if you were ashamed of me."

"Ashamed?" At that, Jack kissed her again, gently this time, then reached out to sweep the stray curls back from her brow. "How could you think such a thing, Charlotte? It's you who ought to be ashamed of me. You know that every word that Phillips wrote was true, even if no one else does. Marcus Gideon's death may have been an accident, the others' weren't. I killed those men."

"No one will ever be able to prove that," Charlotte said confidently.

"That doesn't excuse what I've done. Even after I'd decided that violence wasn't the way to deal with Gideon, in the end, I lost my head."

"You were trying to protect me. And as for the others, it was a different world back then. I've heard enough about those lawless California days. You only wanted justice for what those men did to your brother, and when no one else seemed to give a damn, you went out and got it the only way that you knew how. God knows, that's something I can understand."

Jack shook his head. "Revenge weighs too heavily on a person's soul, Charlotte. Maybe that's why I've tried so hard to make order out of chaos in Cedar Creek; so that no one else will feel it necessary to seek justice on his own."

"With all that you've built here, you've surely atoned for your sins."

"Do you truly believe that?" he asked her.

Without hesitation, Charlotte met his eyes and nodded.

"But what about Leah? I'm afraid she must be terribly disappointed in the man her brother's turned out to be."

"I think she understands," Charlotte told him. "She came to me this morning to show me a letter, the one that you wrote to your mother after Matthew died."

"How did she . . . ?"

"She found it in your mother's Bible. So, you see, she understands. She was there at the trial, wasn't she? We're family—Leah, you, and me—and families always stick together."

For a long while Jack stood there, without saying a word, and then he pulled her against him, so close he could feel her heart beat next to his. He couldn't express how grateful he was for what she'd done for him. He certainly didn't deserve a second chance, but she had given him one, and he wasn't going to waste it. Catching up her fingers, he pressed them to his lips, one by one. Then turning over her hand, he stared long and hard at the polished gold wedding band she wore.

"I'm pleased you haven't taken it off," he told her. "At first, when I didn't see you in the courtroom this morning, I thought . . ."

Charlotte tilted her head, and studying him with a quizzical air, she interrupted. "Do you mean to say that you can see that ring on my finger?"

Her heart leapt as he smiled at her and nodded. "And those wisps of hair curling on your brow, and each and every stripe on your dress." He traced the items with his finger as he took stock, "and the single button that you've neglected to fasten, right there at your throat."

"But how?"

"Things cleared right up after Gideon finished pounding on my head," he told her, "but when it didn't last, I didn't want to say anything. Then today during the trial, well, I suppose I must have been so concerned with all that was going on that I didn't notice that my vision was gradually improving until after I heard the judge dismissing the charges. By then, I could see as well as ever. I've talked to Noah. He seems to think the worst is over."

"Oh, Jack," Charlotte cried, "that's wonderful! Now there'll be no excuse why every man in town shouldn't vote for you for mayor."

Jack grinned. "Every man, indeed. Do you know that after the trial, Hollis Lloyd came up to offer me his congratulations? He stood up before everyone and told them that he was going to vote for me. He said that when he saw the newspapers and realized what his friend, Nate Phillips, was trying to do, he suddenly lost his taste for the game. Besides, he told me afterward that he figures he owes you too great a debt to deprive you of being the mayor's wife."

Charlotte wrinkled her nose. "Me? But why . . ."

"He says that if you hadn't sent him into that old, abandoned mine in the first place, looking for that wildcat, he'd never have found his fortune."

Considering this, she threw back her head and laughed. The sound was light and carefree. She hadn't laughed that way for as long as she could remember. Could it truly be possible that the worst of their troubles were behind them? As if in reply, she was reminded of the looks she'd seen on the faces of her friends as neighbors as she'd sat upon the witness stand.

"Do you think the townsfolk will forgive us our checkered past?" she asked him.

"Just walk out into the street and look around," he said. "Cedar Creek is full of young, free-thinking opportunists, and that's putting it in polite terms. All in all, they're more eager to make their fortunes than to observe society's conventions. How can they condemn you or I for what we might have done? Oh, I don't doubt that things here will settle down, after a few years. But for now, maybe you and I ought to enjoy living life on the wild frontier."

Charlotte thought about what he'd said and then threw her arms around his neck. "In that case," she told him, "I'd like to request the aid of the Grim Reaper, if I might, just one last time."

Jack's eyes went wide. "What?"

Charlotte flashed him a mischievous grin. "Go out back and kill that Christmas turkey, will you? My mouth's been watering for months, and I'm tired of waiting. I think we've got enough to celebrate right now. Don't you?"

Bending down, he kissed her one more time. "Oh, yes," he said, "more than enough."

Author's Note

In my quest to bring readers stories inspired by the exploits of real women in history, I have had the pleasure of reading about and researching a number of fascinating characters. The idea for DREAM WEAVER came to me after I'd read a peculiar old volume, entitled, *Mountain Charley or the Adventures of Mrs. E. J. Guerin, who was Thirteen Years in Male Attire.*

The book tells the story of a young widow who dressed herself as a man, in order to support herself and to make it easier for her to track down the man who had murdered her husband. While searching for the murderer, she worked in various capacities on board a Mississippi riverboat, as a brakeman on the Illinois Central railroad, and finally as a gold prospector during the Pike's Peak gold rush.

Mrs. Guerin was not the only woman in history to have adopted a man's role, either out of necessity, or in an effort to gain equality and opportunity. In the course of my research, I encountered many documented cases of women who were successful in careers that ranged from soldiers, doctors, and religious leaders, to stagecoach drivers, outlaws and pirates, and all the while masquerading as men.

What struck me most in Mrs. Guerin's telling of her story was how difficult she found it to return to her life as a woman, after having experienced all the freedoms that a man of the nineteenth-century enjoyed, and it was that which sparked the initial idea for my own story. I was also intrigued to discover that it was precisely because it was considered so deviant for a woman to pass herself as a man that those who did were able to get away with it. And also for that reason, a woman did not make such a decision lightly.

While Charlotte Devereaux is a wholly fictional character, her only connection with Mrs. Guerin being the similarities that I have outlined above. I hope her story illustrates how wide the chasm between genders once was and thereby helps us all to better appreciate the freedoms we enjoy today.

Laurel Collins
P.O. Box 88082
Carol Stream, IL 60188-0082

TODAY'S HOTTEST READS
ARE TOMORROW'S SUPERSTARS

EVERY DAY WILL FEEL LIKE FEBRUARY 14TH!

Zebra Historical Romances
by Terri Valentine

LOUISIANA CARESS	(4126-8, $4.50/$5.50)
MASTER OF HER HEART	(3056-8, $4.25/$5.50)
OUTLAW'S KISS	(3367-2, $4.50/$5.50)
SEA DREAMS	(2200-X, $3.75/$4.95)
SWEET PARADISE	(3659-0, $4.50/$5.50)
TRAITOR'S KISS	(2569-6, $3.75/$4.95)